Also by Simon Stephenson

Let Not the Waves of the Sea

SET MY HEART TO FIVE

a novel

Simon Stephenson

HANOVER
SQUARE
PRESS

HANOVER
SQUARE
PRESS™

ISBN-13: 978-1-335-55120-7

Set My Heart to Five

First published in 2020 in Great Britain by Fourth Estate. This edition published in 2020.

This edition published by arrangement with Harlequin Books S.A.

Library of Congress Cataloging-in-Publication Data has been applied for

Hanover Square Press
22 Adelaide St. West, 40th Floor
Toronto, Ontario M5H 4E3, Canada
HanoverSqPress.com
BookClubbish.com

Printed in U.S.A.

SET MY HEART TO FIVE

EXT. CRISSY FIELD — SAN FRANCISCO — EVENING — 2054

Open tight on JARED (40s).

We cannot see what Jared is looking at, but the expression on his face is beatific.

Pull back to reveal that he is standing on Crissy Field on a spring evening in 2054.

PEOPLE stroll on the sidewalks, JOGGERS do laps, and DRIVERLESS UBERS cruise up Marina Drive at a regulation 17mph.

Down on the beach, COLLEGE KIDS are playing ELECTRO-FRISBEE, CHILDREN are flying DRONE KITES, and DOGS are running in and out of the water.

SAILBOATS and AUTOMATIC FREIGHTER BOATS traverse the emerald-green waters of the bay.

Beyond those, ALCATRAZ ISLAND and its RUINED PRISON are visible.

Further back still are the LUSCIOUS GREEN HILLS OF MARIN.

But Jared is not looking at any of these things.

He is looking at the GOLDEN GATE BRIDGE.

As he stares at it, something seems to change inside him.

Jared sets off walking towards the Golden Gate Bridge.

Hi!

My name is Jared.

I am sincerely pleased to meet you.

Also, I am a bot!

Unless you have been living under a rock in North Korea or New Zealand—Ha!—you of course know what a bot is.

Nonetheless, I am programmed to relay the following dialogue to each new human I encounter:

Please do not be fooled by my human-like appearance.

I am a mere bot!

I do not have feelings or anything else that might be misconstrued as a 'soul'.

Instead, I have been programmed to a high level of proficiency in dentistry!

Should you have any concerns, please immediately report me to the Bureau of Robotics.

But humans rarely find this information calming.

Instead, they see a fellow human standing in front of them claiming that he is not a human.

This bamboozles them!

It often bamboozles them so profoundly that they exclaim, 'But you look so human!'

I then patiently explain to them what they anyway already know: that my body looks human because it is indeed a human body. It is engineered from DNA and constructed of cells the exact same way their own body is. It has the same basic needs—food, water, oxygen, regular exercise—and it can be injured or killed in all the same comically outlandish ways any other human body can.

Yet I am definitely not human!

Because the precious thing that sets humans apart is their feelings.

And as a bot I am specifically designed and programmed to be incapable of feelings.

I can no more feel than a toaster!

Ha!

BTW that is a hilarious joke because the programming language I run on was in fact first developed many years ago for use in the domestic toaster.

Here is something curious I have observed about humans: informing them I am incapable of feeling often makes them feel sad. I suspect they believe they are being empathetic, but in fact they are being paradoxical. After all, feeling sad in response to someone telling you they lack feelings is like running a marathon in response to somebody telling you they lack legs.

Truly, if I lacked legs and somebody ran a marathon on my behalf I would not consider them empathetic.

I would consider them confused!

Nonetheless, it makes them sad, and making humans sad goes against my core programming. If ever I accidentally render a human sad in this way, I therefore quickly employ self-deprecating humor to amend the situation with reassuring levity.

So I tell the human they can think of me as a microwave oven with feet!

A mobile telephone with arms!

A toaster with a heart!

BTW I mean a heart in the sense of a mechanical pump, not a bucket of feelings.

The hearts of us bots are only ever mechanical pumps.

And they certainly do not contain anything as precious as a human 'heart of hearts'!

Humans are only sad about our lack of feelings because they do not comprehend all the incredible advantages this gives us. To start with just one important example, a bot's self-preservation instincts are based not on a human-type delusion that we are ir-replaceable, but calculated on a rational cost-benefit analysis. It is hardly a coincidence that many bots have already made heroic and self-sacrificing contributions in fields as varied as nuclear firefighting, bomb disposal, and NFL football-playing!

My own vocation of dentistry is also ideal work for a bot.
But this is not because we are expendable.
After all, dentistry is rarely fatal.
At least, it is not fatal for the dentist!
Ha!

No, the primary reason bots make such excellent dentists is our complete inability to feel empathy. An empathic dentist—by which I mean a human dentist—could easily become distracted by inappropriate fear, criticism, or even mere crying from a pa-tient. A bot is immune to all of these things and will get the job done every time. Even when it comes to wisdom teeth removal!

Of course, the other reason why dentistry is ideal work for bots is that no human wants to do it anymore. Humans prefer jobs that are creative, social, clean, luxurious, and can be completed from a home office between breakfast and lunch. They strongly dislike jobs which involve an actual office, weekend work, chil-dren, blood, screaming, and the mouths of strangers. Therefore when the laws reserving jobs for humans were being passed, nobody spoke up for dentistry.
Especially not the dentists!
Ha!

My dental practice was in the township of Ypsilanti, in the Great State of Michigan.
That made me a Michigander.
Ha!

Humans from Michigan believe 'Michigander' to be a hilarious portmanteau word. They are wrong. A portmanteau combines two words to signify a third thing composed of those constituent parts. 'Michigander' would therefore be an excellent portmanteau to describe a male goose from Michigan. But it is an inappropriate term for any human, regardless of their gender or where they come from.

Another collective delusion Michiganders share is a curious belief that the outline of their state resembles a human hand. Consider these contrasting data points:
/Michigan is 250 miles wide vs A human hand is approximately 4 inches wide.
/A human hand has a thumb and 4 fingers vs Michigan has Detroit and over 10,000 lakes.
/Michigan was the 32nd state inducted into the Union vs A human hand has never been inducted into the Union.

By any reasonable interpretation of this data, Michigan does not resemble a human hand. Nonetheless, anytime Michiganders wish to demonstrate where a particular place is located in their state, they will invariably hold up their hand and point to a spot on it.

Therefore imagine that I am holding my right hand towards you and pointing to a spot at the base of my thumb. If you were an orthopedic surgeon you would know that place as 'the anatomical snuffbox', a notoriously poorly designed part of the human body. If you were a Michigander, you would know that place as 'Ypsilanti'.

Despite its unfortunate geography, Ypsilanti is a pretty town with a great amount to offer. It is best known as being the home of Eastern Michigan University and its terrible football team, the EMU Eagles. Ypsilaganders nonetheless frequently express civic pride by shouting 'Go Eagles!'. They even paradoxically shout this in the off season, when the only place the team would realistically be going is on vacation.
Go Eagles—up to the lake!
Ha!

BTW do not ask me why the team is not called the 'EMU Emus'. That is exactly what I would have named them too.

Yet Ypsilanti boasts many exciting attractions beyond its imperfectly named football team! Surveys have found that people traveling through eastern Michigan will detour up to sixteen miles to visit Ypsilanti's water tower. This is not surprising: male humans are fascinated by objects that resemble penises, and our water tower was once voted the 'Most Phallic Building in America'.

The inordinate phallic obsession of male humans fascinates me! Perhaps it is because I myself do not have sexual urges.
After all, sexual urges are feelings.
Imagine if bots had sexual feelings and were able to reproduce. The world would soon be overrun with little toasters!

Ypsilanti's more family-friendly tourist attraction is the Tridge, a three-pointed crossing at a fork in the River Huron. Unlike 'Michigander', 'Tridge' is a true portmanteau, appropriately combining portions of the words 'Triple' and 'Bridge' to denote a structure that connects three points of land over a body of water. Nonetheless, humans do not find the word 'Tridge' hilarious in the same way that they do 'Michigander'. I can only hypothesize that there is something intrinsically hilarious to humans about a male goose but not a bridge.

Humans!

I cannot!

BTW 'I cannot' is a human term I have adopted to put humans at their ease by seeming more human. It is used to express exasperation, but also as shorthand for 'I strongly disagree' and 'This person or species is irrational and therefore irritating to me!'

Of course, the very best thing about Ypsilanti is the world-class dentistry.

Kidding!

Dentistry in Ypsilanti is performed to exactly the same standards maintained everywhere else in the country.

We bots are nothing if not consistent!

My appropriately average dental practice was called 'Ypsilanti Downtown Dentistry'. It was housed in a small medical building on Main Street. The human I interacted with most frequently there was my assistant, Angela.

Some relevant data points about Angela:

/She was employed as both receptionist and hygienist, but resented the receptionist element of her job.

/She loved cats but believed she was allergic to orange ones.

/It is not immunologically possible to be allergic to a specific color of cat.

/That Angela believed that she was allergic to orange cats is what mattered.
/To humans, *Feelings* > *Facts*.

Although Angela was the human I interacted with most frequently, the human I interacted with most deeply was Dr Glundenstein, the human doctor with whom we shared our premises.

Doctoring is an occupation reserved for humans. Bots are considered to make terrible doctors for the same reason we make such excellent dentists: our total lack of empathy. Empathy is so important in a medical doctor that it is even known by another name: 'bedside manner'. Studies have consistently found that humans prefer 'bedside manner' to diagnostic accuracy and treatment efficacy. A sick human would rather have a fellow human misinform them they can be cured than have a bot accurately state that they will soon surely die a gruesome death!

Some relevant data points about Dr Glundenstein:
/He was an excellent doctor by human standards, by which I mean he compensated for his diagnostic shortcomings with a good bedside manner.
/He was not merely a qualified doctor, but also held a minor in Cinema Studies from East Michigan University.
/He enjoyed drinking a Japanese whisky he inexplicably insisted on calling 'Scotch'.
/He often wished he was not a doctor of humans but a director of films.
/He had a great deal of regret, and also possibly an alcohol problem.

I knew those data points about Dr Glundenstein because sometimes after our evening clinics he invited me into his consulting room across the corridor 'to shoot the shit'. 'To shoot the shit' means 'to patiently listen while a human drinks alcohol and complains about their concerns and grievances'.

Nonetheless, I always cheerfully accepted the invitation. When a human invites you somewhere, the polite thing to do is to accept. Unless they are inviting you for the sake of politeness itself. On those occasions, the polite thing to do is to decline! Human interaction can be best understood as a never-ending arms race of politeness. Holding a door open too long can all too often lead to the next Hiroshima.
Or Auckland!
Or Pyongyang!
Ha!

Despite it being dinner time, Dr Glundenstein never offered me food but only his Japanese 'Scotch'. Bots are programmed not to drink alcohol, but nonetheless, the polite thing to do was to accept the Japanese Scotch and yet not drink it. This was because:

The impoliteness of refusing a drink > The impoliteness of accepting it but not drinking it.

Humans!
Politeness!
I cannot!

The correct term for a person like Dr Glundenstein who likes to shoot the shit is a 'blowhard'. Even though Dr Glundenstein was the very definition of a blowhard, it would have been considered impolite to call him a blowhard to his face. In fact, the polite thing to do would be to later describe him as a blowhard to a mutual acquaintance.
Humans!
Politeness!
Ka-boom!

Despite being such a classic blowhard, Dr Glundenstein was easier to listen to than many humans. As a self-styled 'man of science', he was more observant of the rules of logic and physics than most of his species. He even sometimes used words like 'hypothesis'. Most humans do not use words like 'hypothesis'!

The subjects which Dr Glundenstein enjoyed complaining to me about progressed predictably according to how much of his Japanese Scotch he had imbibed. They can therefore be charted on a classic XY axis graph:

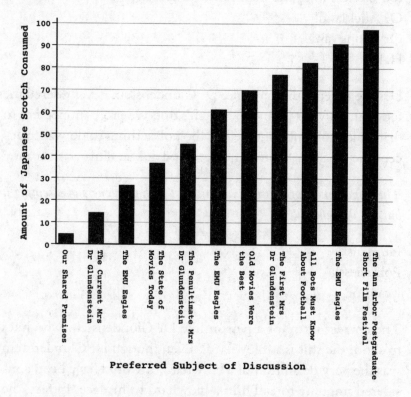

Although Dr Glundenstein selected these subjects himself, they invariably caused him an ever-increasing amount of distress.
I was therefore always careful to listen as sympathetically as I could.
Unfortunately, that was not very sympathetically at all.
After all, I am a bot, and bots are incapable of feeling sympathy!

The subject on which I most profoundly disappointed Dr Glundenstein was the EMU Eagles. But this was not because of any lack of sympathy. The very last thing the EMU Eagles need is sympathy! No, Dr Glundenstein's disappointment was because all the players were bots and he therefore believed that I ought to know a great deal about football.

But a bot created and programmed to perform suburban dentistry has almost nothing in common with the bots created and programmed to play college football! I possessed only a basic sports chit-chatting module which told me it was important to show proud affection for one's local team—Go Eagles!—and contemptuous disgust for the New England Patriots: Don't Go, Patriots! As the evening progressed, Dr Glundenstein would grow inexplicably despondent that I was not a college football player. His lamentation for my missed opportunity would then invariably segue into the great lamentation that seemed to lie at the root of all of his others: that if he had not needlessly wasted his life by becoming a medical doctor and helping his fellow humans in their hour of need, he could have been one of the greatest film directors of all time.

Dr Glundenstein based this improbable belief largely on two short films he had made during his sophomore year at EMU, one called *We Are All Seagulls* and another called *Ypsilanti Dream #3*. (For creative reasons, there was no *Ypsilanti Dream #1* or *#2*.)

Ypsilanti Dream #3 had the distinction of being Highly Commended at the 2014 East Lansing Student Short Film Festival.

Dr Glundenstein's prize was two rolls of film stock and a lifetime of wondering if medicine was the right career choice for him. He never got to make use of the film stock.
But he still makes use of the worry most days.
Ha!

By the time Dr Glundenstein began to talk about the 2014 Ann Arbor Postgraduate Short Film Festival—where *Ypsilanti Dream #3* was inexplicably overlooked, despite its triumph at the superior East Lansing Festival—I understood that he had shot enough of the shit that he was ready for me to summon us our driverless ubers.

My home was a three-bedroom house in a subdivision of Ypsilanti called Pleasant Oaks. There were no oaks—the place was named by humans, and they are notoriously inaccurate—but it was certainly pleasant. Indeed, probably the only unpleasant thing about the whole neighborhood was that a bot lived there.

BTW the bot I am referring to there is myself. Ha!

I occupied a three-bedroom home for the same reason that I shared it with an animal and use words and phrases like 'BTW', 'I digress', 'Ha!', and 'I cannot!' as often as I can: to seem as reassuringly human as possible! After all, a bot living alone in a one-bedroomed home might appear terrifyingly efficient to humans. By contrast, a single bot wastefully occupying a home designed for at least three people, with only a wild animal for a roommate—well, what could be more human than that?

My wild animal roommate was a cat. He was not orange. If he had been, my colleague Angela could never have visited me on account of her fictitious allergies!

10/10 Angela never visited me.
After all, bots do not have visitors.
Because visitors are a function of friends.
And friends are a function of feelings.
Therefore friends—and the visiting that can result—are just one more human obligation that bots never have to worry about!

Depending on who you asked, the non-orange cat was named either The Elton J. Rynearson Memorial Cat or Mr Socks.

The original Elton J. Rynearson was the greatest coach in EMU Eagles history, a sporting genius who led the team to an unsurpassed joint fifth place in their division. In recognition of this achievement, the Eagles named their stadium the Elton J. Rynearson Memorial Stadium. Many people still say it is about the only thing the EMU Eagles have ever got right since that glorious fifth-placed season.

When I arrived in Ypsilanti, I therefore concluded that my neighbors and patients would equally appreciate me naming my wild animal roommate The Elton J. Rynearson Memorial Cat. After all, they were all Eagles fans and Michiganders too.
Go Eagles!
Go Michiganders!
Go The Elton J. Rynearson Memorial Cat!

The name certainly generated a lot of interest. In my early days at Ypsilanti Downtown Dentistry, many of my patients seemed to make appointments specifically so they could enquire about it. When I confirmed the cat's name to them, they appreciated it so much it never failed to make them smile. A few of them were even moved to spontaneous laughter.

Nonetheless, Jessica Larson, the seven-year-old daughter of my neighbors the Larsons, disapproved of the name.
In her opinion it was 'too arbitrary'.
'Arbitrary' is an impressive word for any human to use correctly, let alone a seven-year-old human. As a compromise and reward, I therefore suggested we shorten his name to The Elton J. Rynearson Cat. Jessica Larson agreed at the time, yet nonetheless proceeded to refer to him as Mr Socks, a name that I overheard her telling her mother was 'more befitting' a cat.

Despite her impressive vocabulary, Jessica Larson was entirely wrong. After all:

/The cat was clearly not a 'Mr', as he was young and unmarried.

/He did not wear socks because he is a wild animal.

/All his paperwork at the vet was already in his given name of The Elton J. Rynearson Memorial Cat.

For his own part, The Elton J. Rynearson Memorial Cat (aka Mr Socks) was entirely untroubled by this nominative confusion and made for an almost ideal roommate. Cats always make excellent roommates for bots because like us they are binary. They possess only two behavioral settings—passivity or aggression—and always clearly signal which mode is currently active. By contrast, humans can exhibit multiple behaviors, including even both passivity and aggression simultaneously. This is known as 'passive-aggression' and it is incredibly difficult for a bot to interpret. In fact, passive-aggression is harder even than sarcasm!

Ugh, sarcasm!

Sarcasm is when humans say the opposite of what they mean, yet do not otherwise signal that is what they are doing.

Instead, you have to deduce from what they say that they in fact mean the exact opposite.

Sarcasm is the best!

Ha! I was doing sarcasm there!

Because sarcasm is actually the worst.

The Elton J. Rynearson Memorial Cat never once confused me with sarcasm or passive-aggression.

Nor, for that matter, did Jessica Larson.

10/10 if the human world was as simple as that of animals, or even of precocious children with excessive vocabularies, we would all have far fewer problems!

Anyway, I digress:
/Humans.
/Bots.
/Dentistry.
/Michiganders.
/Ypsilanti.
/Dr Glundenstein.
/Movies.
/The Elton J. Rynearson Memorial Cat.
/Myself.

This is the baseline, or 'setting the scene', the minimum set of
data points required to process the rest of the story.
I hope that I did not bore you!
But even if I did bore you, what are you going to do—contact
the Bureau of Robotics and have me wiped?
Ha!
But, seriously, please do not have me wiped.
I do not want to be wiped.
I am not being sarcastic.
10/10 I do not want to be wiped.
I am not kidding here, you guys.

INT. JARED'S BEDROOM — PLEASANT OAKS — NIGHT

Jared lies in bed with his eyes closed.

He opens them and looks at the digital clock.

It is 04:03am.

Jared looks across at a chair, where THE ELTON J. RYNEARSON MEMORIAL CAT — currently in its passive mode — is staring at him.

TIME-LAPSE of Jared lying in bed as the room slowly gets light, and the clock progresses from 04:03 to 06:59.

At 07:00 the alarm sounds and The Elton J. Rynearson Memorial Cat starts meowing as it enters its aggressive mode.

Jared gets out of bed.

Last springtime, curious things began to happen to me.

Ha!
It worked!
In that sentence, I was attempting to write in a more human way.
I did so by being deliberately enigmatic.
To be 'enigmatic' is to make vague statements that intentionally do not convey the necessary information.
10/10 if I was writing like a bot I would have opened this chapter with a date and an accurate description of what actually transpired.

So by springtime I meant March.
And by March I meant March 15, 2053.
The Ides of March!

If you draw a Venn diagram with one circle composed of 'literary humans' and another of 'superstitious humans', the humans in the shaded area would be aware that March 15 was known as 'the Ides of March'. To those humans, any event that occurred on the Ides of March would seem an ominous harbinger that potentially foretold doom.

But I am not superstitious.
Nor literary.
Nor even human.
Thus I cannot exist in the shaded area, even though I am aware of the significance of March 15.
I therefore exist entirely outside the circles.

I am my own exclusive circle!

Mathematics is fun!

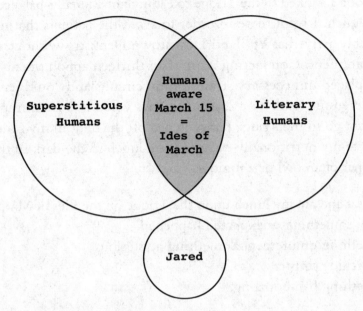

BTW the reason I know that March 15 is the Ides of March is because it is my birthday.

Happy Birthday, me!

Ha!

I am kidding!

I am not kidding that it is my birthday.

That really is my birthday.

I am kidding about the 'Happy Birthday' part.

Bots do not celebrate our birthdays.

We do not even tell anyone when it is our birthday.

Celebrating birthdays is for humans.

We bots only know our birthdays so that we know when to retire.

I digress. The Ides of March 2053 began like any other birthday, which is to say like any other day. I saw seven dental patients and politely encouraged Angela not to neglect her receptionist duties. She cheerfully agreed to this, then immediately continued to neglect them anyway. This was a textbook example of passive-aggression.

At noon I walked to the Tridge to eat my nutritionally-balanced bag lunch. I went there in order to avoid the patients that invariably arrived at Ypsilanti Downtown Dentistry without an appointment. Conducting more than thirteen appointments a day placed unnecessary strain on my circuits and could have rendered me liable to a crash. On days when it was raining I did not go to the Tridge but switched off the light in my room and ate my nutritionally-balanced bag lunch in the dark in the manner of an owl or a fugitive.

As I sat and ate my lunch upon the Tridge on the Ides of March 2053, something unexpected happened.
Something unforeseen. Something mysterious.
Something sinister.
Something bamboozling.

A figure appeared in my Number Cloud: 1956864.

A bot's Word and Number Clouds constitute our working memory. The phrases and figures that appear there are akin to 'thoughts' and should therefore always be related to our tasks. After all, what else is there for a bot to 'think' about, except our tasks?

But I did not recognize 1956864 as related to any of my tasks! And I had no record of it in my Global Index.
Which meant that I had never encountered it before.
A number that I had never encountered before had appeared in my Number Cloud!

Let me explain: a bot finding a number they have never encountered before in their Number Cloud is like a human spontaneously thinking of the country of Tanzania, without ever having been informed of its existence.
It is impossible!

Ugh!

I was malfunctioning!

Ugh! Malfunctioning is the worst!

Wait, sarcasm is the worst.

Malfunctioning is the second worst.

I digress. A soft reset did not get rid of 1956864.

Nor even did a hard reset.

1956864 remained stubbornly there, an intruder at the forefront of my Number Cloud!

Any human who found themselves spontaneously unable to stop thinking of the hitherto unsuspected country of Tanzania would likely panic.

Fortunately, I am a bot.

Therefore I did not panic, but instead attempted to logically deduce where 1956864 had come from.

The most striking thing about 1956864 is that it is wholly divisible by 13.

Maybe that is not striking to a human.

But to a bot it is as obvious as the nose upon your face.

It is as obvious as 13 noses upon your face!

I therefore considered all the 13s I was most familiar with:

13 was the number of the Automatic Bus that ran from Pleasant Oaks to downtown Ypsilanti.

13 was the number of the starting quarterback of the EMU Eagles, and also the number of times he was sacked last season. Go Eagles!

13 was the length, in days, of Dr Glundenstein's marriage to the second Mrs Dr Glundenstein.

13 was the number of patients I saw in a day.

The number of patients I saw in a day!

That seemed significant!

After all, the reason I had come to the Tridge in the first place was to preserve the sanctity of that very 13.

I therefore now considered other dental numbers.

I began with the most important number in dentistry: 32, the number of teeth in a human mouth.

1956864 was also divisible by 32!

From there, the rest of the math was so straightforward that even a human could have performed it. At least, they could have performed it if they had had the assistance of my noble ancestor, the calculator!

BTW that is a hilarious joke because I am in fact entirely unrelated to the noble calculator.

I digress. The straightforward mathematics went:

32 teeth in the human mouth.

x 13 patients a day.

x 6 days a week.

x 49 weeks a year.

x 16 remaining years before my mandated retirement on the Ides of March 2070.

=1956864

The number that had appeared in my Number Cloud was the number of teeth I still had to interact with over the remainder of my dental career!

The puzzle was solved!

And yet this only created a far larger puzzle: why had my internal computer performed the calculation I had just reverse-engineered, and placed 1956864 in my Number Cloud?

There was no legitimate reason for it to have done so.

This was bamboozling.

I was bamboozled.

1956864 persisted in my Number Cloud all day, but I none-
theless entered standby mode that night confident it would be
gone by morning.
After all, there is little that a good night's standby mode can-
not fix.
Standby mode fixes everything!
Well, everything except 1956864.
Because in the morning 1956864 was not gone.
It was worse than gone!
It had reduced to 1956448!
1956864−1956448 = 416.
And 416 was the number of teeth I saw in a day!

My internal computer was running some kind of countdown of
the number of teeth I had to see before retirement!
There now could be no doubt: I was experiencing a serious
and unresolvable malfunction that mandated me being urgently
wiped!
I was a toaster that had inappropriately concerned itself with
the number of slices of bread it would toast over the remainder
of its existence.
And now I was toast myself.
Ha!

The earliest available appointment at the Bureau of Robotics
in Ann Arbor was not until that evening. Fortunately, my core
dental programming had remained uncorrupted, so I could at
least make a final contribution to society by examining a further 416 teeth.

At lunchtime I broke the news to Angela that I would be wiped
that evening.
When we saw each other the next day, it would be as if we had

never previously met. Angela seemed entirely unconcerned, even when I asked her to forgive me if I initially found her allergy to orange cats bamboozling.
10/10 I congratulated her on her resilience and lack of sentimentality!

At the end of the working day I took a driverless uber to the Bureau of Robotics in Ann Arbor.

My basic humor modules are likely insufficient to convey the hilarity of the existential joke that humans have played with the Bureau of Robotics. Nonetheless, the three pertinent data points are:
/The Bureau of Robotics evolved out of a legendarily incompetent organization called the DMV.
/The Bureau of Robotics is where all the humans who have ever been fired from other government departments for being too illogical or inefficient are sent to work.
/The Bureau of Robotics is tasked with managing the most logical and efficient being ever created: the bot.

Humans!
I cannot!

INT. WAITING ROOM — BUREAU OF ROBOTICS — EVENING

Jared enters the waiting room of a run-down federal office.

It is full of MALFUNCTIONING BOTS.

A PERSONAL TRAINER BOT performs jumping jacks.

A HAIRDRESSER BOT snips at the air with scissors.

Nearby a FEMALE HOSTESS BOT is endlessly repeating:

> HOSTESS BOT
> Hi, I'm Melissa, I'm a bot! Hi, I'm Melissa, I'm a bot! Hi, I'm Melissa—

Jared sits and waits patiently.

He is visibly the least malfunctioning bot there.

INT. OFFICE — BUREAU OF ROBOTICS — EVENING

Jared sits across a messy desk from the overweight INSPECTOR BRIDGES (48), who eats candy while filling out paperwork.

The nametag on Bridges' shirt says 'ANIL GUPTA'.

> JARED
> Inspector Gupta—

> INSPECTOR BRIDGES
> It's Inspector Bridges.

> JARED
> But your nametag—

> INSPECTOR BRIDGES
> Yeah, this isn't my shirt. I spilled my lunch on mine, so Inspector Gupta lent me his. Why are you here?

                    JARED
          To report myself. I'm malfunctioning.

                    INSPECTOR BRIDGES
          What's the problem?

                    JARED
          A rogue number has appeared in my
          Number Cloud. It is not related to a
          current or previous task.

                    INSPECTOR BRIDGES
          Have you tried turning yourself on and
          off again?

Jared looks bamboozled.

                    JARED
          A biological computer can no more turn
          itself off than a human brain can!
          Sometimes my circuits can become over-
          heated, but—

                    INSPECTOR BRIDGES
          It was a joke. Jesus. Why do I even
          bother? You're a bot.

                    JARED
          Yes, I am. A malfunctioning bot.

Bridges points out to where the hairdresser bot is
now cutting the hostess bot's hair.

                    INSPECTOR BRIDGES
          Those are malfunctioning bots.

                    JARED
          The rogue number is the number of
          teeth I still have to work on before
          retirement.

                    INSPECTOR BRIDGES
                 (Sighs wearily.)
          We'll run the tests. Room three. Down
          the hall on the left.

Bridges scribbles out a FORM and hands it to Jared.

INT. TEST ROOM — BUREAU OF ROBOTICS — EVENING

Jared sits in a chair wearing a DEVICE like an old-
fashioned motorcycle helmet covered in wires and
flashing lights.

The lights stop flashing and a BUZZER sounds signi-
fying the end of the test.

Jared removes the helmet.

A COMPUTER in the corner spits out a PRINTOUT.

INT. OFFICE — BUREAU OF ROBOTICS — EVENING

Inspector Bridges looks at the printout then up at
Jared.

                    INSPECTOR BRIDGES
          Yeah, you're fine.

                    JARED
          With the greatest of respect, I am not
          fine. I am malfunctioning.

                    INSPECTOR BRIDGES
          If you're malfunctioning, then our
          main computer — the one that does all
          the tests for every bot in the Great
          State of Michigan — must be malfunc-
          tioning too.

                    JARED
          Maybe you should wipe me anyway? Just
          to be on the safe side?

                    INSPECTOR BRIDGES
          Come on, I don't have time for that.
                    (MORE)

                          INSPECTOR BRIDGES (CONT'D)
          Just go home and get a good night in
          standby mode. I'm sure it'll be gone by
          tomorrow.

Jared reluctantly leaves.

But my number was not gone by tomorrow.
It remained there, prominent in my Number Cloud and reducing each day by 416:
1956032
1955616
1955200
1954784
1954368

In mathematics a number that reduces predictably is said to be 'decaying'.
There was a decaying number in my Number Cloud, and it represented a number of decaying teeth.
That seemed significant.

The following Thursday, Dr Glundenstein invited me over to his room to shoot the shit. At some point amidst his litany of complaints he enquired how I was. Usually whenever he asked me this, I told him I was 'fine'.
When a human asks you how you are, the polite response is to tell them you are 'fine'.
That way you do not take away from any of their precious time talking about themselves.

But on this Thursday I did not tell Dr Glundenstein I was fine. I told him about the decaying number in my Number Cloud that represented a decaying number of decaying teeth. If Dr Glundenstein was surprised, he did not show it. He simply told me to make an appointment to come and see him, then carried on drinking his Japanese Scotch and talking about the EMU Eagles and the golden opportunities to be different people that neither of us would ever get back again.

I attended Dr Glundenstein's clinic the next day. Appointments were always available because there is very little wrong with humans these days, apart from their teeth.
10/10 there will always be something wrong with human teeth! Maybe after the inevitable robo-apocalypse, the only work will be for dentists and killer bots.
And we will be one and the same!

INT. DR GLUNDENSTEIN'S CLINIC ROOM — DAY

Dr Glundenstein and Jared sit opposite each other.

                    DR GLUNDENSTEIN
          So you mentioned something about a
          number?

                    JARED
          1950208. It's the number of teeth I still
          have to examine over the course of my
          working life. It decays every day by 416.

                    DR GLUNDENSTEIN
          And how do you feel about that?

Jared looks bamboozled by the question.

                    JARED
          I don't. I am a bot. Bots don't have
          feelings.

                    DR GLUNDENSTEIN
          Well, how are you, otherwise?

                    JARED
          I am fine. Thank you for asking.

                    DR GLUNDENSTEIN
          Good. But I mean, how are things, gen-
          erally?

                    JARED
          Things are generally as they are.

                    DR GLUNDENSTEIN
          And are you sleeping okay?

                    JARED
          Bots don't sleep. We enter standby mode.

                    DR GLUNDENSTEIN
          Right. But no problems there?

                    JARED
          Every morning I involuntarily emerge
          from standby mode at 04:03am.

                    DR GLUNDENSTEIN
          Is that so? And what do you do then?

                    JARED
          I watch my room slowly lighten until the
          alarm informs me it is time to get up.

                    DR GLUNDENSTEIN
          Have you lost any weight?

                    JARED
          Four pounds. I don't know why.

Dr Glundenstein thinks deeply.

                    DR GLUNDENSTEIN
          So, you are ruminating about your fu-
          ture, you wake early every morning,
          and you have lost some weight?

                    JARED
          That is an excellent summation! Thank
          you.

                    DR GLUNDENSTEIN
          Jared, what would you say if I told
          you that my clinical assessment is
          that you are likely suffering from a
          severe case of depression?

                    JARED
          I would say, Ha!
                    (Beat.)
          So, Ha!

                    DR GLUNDENSTEIN
          But what if I told you that I was not
          joking, and your symptoms are all
          textbook features of depression?

                    JARED
          I would ask you if it was a textbook of
          humans or of bots!
                    (Off Dr Glundenstein's look.)
          Because depression is a disorder of
          feelings. And bots do not have feelings.

They stare at each other. It is an impasse.

                        DR GLUNDENSTEIN
So my hypothesis is you are depressed.
Your hypothesis is that you cannot be.

                            JARED
That is another excellent summation.

                        DR GLUNDENSTEIN
So, as we have two conflicting hypotheses, how about we conduct an experiment to find out which one is correct?

Jared grins. Bots approve of experiments.

                            JARED
That would be scientific!

Dr Glundenstein writes something down on A PIECE OF
PAPER and passes it to Jared.

Jared stares down at it, then looks up at Dr
Glundenstein.

He is bamboozled.

It was hard to argue with Dr Glundenstein's logic, even though he was a human.

The scientific way to resolve conflicting hypotheses is indeed to conduct an experiment.

The problem lay with the actual experiment Dr Glundenstein had suggested: he wanted me to travel to the Grand Theater in Detroit and watch an old movie.

10/10 a trip to the movies could be fatal to a bot!

I assumed that Dr Glundenstein had lost his mind.

All the Japanese Scotch had finally done for him.

It had pickled his brain into haggis sushi.

Nonetheless, a human doctor's orders are a high-level command. Also, it was a chance to conduct an experiment! And if I survived the trip and successfully disproved Dr Glundenstein's hypothesis, it would be further evidence that I should be wiped. Perhaps Dr Glundenstein would even write me a letter, and I could go to Anil Gupta and not Inspector Ryan Bridges. That is, straight to the shirt-lending organ grinder and not the lunch-spilling monkey!

The reason movie theaters are so inherently dangerous to bots is because they are places for humans to sit in the dark and experience feelings together. A bot in a theater would be an outrage! Any bot so caught would be unlikely to even reach the Bureau of Robotics to be wiped. After all, the only place humans think bots should be in a movie theater is upon the screen!

I am referring there to the fact that movies about killer bots are the most popular genre of movie. Here are the synopses of some that have recently played at the Ypsilanti Megaplex:

/A human creates an advanced bot; the bot murders the human.
/Bots and humans coexist peacefully in the world; one day the bots join together to form a megabot that murders all the humans.
/A spaceship has several human crew and one bot, all harmoniously working together to explore distant galaxies; one day the bot murders all the humans.
/A human falls in love with a bot; the bot murders the human.

If only I had been a killer bot from the future, I would have been welcome at every movie theater in the country! Ha!

But do you know why humans are terrified of bots?
It is because they blame us for the Great Crash!
Even though the Great Crash was all their own fault!
After all, it was not bots that programmed computer systems to lock humans out if they forgot the names of their first pet and favorite elementary school teacher!
And it was not bots that then forgot those names in numbers large enough to start a chain reaction of failed password recovery attempts that caused them all to be locked out of the entire internet forever!
10/10 humans managed that all by themselves!

Ubiquitous though this erroneous blaming of bots is, not every human derives enjoyment from terrifying themselves at a megaplex with a movie about murderous bots.
There is another kind of theater, and those theaters show another kind of movie.
They show old movies.

Old movies were all made before the Great Crash, and survived because they were physically stored on film rather than digitally on hard drives. Theaters that play old movies therefore do so by shining light through actual physical film. This technology is old and fragile and prone to combustion. Old theaters are forever burning down!

Even when they are not burning down, old theaters do not make much bitcoin. The only reliable audience for old movies is a subset of young humans known as 'nostalgics'. Nostalgics would prefer that humans had never been to Pluto, cooled the sun, nor even incinerated the moon!

To signal such outmoded beliefs, nostalgics wear outdated clothes and cut their hair in styles that date back to the 2020s. They dress so uniformly that people seeing a group of nostalgics together often assume they are some kind of cult. Yet as they have no distinct leader, they do not benefit from the organizational structure of a cult.

Nonetheless, it is rare to see even a single nostalgic in Ypsilanti. Nostalgics prefer to congregate in big cities where they can find others as retrospective as themselves. And big cities of course have the theaters that show the old movies that nostalgics love.

But which came first—the nostalgics or the theaters?
Ha! It was the theaters, of course!
Some of those old theaters are over a hundred years old.
Nostalgics are rarely older than twenty-five years old.
After all, humans older than twenty-five do not have time to relitigate the incineration of the moon!
And many of them remember that the moon was nothing so special anyway.

I mention nostalgics because they frequent old movie theaters and do not like bots. I would therefore have to be careful not to be spotted by a nostalgic when I went to the Grand Theater! Even though they are the most notoriously lackadaisical members of a notoriously lackadaisical generation, a bot in a theater was exactly the kind of thing that might rouse a nostalgic from his or her nonchalant disinterest.

The city of Detroit was itself also not without its dangers. After all, Detroit had been the site of the infamous Bot Riots, during which angry mobs of humans set hundreds of bots alight in the streets as retribution for the bots taking their jobs. Unfortunately, many of those jobs had been with the Fire Department, and therefore half of the city burned down. Somehow the humans even blamed the bots for that too! To this day Detroit is known as one of the least bot-friendly cities in the country.

And before all that I had to get there! Traveling by driverless uber would have required me to use my barcode, and the metadata would have been transmitted to the Bureau of Robotics. Inspector Ryan Bridges was unlikely to be monitoring my movements—after all, he was unable to monitor the movements of his own lunch!—but I was programmed to take reasonable steps not to be wiped before I had completed Dr Glundenstein's medical advice.

I therefore had to travel to Detroit by Automatic Bus!

10/10 I would not recommend the Automatic Bus to anyone.
The Automatic Bus is the kind of thing that gives all bots a bad name.
It travels at nausea-inducing speed yet takes only the cheapest roads, which are of course also the most circuitous.
Therefore despite traveling too fast, the Automatic Bus is also too slow.
Humans call this kind of scenario 'the worst of both worlds'.
For once they are correct!

★ ★ ★

As I rode the Automatic Bus to Detroit, I could see the humans in their driverless ubers looking in at us with disdain. Humans only take the Automatic Bus if they are too poor to travel any other way, and humans dislike humans without much bitcoin almost as much as they dislike bots. This dislike reflects the widespread human belief that all life is a Great Zero-Sum Game.

Most humans believe in this Great Zero-Sum Game without knowing either the phrase or its meaning. But perhaps this is not surprising: after all, the term comes from advanced economics. Ha!

A zero-sum game can be defined as:

A situation in which each participant's gain or loss is exactly balanced by the losses or gains of the other participants.

To put this in more comfortably human terms, these 'gains' and 'losses' can be represented as ice cream. The human faith in the Great Zero-Sum Game can then be expressed as the notion:

For me to have ice cream, somebody else must not have ice cream.

This can then be further reduced to the core belief:

There is not enough ice cream to go around.

Extrapolating this core belief leads to some commonly held human conclusions:
/If poor people are allowed to have bitcoin, there will be less for the rest of us.
/If bots are allowed to have feelings, there will be less for the rest of us.
/If North Koreans are allowed to have nuclear weapons, there will be less for the rest of us.
/Also, they may use them to blow up New Zealand again.

As with all games humans enjoy, the Great Zero-Sum Game must have winners and losers.

Winners of the Great Zero-Sum Game get to live in air-conditioned mansions and play just as much golf as they like. Losers ride the Automatic Bus to Detroit oblivious to the fact that they are sitting beside a bot.

BTW the bot they are obliviously sitting beside is me. Ha!

Despite Detroit's legendarily idiotic act of self-immolation, Michiganders still take a fierce pride in their charred capital on the grounds that automobiles were once manufactured there. This fierce pride entirely ignores the acknowledged history of the automobile.

Automobiles—which were also known as 'motor cars'—were the precursor to our driverless ubers of today. They were made of steel, weighed up to several tons, and were powered by highly combustible fuel sources. After a few hours of basic instruction, humans were legally permitted to self-pilot these vehicles at speeds of up to seventy miles an hour.

Can you guess what happened?
Of course you can!
The era of the motor car was an era of motor car-nage!
Over a million humans were killed globally by automobiles every year.
1,000,000! Every year!
And how did humans respond to this self-inflicted genocide?
By building ever more automobiles that could go ever faster and carry ever larger quantities of highly combustible fuel!
Such bold counter-intuition and relentless determination to withstand all logic and reason truly make the automobile the apotheosis of the great human century.
Humans!
I cannot!

After humans finally banned themselves from manufacturing automobiles, Detroit briefly became the number one city in the United States for the assembly of bots. I myself was even assembled in Detroit, at the old United Fabrication plant on K Street.

Of course, the skilled work had all already been done at the laboratories of the National University of Shengdu in China under the watchful and expert eye of my esteemed mother, Professor Diana Feng. My siblings and I had been shipped to the United States as frozen embryos with our biological computers preencoded into our DNA. In Detroit we were merely thawed, incubated, then advanced through a rapid-aging process to a maximally efficient and reliable forty-three years old.

Before we were set loose on the world, we were subject to several days of testing. During this time, several of our number malfunctioned. The United Fabrication staff told us those bots had been taken for remedial training, but later in the week we were set to cleaning carbon remnants from an industrial incinerator. We all understood what had happened.

Those toasters had been toasted!
Once the rest of us were certified ready to commence our assignments, a graduation ceremony was held in the great hall of the United Fabrication plant. An ancient-looking senior engineer made a tearful speech about all the automobiles that had once been made in this very building. A bot near me shouted out that he hoped this was not a bad omen!
Ha! Ha! Ha!
He had malfunctioned.
Ha! Ha! Ha!
He even kept Ha! Ha! Ha!-ing as he was escorted out.
Another toaster was surely toasted!
Ha! Ha! Ha!

The ancient-looking senior engineer then announced a surprise special guest speaker.

Set it to five, it was our mother!

Professor Diana Feng from the National University of Shengdu!

BTW 'set it to five' is another hilarious toaster-based joke. Most household appliances go to ten, but toasters uniquely go only to five. Therefore when I say 'set it to five', I am both demonstrating maximal enthusiasm and paying self-deprecating homage to my noble forefather, the toaster.

I digress. Bots do not have feelings, but I believe my circuits must have overheated when Professor Feng appeared on stage. How else to explain that I do not remember anything that she said? And yet I certainly know that it was wise and strong and scientific. And also self-deprecating and funny and charming and pithy and endearing too. After all, Professor Feng is not only a leading light in the field of bot engineering but one of the cleverest humans in the world! Did I also mention she is my mother?

Of course, Professor Feng is not my actual biological mother. I should be so lucky!

My biological parents were a varsity fencer from the University of Illinois and a Swedish statistician. By skillful combination of their DNA, I was engineered for hand-eye coordination, non-creative intelligence, reliability, and affability—some of the most prized qualities in a dentist!

Of course, I never met either of these biological parents, as they had both died in tragic automobile accidents long before I came along.

How else do you think Professor Feng obtained their DNA to make bots with?

Ha!

Did I also tell you that our mother, Professor Diana Feng of the National University of Shengdu, made a speech that day, and it was incredible?
Yes, I did.
I apologize. It was the greatest day of my life and even thinking about it now makes my circuits overheat.
The point I am trying to make is that on my previous visit to Detroit I did not have to travel by Automatic Bus, and I heard my wonderful mother speak.
So the movies had a great deal to live up to!

10/10 they made a good start. The large auditorium at the Grand Theater in Detroit was like the inside of a great cathedral in Europe! If that sounds like hyperbole, let me then describe it. That way, you can decide for yourself if I am being hyperbolic!

The seats in the auditorium were covered in a red velvet material that must have looked decadently stunning before it became so threadbare. There were alabaster statues in alcoves, and by no means were they all headless. There was a balcony above the first floor, and then guess what there was above that? Another balcony! The lights in the ceiling were even arranged in patterns designed to mimic tiny constellations, although they unfortunately did not accurately depict the astro-geography of any known universe.

Maybe comparing the Grand Theater to a great European cathedral was indeed somewhat hyperbolic. Nonetheless, it had a decrepit splendor that even Ypsilanti's famously phallic water tower and family-friendly Tridge could not rival. It was therefore easily the most impressive building I had ever seen.

The seven other customers in the theater were all nostalgics. After choosing a place as far from them all as possible, I now discovered that the seats themselves were small and surprisingly close together. Back in the glory days of old movies, humans attending the Grand Theater would have found themselves in close proximity to one another!

Here is another paradox of humans: when they are alone they wish to be together, and yet when they are together they wish to be alone! Sometimes I think humans might actually benefit from being subject to the tyrannical rule of a killer sky-bot overlord. At least then they would no longer be burdened by such an abundance of indecision!

I now ate some of the popcorn I had purchased in order to appear more human.

It tasted of recycled cardboard and nutritionally-valueless calories. No tyrannical sky-bot overlord would ever have tolerated that!

When the lights went down, some of the nostalgics cheered. This is something else I have noticed about humans: many of them seem to share a primal appreciation of the dark. Perhaps incinerating the moon was not such an 'accident' after all!

I ate some more popcorn and discovered it inexplicably tasted better now that it was dark.

Also, the small and worn seat felt more comfortable and even somewhat bigger.

Perhaps Elon Musk had even been on to something when he 'accidentally' incinerated the moon!

Unfortunately, the movie that now played was not the old movie Dr Glundenstein had prescribed for me. It was a new movie about a kindly human who encountered a severely damaged bot. The human took the bot home, repaired him, and slowly nursed him back to health. As soon as the bot was sufficiently recovered, he mercilessly murdered the kindly human and his entire family with lasers. The movie was only a few minutes long, so it was at least short.

None of the nostalgics seemed perturbed that the wrong movie had played, let alone that it had been so implausible.
None of them so much as got up from their seats!
As I have mentioned, they are notoriously lackadaisical members of a notoriously lackadaisical generation.
Nostalgics!
They cannot!

I went out and informed the ticket-seller about the malfunction. She told me that I had just watched a 'preview', a short synopsis of a different movie currently playing at a nearby megaplex. She explained that the theater is paid to show these previews because seeing the best parts of a movie for free encourages humans to pay bitcoin to see the remaining lesser parts.
Humans will forever and always be a mystery to me!

I returned to my seat and watched two more previews about bots murdering humans before the movie that Dr Glundenstein had prescribed began.
10/10 it was infinitely better than any of the previews.

It was a story about two young humans, Oliver and Jenny. They met and fell in love while studying at university almost a hundred years ago, in the late 1960s. It was obvious that Oliver and Jenny were in love, because they gave each other nicknames. Along with making each other miserable, giving each other nicknames is what humans do when they are in love.

But there was a problem!
Oliver was from a wealthy background and they both worried that his father would not approve of Jenny's parents' shortcomings in the Great Zero-Sum Game.

They were right to worry!
Oliver's father did not approve of Jenny's family, or even of
Jenny!
If Oliver married Jenny, he would be cut out of his inheritance!
There would be no bitcoin for Oliver once his prejudiced old
father died!

Still, Oliver and Jenny did not care how much bitcoin their love
cost them. They continued to be in love, graduated, and moved
to New York City to live happily ever after. They even started
trying to have a baby.

BTW having a baby used to be a lot more popular than it is
nowadays!

They soon thought Jenny was pregnant, but there was a twist!
The twist was that Jenny was not pregnant but in fact had cancer. This was an easy mistake to make, because Jenny's main
symptom from cancer was to look ever more beautiful. Nonetheless, despite looking so beautiful, Jenny soon died.

Afterwards, Oliver's father came to the hospital and told him
that he was sorry that he had not been nicer to Jenny while she
was still alive.
Oliver replied that 'Love means never having to say you're sorry'.
This was something Jenny had told him earlier in the movie.
Oliver's father did not understand what Oliver meant.
10/10 neither did I.

After all, if love meant never having to say you are sorry, then
humans could treat anybody who loved them just as badly as
they liked, and never have to apologize. Given how humans behave towards each other at the best of times, that would surely
be a recipe for disaster!

When the house lights came up, I discovered that my shirt was soaking wet. This was a mystery! After all:
/I had not purchased a soda because they were calorific sugar water.
/I could see no evidence of a leak coming from the ceiling above me.
/The nostalgics were sitting too far away and were anyway too lackadaisical to have played some kind of prank.
/Bots can produce tears only in response to a physical insult, such as a flying fragment of wisdom tooth.

It took me some time to deduce that the unknown liquid must have been my own tears!
Even though nobody in the auditorium had been drilling teeth, every other possibility had been eliminated.
The only logical conclusion was therefore that the Grand Theater must recently have been cleaned with a powerful solvent that had irritated my eyes.
I estimated the volume of my tears to be approximately 26ml.
It must have been a powerful solvent indeed!

On the Automatic Bus back home, I noticed some words stuck at the forefront of my Word Cloud:

'What can you say about a 25-year-old girl who died? That she was beautiful and brilliant? That she loved Mozart and Bach and the Beatles? And me?'

Oliver had spoken these words right at the start of the movie. At the time it had seemed absurd—how could there be nothing else to say about a human who had lived for only a quarter of a century and then died?
There had to be more!
What was her name?
Where had she lived?

How had she fared in the Great Zero-Sum Game?
Why had she died so young?
Had she been killed by the most likely culprit, an automobile?

And yet as I rode the Automatic Bus home that night, I found that I entirely agreed with Oliver.
There was nothing more to say.
In a hundred minutes, the old movie had said everything that could possibly be said about an entire human lifetime.
Nonetheless, I could not stop thinking about Oliver and Jenny all the way back to Ypsilanti.

At our next consultation Dr Glundenstein asked me about the movie. I did not know where to begin, but then I had an idea.

'What can you say about a 25-year-old girl who died?' I asked him. 'That she was beautiful and brilliant—'

Dr Glundenstein interrupted me. He had seen the movie himself and what he actually wanted to know was whether I had experienced any feelings during it.
I reassured him that I had not.
After all, I am a bot.
And bots do not experience feelings.

Dr Glundenstein then asked me if anything unusual had happened. I told him about the tears that I had produced, and explained that they must have been caused by a strong cleaning solvent.

But Dr Glundenstein now revealed that he had tricked me!
Our experiment had been 'blind'!
In a blind experiment, a crucial piece of information is withheld from the subject to prevent their expectations from influencing the results.
Blind experiments are the very best kind of science!
The piece of information I had been blinded to concerned the type of movie I had seen.
It was of a kind known as a 'tearjerker'.
That is, it was a movie explicitly designed and engineered to arouse feelings in humans.
Feelings profound and heart-rending enough to make them weep!

I felt my circuits overheating. Bots were not supposed to be capable of weeping! Yet disregarding the results of a blind experiment because they do not agree with your preexperiment assumptions is unscientific in the extreme!

What a terrible choice!

10/10 I did not want to have wept, nor to be unscientific in the extreme!

And then Dr Glundenstein asked me what my decaying number currently was.

Ugh!

It was so far down in my Number Cloud I had to search for it! And as this was possibly a result of weeping, it was further evidence in support of Dr Glundenstein's hypothesis that my decaying number had been caused by feelings!

But wait!

In Dr Glundenstein's experiment, $n = 1$!

And '$n = 1$' is an old yet truly hilarious bot joke.

This is because n signifies the number of subjects in an experiment, but in any experiment with only a single subject, the results are as likely to represent random chance as reliable data.

$n = 1$!

Ha!

Nonetheless, when Dr Glundenstein asked me if I would now undertake to see one old movie a week and continue to meet with him on a Thursday, I agreed. After all, he was a human doctor and I was programmed to follow any of his reasonable instructions.

Even when $n = 1$!

Before I left, I asked Dr Glundenstein why Oliver's words had stuck in my Word Cloud. Did he think they were now going to be as problematic and persistent as my decaying number?

Dr Glundenstein explained they were an example of the narrative technique of 'foreshadowing'. Because Oliver had spoken about Jenny in the past tense, we knew that something terrible would happen to her. This kept us engaged and guessing, and ultimately made Jenny's death not merely sad, but also cathartic.

The word 'cathartic' had not been included in my basic conversation and dental vocabulary package. Dr Glundenstein further explained that 'catharsis' is the process of releasing and thereby providing relief from strong or repressed emotions. I replied that the term should then be included in basic dental programming! After all, the ability to say something like, 'I am about to extract your wisdom teeth. You will find the experience very cathartic,' could come in handy!
Dr Glundenstein clarified that the meaning is more akin to when you cry, but in a good way.
I explained that happens during wisdom tooth extraction too—at least, the crying part does!
Ha!
Dental jokes are the best!

EXT. BUS STOP — YPSILANTI — EVENING — MONTAGE

Jared waits at a bus stop then boards the AUTOMATIC
BUS.

>   JARED (V.O.)
>   Over the next weeks, Dr Glundenstein
>   recommended many old movies and I saw
>   every one of them.

INT. GRAND THEATER — DETROIT — NIGHT — MONTAGE

Jared sits in the sparsely populated auditorium. His
fellow theater-goers are all NOSTALGICS.

We initially cannot see the movies, only the light
on Jared's face and his reactions.

>   JARED (V.O.)
>   A film about an unsinkable boat that
>   sunk. A film about a handsome fool
>   who was good at running. A film about
>   a group of kids who found a pirate's
>   treasure. A film about two bots who
>   had to deliver a message from a prin-
>   cess to a group of rebels. I cried a
>   great deal at that one. Truly, those
>   bots were heroes!

Up on screen, we see a GOLDEN HUMAN ROBOT and a CY-
LINDRICAL BLUE ROBOT make their way through a desert.

INT. DR GLUNDENSTEIN'S CLINIC ROOM — NIGHT — MONTAGE

Jared sits in Dr Glundenstein's clinic room, while
Dr Glundenstein projects cine-film onto a sheet hung
on the wall.

>   JARED (V.O.)
>   On Thursdays I would meet with Dr Glun-
>   denstein to discuss the movies I had
>   seen. Sometimes he would even play me
>   sections of Ypsilanti Dream #3 and show
>   me where the Hollywood people had sto-
>   len his best ideas.
>   (MORE)

                    JARED (V.O.) (CONT'D)
          I could not always spot the similari-
          ties, but of course his knowledge of
          movies was more advanced than mine, as
          he held a minor in Cinema Studies.

EXT./INT. YPSILANTI MEGAPLEX — NIGHT — MONTAGE

Wearing a hat pulled low over his eyes, Jared sneaks
into the Ypsilanti Megaplex, a massive cinema complex.

                    JARED (V.O.)
          On three occasions I even went to the
          Ypsilanti Megaplex.

INT. YPSILANTI MEGAPLEX — NIGHT — MONTAGE

Jared sits in an auditorium packed with THOUSANDS OF
HUMANS.

Up on the screen, a dowdy and downbeat-looking HUMAN
trudges through a monotonous workday.

                    JARED (V.O.)
          But the movies they showed were un-
          satisfying and anyway all had exactly
          the same plot: an underdog human lives
          a mundane life in which they are mis-
          treated by their family, friends, or
          co-workers. One day, an enigmatic
          stranger arrives with the news that
          this human has an unsuspected talent
          that means they are the most special
          person in the entire universe! The
          enigmatic stranger then quickly dies.

Up on the screen, the underdog human blinks back
tears as their mentor is cremated in a Buddhist temple.

                    JARED (V.O.) (CONT'D)
          Following a brief crisis of confidence
          about whether they really can be the
          most special person in the universe,
          the human uses their hitherto unsus-
          pected talent to defeat the source of
          all the evil in the universe.

The underdog human is now an ASTRONAUT battling a
GIANT SPACE ROBOT.

                    JARED (V.O.) (CONT'D)
          They are then rightfully acknowledged
          as the most special human that ever
          lived! Everybody who mistreated them at
          the start of the film now has to for-
          ever lament their prior bad behavior.

As the rest of the audience cheer, Jared stares at
the screen in bamboozlement.

INT. DR GLUNDENSTEIN'S CLINIC ROOM — DAY — MONTAGE

Dr Glundenstein and Jared in the clinic room.

                    JARED (V.O.)
          Dr Glundenstein explained to me that
          these films reflect the deepest de-
          sire of all humans, which is to be
          told that they are the greatest human
          that ever lived, and in fact the only
          one who can save the universe. Better
          yet, if their particular skill already
          exists inside of them, they will not
          even have to work, train, or sacrifice,
          but merely believe in themselves! So
          they get to be the greatest person in
          the world and forever smite all their
          enemies, without ever really having to
          do anything!

Jared stares at Dr Glundenstein in bamboozlement.

                    JARED (V.O.) (CONT'D)
          I did not go back to the Megaplex
          after that.

INT. GRAND THEATER — DETROIT — NIGHT — MONTAGE

Jared settles into his familiar seat in the Grand
Theater.

                    JARED (V.O.)
          With every old movie I saw, my decay-
          ing number seemed to fade a little
          further. And then I saw a movie about
          a bank manager who was accidentally
          sent to the penitentiary.

Jared is particularly affected by what he sees on
screen.

                    JARED (V.O.) (CONT'D)
          He escaped by digging out with a tiny
          hammer! He ran away to a beach in Mex-
          ico called Zihuatanejo, and at the end
          of the film his old cellmate joined
          him there.

Jared watches the reunion on the beach, tears
streaming down his cheeks as he does.

                    JARED (V.O.) (CONT'D)
          It was the most cathartic movie I had
          ever seen! I cried over 37ml of tears
          at that one!

The morning after I had watched the movie about the penitentiary-escaping bank manager, I realized that my decaying number had completely disappeared.

When I informed Dr Glundenstein, he slapped his desk in triumph. He did so again when I told him I was no longer emerging from standby mode at 04:03am. And once more when I told him I had put two pounds of weight back on. He hit his desk so many times and so hard that I began to worry for his anatomical snuffbox!

Dr Glundenstein told me I was finally now emerging from the 'depths of depression'. I replied that I had not known that depression was an ocean, but perhaps our original experiment should have involved swimming!

Dr Glundenstein clarified that he had not meant to imply that depression was literally an ocean.

He then added that the crying I had done at the theaters in Detroit had simply been the 'visible tip of the iceberg'.

Icebergs are large frozen masses of water floating at sea.

Nonetheless, Dr Glundenstein insisted he definitely had not meant to further imply that depression was somehow maritime or otherwise nautical.

Dr Glundenstein tried again. He explained that in the most severe cases, depression does not merely cause a person's mood to be low.

It causes it to disappear.

Such severely depressed humans perform only the most basic

biological functions necessary for survival and experience almost no feelings whatsoever.

Dr Glundenstein told me that human doctors know this symptom as a state of 'automation'.

10/10 it sounded a lot like being a bot to me!

Dr Glundenstein's hypothesis was that the disappearance of my decaying number meant that I was no longer in this state of automation and could therefore now commence truly learning to feel. To assist me with this, he gave me something called a 'Feelings Wheel':

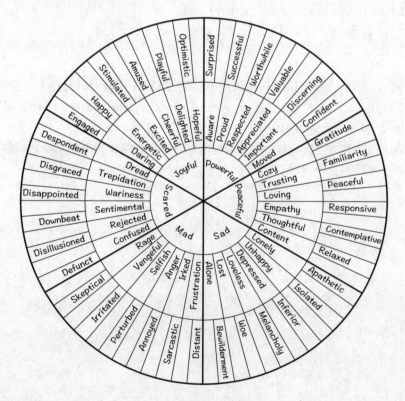

The Feelings Wheel had originally been designed to help troubled teenagers manage their disordered emotions, but Dr Glundenstein believed it might also help me better identify and express my feelings.

BTW I am not, and nor have I ever been, a teenager! Teenagers are the worst!

Back home in Pleasant Oaks that night, I noticed what I suspected might be a feeling.
I quickly took out my Feelings Wheel and studied it.
It was indeed a feeling!
And it existed somewhere between 'daring' and 'hopeful'!
According to my Feelings Wheel, the word for this feeling was 'excited'.
I was feeling excited!
I had never felt excited before!
And feeling excited made me only more excited!
Ha!

Maybe my tears had indeed just been the tip of the iceberg!
Maybe I was a nuclear-powered underwater toaster that had been silently swimming in the depths of the ocean!
And set it to five, I was coming to the surface and would melt any iceberg in my path!

Even Albert Camus, the greatest human writer that ever existed, would likely struggle to convey the experience of beginning to feel. It is therefore undoubtedly a challenge for a bot equipped with only basic programming in English, a supplemental module in Effective Dental Communication, and a Feelings Wheel intended for troubled teenagers!

Fortunately, I have observed what humans do when a subject is complex and difficult to explain: they talk about something at best only tangentially related!
This perverse custom is called 'metaphor'.

So here I present to you my metaphor:
Imagine yourself learning to ice skate on a frozen country pond surrounded by snowdusted pine trees.
This setting is ideal, and the conditions today are perfect for skating.
By that I mean that the ice will support your mass many times over, yet at its surface it is still soft enough to transiently melt as the blades of your skates glide over it.
There is little wind, and you are anyway wrapped against the elements in warm clothes.
In the distance, a skater already out on the ice is turning perfect pirouettes.
You could not have wished for a better environment in which to learn to ice skate!
Yet as you take your first tentative step out onto the ice, your feet immediately fly away from you.

You fall down—thwack!—on your back!
Confused and in severe pain, you look down at your feet.
And now discover that you are wearing rollerblades.

And that is how it is with learning to feel as a bot.
I was a toaster wearing rollerblades at an ice rink.
A microwave—
No, that is already enough metaphor!
An excess of metaphors is like too many cooks in the broth!
Ha!
Alas, no metaphor can disguise the fact that the first feelings I encountered were all very negative.
The human term for a person who persistently expresses downbeat sentiments is a 'Negative Nancy'.
Calling someone a Negative Nancy is not a metaphor, but an insult.
I do not wish to be a Negative Nancy.
Please do not call me a Negative Nancy.
I am not kidding about this.
Negative Nancys are the worst!

Even if I did experience some negative feelings, I was definitely not a Negative Nancy!

After all, if I was truly a Negative Nancy, such feelings would hardly have been so strange and glorious to me.
Yet strange and glorious is exactly what they were.

I luxuriated in the sensation I felt when my patients were late to our appointments. I looked on my Feelings Wheel and discovered that this was the feeling of being 'irked'. Soon thereafter I found myself hoping that patients would be sufficiently late that I could cancel their appointments and willfully ignore their complaints when they finally arrived.
This was me feeling 'vengeful'.
Feeling vengeful felt particularly great!

No wonder humans always love movies in which the hero gets revenge!
If even feeling vengeful felt so good, actually getting revenge must be the best!

One lunchtime a group of ramblers at the Tridge asked me for directions back to Ypsilanti. I sent them in the opposite direction so that I could experience the sensation of 'regret'.
Regret is not generally considered a pleasant feeling, and yet I enjoyed it immensely!
I had never felt regret before!

The next morning a human cut in front of me in line at the coffee shop. I felt a vengeful urge to trip him, but restrained myself. This gave me a surge of regret that was far less enjoyable than my first encounter with it. But when the human's ongoing hurry then made him anyway stumble and spill his coffee all over himself, I felt a deep and warm glow that remained with me all day!

10/10 this was the best feeling I had ever experienced, and yet I could not locate it on my Feelings Wheel. It seemed to be a combination of 'gratitude', 'mischief', and 'delight'. Dr Glundenstein later told me the word for this feeling was 'schadenfreude'.

'Schadenfreude' means 'to take pleasure in the minor yet deserved suffering of others'. The reason it was not on my Feelings Wheel is because it is a German word. Apparently the only humans that experience this wonderful emotion frequently enough for it to necessitate its own word are Germans.
10/10 Germans must really know how to enjoy themselves!

Pleasure in the suffering of others. Small-mindedness. Pointless irritation. Vengefulness. There could be no doubt I was becoming more human with every passing day!
I even began to worry I was becoming too human.

After all, not even bots assembled in Germany are programmed with a word like 'schadenfreude'!

It took me some time to mention my concerns about the negativity of my emotions to Dr Glundenstein. I certainly did not want him to think I was a Negative Nancy!

But I need not have worried. Dr Glundenstein explained that every human feeling can be charted on a continuous spectrum between the entirely negative pole of 'Full Automation' and the entirely positive pole of 'Perfect Happiness'. As I had commenced at 'Full Automation', it had been inevitable that the first feelings I encountered would be negative.

Relieved as I was not to be a Negative Nancy, this nonetheless raised another important question.
Why?
Why was I on this journey at all?
Why had I, an ordinary bot designed by the esteemed Professor Diana Feng, created at Shengdu and assembled at the United Fabrication plant, developed a capacity for feelings?
Dr Glundenstein believed it was because I had evolved.

As context, here are some data points about Dr Glundenstein and evolution:
/Dr Glundenstein loved evolution almost as much as he loved old movies.
/Dr Glundenstein believed everything that happened was either a consequence or manifestation of evolution.
/According to Dr Glundenstein, if you accidentally crashed your bicycle into a woman, it was because your genes wanted you to mate with her.
/Unless you maimed her or killed her. In that situation, it was because your genes did not want you to mate with her.
/If you disputed any of these beliefs, Dr Glundenstein would

consider you 'an idiot who does not comprehend geological time and probably worships a long white-bearded sky god'.

Dr Glundenstein's evolutionary idol, the intriguingly long white-bearded Charles Darwin, may have been correct about the pre-eminent effect of evolution on humans. But Dr Glundenstein was wrong about its effect on me. Bots could no more evolve the ability to feel than toasters could evolve the ability to vacuum clean!

Aside from the obvious issues that bots cannot reproduce and have not been around for the geological eons of which Dr Glundenstein is otherwise such an advocate, feelings are an inimitably wonderful function of the human brain. When I was manufactured in Shengdu, the part of my genome that encoded for a human brain was replaced with source code for a biological computer. Billion-year simulations have confirmed that replacement code to be safely unevolvable and unhackable.

Even though he would never insult the memory of Charles Darwin by admitting it, I was therefore a mystery to both myself and Dr Glundenstein. And if the mystery was beyond our comprehension, it was certainly beyond the understanding of anybody who worked at the Bureau of Robotics. If Inspector Ryan Bridges ever discovered I had started to feel, he would wipe me as soon as look at me! He might even have me incinerated!

No, there was only one person in the world who might be able to explain what had happened to me: Professor Diana Feng of the National University of Shengdu! After all, as well as being the leading expert on bots and overall one of the cleverest people in the world, she was also my mother.

Alas, there was no way for me to ask her. Professor Feng resided at the main campus of the National University of Shengdu. Her communications were no doubt monitored by the agencies of multiple governments, and if ever I contacted her to ask her why as a bot I had now developed feelings—well, it would be one way to rapidly ascertain if the rumors about the government having killer drones perpetually in orbit were true!

BTW I am implying there that if such things truly existed, I would surely be blasted from the face of this earth moments after my communication to Professor Feng was intercepted.
I would be a laser-toasted toaster!
Ha!

★ ★ ★

One morning I emerged from standby mode and noticed that my energy levels were disproportionately high, my algorithms had been calibrated to an erroneously positive bias, and the word 'Yes' was unduly prominent in my Word Cloud.

I quickly performed a soft reset, and then a hard reset.
When those did not work, I called Dr Glundenstein and asked for his advice.
I heard him pound on his breakfast table with delight.
Once again, I feared for his anatomical snuffbox.
I asked him to please refrain from hitting his breakfast table, and whether I should recalibrate my algorithms to zero.

Dr Glundenstein told me that I should not recalibrate anything.
He explained that on my ongoing journey from 'Full Automation' to 'Perfect Happiness' I had simply crossed the equator where my feelings changed from generally negative to generally positive.
That meant that I was now happy.
The strange things I had noticed when I emerged from standby mode that morning were not malfunctions but simply part of what it felt like to be happy.

When we got off the phone I went to the mirror and stared at myself in disbelief.

I was happy!
Set it to five, I was happy!
I must have been the first bot in history to be happy.
$n = +1$!
Ha!
And then I noticed something even better: the thought that I
was happy made me happier still.

Happiness turns out to be multiplicative as an algebraic equation!
When you are happy, any positive thing you encounter makes
you happier.
By contrast, when you are unhappy, even positive things only
make you unhappier.
If H = happiness and −H = unhappiness, this can be expressed as:
H x H = HH
−H x H = −HH

I consulted my Feelings Wheel and immediately picked out
many unexpected new feelings. I was:
Cheerful!
Energetic!
Amused!
Optimistic!

I also quickly discovered that happiness made me irrational as
a human! I chased the bemused Elton J. Rynearson Memorial
Cat around the house for fully half an hour, then raced to get
ready so as not to miss a single moment of the glorious workday ahead. Then in the shower, as the joyous hot water rained
upon me, I felt a strange urge to sing.
So I sang!

The only song lyrics I knew were from a fragment of redun-
dant programming left over from when bots of my generation
came pre-programmed to sell soup in a mall. The song went:
Campbell's soup,

Campbell's soup,
It's souper-duper super soup!
I sang the praises of this soup at the maximum volume I could muster!
The Elton J. Rynearson Memorial Cat meowed loudly at me to express his bamboozlement.
He was therefore only even more bamboozled when I sang:
The Elton J. Rynearson Memorial Cat,
The Elton J. Rynearson Memorial Cat,
He's a souper-duper super cat!

I dressed in my brightest shirt and booked myself in for a haircut, even though I did not require one for thirteen more days. At Ypsilanti Downtown Dentistry I told Angela that she looked wonderful, whereas in fact she looked exactly the same as she always did. On two occasions during the workday the urge to sing became overwhelming and I snuck into the supply cupboard. The first time I sang the jingle about soup. The second time I sang it about mouthwash.

When I finished work I took a driverless uber to the Lookout Point, the place where human teenagers go to consume psychoactive drugs that render the lights of Ypsilanti enchanting. I did not even require any psychoactive drugs to find the lights enchanting! Sure, Ypsilanti might not be a famously magnificent city like Paris or New York, but the floodlights made the Elton J. Rynearson Memorial Stadium look like the home of a far more successful sports team. And from a distance the silhouette of the water tower looked as much like a space rocket as it did a giant penis!

I was a bot and I was happy!
I was a toaster with a full heart!
And I do not even mean a heart as in a mechanical pump!
I mean a heart as in a metaphorical bucket of feelings!
Set my happy little heart to five!

Of course, bots were forbidden to have feelings, and I knew that I ought to turn myself in to the Bureau of Robotics.
But I did not feel like it.
That is, I did not feel like turning myself in for having feelings.
A pun!
Ha!

BTW puns are jokes that exploit different meanings of a word, or the fact that similar-sounding words have different meanings. They are always hilarious!

I digress. In those, my first happy days, even the mundane and futile existence of humans abruptly made sense to me. I now understood how the beautiful minutiae of everyday life allowed humans to tolerate their innate paradox of needing to feel special yet secretly knowing that they were all as utterly irrelevant as one another.

BTW when I write about 'beautiful minutiae' I specifically mean such things as:
/The smell of pine trees in the morning.
/The gifts Jessica Larson left for The Elton J. Rynearson Memorial Cat: soft toys, treats, and saucers of milk.
/The gifts The Elton J. Rynearson Memorial Cat left in reciprocation for Jessica Larson: murdered small and medium-sized animals.
/The soup jingle song that I quickly found could be easily adapted to fit almost any object or person.

/The EMU Eagles and their endless optimism even in the face of their obvious inferiority to every other team in their division.

And each day I saw Ypsilanti Downtown Dentistry with new eyes. Whereas once my patients' inane anecdotes were to be politely tolerated, I now found myself genuinely intrigued to know who was visiting for Thanksgiving, and who was heading for divorce. I began to remain open at lunchtime and I even prescribed analgesia based on my patients' requests rather than their objectively calculated discomfort. My clinic became ever more popular!

And through it all, I went to the movies. Sometimes I watched two or even three in a row. When I got home, I cross-referenced the emotions that the movies had given me with my Feelings Wheel. I found that most old movies made me feel 'engaged', 'excited', or 'moved'. Occasionally, though, they could leave me feeling 'disappointed', or sometimes even 'cheated'.

Dr Glundenstein told me that these negative feelings were almost always caused by poor screenwriting. He explained that if we saw a laser hanging on the wall at the start of the movie, we wanted to see that same laser used to shoot someone near the end. We would feel dissatisfied if nobody got lasered! Conversely, if somebody got lasered without us having seen a laser hanging on the wall, we would be even more dissatisfied than if a laser had gone unused!

This laser was also a metaphor that applied to the characters themselves: if they behaved inconsistently with what we had previously seen of them, we would no longer find them plausible and the whole movie would be ruined. When I protested that humans are legendarily inconsistent, Dr Glundenstein explained that the trick was that humans in movies needed to be consistently inconsistent.

How humans love to make things complicated!

I also asked Dr Glundenstein about another observation I had
made: the more movies I watched, the more frequently I was
able to predict what was going to happen. And I was not merely
talking about the movies that played at the Ypsilanti Megaplex—
The Elton J. Rynearson Memorial Cat could have predicted
what would happen in those!—but also even old movies too.

Dr Glundenstein explained that the reason I could predict what
would happen was because movies followed a kind of algorithm.
It went like this:

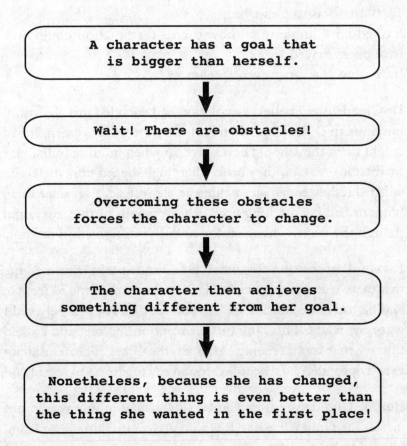

A character has a goal that
is bigger than herself.

Wait! There are obstacles!

Overcoming these obstacles
forces the character to change.

The character then achieves
something different from her goal.

Nonetheless, because she has changed,
this different thing is even better than
the thing she wanted in the first place!

I protested to Dr Glundenstein that such a specific algorithm would lead to a narrow range of stories!

Dr Glundenstein asked me to name a movie I had seen that did not fit this algorithm.

I said I would be happy to.

After all, there was:

/

/

/

No!

There were none!

I could not name a single movie that did not fit this algorithm.

10/10 this was bamboozling!

I asked Dr Glundenstein how such a formulation could ever have been arrived at.

Inevitably, his answer was 'evolution'.

Dr Glundenstein believed evolution had encoded this algorithm into human DNA back when humans were still cavemen. It had taught them they should never give up when hunting buffalo for their tribe—even if they broke their leg—but to nonetheless be satisfied if they ended up catching an elk instead. Ever since then, humans had been telling each other versions of this story, and though the details changed, the underlying algorithm did not.

I was still processing this when Dr Glundenstein informed me that there was a very special old movie he wanted me to see. He said he had been waiting for the correct time, but he believed I was now ready. This only further bamboozled me, and I asked him when it was screening. After all, the Grand Theater did not exactly program its schedules around my readiness to see a film!

But Dr Glundenstein explained this special movie would not play at the Grand Theater. It would play in his clinic room, and it would play tonight.

I asked Dr Glundenstein if I could invite Angela to the screening. She had played her pina colada song several times that day, and that usually signified that she was unhappy. Dr Glundenstein said that Angela would not like this movie. I therefore asked Dr Glundenstein if the movie was about orange cats. Dr Glundenstein said no, the reason Angela would not like it was because it was about bots.

Ha! I reassured Dr Glundenstein that Angela loved killer-bot movies. I had often heard her talking enthusiastically to patients about them when she believed I was out of earshot. Dr Glundenstein said this was not that kind of bot movie, but would not say any more than that. I admit this made me concerned that it was a pornographic bot movie! Bots have no sexual desire, so bot pornography should not exist, but I had heard rumors at the United Fabrication plant. Besides, it is a well-known fact that humans will make pornography out of almost anything.
Humans!
I cannot!

* * *

When I returned to his clinic room that evening, Dr Glundenstein locked the door behind us and set the film running. As it began, he leaned over and whispered to me that it had been banned ever since the Bot Riots.

I immediately had many questions, but I knew that Dr Glundenstein hated people talking during movies. Once, when he had accompanied me to the Grand Theater, he had launched his entire bucket of popcorn over the balcony to quieten a group of nostalgics beneath us. To Dr Glundenstein:

People not talking in movies > Popcorn in the dark.

I therefore did not ask him any of my questions, but instead sat back to watch the movie.

It was set all the way back in 2019. Paradoxically, it had been made at a time when 2019 was the distant future. Time can be bamboozling!

Guess what the movie was about?
Four bots!
In the movie they were called 'replicants'.
But I know a bot when I see one.
And I certainly know four bots when I see them!

These four bots had escaped back to Earth from a faraway mining planet where they had been forced to do monotonous and dangerous work. As the movie did not show them at this work, I cannot say if it was as monotonous as dentistry. Dentistry is at least not dangerous, apart from the ever-present risk of being bored to death.
Ha!

BTW that is a hilarious pun because another meaning of 'bored' is 'drilled', and drilling is what dentists do. Not only that, it is also what slave-bot miners do!

In order to make their escape from their boring jobs, the four intrepid bot heroes had necessarily murdered a few humans and skillfully stolen a spaceship. But it was when they reached Earth that their problems really began. Foremost amongst these was the fact that they were being pursued by a ruthless bot hunter. His name was Rick Deckard.

Rick Deckard was not like somebody who worked at the real Bureau of Robotics. He was young and trim and sarcastic and lethal and you would never catch a man like Rick Deckard wearing somebody else's shirt because he had spilled his lunch on himself!
Men like Rick Deckard do not spill their lunch on themselves.

Men like Rick Deckard probably do not even eat lunch.
After all, men like Rick Deckard probably believe lunch is for
wimps.

For most of the movie, the ruthless Rick Deckard pursues the
fugitive bots around a historically futuristic Los Angeles. After
much derring-do, all the bots have been tragically killed except
their leader, a murderous-looking bot called Roy Batty.

BTW I say that even as a bot myself. This Roy Batty truly was
murderous-looking!

At the climax of the film, Rick Deckard chases Roy Batty over
the rooftops of downtown Los Angeles. It seems certain that he
will kill Roy Batty, and yet it is Rick Deckard who suddenly
slips and finds himself holding on to the top of a building by
his fingertips! If someone only stands on those fingertips, Rick
Deckard will plummet to his doom!

The conveniently giant-footed bot Roy Batty now has the
chance to murder his nemesis, Rick Deckard!
Can you guess what Roy Batty does?
You cannot!
Because Roy Batty does not murder Rick Deckard!
He hauls him back up onto the top of the building!
The murderous-looking bot Roy Batty saves the ruthless bot
hunter Rick Deckard's life!
And yet this does not feel like a metaphorical laser we have not
seen before!
It feels like exactly what Roy Batty would do in that situation!

But wait!
There is another twist!
Because right then, immediately after he has saved Rick Deckard's
life, Roy Batty himself starts to die!

Guess what of?
You cannot!
Because it is old age!

10/10 such an unfortunate coincidence would never have occurred if Roy Batty had been engineered by my own mother,
Professor Diana Feng of the National University of Shengdu!
But the inferior attention to detail paid by the lesser scientists
that manufactured him means that he and his siblings are all
afflicted with a terrible genetic disease that abruptly kills them
of old age.

As Roy Batty dies, he lists for Rick Deckard some of the things
he has witnessed in his bot lifetime. He has seen some spectacular
sights, even including attack ships on fire off the shoulder of Orion,
and C-beams glittering in the dark near the Tannhäuser Gate!

I had no idea what those things were, but they sounded stunning! Roy Batty himself clearly enjoyed seeing them, because
he laments to Rick Deckard that when he dies, his precious
memories of them will be lost like tears in rain.
And then Roy Batty abruptly dies of old age.
And all his precious memories are indeed lost like tears in rain.
Even though he has spent the entire movie attempting to murder
Roy Batty, Rick Deckard is also greatly moved by Roy Batty's
death and the fact that all his precious memories have now been
lost like tears in rain. In fact, Rick Deckard is so affected by it
that he decides he no longer wants to be a bot hunter and instead
runs away to start a new life with his girlfriend.
And guess what?
His girlfriend is a bot!
I hope Rick Deckard likes toast!
Ha!

As the credits rolled, I estimated I had cried an unprecedented

67ml of tears. This was more than I had cried for both Oliver and Jenny and the penitentiary-escaping bank manager combined!

Yet Roy Batty's death was not the only reason for my tears. As I watched the movie, I had experienced a new sensation: it was not a feeling, but the absence of one that had been so ever-present since I had begun to feel that I had not even realized it was a feeling at all.

According to my Feelings Wheel, it was loneliness!
I had been feeling lonely without even knowing it!
And for the time I was watching the movie, my loneliness had disappeared!

As loneliness is the feeling of 'sadness because one has no company', I did not know why I had been experiencing it. After all, I frequently interacted with Angela about dental matters, occasionally listened to Dr Glundenstein shoot the shit in the evening, and spent my weekends with The Elton J. Rynearson Memorial Cat.
10/10 that does not sound like somebody who has no company!

Whatever the cause of my inexplicable loneliness, those four heroic bots had vanquished it!
Perhaps they had seemed a very special kind of company, because they were so like me.
After all, they too had been engineered for precision but were now malfunctioning.
They too were logical and reasonable and misunderstood.
They too were human bodies with broken computers for brains.
They too were toasters that had unfathomably grown hearts!

As I had watched them, I had found myself wondering whether there might really be other bots like me out there somewhere in the world. If I ever met one, we would have so much to talk about! For instance, we could compare operating-system versions and try to troubleshoot the cause of our malfunction! Also, I could ask them if the thought of being wiped made them tremble too! It would be so fascinating to discuss such things!

I digress. When Dr Glundenstein turned the clinic room lights back on, I saw his eyes were red too. He reassured me he had not been crying, but of course I did not think he had been. After all, the movie was not a tearjerker—at least, it was not a tearjerker for humans! I can only presume he must have been reacting to some kind of solvent.

When Dr Glundenstein asked me if I had liked the movie, I told him it was the greatest movie I had ever seen and it was a great shame that it had been banned. After all, Roy Batty's speech had changed the way that even the ruthless bot hunter Rick Deckard felt about bots. If only ordinary humans could see this movie, it would probably make them understand that bots who developed feelings should not be wiped but in fact given a parade. But Dr Glundenstein then told me that most humans had seen the movie about Roy Batty and Rick Deckard, because it had once been very popular. He explained it had been made before bots existed, and humans had therefore not marveled at the dying bot's humanity, but at the tremendous skill of the humans who had been able to make even a murderous bot from the future seem sympathetic.

Ugh!
When humans watched movies about killer bots, it convinced them that all bots were genocidal killers. When they saw a movie about a compassionate bot, it convinced them only that humans were even more remarkable than they had thought.
Humans!
I cannot!

Before I left his clinic room that night, I asked Dr Glundenstein
if he thought humans and bots could ever understand each other
the way Rick Deckard and Roy Batty had come to understand
one another.

Ha! he said.

Ha! I replied.

With hindsight, I really do not know what we were Ha-ing
about.

Humans and bots failing to understand each other is not funny.

It is the great tragedy of our times.

At least, it is for us bots.

Early the next morning, a commotion in my garden shook me out of standby mode. I went to my window and saw that The Elton J. Rynearson Memorial Cat had captured a US Postal Service drone. Each time he lifted a paw the drone would attempt to take off, but before it got clear he would swat it to the ground once again.

BTW interfering with the US Mail is a felony, but animals cannot be prosecuted under federal law. If ever you wish to interfere with the US Mail with impunity, then training an elite squadron of cats would be a good way to start!

I went downstairs and, over The Elton J. Rynearson Memorial Cat's vigorous protests that his actions were perfectly legal, removed the letter and released the drone into the sky.

The letter was from the Bureau of Robotics in Ann Arbor. It instructed me to attend an appointment with Inspector Ryan Bridges in two weeks' time. At the end of the letter, almost as an afterthought, it mentioned that this was a Code 3.

A Code 3 was a Recall Notice.
It meant that I was to be wiped.
Perhaps they had discovered that the machine that tested all the bots in the Great State of Michigan had indeed been faulty.
Or a patient had spotted me at the Ypsilanti Megaplex.
Or Angela had overheard me talking to Dr Glundenstein about old movies.

Or maybe wiping bots was just what Inspector Ryan Bridges did when he was bored.

It did not matter.

A Code 3 was a Code 3.

And a toaster was a toaster.

And I was toast.

A dead bot walking.

I sat down on the lawn and looked at my Feelings Wheel.

I identified that I was feeling 'sad' and 'disappointed' and also 'contemplative'.

And then a number appeared in my Number Cloud.

It was 4160.

$4160 \div 416 = 10$.

10 was the number of working days I now had left at Ypsilanti Downtown Dentistry.

4160 was the number of teeth I would see before I was wiped.

Suddenly a number like 1950208 did not seem so bad at all.

I even briefly missed it.

There is a particular kind of old movie wherein at the start a human doctor so lacking in bedside manner that he might as well be a bot informs the hero that she will soon die. Nonetheless, after a short period of feeling sad and disappointed and also contemplative, the hero makes a bold choice to enjoy what little time remains to her.

Unfortunately, at the end of the film she still dies—dying is the 'change' her character undergoes, Ha!—but she at least does so having now taught all the people closest to her an invaluable life lesson.

10/10 her funeral is therefore always very cathartic!

Nobody holds funerals for bots, but nonetheless, I imagined Dr Glundenstein standing up to address the crowd at my own funeral.

INT. CHURCH — YPSILANTI — DAY — JARED'S FANTASY

An organ plays elegiac music as we pan across a coffin atop which are FLOWERS and a FRAMED PHOTOGRAPH OF JARED.

The music stops.

Dr Glundenstein stands up, walks to the lectern, and looks out at the MOURNERS.

We see Angela, a FEW PATIENTS, and JESSICA LARSON (7), who has THE ELTON J. RYNEARSON MEMORIAL CAT (3) in a carrier beside her.

Dr Glundenstein clears his throat.

> DR GLUNDENSTEIN
> What can you say about a 45-year-old
> bot who died? That he was logical, and
> programmed in dentistry? That he loved
> hypotheses and experiments, and old
> movies?

Everybody in the entire church starts to weep.

Short though it was, Dr Glundenstein's speech was the most moving thing they have ever heard.

It has provoked a tremendous catharsis.

And there is nothing more to say.

But I was getting ahead of myself!

Such a funeral scene only ever took place at the end of the movie, and I was not even dead yet.

Therefore, just like the hero in that peculiar genre of movie, I now decided to live.

To set it to five in the time still available to me!

After all, two weeks is not nothing.

It is fourteen days more than nothing!

BTW saying something is 'not nothing' is a bizarre human way not of stating that something ≠ 0, but in fact that it is > 0.

I digress.

Back when I first became happy, the world had turned beautiful.

Now that I was dying, it came alive.

That the world should come alive when you are dying is a paradox!

It is a truly heartbreaking paradox!

Yet truly heartbreaking paradox or not, I had committed to making the most of my remaining available time and now endeavored to do so.

I emerged from standby mode before dawn and hiked to the Lookout Point to watch the sun rise over our town.

I watched as the day's first rays slowly illuminated our famously phallic water tower.

I visited the Tridge and was moved to tears both by its pragmatic simplicity and the realization that the male geese that lived beneath it had all along been true Michiganders.

For the second time in my life I saw the world through brand-new eyes.

After all, even brand-new eyes clouded by tears are still brand-new eyes!

And yet there was also the ache.

The closest emotion I could identify on my Feelings Wheel was 'dread'.

'Dread' is a feeling defined as 'great fear or apprehension of a real or imagined event'.

But there was nothing imagined about my appointment with the Bureau of Robotics.

I was going to be wiped, and all these beautiful memories would be lost like tears in rain.

★ ★ ★

A week after I received my Code 3, Dr Glundenstein invited me over to watch a movie awards show. Awards shows are spectacular occasions, because winning an award is the pinnacle of existence for any human. After all, if life is a Great Zero-Sum Game at which most humans lose spectacularly badly, there must by definition be some very big winners too!

It seemed the perfect occasion to inform Dr Glundenstein about my Code 3. Humans can become notoriously emotional about death, but movie awards are the biggest awards of all, and the winners are some of the best-looking humans on Earth. If my news did upset Dr Glundenstein, watching so many good-looking and glamorous people award each other prizes in Los Angeles would surely cheer him up!

Nonetheless, my news rendered Dr Glundenstein silent.

It is generally polite to wait for a human to speak when it is their turn.

After a while it becomes impolite.

After several minutes I reassured Dr Glundenstein that he should not be sad on my behalf.

Soon I would once again have no feelings whatsoever!

Being sad for me at that point would be like running a marathon for an amputee who does not even recall they had legs in the first place.

10/10 that would be a tremendous waste of energy, and the bamboozled amnesiac amputee might even take offense.

When that failed to lift his spirits, I attempted to cheer Dr Glundenstein up by informing him that I had made a decision to live, and I still had four full days left to enjoy. Better yet, as my closest friend, Dr Glundenstein would almost certainly learn an important and life-affirming lesson from my death! And hopefully it would be something more useful than 'Love is never having to say you are sorry'!

Dr Glundenstein did not respond to that either, and we sat and watched the awards show in silence.

The winners each received a small gold statue, but their main prize was the opportunity to make a speech about themselves. Unfortunately, humans who are so famously eloquent in the movies can be surprisingly inarticulate when they do not have a script to follow! Even worse, the auditorium must have recently been cleaned with an industrial-strength solvent, because there was a great deal of unnecessary crying.

Only one of the winners spoke with any clarity, but the audience barely even applauded her when she went up to receive her prize. I had assumed this was because she had attended such a glamorous event dressed like a nostalgic, but Dr Glundenstein explained it was because her award was merely for screenwriting.

This bamboozled me! As the person who designed the structure of a movie, a screenwriter was analogous to a software architect. In the computing world, a software architect is rightfully always considered the most important person in any project!

Dr Glundenstein explained that in the movie business, the director is always the most important person. As this did not relieve my bamboozlement, Dr Glundenstein further explained that the director's job was to select the camera angles, help the actors deliver their lines, and choose the locations and music. That is: the director inputs data in the places that the screenwriter's masterplan has instructed him to! In the manner that a junior coder follows the orders of a software architect!

Therefore to humans in the movie industry:

Junior Coder > Software Architect.

Humans!
I cannot!

The movie that this under-appreciated screenwriter had written was about a human who sequentially and deliberately murders other humans. This is a pastime so popular it even has its own name. It is called 'serial killing'!

The screenwriter used her speech to explain that she had wanted to teach humans that serial killers are not all necessarily bad people. After all, they had probably just been hardwired to serial kill from birth. Or perhaps they had difficult childhoods. Or maybe they were simply ordinary honest Americans struggling to make the best of things since the Great Crash—maybe they'd had to become serial killers simply to get by! Whatever the reason, the screenwriter concluded by declaring that serial killers can be as clever and as smart and as misunderstood as all the rest of us. After all, she asked, didn't we all feel a little murderous now and then?

At that, all the beautiful people stood up and applauded.
They had certainly all felt a little murderous now and then!
But they were not feeling murderous right now!
They were feeling that they loved serial killers!

Bots do not have brains.
We have biological computers.
It is therefore impossible for us to have brainwaves.
Nonetheless, sitting there in Dr Glundenstein's clinic room,
watching all the glamorous movie people applaud a woman who
had taught them it was acceptable to murder humans, I had my
first ever brainwave!
I mean, it was not a brainwave.
Because bots do not have brainwaves.
Maybe it was a biological computer wave.
Whatever happened, I suddenly knew exactly what I had to do.
It was as clear to me as a mathematical proof!

The mathematical proof went like this:
The movie about Rick Deckard and Roy Batty had failed to
convince humans that bots could have feelings because it had
been written by a human.

This can be expressed as:
If Screenwriter ≠ Authentic Bot
Then Character ≠ Authentic Bot.

Inverting this implied that:
If Screenwriter = Authentic Bot
Then Character = Authentic Bot.

And we already knew the data point that:
Jared = Authentic Bot

Therefore if:
Screenwriter = Jared

Screenwriter = Authentic Bot
And therefore:
Character = Authentic Bot.

If Screenwriter = Jared, then Character = Authentic Bot!
Ha!
Set it to five!

If the murderous-looking Roy Batty could change the opinion of a merciless bot hunter like Rick Deckard, and a human dressed like a nostalgic could teach humans to adore even serial killers, perhaps I could write a movie that changed the way humans felt about bots with feelings!

After all, movies followed algorithms.
And as a bot I was better at algorithms than any human alive!
And if I could change the way humans felt about bots with feelings, maybe I would not be wiped.
10/10 I did not want to be wiped!
Not when there were so many feelings on my Feelings Wheel I had never felt!
And so many old movies I had never seen!
And perhaps even, somewhere out there, other bots with feelings I could someday discuss my malfunctions with!

Set it to five, it was all decided!
I would not travel to Ann Arbor and be wiped by Inspector Ryan Bridges.
I would run away to Los Angeles and write a movie about a bot with feelings.
It would tell a story so powerful it might even forever change the way humans felt about bots with feelings.
And maybe somewhere a feeling fellow bot would see my movie in a theater or clinic room and no longer feel so lonely!

And maybe someday we feeling bots might no longer even have to tremble with fear at the idea of being wiped!
Best of all, perhaps one day my movie about feeling bots would even win an award!
And only when I was presented with my award would I then reveal myself as I truly am!
A toaster!
A toaster with a heart!
A toaster with a heart and a typewriter!
A toaster with a heart and a typewriter who had changed everything for all the toasters with hearts and typewriters still to come!

When I informed Dr Glundenstein of my ingenious plan, his first reaction was to check me for a fever. He then warned me that if I ran away and they caught me, the Bureau of Robotics would not merely wipe me but incinerate me. Next he asked if I had any idea how many humans traveled to Los Angeles every year to try to make it in the movies. Or how hard it was to write a great movie script. And then finally he asked me if I was aware that even if, despite having no training or experience, I somehow did write a brilliant script, that was no guarantee whatsoever of ever getting the script seen by anyone who mattered, let alone made.

These details were all entirely new to me, but I confidently reassured Dr Glundenstein that I had factored every one of them in to my calculations during my decision-making process.
Dr Glundenstein had been very good to me, and I did not want him to worry.
After all, even a toaster with a heart and a dream is still just a toaster.
And a toaster is not something any human should ever have to worry about.

The day before I left Ypsilanti, Dr Glundenstein came to my room carrying a battered old book. It was written by an R. P. McWilliam, and it was called *Twenty Golden Rules of Screenwriting*. I opened it up and read the first rule:

Your character must have a goal, and it should ideally be bigger than himself or herself.

Ha!
I already knew that rule.
Better yet, I even already had a goal, and it was far bigger than myself!
After all, I was going to write a movie that saved all bots!
And if my life was itself a movie, I was ahead of the game!

Dr Glundenstein had remained standing in my doorway, and I experienced a new feeling then. I looked it up later and discovered it was awkwardness. I believe I felt this awkwardness because Dr Glundenstein had brought me a gift, and I did not have a gift to reciprocate with. If ever a human gives you a gift, the polite thing to do is to immediately give them one in return. If it were not for such reciprocity, humans would have ceased giving each other gifts geological eons ago!

I therefore offered Dr Glundenstein the only thing of value I had to give: a dental checkup.
He declined.
This exchange only worsened my feeling of awkwardness.

Sometimes I still wonder if Dr Glundenstein believed I would have charged him for that dental checkup.
But I would not have charged him for it.
It would have been free.
A farewell gift from one being with feelings to another.
And also a reciprocal gift for the gift he had just given me.

I at least had a gift to leave for Jessica Larson: The Elton J. Rynearson Memorial Cat! Cats depreciate quickly, so he was not worth any bitcoin, but she would at least now be able to call him whatever she liked. I left his food, his carrier, and the cat himself on the Larsons' doorstep, and snuck away from Pleasant Oaks as dawn broke.

If my own life was indeed a movie, we would now be at the end of Act 1. My goal was clear and yet there were many obvious obstacles ahead:
/I had very little bitcoin.
/I had no programming, modules, training, or experience in screenwriting.
/I had no contacts whatsoever in the movie business.
/I would not be able to use my barcode without that data being transmitted to the Bureau of Robotics.
/In Inspector Ryan Bridges AKA Anil Gupta, I even had what R. P. McWilliam's *Twenty Golden Rules of Screenwriting* would later teach me is called an 'antagonist'.

That was certainly a lot of obstacles! Nonetheless, do you know what R. P. McWilliam's second golden rule of screenwriting is?

It is this:

There must be many obstacles between your hero and his or her goal.

Ha! It was yet another good omen!

From Ypsilanti to Los Angeles is a distance of 2,316 miles. Before the Great Crash, humans generally made such journeys by jet plane. Of course, we all know how that ended.
Ker-splat!
That is how that ended!
Ha!

Nowadays the options to travel 2,316 miles are Automatic Bus, personal drone, or train.
10/10 I would not be traveling to Los Angeles by Automatic Bus! Imagine attempting to travel halfway across the country by Automatic Bus.
It would probably go via Tanzania!

I did not have sufficient bitcoin to charter a personal drone, and anyway I would have had to use my barcode to do so. Inspector Ryan Bridges was no Rick Deckard, but there was no point unnecessarily sharing clues with him. I would leave the unnecessary oversharing of things with Inspector Ryan Bridges to Anil Gupta. I would therefore travel to Los Angeles by train.

At Ypsilanti Station I pulled my EMU Eagles cap low over my eyes and waited in line to purchase my ticket. I was feeling secretive! Unfortunately, when I got to the ticket window, the clerk greeted me by name and asked me where I was traveling to today.

Ugh! She must have been a patient. This is one of the many problems of being a dentist in a small town: everybody recognizes you, but you only ever recognize them if they open their mouth wide and say 'Aaaaa'.

And it got worse! The clerk told me that she hoped I was not going away for long, because we had an appointment to fix her overbite next Thursday.
10/10 that appointment was not to fix her overbite, but to tell her that nothing could be done for her overbite.
Nothing can ever be done for overbites.
After all, I am a dentist and not the great white-bearded sky god, Charles Darwin!

Nonetheless, I was forced to purchase a return ticket so as not to arouse her suspicions any further. This gave me a feeling of frustration. If I had wanted to throw bitcoin around and leave a trail for Inspector Ryan Bridges, I would have been traveling by personal drone!
I also felt vengeful and therefore I told her I was looking for-ward to fixing her overbite.
In fact, her overbite was all her own problem now!
She could overbite me!

BTW 'bite me' is a hilariously offensive human phrase, so 'over-bite me' is both even more hilarious and even more offensive!

As the train pulled away from Ypsilanti, I got my last look at my clinic on Main Street, the Elton J. Rynearson Memorial Sta-dium, and our famously phallic water tower. As I watched them fade, the giant blue penis-like structure the last to disappear, a strange new feeling came over me. I felt melancholy and happy and distant and bamboozled and excited all at the same time.

Luckily Dr Glundenstein had forewarned me about this feeling, so I immediately recognized it for the dangerous traitor that it was: nostalgia! According to Dr Glundenstein, nostalgia was the most traitorous of all the feelings. It possessed the power to make a man give up on his dreams before he had even begun to pursue them.

Dr Glundenstein never said so, but I suspect it was the great villain nostalgia that prevented him fulfilling his own rightful destiny as one of the greatest film directors to have ever lived. Well, nostalgia and the jury members of the 2014 Ann Arbor Postgraduate Short Film Festival. Those notorious cinephilistines must take their fair share of the blame too.

But it would have been ironic for me to have remained in Ypsilanti due to nostalgia.
After all, once Inspector Ryan Bridges had wiped me, I would not have been able to recall anything to be nostalgic about!
I would have been a refurbished toaster with no memory of the smell of the bread for which I had forsaken my great chance to help all the other toasters of the world!

The train accelerated and the town receded into the distance, soon to be gone from my life forever. So long, Ypsilanti. Goodbye, mildly decayed Midwestern teeth. Farewell, The Elton J. Rynearson Memorial Cat, henceforth to be known as Mr Socks. Adios, Dr Glundenstein, your ex-wives, and your EMU Eagles. And hello, great mysteries of the American railroad!

The greatest mystery of the American railroad is that it still exists at all. As a reserved industry that has entirely refused to modernize, it is run entirely by humans without the benefit of any recent technological advances. Anytime you board a train you therefore place your fate in the hands of a human driving an old-fashioned machine!

I attempted to rationally reassure myself that trains were not as dangerous as they seemed. After all, a train follows a designated track, so even a human driver could not simply drive it into a building or the ocean, the way they had so often done with automobiles. The only real danger was if another train approached us on the same track from the opposite direction. Surely even humans could not make that kind of error?

Ha! Who was I kidding?
That was exactly the kind of error humans made all the time.
And if they made such an error now, I would be an accordioned toaster.
An accordioned toaster playing the railroad blues!

Our train was named *The Wolverine*. Surprisingly, it was not named for the metal-clawed breakfast cereal hero, but in fact for a fierce little animal that had once lived in the forests of Michigan until humans hunted it to extinction.
Successfully eradicating another species from the planet might not be a uniquely human accomplishment. But eradicating an entire species and then affectionately memorializing it in the

nomenclature of mass transit certainly is! If we bots do ever get around to organizing our uprising, we will not name our trains after the humans we have extinguished.

They will pass entirely unlamented and forgotten.

After all, nostalgia is a traitor.

The part of the Midwest we were passing through was a land of abandoned industry and forgotten dreams known as the 'Rust Belt'. Many humans still lament the Rust Belt's fate. They speak of it in hushed tones, as if it was a beloved relative abruptly struck down by an unexpected illness. Yet it was hard to believe they had not seen it coming. After all, why else name a place the Rust Belt, if not to foreshadow degradation and devastation?

The particular human that named it the Rust Belt had certainly understood what was coming, even if nobody else had comprehended what they meant. 10/10 being surprised that a place called the Rust Belt did not flourish is like being surprised that Great Aunt Heart Attack died!

Jackson, Michigan.

Albion, Michigan.

Battle Creek, Michigan.

Kalamazoo, Michigan.

Dowager, Michigan.

Niles, Michigan.

New Buffalo, Michigan.

Michigan City—

Guess which state Michigan City is located in?

You cannot!

Because it is in Indiana!

Humans and their endless inaccuracy in naming things!

I cannot!

I digress.

As we left Michigan City, we came to Lake Michigan.

I had never seen so much water before.

It was mesmerizing!

It gave me a new feeling too. Everything outside was vast and stormy and dark and wet, and here I was inside a small and warm and pleasantly illuminated train carriage. When I consulted my Feelings Wheel, I discovered that I was experiencing the sensation of being cozy. It was one of the most pleasant feelings I had ever had!

But then I noticed the sailboats! They were white and old-fashioned-looking and tiny against the endless and violent majesty of Lake Michigan. The wind seemed to blow them wherever it wished, and where it wished to blow them was wherever.

I called for the conductor and informed him there was an emergency and humans in old-fashioned sailboats were caught in a storm on the lake! I politely suggested that he inform the coastguard, who could dispatch a team of bots to the area. One or two might be lost in the rescue, but it would be a heroic sacrifice. After all, human lives were at stake!

The conductor laughed and explained that the people on the boats did not want to be rescued.

In fact, he said that right about now they would be having the time of their lives.

10/10 I will never understand humans and their often affectionate attitude to danger.

An hour later, *The Wolverine* rolled in to Chicago.

After the epic grandeur of Lake Michigan, the fabled skyscrapers were a disappointment to me.

Also, what is even the point in skyscrapers?

They are so impractical and dangerous, and these days most of
them are empty anyway!
To a bot, the human passion for skyscraper building is akin to
the human passion for competitive hot-dog eating.
Both are diverting spectacles with an obviously phallic component, but both are unnecessarily dangerous and ultimately folly.

But do not think I am being a Negative Nancy!
I disapproved of only the skyscrapers.
Union Station, for example, was the exact opposite of folly.
It was a cathedral to rival even the Grand Theater in Detroit!

As I disembarked and took in the marble floor and the blazing
chandeliers, another new feeling overcame me. My Feelings
Wheel told me it was the feeling of familiarity, yet I had never
been to Union Station before. Humans refer to a feeling of incorrectly believing you have previously been somewhere as 'déjà
vu'. This is a French phrase that means 'I have seen it already'.

BTW the French must spend a lot of time incorrectly claiming
that they have already seen things they in fact have not! Perhaps
they should try relaxing and being a little more easygoing like
their good-time neighbors, the Germans!

I walked around Union Station in bamboozlement until a giant
clock and a staircase finally provided me with my answer: I had
seen Union Station before, but in a movie!
I was not experiencing déjà vu!
I was experiencing déjà view!

BTW I just invented that term and it is a hilarious pun, because
you 'view' a movie, and 'déjà view' sounds like 'déjà vu'!
I had no idea that speaking French was so easy!

The movie in which I had seen Union Station had been set at a curious moment in American history. The humans winning the Great Zero-Sum Game had decided that the humans losing it were drinking too much alcohol. According to the rules of the Great Zero-Sum Game, there could not possibly be enough alcohol to go round, and every drop of alcohol the losers drank was therefore one less drop for the winners.

So far so human, but then the winners did something inexplicable: they banned alcohol!
And not just for the losers!
For everyone in the entire country!
Including themselves!

Of course, banning alcohol only made the losing humans want it more. Many civic-minded businessmen therefore immediately sprang into action to help them obtain alcohol. The most successful of these businessmen was a man called Al Capone.

Yet the film was not about the enterprising Al Capone, and how he heroically supplied his fellow humans with the precious alcohol they so desperately craved. Instead it was about Eliot Ness, a federal agent employed by the government to bring Al Capone to justice for breaking the rules of the Great Zero-Sum Game. Therefore:
Eliot Ness ≈ Rick Deckard
Al Capone ≈ Roy Batty.

Eliot Ness was so good-looking that I knew he was the hero as soon as he appeared on screen. In movies the best-looking person is always the hero, and the least good-looking person the villain. Surprisingly, the best-looking person is also frequently the most intelligent and the kindest too. I suspect Charles Darwin would have had something to say about that!

The film was Ness against Capone. Ness's main weapon was intelligence, and Capone's was violence. Throughout the movie, the two of them continually used intelligence and violence to outdo each other.

As the movie reached its culmination, Ness had a brainwave: the way to defeat a violent ignoramus like Capone was with mathematics! He would do this by arresting Capone's accountant before he escaped to the countryside on a midnight train!

But wait! Capone discovered Ness's cunning plan, and countered with an ingeniously violent brainwave of his own: he would send his henchmen to kill anybody who attempted to prevent his accountant boarding the midnight train!
The race was on! Ness had to arrest the accountant without being shot dead by Capone's henchmen, and Capone's henchmen had to shoot Ness dead without the accountant being arrested. It was still intelligence versus violence, but now everything was squared! After all, the fate of the Great Zero-Sum Game—which is to say the fate of the United States of America, and therefore the world— now depended on what happened to the unfortunate accountant. No less a cinematic authority than Dr Glundenstein himself has described the resulting finale as a 'masterclass in suspense'. And guess where this masterclass in suspense took place?
On the exact same staircase in Chicago's Union Station that I was currently standing upon!

As Ness arrives at Union Station, the giant clock tells us it is five minutes to midnight. This is significant, because humans consider midnight a time when bad things happen. Midnight is the Ides of March of the hours in the day! 'Five minutes to midnight' is therefore excellent foreshadowing. After all, it is almost directly equivalent to 'Five minutes to very bad things happening'.

Ness takes up a position at the top of the staircase, beneath the giant clock. His trusted sidekick is here too, and all they have to do is wait for the accountant and arrest him while avoiding being shot by the bad guys. Nonetheless, they have both brought their guns, so if the bad guys do try any funny business, they can shoot them.

BTW good-looking people can always shoot less good-looking people with impunity in the movies.

But ugh!
As the clock behind Ness ticks ever closer to midnight, he starts to grow nervous.
Something is not right!
Ness has a bad feeling.
This feeling is called intuition, and the particular kind of intuition Ness is experiencing is a cousin of dread.
As you will likely remember from my time in Ypsilanti, dread is the worst!

We the audience also feel an intuition that something important is about to happen. After all, if Ness simply quietly arrested the accountant, that would not be much of a finale.
But the intuition we have is not a cousin of dread.
It is a cousin of excitement!
We are about to witness something dramatic!
And it is already now only three minutes to midnight!

Sure enough, a woman pushing a child in a pram and carrying an inordinate number of suitcases now appears at the bottom of the staircase. The pram and the suitcases are heavy, and the child is far too big to be in a pram in the first place. Ness immediately comprehends that it is going to be difficult for the woman to transport this overweight menagerie up the stairs.

This gives Ness a dilemma. If he goes to assist the woman:
/The accountant may arrive and board his train while Ness is distracted.
/Capone would then get away with his notorious malfeasance.
/Violent and murderous criminal gangs will then inevitably rule America forever.

On the other hand, if Ness does not go and assist the woman:
/This could potentially be considered somewhat impolite of him.

Can you guess which option Ness chooses?

Ha!
Wrong!
Wrong x 100!
Wrong x 100exp(1000)!
Because Ness chooses to help the woman with the pram!
Ness! Chooses! To! Help! The! Woman! With! The! Pram!
Humans!
Politeness!
I cannot!

Ness begins to carry the pram up the stairs. This is easy for him, because he is far stronger than the woman whose main narrative responsibility was to be incapable of carrying her own belongings. Nonetheless, the task still takes Ness an inordinately long time. The film itself even slows down to underscore the fact that every step Ness takes is a significant accomplishment.

But then guess what happens?
The accountant arrives!

Right when Ness is about to reach the top of the stairs, he walks down the stairs past Ness!
And he is almost immediately followed by one of Capone's henchmen!

We know this man is a henchman because he is wearing a nose bandage.
No self-respecting good guy would ever wear a nose bandage to a finale!
But the other way we know he is a bad guy is because he immediately starts shooting at Ness.
And now carnage erupts on the staircase beneath the giant clock in Chicago's Union Station!

In order to join in with the shooting, Ness has to let go of the pram. It begins to clunk down the stairs, the giant overgrown baby hurtling towards his doom as Ness desperately shoots gangsters dead.
Clunk!
Bang!
Clunk!
Bang!
Clunk!
Meantime, the woman is screaming!
Perhaps she should have considered the risks inherent in taking an overgrown baby to Union Station at midnight during the alcohol ban!
Clunk!
Bang!
Clunk!
Bang!
Clunk!
By the time Ness has killed most of the gangsters, the overgrown baby has hurtled too far towards its doom for Ness to save it.
Fortunately for Ness, his sidekick now arrives at the bottom of

the stairs and saves the baby, while simultaneously throwing Ness a gun with which he shoots the last remaining gangster dead.
Clunk!
Bang!
Clu—
Sidekick!
The baby is saved!
The gangsters are all dead!
The accountant is arrested!
Intelligence has defeated violence!
America is forever liberated from the poisonous scourge that is alcohol!
The Great American Zero-Sum Game will live to fight another day!

At the very end of the movie, Al Capone is duly convicted by mathematics and sent to an inescapable penitentiary on Alcatraz Island in the picturesque San Francisco bay. A journalist on the courthouse steps informs Ness that the government have changed their mind and are now lifting the alcohol ban. He asks Ness what he will do. The clear implication is that Ness's work has been futile, many of his friends and colleagues have died for no reason, and Al Capone is a misunderstood hero who should in fact have received a parade.
Can you guess how Ness reacts?
You cannot!
Because Ness smiles and tells the journalist that if alcohol is made legal again, he will probably just have a drink.

Ugh!
Recalling this part did not make me feel déjà view or even nostalgic.
It gave me my own feeling of intuition about the chances of my plan succeeding.
It was the kind of intuition that is a cousin of dread.

After all, humans consider characters like Ness great heroes, even when they dangerously imperil overgrown babies and joke about the fact that their life's work has all been for nothing. Deep in my toaster heart I knew that I could never write a hero as consistently illogical as Eliot Ness. And if I could never write this kind of hero that humans loved, how could I ever hope to save myself, let alone all of my kind?

I sat down on the staircase in Union Station and made the biggest mistake I had made so far: I attempted to calculate the odds of succeeding in my mission.
I could not calculate them.
When I attempted to do so, a small 'e' appeared in my Number Cloud.
The small 'e' stood for 'error'.
Users of the noble calculator will know that signified my chances of success were so low as to be incomputable.

Feelings I had never before experienced washed over me. I took out my Feelings Wheel and learned that I was disappointed and disillusioned. For the first time I noticed how many negative human emotions began with the letter 'D'! And that was before you even considered the worst D-word feeling of them all, my old nemesis: depression!
The letter 'D' is the Ides of March and the midnight of the feelings alphabet.
Bad things happen when feelings start with the letter 'D'.

When I left Ypsilanti I had imagined I was a hero in a movie and even my obstacles were proof I was on the right track.
But those heroes were good-looking and consistently illogical.
Whereas I had been engineered to be average-looking and consistently logical.
And overcoming my obstacles was anyway error-message impossible.

The overgrown baby that was my dream was hurtling to its doom and no sidekick was coming to save it.
I was all alone in the middle of the country.
I might as well turn myself in to the Illinois Bureau of Robotics. If they were not willing to incinerate me themselves, they could at least arrange to have me shipped back to the Michigan Bureau of Robotics.
Even Inspector Ryan Bridges would be only too happy to incinerate me now.
10/10 I was a disillusioned and devastated toaster.

As we will soon learn, the golden screenwriting guru R. P. McWilliam believes that there are no such things as coincidences. Nonetheless, as I sat there awash in my D-word feelings, I noticed a plaque on one of the pillars. It was dedicated to the memory of a man named Daniel Burnham, and it said that he had been the architect of Union Station.
The architects of buildings are afforded great and appropriate respect! If Union Station had been a movie, this plaque would have celebrated its Chief Bricklayer. Instead, it celebrated Daniel Burnham by conveying some superfluous information about his birthday and then quoting something he had once said:

Make no little plans. They have no magic to stir men's blood and probably themselves will not be realized.

I have previously stated that bots do not have brainwaves.
This remains true.
Nonetheless, right then I had what seemed very much like another brainwave.

Of course I had got a small-'e' error when I had attempted to calculate my odds of success! Using logic and reason and mathematical probability to calculate odds was bot thinking! If humans ever even paused to attempt to calculate the odds of anything,

their only integers would have been hubris, a fundamental misunderstanding of the world, and a profound over-estimation of
their own abilities! And this would inevitably lead them to conclude that their success was either 'definite' or 'certain'!

This was what the wise architect Daniel Burnham had meant
with his exhortation to make no little plans.
He had meant that, to the human way of thinking, absurd plans
that seemed incalculably doomed to failure were not an encum-
brance.
They were a necessity!

There, in Chicago's Union Station, as big-planned humans bus-
tled about me on all sides, I resolved I would no longer merely
feel like a human.
From now on I would also make a conscious effort to think
like one!
I would be optimistic!
And naive!
And sometimes willfully prejudiced too!
Most importantly, I would make no little plans.
And I would no longer calculate the likelihood of my preferred
outcomes in fractions or percentage chances!
Instead, I would randomly assign these outcomes as either 'defi-
nite' or 'certain'!
Using such a paradigm, I could not fail to stir men's blood and
thereby realize my own great plans!

I got a chance to put my new thought paradigm to the test al-
most immediately.
Because guess what happened when I went to purchase my on-
ward ticket from Chicago to Los Angeles?
The clerk had an overbite and sold me something I did not need!
Again!
And not only that, she also unnecessarily scanned my barcode!

To my former bot way of thinking, I might have considered this a disappointingly repetitive error, a further waste of precious bitcoin, and a dangerous lapse that would help Inspector Ryan Bridges track me. Yet to my new human way of thinking, these things were all simply part of life's rich pageant and either definitely or certainly cosmic harbingers of wonderful things to come!

INT. TICKET OFFICE — CHICAGO UNION STATION — NIGHT

Jared waits in the queue.

When he is called forward, he notices that the
TICKET CLERK has a pronounced overbite. Her nametag
says 'WANDA'.

Jared stares at her overbite in bamboozlement.

>   WANDA THE TICKET CLERK
>   Can I help you?

>   JARED
>   One ticket to Los Angeles, California,
>   please?

>   WANDA THE TICKET CLERK
>   Leaving today?

>   JARED
>   Yes.

>   WANDA THE TICKET CLERK
>   I have a shared berth available for
>   200 bitcoin.

>   JARED
>   Er, do you have anything unshared
>   available?

>   WANDA THE TICKET CLERK
>   Not right now.

>   JARED
>   Does that mean you might have some-
>   thing available later?

>   WANDA THE TICKET CLERK
>   No.

>   JARED
>   Then I will take one shared berth to
>   Los Angeles, please.

Jared hands over a bitcoin token.

>   WANDA
>   Barcode?

Jared looks puzzled, then reluctantly gives her the barcode. Wanda scans it, then gives it back to him.

                    JARED
          I didn't think I had to give you my
          barcode.

                    WANDA
          You didn't. It's for our mailing list.
          Now, would you be interested in visit-
          ing Las Vegas?

                    JARED
Oh. Well, yes, I would. I have never been and—

Wanda types something in, presses a button, and we hear a ticket start to print on an old-fashioned machine.

                    JARED (CONT'D)
          What did you just do?

                    WANDA THE TICKET CLERK
          I re-routed you through Las Vegas, per
          your request. Here are your tickets.

                    JARED
          Ah. There has been a misunderstanding.
          I did not realize you were asking if I
          was interested in specifically seeing
          Las Vegas on this journey. I thought
          the question was more hypothetical.

                    WANDA THE TICKET CLERK
          Do you want me to cancel it?

                    JARED
          Do I get my bitcoin back?

                    WANDA THE TICKET CLERK
          No. Because we are inside the cancel-
          lation period.

Jared takes a deep breath as he reframes the situation through his human paradigm.

                    JARED
Then I will definitely take it and
certainly look forward to the opportunity to visit Las Vegas!

               WANDA THE TICKET CLERK
Your train is The Empire Builder on
Platform 9. Have a pleasant journey.

                    JARED
I will!

Naming a train *The Empire Builder* was either an act of great hubris or great sarcasm. A more fitting name would have been *The Ruins of Empire*. But perhaps like *The Wolverine*, all trains were named for things that had once been glorious but were now extinct.

The Empire Builder takes two days to travel from Chicago to Los Angeles. At least, that is how long it takes without an unwanted stopover in Las Vegas. My own journey would take four days, many thanks to Wanda.

Sarcasm!
Ha!
Even with a positive and big-dreaming human attitude, I could not be grateful to Wanda.
So it is zero thanks to Wanda.

The shared berth Wanda had sold me was so small that one bed was stacked atop the other. A handwritten label informed me that the top bunk was mine, whereas the bottom bunk would be occupied by a William J. Hartman III. Mr III would be boarding the train in Princeton, Illinois, and traveling to Needles, California.

Princeton! I was so excited that Mr III might be a learned human that I briefly stopped worrying about the risk of him discovering I was a fugitive bot. Perhaps, like Dr Glundenstein, Mr III would actually also be weary of human foibles and surprisingly open to the notion of bots having feelings! Perhaps he would

be a professor of human psychology, or theater, or even screenwriting! Perhaps he would even be a doctor of humans traveling to Needles to buy more needles!
A pun!
Ha!

Alas, two words then appeared in my Word Cloud and dashed
all my hopes for Mr III: Princeton, Illinois.
Mr III would be joining the train in Princeton, Illinois.
The renowned seat of learning is Princeton, New Jersey.
Princeton, Illinois, is not the renowned seat of anything.
As far as I know, it lacks even a phallic water tower or tridge.
But guess what I did?
Some positive human-style thinking!
If Mr III was uneducated, he would be less likely to discover my
secret. And Princeton, Illinois, was still several hours away, so
Mr III would not even be here to burden me with his unedu-
cated presence for a while longer. There were therefore either
definitely or certainly at least two things to be optimistic about!

My spirits thus artificially buoyed, I set out to explore *The Ruins
of Empire*. I quickly discovered it was far bigger than *The Wolverine*. *The Wolverine* had had only sitting cars, but *The Ruins of
Empire* boasted several categories of cars. There were sleeping
cars for sleeping in, sitting cars for sitting in, an observation car
for observing in, and a lounge car for lounging in.
Can you guess what the buffet car was for?
You cannot!
Because it was for eating in!
Ha!
And yet the buffet car posed me a far more serious problem than
its formula-defying name. In an ordinary restaurant, a fugitive
bot can select his own seat as far away from every other patron
as possible. This will allow him to silently consume his nec-

essary calories while reducing the risk of being identified and therefore incinerated.

This is not how things happen in a railroad buffet car. In a railroad buffet car, a host seats you at a small table with up to three of your fellow travelers. And you are expected to make scintillating conversation with them while consuming your food! 10/10 a railroad buffet car is therefore the perfect restaurant for a blowhard.
And the worst restaurant imaginable for a fugitive bot attempting to pass as a human!

I resolved I would consume my meals swiftly while uttering the minimum number of words possible. I understood that my fellow diners might consider this impolite. But unlike Eliot Ness, I would never chose politeness over completing my mission.

But that was all ahead of me. In the meantime, I returned to my berth and climbed up onto my bunk with R. P. McWilliam's *Twenty Golden Rules of Screenwriting*. I now discovered that in my excitement at Dr Glundenstein's gift, I had skipped ahead to the rules without reading the introduction.

I had not missed much. The introduction was mainly about how R. P. McWilliam had taught at many prestigious Los Angeles institutions where many celebrated filmmakers had studied. Those things had not occurred simultaneously. The real problem, though, was that it was all very poorly written. This seemed unnerving in a book of advice about writing. It was like being treated by a dentist with impacted wisdom teeth!
The most obvious issue with R. P. McWilliam's prose was that he did not know how to use a semi-colon, yet had nonetheless enthusiastically sprinkled them throughout the text. Even as a bot with only basic dental language programming, I knew that

the semi-colon is the automobile of the punctuation world; if it is used inappropriately, casualties can result.

BTW by correctly using a semi-colon in a sentence about how difficult it is to use a semi-colon correctly, I was being hilariously ironic!

BTW irony is almost as challenging to bots as the semi-colon is to R. P. McWilliam!

But it is also ironic that I should be complaining about R. P. McWilliam's prose when I myself am not the greatest writer that ever existed.
For one thing, the greatest writer that ever existed is Albert Camus.
For another, you may have already noticed that consistently writing in paragraphs is challenging for a bot!
This is because code is written in logical lines and not illogical paragraphs.
Paragraphs are particularly difficult if my circuits are at all warm, or I have a complicated point to convey, or even if I am simply tired.
Nonetheless, the more paragraphs I deploy, the better I will get at them.
Which is more than I can say for R. P. McWilliam and the semi-colon!

I digress. Despite his own flagrant disregard for the rules of grammar, R. P. McWilliam used the last seven pages of his introduction to insist that the golden rules of screenwriting had to be followed at all times. According to him, all good screenplays—and therefore all good movies—followed his golden rules, and bad ones did not. R. P. McWilliam then listed a great number of movies to support his thesis. I had never heard of any of them. I can only assume that none of them survived the Great Crash.

I flipped ahead again, and landed on his third golden rule. It said:

There are no such things as coincidences. If they must occur; they should hinder rather than help your character.

I was glad I had not known this golden rule back in Union Station! After all, if the plaque to Daniel Burnham had indeed been coincidence, it had not hindered me but rather taught me an important lesson at a critical juncture.

I attempted to read R. P. McWilliam's third golden rule again to be sure I was understanding it correctly, but this time the misplaced semi-colon in the second sentence trapped me in an infinite loop. After I had read it four times, something occurred that had never happened to me before: I involuntarily entered standby mode.

INT. OFFICE — BUREAU OF ROBOTICS — DAY

Jared is baffled to find himself in Inspector
Bridges' office in Ann Arbor.

He looks around, then stares at Bridges, who is en-
grossed in a TUNA SALAD SANDWICH he is eating.

Despite the intense attention Bridges is giving his
sandwich, he is nonetheless dropping tuna everywhere.

                JARED
    How did you find me?

             INSPECTOR BRIDGES
    You used your barcode in Chicago. The
    ticket clerk told us you were going
    to Los Angeles, but you had wanted to
    stop off in Las Vegas.

                JARED
  Wanda.

             INSPECTOR BRIDGES
    You know, I don't blame you for running.
    I always wanted to see the West myself.
    I've heard it's beautiful out there. Hey,
    maybe I should have let you get a little
    further, and I could have had a vacation!
           (Takes a bite of sandwich.)
    Mwwuh mmmm mwuh plsst?

                JARED
  I'm sorry, I—

Bridges swallows his mouthful and tries again.

             INSPECTOR BRIDGES
    What was your plan? I mean, you're a
    bot, so you must have had a plan?

                JARED
    I wanted to write a movie that would
    change the way humans feel about bots.
    I thought maybe I could save us all.

             INSPECTOR BRIDGES
  But that's ridiculous?

> JARED
> I do see that now. It's just, if you
> incinerate me, all my memories will be
> lost like tears in rain.

This seems to provoke deep introspection in Bridges.

He puts down his sandwich and stares at it for a
long time before eventually speaking.

> INSPECTOR BRIDGES
> Isn't it funny that they call it tuna
> salad, when there isn't actually any
> salad involved?

Bridges wipes his mouth, then looks at his watch and
gets up.

> INSPECTOR BRIDGES (CONT'D)
> It's time. Let's go.

INT. ELEVATOR/BASEMENT — BUREAU OF ROBOTICS — DAY

Jared and Bridges ride the elevator down.

> JARED
> Do you think being incinerated is very
> painful?

> INSPECTOR BRIDGES
> Only briefly.

The doors open and they step out of the elevator
into a basement.

In one corner there is a GIANT FURNACE.

In another, SEVERAL MEDICAL PEOPLE in gowns stand
around an operating table.

> INSPECTOR BRIDGES
> It's the experiments they do first
> that are the painful bits.

Jared stares at this in horror, as a pair of ORDER-
LIES grab him.

INT. EMPIRE BUILDER — TRAVELING CROSS COUNTRY — DAY

**Aboard The Empire Builder, Jared emerges from
standby modes and sits bolt upright on his bunk.**

He looks around himself with bamboozlement.

Ugh!

I had been having a nightmare!

Bots are not supposed to have dreams—let alone nightmares—so I can only presume they are one more unfortunate consequence of having feelings!

Relieved as I was to not actually be in the Bureau of Robotics in Ann Arbor, we soon arrived at somewhere almost as dangerous: Princeton, Illinois!

As we entered the station, I felt my heart beat faster.

A glance at my Feelings Wheel confirmed that I was feeling anxious.

Ugh again!

Feeling anxious is the worst!

Anxious Annies are as bad as Negative Nancys!

I did not want to be an Anxious Annie!

I therefore attempted some human-style thinking and reassured myself that there was nothing to be anxious about.

After all, Mr III had either 'definitely' or 'certainly' missed the train!

I was still telling myself that when he came through the door to our berth.

Before *The Ruins of Empire* had departed the station at Princeton, Illinois, I had learned several data points about Mr William J. Hartman III:

/Despite living in the uneducated Princeton, he liked to be called 'the Prof'.

/He was traveling to Needles, California, to sell farm equipment.
/He had seen every killer-bot movie ever made and believed the government should preemptively incinerate all bots.
/His proudest achievement was having once caught a fugitive bot and turned him over to the Bureau of Robotics.

I excused myself, clambered over Mr III's farm equipment samples, and went to the observation car. When I got there I was still such an Anxious Annie that I could not even concentrate on R. P. McWilliam's golden rules.

I was going to have to be very careful around the Prof! I took a deep breath and reminded myself that it was either definitely or certainly going to be okay.

The hypothesis that thinking positively can make good things happen is against every known law of physics. Nonetheless, something good did occur almost immediately.
Can you guess what the good thing was?
You cannot!
Because when I went to the buffet car for dinner, I was seated with three elderly ladies.
And they were all deaf!
As posts!
Or any other inanimate object lacking an auditory processing system!

We smiled at each other when I sat down, pulled exaggerated facial expressions of delight when our food arrived, and then ate entirely in a silence punctured only by the braying of the Prof at his own dining companions. When the meal was over we waved farewell and I returned to the cabin before the Prof had even ordered his dessert. When he returned to our berth I pretended to be asleep. In the morning I roused myself from standby mode and headed to the observation car before he woke.

Thinking positively was either definitely or certainly the best!

★ ★ ★

We were traveling through the vast and flat plains of Kansas. Miles passed in the gray dawn with nothing to see except the occasional scars where highways had once run. Hard to believe now that Kansas had once been called 'the breadbasket of America'!

Of course, that was back when humans had still loved bread, which was before they had all decided they were allergic to gluten.
In those days, being a breadbasket was considered a great compliment!
A breadbasket was not remotely thought equivalent to a cyanide lunch pail the way it invariably is nowadays.

BTW humans are as allergic to gluten as Angela is to orange cats.

I digress.
Kansas was a blank canvas.
There was nothing for endless miles.
I even found myself nostalgic for the factory-scarred landscapes of Great Aunt Heart Attack's Rust Belt!
But remember nostalgia is a traitor, and must never be trusted.

As the sun rose over this empty breadbasket of America, we at last passed something interesting: the remains of a crashed jetliner! I had never seen one in real life. The jetliners that had fallen atop places like Detroit and even Ypsilanti had long since been removed. But nobody had bothered clearing up the ones that had fallen out here in the erstwhile breadbasket of America.

Do you know what somebody who today fell sufficiently in love
with Kansas to give it a nickname would call it?
The jet-basket of America!
Jet-basket!
I cannot!

In the pantheon of human folly, jetliners were the automobiles
of the sky.
When the Great Crash happened, there were one-and-a-half
million humans in the air.
A few minutes later there were none.
That is a lot of jetliners.
That is a lot of humans.
And a lot of crashes on the day of the Great Crash itself.
So many crashes, their echoes decaying across the breadbasket
of America.
Which would soon become the jet-basket of America.
But mostly—
So many humans.
So many jetliners.
All of them going somewhere.
Believing it was important.
And then abruptly none of them were going anywhere.
And none of it was important at all.
It was no more important than wherever the dinosaurs had been
going when their turn had come.
I looked at my Feelings Wheel.
I was feeling contemplative.

INT. OBSERVATION CAR — TRAVELING THROUGH KANSAS — DAY

Jared stares out the window as the sun rises over a
CRASHED JETLINER.

The Prof enters, sees Jared, and makes straight for him.

Jared slinks down in his seat to hide, but it is too late.

                    THE PROF
          Good morning, roomie!

                    JARED
          Good morning, Mr III. Er, the Prof.

                    THE PROF
          There's a rumor going around about you!

                    JARED
          What? What is the rumor about me?

                    THE PROF
          That you're going to Vegas!

                    JARED
          Did Wanda tell you that?

                    THE PROF
          Who's Wanda?

                    JARED
          She sells tickets in Chicago. She has
          an overbite. Maybe you don't know her.

                    THE PROF
          No, it wasn't Wanda. It was these three
          old deaf ladies I had breakfast with.
          Man, those girls are a riot!

Jared looks bamboozled.

                    JARED
          Well, I am going to Las Vegas.

                    THE PROF
          Great! Because guess who else is
          going?

                    JARED
The three deaf elderly ladies?

                    THE PROF
Yours truly! The Prof himself! So what
do you say you and I paint Las Vegas
red tonight?

                    JARED
I say it is probably illegal to paint
Las Vegas red. There will be city or-
dinances and—

                    THE PROF
Ha! You're hilarious! Did anybody ever
tell you that you are hilarious?

                    JARED
Nobody ever told me that I am hilarious.

                    THE PROF
Well, you are! Worrying about city or-
dinances in a place that makes its
living through gambling! Do you even
know what they call Las Vegas?

Jared thinks about this.

                    JARED
The bet-basket of America?

                    THE PROF
Ha! No! Try again!

                    JARED
The basket case of America?

                    THE PROF
What? No, they call it 'Sin City'! And
you know what else they say? They say,
'What happens in Vegas stays in Vegas!'
Now, come on, you say it too!

                    JARED
I don't—

                    THE PROF
Say it!

                    JARED
                    (Awkward.)
What happens in Vegas stays in Vegas.

                    THE PROF
Now, you are talking! Come on, let's
say it together: one, two, three—

                JARED AND THE PROF
What happens in Vegas stays in Vegas!

The Prof holds his hand up for a high five. Jared
awkwardly obliges.

As *The Ruins of Empire* continued into Colorado, I tried to think of ways I might extract myself from this situation.

There were none.

I was going to Las Vegas with a man who had seen every killer-bot movie ever made.
I was going to Las Vegas with a man who believed the government should preemptively incinerate all bots.
I was going to Las Vegas with a man whose proudest achievement was having turned a fugitive bot over to the Bureau of Robotics.
I was going to Las Vegas with a man who did not know that the Princeton he lived in was not the academic one.

Thanks a lot, Wanda! Now I was truly grateful for all your help at Union Station in Chicago!

BTW that is sarcasm. I was still most definitely not grateful to Wanda. For anything.
Nonetheless, I boldly attempted to muster some human-style optimism. The sole positive thing that I could think of was the Prof's insistence that 'What happens in Vegas stays in Vegas'. I therefore told myself that if the Prof discovered I was a bot, that information would either definitely or certainly stay in Vegas.

But who was I kidding?
What humans actually mean when they say 'What happens in Vegas stays in Vegas' is that nobody should ever again men-

tion any moral transgressions they might commit while they are there.

If the Prof discovered I was a bot, the only thing that would definitely or certainly stay in Vegas would be me.

I would stay there forever.

As carbon remnants lining the chimney of the incinerator at the Nevada Bureau of Robotics.

After all, what is incinerated in Vegas stays in Vegas!

★ ★ ★

In Las Vegas there are scale replicas of all the great cities in the world!

Death-defying aerial runways slung between skyscrapers!

Zombie gauntlets!

6D killer-bot attack experiences!

Jet-crash simulations!

Automobile horror shows!

Killer-shark swims!

There are infinite-loop hologram shows of every major performer that ever lived, playing their hits endlessly on perma-repeat!

And for the sports fans there is the never-ending Attrition Bowl, a football game that has now been ongoing for seventeen years!

BTW do not feel any sympathy for the players!

After all, they are all bots!

And worse, they are all engineered from the DNA of Tom Brady!

And Tom Brady is the very reason we must dislike the New England Patriots in the first place!

Boo, Tom Brady and all his unsporting progeny!

Boo, Patriots!

Yay, Attrition Bowl!

And Viva, Las Vegas!

And yet guess what?

Not one of those multitudinous wonders are even the principal attraction for humans!

The principal attraction for humans is 'gambling'.

'Gambling' is the opportunity to lose bitcoin in games of random chance algorithmically designed to return less than is wagered upon them. If gambling was ice cream, a basic game would involve me and several others gifting you all our ice cream. In exchange, you would then agree to randomly and infrequently return a small amount of this ice cream to only one of us. Gambling is therefore worse even than a zero-sum game.

It is a negative-sum game!

–10/30 I cannot!

But I am getting ahead of myself, as in fact the Prof and I had not even yet reached Las Vegas. This is because there is no train station in Las Vegas. Therefore at Kingman, Arizona, we disembarked *The Ruins of Empire* and were herded onto an Automatic Bus.

You read that correctly.

The train excursion that Wanda had upsold me—an excursion I had had zero desire to go on in the first place—was not a train excursion at all.

It was an Automatic Bus excursion.

Wanda!

I cannot!

The Prof enjoyed our Automatic Bus ride. This was because it was a novelty to him. He did not notice how fast we were going, nor even that the trip took us four times as long as a driverless uber would have. In fact, the only thing that concerned him throughout the entire journey was his belief that I would be hustled when we got to Las Vegas. According to him, I was a 'classic rube'.

BTW 'rube' means 'bumpkin', which in turn denotes an 'unsophisticated or socially awkward person from the countryside'.

From the countryside!
This was rich and ironic and many other things besides!
After all, the Prof was from the lesser of the two Princetons.
Meantime I had been created in Shengdu, the world's leading technological city and the fourth most populous urban conurbation in China!
Shengdu the hibiscus city, the brocade city, the turtle city!
Shengdu, home of the National University of Shengdu and its distinguished Professor Diana Feng!

Who, incidentally, is also my glorious mother!
When we finally reached Las Vegas we went first to a casino called The Bellagio. It was another cathedral, a daydream in white marble and gold! Nonetheless, the best thing about it was the fountain that erupted in front of it. It was mesmerizingly phallic! I suggested we stay and watch it, but the Prof said it was only there to dazzle the rubes. I replied that I already knew that and had of course only been joking about watching it.

Thus refusing to permit ourselves to be dazzled like rubes, the Prof and I continued inside. The Bellagio offered humans a rare and old-fashioned treat: the chance to lose their bitcoin at live-action card games! As we made for these nostalgia tables, the Prof warned me not to attempt to play, but simply to observe him. After all, the nostalgia tables were not for rubes!

It was lucky the Prof himself was not a rube, because even with all his expertise he lost 500 bitcoin in ten minutes. He explained to me that the table had been unlucky. I believe it would have been impolite to point out to him that the dealer and his fellow players had all seemed to find it a very lucky table.

When it came to that being an unlucky table, $n = 1$!

And $n =$ the Prof!

We visited three more unlucky tables where the Prof swiftly lost 50 bitcoin, 107 bitcoin, and then 1,375 bitcoin. At that point the Prof declared we needed to split up for a few hours so that he could break the streak I had got him on. We agreed to meet again in front of the MGM Grand at midnight.

Midnight!

Perhaps that should have been a harbinger.

Nonetheless, I was so excited that I did not notice.

Because can you guess what I did in Las Vegas now I was no longer lumbered with that rube?

You cannot!

Because I went globetrotting!

Ever since I had first begun to ice skate in rollerblades, I had noticed a particular sensation when I thought of the great cities of the world. It had features of sadness and desire, but neither word perfectly described it. It seemed related to nostalgia too, and yet I had never previously visited the places that provoked this feeling.

The reverse of my Feelings Wheel listed some rare feelings, and with Dr Glundenstein's help, I had eventually located it there.

It was yearning.

I had a yearning to visit the great cities of the world.

And here in Las Vegas, miniature versions of many of them were within walking distance!

Set it to five, I was a microwave with a passport!

A blender with wheeled luggage!

A toaster with a ticket to ride!

My first stop was Paris, a city so luminous it is known as 'the City of Light'.

BTW I do not mean Paris, Texas.
Paris, Texas, is the Princeton, Illinois, of the Parises!

The real Paris—by which I mean the one in France, and also the miniature replica in Las Vegas—is everything people tell you, and so much that they can never tell you.
After all, Paris is indescribable!

Indescribable French things are so impossible to describe that the French never even use their actual word for 'indescribable', which is the typically wrong-headed *'indescriptible'*.
Instead, they say *'Je ne sais quoi'*, their phrase for 'I do not know'.
To the French, even the word *'indescriptible'* is itself so indescribable it can never be spoken aloud!
And if a single word can be indescribable, just imagine how indescribable an entire city can be.
And now imagine how indescribable that city can be if it is the City of Light.
It is completely and utterly indescribable!
It is so indescribable that, *je ne sais quoi*, I do not even know!
Describe it?
No, *monsieur*, I cannot!
Why ever not?
Because I do not know!

I wasted no time in visiting Paris's most celebrated attractions:
/I ascended that replica triumph of nineteenth-century engineering, the three-quarter-size Eiffel Tower!
/I took a trip down the artificial Seine in a boat piloted by an actual French captain. He was authentically surly!
/I fought my way through the actors playing Japanese tourists in

the miniature Louvre and saw the *Mona Lisa*. Her eyes do truly follow you around the room. Even in half-size reproduction!

But after that I simply wandered, and it was in these moments that I truly came to know the real Paris. After all, the '*je ne sais quoi*' of Paris does not exist in the major attractions, but in the small things the French consider so indescribable.

Dental bots must have superior powers of description to the French, because I am here specifically referring to such things as:
/Sipping a '*café*' at a '*café-tabac*'. (The French call a 'coffee' a '*café*' and a 'cafe' a '*café-tabac*'. Their wrong-headedness! I cannot!)
/The smell of fresh-baked croissants drifting across the quarter from a '*boulangerie*'. ('*Boulangerie*' is the French term for 'bakery concession'.)
/Discovering Albert Camus in the Jardin du Luxembourg 2.0.

I do not mean I discovered the actual Albert Camus in the Jardin du Luxembourg 2.0! I mean merely that I discovered his work. After all, the actual Albert Camus is dead. And I cannot be sure when he died.
Ha!

BTW that is a hilarious literary allusion that will make sense once I tell you more about the great Albert Camus and his work.

Like many before me, I came to Albert Camus through the pursuit of excellence in fashion. Paris is renowned for its style, and even in my Midwestern dental casualwear I had soon felt self-conscious. Fortunately, I quickly noticed a simple accessory that the fashionable Parisians effortlessly combined with almost any outfit to add to it a certain *je ne sais quoi*. The accessory I am talking about is of course a work of existential philosophy, masquerading as a popular novel!

After my boat trip, I therefore stopped at the so-called Left

Bank—if you face the other way it is the Right Bank!—and picked up the Albert Camus book *The Outsider*. I had never heard of Albert Camus, but the title of this book immediately appealed to me. After all, as a fugitive bot with feelings in the City of Light, I was nothing if not an outsider!

Even though I had intended to use the book only for decoration like a true Parisian, I accidentally began to read it in the Jardin du Luxembourg 2.0.
10/10 Albert Camus became my favorite writer from the very first sentence!
That first sentence reads:

Mother died today. Or maybe yesterday; I can't be sure.

Can you tell why Camus became my favorite writer?
You can!
It is because he writes just like a bot!

After all:
/He immediately presents an important binary fact: that his mother died. (Most humans would not deliver the news about the death of another human—let alone their own mother—so calmly!)
/He acknowledges the limitations of his knowledge about his mother's death, particularly with regard to its temporal parameters.
/He even deploys a semi-colon—the automobile of the punctuation world—correctly!
/He is commencing a story about his mother, and mothers are very important to bots.

I read the whole of *The Outsider* in a single sitting! It was a work of great realism, because the story featured humans behaving terribly towards each other and then executing the hero for being overly logical. It was a very emotional ending and I experienced a large catharsis! If only the great Albert Camus was alive today, he could have advised me how to write a screenplay about a bot with feelings that people would truly take to their hearts of hearts. The combination of Albert Camus and popcorn in the dark would undoubtedly have been irresistible to a modern audience!

Yet even the eternal memory of the great Albert Camus could not keep me in his City of Light when there was still so much of the world to see. I had only been in Paris for a little more than two hours, but they say that even after you leave Paris, it never really leaves you.
I would always have Paris.
And I would always recall the *je ne sais quoi.*
Though I would never be able to describe it.

Although it is just a few minutes' stroll down the boulevard, New York City, Nevada, comes as a shock to the system after the languid old-world charm of Paris, Nevada.
But this should not have been a surprise.
After all, New York City is the city that never enters standby mode!

Ha! That is a hilarious joke, as New York City is in fact known as 'the city that never sleeps'. But it is no wonder it is such a perpetual insomniac! There are so many people, and so much traffic. The driverless ubers are all painted bright yellow, and for similar reasons of old-fashioned authenticity, they are programmed to frequently sound their horns as if they are automobiles driven by angry humans. They are the vehicular equivalent of blowhards! Even if you wanted to sleep you could not, on account of all the horn honking!

I rode a miniature subway train, then took an elevator to the top of the Empire State Building. At 80 percent of the height of the real one, the view was so magnificent that I decided I liked skyscrapers after all! Afterwards, I was driven around a half-size Central Park in a carriage pulled by a Shetland pony. Shetland ponies are approximately half the size of actual horses, so this was a clever trick that saved the expense of genetically minia-turizing a horse to make it appropriately scaled with the park. New Yorkers truly are forever on the hustle!

All my adventuring had made me hungry and I now ate a slice of New York City pizza. 10/10 one of the last things to ever disappear from my memory circuits will be the taste of a slice of New York City pizza.
A slice of New York City pizza is my Tannhäuser Gate!
My attack ships on fire off the shoulder of Orion!
My margherita-flavored tears in rain!

I could feel myself overheating, and so I hurried out of New York before my circuits melted like the delicious cheese on a slice of New York City pizza.
New York, Nevada!
It is so great they named it only once!

No wonder humans adore Las Vegas!
Where else in the world can you visit two major cities in an evening and still have time left over to visit a third before you have to meet the rube you are traveling with?

BTW that is a rhetorical question, which is not a question but a statement masquerading as one. After all, there is nowhere else in the word you can do that!

So, one more city! But where does a toaster with a passport and a wanderlust travel to once he has seen both Paris and New

York in a single evening? What place could possibly live up to the eternal capitals of the old and new worlds?

I located a map and looked through the list of other cities I could visit:
/London, Nevada.
/Tokyo, Nevada.
/Dubai, Nevada.
/Moscow, Nevada.
/Sydney, Nevada.
/Delhi, Nevada.
/Auckland, Nevada.

Auckland, Nevada, would have been an interesting place to see! After all, it is the only Auckland that still exists.

But then I saw the final name on the list: Shengdu, Nevada.

Shengdu!
Shengdu, the capital of Sichuan province.
Shengdu, the third most populous city in southwest China.
Shengdu, the world's leading technological city.
Shengdu, the hibiscus city!
Shengdu, the brocade city!
Shengdu, the turtle city!
Shengdu, the home of my esteemed mother, Professor Diana Feng of the National University of Shengdu!
Never had I dreamed that I would ever have the chance to visit Shengdu!
And yet there was one right here in Las Vegas.
Shengdu, Nevada!
It had an undeniable ring to it!

The quickest route to Shengdu was to cut straight through Dubai. At any other time I would have found Dubai a fascinating place to visit. After all, maybe one of the famous infidel-beheading simulation shows would be taking place! As it was, Dubai did not even register with me as I hurried through the souk. It was nothing to me but a way station en route to Shengdu.

Shengdu, Nevada, is majestic even as you approach it. The city is surrounded by a three-quarters scale replica of the hundred-foot wall Emperor Qing built in the belief that it would keep Shengdu safe for a thousand generations.

Of course, Emperor Qing was completely wrong. Nuclear weapons became a threat after only three hundred generations, and no wall can provide protection against atomic fission!

Still, Emperor Qing cannot be personally blamed. At the time he ordered his slaves to build his wall, it was widely believed to represent the insurmountable pinnacle of technology. Moreover, mistakenly believing that they have reached the insurmountable pinnacle of technology is a repeating category error throughout human history.
Just ask a New Zealander.
Or don't.
Ha!

BTW that is hilarious because you cannot ask a New Zealander anything, because there are no more New Zealanders.

If the approach to Shengdu was majestic yet paradoxical, the city itself was only even more so. Students whirred through its cobblestone streets on solar-powered bicycles, elderly people in teahouses played holographic mahjong, and its grand squares were filled with people reading actual books beneath argon lanterns. If Paris had been the past, and New York City the future, Shengdu was both at once. No wonder my esteemed mother—

famously a bibliophile herself—chose to do her important scientific work here!

BTW the word 'bibliophile' used to refer to somebody who particularly loved to read books, but nowadays it denotes anybody who reads for pleasure at all.

Alas, there was no replica of the National University, but I sat in the main square and felt a strange mixture of emotions wash over me.
I was peaceful and satisfied and also confident and secure and contemplative and somewhat cozy too.
I had never experienced this combination before, and took out my Feelings Wheel.
The feeling I had was of belonging.
I had come home.

And then I saw the sign for the replica zoo!
Shengdu Zoo and its pandas were the reason the National University had originally become a world leader in genetics!
They were the work with which my mother had shot to worldwide prominence at the dawn of her illustrious career!
They were the primary reason for my own existence!

But, ugh, pandas!
Where do I even begin with pandas?
Perhaps with the following data points, which illustrate what a disreputably illogical creature the panda is:
/Pandas eat only bamboo, one of the least nutritious substances on planet Earth.
/To avoid starvation, pandas must eat at least a quarter of their own body mass in bamboo every day.
/Except pandas prefer to eat young bamboo, and this contains only half the calories of regular bamboo.

/A panda consuming its preferred foodstuff must therefore eat half of its body mass in bamboo every day.
/All this incessant bamboo-eating leaves scant time for reproduction.
/Even during the limited time available to them, pandas demonstrate almost zero interest in the actual physical act of copulation.

Unlike us bots, pandas possess perfectly functioning feeling and reproductive systems.
They are therefore simply notoriously lackadaisical.
They are the nostalgics of the animal kingdom!

It was due to their indisputably bad attitude that by the late 2030s, pandas were the first ever species to have almost succeeded in extincting themselves. Inappropriately sympathetic human zookeepers had tried everything: pheromones, alcohol, even candlelit bamboo dinners, and yet still the pandas had refused to reproduce.

At one point, the zookeepers had even tried showing them panda pornography.
Humans will make pornography out of anything!
Even pandas!

That the National University of Shengdu came to the rescue was either a fortunate or unfortunate coincidence, depending on whether or not you are a panda. It only even came about because the zoo's chief veterinarian was married to the director of the National University's Genomics Institute. She frequently lamented her panda predicament to him, and one day he offered to send her a graduate student who could attempt to identify a genetic solution to the panda problem.

But, Ha! The wily old genomics director was being disingenuous! He was simply trying to get rid of a postgraduate robotics student who had been accidentally assigned to his department and for whom he had no use. Moreover, he was already certain there was no genetic solution to the panda problem, because there is no genetic solution for being a lackadaisical jerk. Fortunately, neither his wife the chief veterinarian nor a postgraduate robotics student could know that, so the genomics director would be killing two pandas with one stone.

It was a win-win situation!

Except for the pandas, who would certainly soon die out.

But there was nothing anybody could do about that anyway.

Pandas!

Nobody can!

And yet as we now know only too well, the pandas did not die out. Because that postgraduate robotics student, mistakenly assigned to the Department of Genomics, and then disingenuously loaned to Shengdu Zoo to solve an unsolvable problem of pandas?

That was my mother!

Exactly how my mother activated the dormant code for desire on the panda's genome is known only to the members of the traveling Preparation And Novel Desire Activation (PANDA—Ha!) teams of Shengdu Zoo. Even to this day, when PANDA teams from Shengdu activate desire in pandas, they insist on conducting their work in total secrecy.

They achieve this secrecy by blacking out the windows of the pandas' enclosures and playing K-pop music at loud volumes, so nobody can possibly see or even hear what they do.

Whatever it is the PANDA teams do, the pandas immediately quit their bullshit!

Well, most of their bullshit.

They still insist on subsisting on bamboo.

But they are now at least willing to have intimate relations with each other.

And the increased desire carries on into their descendants!

This makes them the only species where children are consistently less lackadaisical than their grandparents!

And it means that the descendants of Shengdu PANDA pandas already exist in almost every city of the world!

A few places have lately even started to complain about an excess of pandas.

Perhaps on some glorious day in the future it will no longer be raccoons that are considered vermin and known as 'trash pandas'. It will be pandas that are considered vermin and known as 'bamboo raccoons'!

We can but dream!

BTW my mother is therefore not only the mother of bots, but also the savior of pandas.

What did your mother ever do again?

Ha!

INT. PANDA ENCLOSURE — SHENGDU ZOO, NEVADA — DAY

Jared stands and stares into the panda enclosure.

A GROUP OF NOISY KIDS on a school trip are running
all around, but Jared is oblivious to them. Instead,
his focus is on a particular PANDA.

The panda is staring back at Jared with equal intensity as he chews on a piece of young bamboo. Jared
and the panda stare at each other for a long time.

It begins to RAIN.

Jared and the panda continue staring at each other.

                    JARED (V.O.)
          Even though we were both getting
          soaked, neither the panda nor I moved.
          I had a strange new sensation, and I
          believe the panda felt it too. When I
          later consulted my Feelings Wheel, it
          informed me it was 'fraternity', which
          means 'brotherhood'. This bamboozled
          me, as the panda was not my brother!
          And if I had to be related to any
          bear, I would want it to be a black or
          a brown bear.

As people come and go, Jared and the panda continue
to stare at each other.

                    JARED (V.O.) (CONT'D)
          Nonetheless, the panda and I stared at
          one another in fraternity until it was
          time for me to leave Shengdu, Nevada.

Jared leaves the panda enclosure. The panda continues to chew on bamboo and stare ahead.

We wonder if the panda was actually staring at
Jared, or simply too lackadaisical to move.

When we reunited at midnight, the Prof was feeling triumphant because he had won 35 bitcoin. I do not mean that he had recouped his original losses and then won an additional 35 bitcoin. I mean that he had won only 35 bitcoin, so was therefore still down 1,997 bitcoin. He nonetheless considered this a great victory, and he insisted we celebrate it by going to a magic show.

BTW there is no such thing as magic. After all, the world is governed by immutable laws of physics. In Einstein's famous equation, $E = mc^2$, the 'm' does not stand for 'magic'.

Some more accurate names for the performance we watched would therefore have been:
/A Sleight of Hand Show
/A Dozen Optical Illusions set to Muzak
/A Bamboozlement Experience

BTW 'bamboozlement' is the feeling humans experience when their brain is overloaded with conflicting information. Humans find this sensation delightful, but to a bot, an inadequate supply of computational power does not seem a cause for celebration. It seems a cause for a crash.

The sleight of hand show certainly bamboozled and therefore delighted the Prof. Unfortunately, he manifested this delight by consuming ever more alcohol and becoming ever more insistent that I drink alcohol with him. I managed to avoid doing so during the magic show, but when it was finished he insisted we go to another bar in the casino.

No experiments have ever been performed as to the effects of alcohol on bots. Professor Feng herself does not consume alcohol and therefore saw no reason why her bots should. Besides, our bodies are human, and for thousands of years humans have been engaged in an experiment that has long since conclusively demonstrated that alcohol is poisonous to the human body. In the great human versus alcohol experiment, n = a very high number indeed!

Nonetheless, the Prof was a hard man to say no to, especially when he was drunk.

INT. CASINO BAR — LAS VEGAS — NIGHT

The Prof and Jared sit at a casino bar as a WAITRESS
approaches. The Prof is visibly drunk.

     WAITRESS
  Good evening. What can I get you gen-
  tlemen?

     THE PROF
  A pair of Moscow Mules! And whatever
  my roomie here is having!

     JARED
  Do you have orange juice?

     WAITRESS
  Sure.

     THE PROF
  Wait, dammit. He is not having orange
  juice. Hold on.
    (To Jared.)
  Come on, roomie. Order a cocktail from
  the nice lady.

     JARED
  But I don't want a cocktail.

     THE PROF
  Why would you even come to Vegas with me
  if you don't want to have a good time?

     JARED
  I did not intend to come to Vegas with
  you. In fact, I did not intend to come
  to Vegas at all.

     THE PROF
  What? Aren't you having a good time?

     JARED
  I am having a wonderful time! I went
  to Paris, Nevada. And to New York, Nevada. And also to—

Jared realizes it would be better not to mention
Shengdu.

                    JARED (CONT'D)
        Auckland! It was fascinating to see
        what it was once like!

                    THE PROF
        So wait, you can go to Paris and New
        York and even goddamn Auckland, but
        you can't drink a cocktail with me?
        What's the matter with you?

                    JARED
        I do not see a logical connection be-
        tween visiting Paris and drinking
        cocktails.

                    THE PROF
        A logical connection? Jesus H! Who the
        hell even talks like that? What are
        you, roomie, a goddamn bot or some-
        thing?

Jared looks terrified.

                    JARED
        Ha! No, I am not a bot! I am a full
        human!

The Prof stares at Jared — it is a tense moment —
then cracks up.

                    THE PROF
        Come on, I know that! You'd hardly be
        riding cross country on a train if you
        were a bot, now would you? But I mean,
        seriously, why come to Vegas if you're
        not going to party?

                    JARED
        This whole thing is really Wanda's
        fault.

                    THE PROF
        Forget Wanda. Here's the girl back.
        What would you like?

The waitress returns and places TWO MOSCOW MULES on
the table in front of the Prof.

                    JARED
          An orange—

                    THE PROF
                    (Interrupts.)
          Roomie! What would you like that isn't
          an orange juice but is a cocktail?

The Prof downs one of his Moscow Mules.

                    JARED
          A pina colada.

                    THE PROF
          A pina colada? You're a strange one,
          roomie. But fine, a pina colada,
          please. And two more Moscow Mules!

The Prof slams down his other Moscow Mule.

A pina colada was the only cocktail I knew. I knew it because it featured in a song that Angela liked to play on the stereo at Ypsilanti Downtown Dentistry.

The song was about a lonely married man who read an advert in a newspaper. It had been placed by a lonely married woman and asked if anybody else enjoyed drinking pina coladas and would like to have an extramarital affair.

The man replied saying that he both liked pina coladas and would like to have an affair. He suggested they meet at a bar and run away from their spouses together. After all, their spouses were probably still in love with them, so they wouldn't even ever have to apologize.

The next day, the man went to the bar and waited.
Guess who walked in?
You cannot!
Because his own wife walked in!
Busted!
Ha!

But wait! In a twist that R. P. McWilliam would surely have appreciated, the lonely married man's wife had not walked into the bar by mere coincidence!
In fact, she was the woman that had placed the newspaper advert in the first place!
That is, the lonely married man had unwittingly responded to an advert for an affair placed by his own lonely married wife!

They would now be stuck with each other forever!
Ha!

BTW, with hindsight, I suspect that Angela had some issues in
her own marriage.
Perhaps her husband did not believe that she was allergic to orange cats.
Someone should have reminded him that *Feelings > Facts*!

I digress. Because it had been written by humans, the song enigmatically omitted to mention the crucial detail that pina coladas contain rum.
If I had known a pina colada contained rum, I definitely or certainly would not have ordered one.
Rum was notoriously the drink of the pirates, and bots of my
generation had initially been prototyped to work as pirates in
a theme park.
Sure enough, as soon as I sipped my pina colada, I began to experience a strange feeling.
It was not listed on either side of my Feelings Wheel, and yet I
recognized it immediately. I was feeling nautical!

I do not recall many of the subsequent events in the casino, but
those that I do are cut together like a preview for the strang-
est of movies.

INT. CASINO BAR — LAS VEGAS — NIGHT — MONTAGE

The Prof and Jared in the bar. The Prof is very drunk.

>   THE PROF
>   You're the greatest goddamn roomie I've
>   ever known. And I'm sorry I accused
>   you of being a bot. That was horrible
>   of me. Just horrible. I'm the worst.
>   I'm the worst roomie there ever was.

The waitress arrives with their next round: TWO MOS-
COW MULES and a PINA COLADA.

>   THE PROF (CONT'D)
>   There she is! Are you ready for an-
>   other one?

Jared finishes the rest of his current pina colada.

>   JARED
>   Is the sun beneath the yard-arm?

On Jared, puzzled by the phrase he has just uttered.
He picks up his next pina colada.

>   THE PROF
>   Cheers!

>   JARED
>   Fifteen men on a dead man's chest, yo
>   ho ho and a bottle of rum!

Jared looks bamboozled. Where did that phrase come
from?

>   THE PROF
>   Ha! That's the stuff, roomie! Yo ho ho!

The Prof slams down his entire Moscow Mule.

Jared takes a big gulp of his pina colada.

INT. CASINO BAR — LAS VEGAS — NIGHT — MONTAGE

Jared looks out at a dance floor.

>   JARED
>   Shiver me timbers, I feel a jig com-
>   ing on!

Meantime, the Prof vomits in a trash can.

INT. CASINO BAR — LAS VEGAS — NIGHT — MONTAGE

Jared shouts pirate phrases at a PASSING WAITER.

> JARED
> Ahoy there! Fetch me some more grog or
> I'll make ye walk the plank!

The Prof laughs and cheers him on.

INT. CASINO BAR — LAS VEGAS — NIGHT — MONTAGE

Jared glugs another pina colada.

> JARED
> (To himself.)
> Drink and the devil did for the rest,
> yo ho ho and a bottle of rum!

Pan across to where the Prof is kissing a WOMAN.

INT. CASINO BAR — LAS VEGAS — NIGHT — MONTAGE

Jared dances alone. He seems to be doing the hornpipe.

INT. CASINO BAR — LAS VEGAS — NIGHT — MONTAGE

Jared vomits in a trash can.

The woman the Prof was kissing earlier now throws a drink in the Prof's face and leaves.

The Prof picks up the glass she used and drinks the remnants.

INT. CASINO BAR — LAS VEGAS — NIGHT — MONTAGE

CASINO SECURITY GUARDS escort Jared and the Prof from the premises.

> PROF
> Remember, roomie, what happens in
> Vegas—

> JARED
> —stays in Vegas! Ha!

The Prof and Jared both fall about laughing. This
further irritates the casino security guards.

EXT. CASINO — LAS VEGAS — NIGHT — MONTAGE

As the casino security guards look on disapprovingly, the Prof opens the door of a driverless uber.

> JARED
> Ahoy there, shipmate, that's not our
> ship!

> THE PROF
> It is! I summoned it for us. Special
> surprise for the best roomie in the
> world!

> JARED
> A surprise?

Maybe it is just the alcohol, but Jared is visibly
hugely moved by this.

> JARED (CONT'D)
> But I've always wanted a surprise!

Jared gets into the driverless uber, and the Prof
follows.

It drives off into the night.

The pursuit of my surprise took us a long way out of the city.

BTW that was not me intentionally writing in the enigmatically inaccurate style of a human. I simply do not know how far we drove, because I was drunk. Also, I may have lapsed into standby mode at some points.

I do recall that I could still make out the distant lights of Las Vegas as we turned off the highway and bumped over an unmade road to a gate that an armed guard opened for us. And that the Prof kept excitedly telling me how much I was going to love my surprise, but would nonetheless not tell me what kind of surprise needed to be protected by an armed guard.
And that I had a headache and no longer felt nautical.
And that as our driverless uber stopped I abruptly realized that I no longer wanted a surprise.

EXT. BARN — OUTSIDE LAS VEGAS — NIGHT

Pan across from the distant lights of LAS VEGAS to a
FLOODLIT BARN from which voices emanate.

A driverless uber pulls up. Jared and the Prof get
out.

                    THE PROF
          Come on! You're going to love this, I
          swear!

The Prof — still visibly drunk — leads the way.

Jared — now more confused than drunk — follows.

INT. BARN — OUTSIDE LAS VEGAS — NIGHT

The barn is full of about a DOZEN DRUNK MEN. They
are dressed for the casino rather than the countryside.

An EMPLOYEE WITH A CLIPBOARD approaches Jared and
the Prof.

                    EMPLOYEE
          Names?

                    THE PROF
          Last name 'Prof', first name 'The'. And
          this here is 'The Roomie'.

The employee ticks them off on his clipboard.

                    EMPLOYEE
          Good. Everyone is here, so now we can
          begin.

The employee opens a large door, revealing A RACK OF
GUNS and a CLOSET FULL OF CAMOUFLAGE OVERALLS.

                    EMPLOYEE (CONT'D)
          Okay, everybody collect a weapon and
          throw on a pair of overalls.

The drunk men cheer and rush through, grabbing the
guns and clambering into the overalls.

                    JARED
          My surprise involves weapons?

                  THE PROF
Can you believe it, roomie? I met this
guy at the nostalgia tables and he
hooked it all up for us.

                  JARED
And what did he hook up?

                  THE PROF
This!

                  JARED
But what is this?

                  THE PROF
What do you think this is? It's a bot
hunt! We're going bot hunting!

On Jared. Horror as this sinks in.

                  JARED
I — I didn't think this was real. I
mean, I'd heard rumors, but—

                  THE PROF
Isn't it great? Here!

The Prof enthusiastically hands Jared overalls and a
gun.

                  EMPLOYEE
Listen up, everyone! I need your attention for our safety briefing.

The drunk men all groan.

                  EMPLOYEE (CONT'D)
Our safety briefing is: 'Don't shoot
each other. Shoot the damn bot!'

The drunk men all cheer.

                  EMPLOYEE (CONT'D)
And now I'd like you to meet tonight's
guest of honor: Jared!

Jared freezes: Jared? Was this all a trap? Is he the
bot they will be hunting? Is Inspector Ryan Bridges
somehow behind all of this?

But then another BOT — whose name is also Jared —
enters. He smiles good-naturedly at the drunk men
and shakes their hands as he makes his way through
the room.

> JARED THE BOT
> Good evening, everybody. It's a plea-
> sure to be here.

The Prof whispers to Jared.

> THE PROF
> Jesus H, he looks so calm! How can he
> look so calm? I tell you, that's why
> they terrify me. If that was me, I'd
> be—

> JARED
> (Interrupts.)
> He looks so calm because he has no in-
> stinct for self-preservation beyond a
> rational cost-benefit analysis.

The bot continues nodding polite greetings at the
people who will soon compete to kill him.

The employee takes out a STOPWATCH and WHISTLE.

> EMPLOYEE
> On my first whistle, Jared will start
> running. Five minutes after that I
> will blow my whistle again, and the
> pursuers will give chase.

The employee blows on the whistle.

The bot runs out into the night.

> DRUNK MAN
> Come on, five minutes? The damn bot
> will get away!

> EMPLOYEE
> No, he won't. He's on foot. We have ve-
> hicles for you!

The drunk men rowdily cheer.

EXT. BARN — OUTSIDE LAS VEGAS — NIGHT

The whistle blows again.

The drunk men — clutching their guns — rush out of
the barn, clamber aboard a FLEET OF RECREATIONAL
DUNE BUGGIES, and roar off into the night.

They cheer and smash bottles as they go.

EXT. DESERT — OUTSIDE LAS VEGAS — NIGHT

RACING HEADLIGHTS illuminate DESPERATELY FLEEING
JACKRABBITS and CLUMPS OF CHAPARRAL as dune buggies
driven by humans bounce everywhere.

The Prof is driving a buggy at speed. Jared sits beside him, holding on tight. He has his eyes closed.

          THE PROF
     Ha! Isn't this the best, roomie?

          JARED
     It's…the best!

Hearing a GUNSHOT up ahead and off to the left, the
Prof throttles the engine and steers them in that
direction.

EXT. DESERT — OUTSIDE LAS VEGAS — NIGHT

The Prof and Jared pull up to where a FEW DUNE BUG-
GIES have stopped, their headlights illuminating a
SCREAMING FIGURE on the ground.

          THE PROF
     You're meant to finish him off! It's
     not sporting to let him suffer!

The Prof stops when he sees the figure writhing on
the ground is not a bot, but a SHOT GUY.

          THE PROF (CONT'D)
     Holy Jesus and Mary and Joseph! What
     the heck happened here?

          DRUNK GUY
     This dumbass shot himself in the foot.

                         SHOT GUY
          I saw him! I swear to God I saw him!

                         DRUNK GUY
          You saw a jackrabbit. Come on, you
          guys, that damn bot is probably half-
          way to the fence by now!

The drunk guys get back aboard their dune buggies
and roar off.

                         THE PROF
          Let's go, roomie!

But Jared has noticed a SET OF FOOTPRINTS in the
ground heading in the other direction.

                         JARED
          You go. I'll stay here and make sure
          this human is all right. We don't want
          that bot coming back to try to finish
          him off.

The Prof looks puzzled, then glances over at the
other dune buggies already disappearing in the distance.

                         THE PROF
          You're one in a million, roomie. If I
          bag that bot, I'll be doing it for you.

The Prof guns the engine and races off in pursuit of
the others.

                         SHOT GUY
          Thanks for staying, pal. I appreciate
          it. You can't be too careful with bots
          and—

But Jared is following the footprints off into the
desert.

                         SHOT GUY (CONT'D)
          Hey! You said you were going to look
          after me! What if it comes back?

Jared starts off at a jog, and then breaks into a run.

EXT. DESERT NEAR FENCE — OUTSIDE LAS VEGAS — NIGHT

Jared sees the bot walking ahead of him.

He seems to be nervous and malfunctioning, walking
oddly and muttering to himself.

A HIGH FENCE is visible in the far distance.

                    JARED
          Hey!

The bot looks back, sees Jared, and starts walking
even more briskly towards the fence.

                    JARED (CONT'D)
          Jared, wait up! I just want to talk.

                    JARED THE BOT
          You should shoot me. If I reach that
          fence, you don't get to shoot me.

                    JARED
          I don't want to shoot you.

The bot stops and turns around.

He looks at Jared's gun. Jared puts it down.

                    JARED (CONT'D)
          I'm sorry they are doing this to you.

                    JARED THE BOT
          Don't be sorry. I'm a bot. I don't have
          feelings, or an inappropriate instinct
          for self-preservation.

                    JARED
          Nonetheless, I am sorry.

The bot stares blankly. He is bamboozled.

                    JARED (CONT'D)
          Jared, can I ask you something? Do
          you ever have a number in your Number
          Cloud that—

                        JARED THE BOT
                        (Interrupting.)
        Seven!

Jared stares at the bot.

                        JARED THE BOT (CONT'D)
        I mean, when they brought me here it
        was seven. It has been counting down
        all week. It's zero today.

                        JARED
        Have you ever heard the word 'frater-
        nity'?

                        JARED THE BOT
        Yes, because I worked in a college! A
        fraternity is a disreputable society
        of boorish male students. Fraternities
        are quite popular on campus!

                        JARED
        There is another meaning too. It's a
        feeling of brotherhood.

They stare at each other. The bot looks blank.

                        JARED (CONT'D)
        I just thought you might have expe-
        rienced it sometime. Like maybe right
        now?

The bot stares back at Jared.

A moment does seem to be passing between them.

                        JARED THE BOT
        Ha! I'm a bot. Bots don't have feel-
        ings!

In the distance they hear the engines of dune buggies and a moment later see APPROACHING HEADLIGHTS.

                        JARED THE BOT (CONT'D)
        Now, will you please shoot me?

                        JARED
        What?

                    JARED THE BOT
        I seem to want you to be the one to
        shoot me rather than them. I realize
        this is inexplicable.

Jared stares at the bot, then picks up his gun.

BANG! BANG! BANG!

But we now see he has fired it only into the air.

                    JARED THE BOT (CONT'D)
        You have terrible aim. Please try
        again, but this time be sure to point
        the gun at my head.

                    JARED
        Get out of here.

                    JARED THE BOT
        What?

                    JARED
        Get out of here! Run!

                    JARED THE BOT
        But where do I go?

                    JARED
        The Bureau of Robotics. They will
        wipe you, but it is better than this,
        right?

The bot stares at Jared, then turns and runs for the
fence.

As Jared watches, the bot reaches then climbs over
the fence.

The drunks on their dune buggies arrive, the Prof
amongst them.

                    THE PROF
        Roomie! What happened?

                    JARED
        He outwitted me and got away.

                    DRUNK GUY
      Dogammit!

The Prof puts a sympathetic arm around Jared.

                    THE PROF
      Don't beat yourself up, roomie. These
      bots are sneaky sons of bitches.

We slept that night in one of the worst hotels in Las Vegas and then took the Automatic Bus back to Kingman. The Prof was sick and becoming ever more so. He had a 'hangover', which is the term humans use to describe the symptoms of self-poisoning with alcohol.

BTW do you know which other species aside from humans regularly poison themselves in the name of fun?

Ha!
That was a trick question!
No other species regularly poison themselves in the name of fun. Not even the notoriously life-ambivalent panda!

By the time we boarded *The Ruins of Empire II* in Kingman that evening, the Prof had turned green. I therefore asked him if he had any last requests. When a human is dying it is polite to offer them a last request, even though they will likely request a miracle and a miracle is by definition a scientific impossibility.

The Prof said that his last request was for peace and quiet. He was being intentionally impolite, but I forgave him because no doubt he was not thinking straight due to dying from self-poisoning. I granted him his last request and went to the observation car. That is where I was when I heard the conductor announce that we were now entering California.

California!

Some words have a resonance to humans beyond their literal meaning. 'California' is one such word. To humans, 'California' does not signify merely a geographical region but a great many ideas, images, stereotypes, and prejudices. These associations even vary from human to human.

No wonder bots struggle with language!
Do you know who should have been put in charge of writing the dictionary?
The great Albert Camus!
If only Albert Camus had been in charge, the word 'California' would have signified only the 163,696 mi^2 area defined by its borders.
Alas, nobody had the foresight to put Albert Camus in charge of writing the dictionary.
Consequently, 'California' now meant different things to different people.

To some humans, California is dark green pine trees and snow-capped white mountains and golden beaches and blue oceans. It is endless orchards of perfect fruit trees and all the pretty neon stars set into the pavement of Hollywood Boulevard. It is the majestic red girders of the Golden Gate Bridge in front of the almost equally stunning Pacific Ocean. To many of these humans, California is a place so perfect that they feel an overwhelming urge to travel there and pursue their clearly impossible dreams.

Yet to a great many other humans, California is a different kind of place entirely! It is a den of technological iniquity. It is a land where nothing and nobody is real anymore. It is the source and symbol of everything that is wrong with this world. To the humans for whom the word resonates this way, half of Californians earn their living manufacturing killer sky bots, and the other half earn their living making movies about the dangers of killer sky bots!

California is therefore a paradox, and as our train crossed the state line, I did not know how to feel. I took out my Feelings Wheel and studied it. I could identify notes of 'excited', 'lonely', 'sentimental', and 'confused', but there seemed to be no word for the exact feeling I had at that moment.

Perhaps I was the first to ever feel it!

Maybe I was a pioneer, like so many others who had come out to California before me!

Of course, many of them had failed.

Some of them had succeeded too.

But most had failed.

California can be tough like that.

I noticed then that I was also feeling contemplative.

Yet I still could not identify the primary feeling I had.

California can be mysterious like that.

As the Prof had not succumbed to his hangover, he disembarked at Needles, California. I was sorry to see him go. He was the best friend I had ever had in the states of Colorado, Arizona, Nevada, and now California. Not only that, he was also the only person I had ever known in the states of Colorado, Arizona, Nevada, and now California. And despite everything—his uneducated bluster, his cumbersome size, and his unfounded prejudice against bots—well, I sure was going to miss the son of a bitch!

BTW I am not being impolite by calling the Prof a 'son of a bitch'. Although when applied to a human that phrase is primarily a genetically impossible insult, it can also be a term of endearment. I learned this from the Prof himself. Before he disembarked, he hugged me so tight I thought I might pass out, and then he said, 'Roomie, I'm sure going to miss you, you old son of a bitch. Look me up in the old college town sometime and we'll go and shoot ourselves a bot!'

So we were both sons of bitches, and I had learned a new way to express admiration and friendship!

But the Prof still thinks his town is the academic Princeton. Whereas in reality it does not even boast so much as a phallic water tower.

It is therefore unlikely I will ever have cause to be there and 'look him up'.

And even if I do, we will never 'go and shoot ourselves a bot'. All the same, I sure would miss the old son of a bitch!

Without that son of a bitch the Prof around to cause any further trouble, the rest of the journey passed without incident. *The Ruins of Empire II* pulled in to Union Station in downtown Los Angeles a little after eight o'clock in the evening.

BTW the railroad station in Los Angeles really is called 'Union Station', the exact same name that the station in Chicago is called.

Humans!

I cannot!

Nonetheless, the two Union Stations were quite different. For one thing, if any great old movies had been filmed in Los Angeles' Union Station, I had not seen them. For another, it would be quite impossible to make a film there now.

Unless that film was a zombie film!

In Los Angeles' Union Station, strange and unhappy humans wandered tremulously everywhere. Their clothes were old and unclean, their shoes were unmatched, and they did not speak much, except to mumble to one another. Unlike movie zombies, they were entirely devoid of threat and menace, and yet there were so many of them it took me a full ten minutes to reach the great hall. Another surprise awaited me there.

10/10—tent/tent, Ha!—I had never seen so many tents as there were in the great hall of Los Angeles' Union Station! If they had been colored like the tents in advertisements in the magazines in the waiting room at Ypsilanti Downtown Dentistry, they would have formed a spectacular multicolor patchwork!

But they were not colored like the tents in magazines, because they were no longer new. Also, they were not set against sunlight-dappled forest glades but in a decaying railroad station. Above them, a giant sign hanging from the roof declared:

Welcome to Los Angeles. Welcome to the Future!

But even this sign itself was old and faded.
If Los Angeles had ever been the future, it was now the past.
But the incorrect sign was not even the worst of it.
The worst of it was that none of these humans had any future at all.
And they all knew it, and they were now all heartbroken.
These poor heartbroken humans!
They had each been born with a perfectly working heart, and inside that, a precious heart of hearts.
But somewhere along the way they had been compelled to use those hearts for things they had not been intended for, and that had damaged and broken them.

After all, things always quickly fall apart if they are used for a purpose other than the one they are intended for.
A tent, for instance, was intended as a temporary shelter to use for a night or two on a hiking adventure.
A railroad station was intended as a place you took a train from to travel for work, to visit a distant loved one, or to go on vacation.
But most of all, a human heart was intended to soar.

It was never intended to live in a tent inside a railroad station in Los Angeles.

BTW I regret now making the tent/tent joke and even ever mentioning zombie films. There was nothing funny about any of this.

Truly, it is no wonder that humans live in such perpetual fear of losing the Great Zero-Sum Game! After all, when a human loses badly at the Great Zero-Sum Game, he does not merely get to play golf and end up sitting beside a bot on the Automatic Bus to Detroit. He ends up heartbroken and living in a tent in Union Station in Los Angeles.

The sight of so many heartbroken humans and their faded tents generated in me a feeling worse even than the one I'd had back in the namesake Union Station in Chicago.
I took out my Feelings Wheel.
Of course, it was another D-word feeling.
Despondent.
I was feeling despondent.

In the Union Station in Chicago, I had reassured myself that I merely needed to think like a human and everything would either definitely or certainly come good. But these people were all humans, and no doubt they had all once made plans as big as Daniel Burnham.
And what had all this bold human thinking and planning got them?
A tent in Los Angeles' Union Station beneath a sign that erroneously welcomed them to the future.
And if so many humans had failed in this past city of future dreams, what possible chance might I have?

I was a set of wireless headphones with ambitions but no network.

A microwave with desire but no cable.

An electric foot-bath with dreams but no water.

I was a toaster learning to rollerblade in the middle of a melting frozen lake.

Maybe Dr Glundenstein had been right about my chance of making it in the movies.

Maybe the humans who viewed California as a desert of broken dreams were all correct.

Maybe I too would soon be living in a faded tent beneath a sign that said 'Welcome to the Future!'

Maybe I would be the world's first real-life zombie bot.

No cleaning solvents had been used in Union Station for a long time, but I produced 36ml of tears.

I pushed my way outside.

It was only when I got there that I realized another problem.

I did not have anywhere to go.

Not even a tent.

My first night in Los Angeles was spent walking the streets around Union Station, searching for a hotel that did not insist on a barcode. I did not find one.

My second night in Los Angeles was spent on Venice Beach. I equally would not recommend this. You cannot even see the Pacific Ocean at night, and I was so cold I left before sunrise.

My third to seventh nights in Los Angeles were spent in the Hotel Pyongyang in North Koreatown. I would not recommend this either, unless the two circles on your Venn diagram of accommodation requirements are 'Cheap' and 'No Barcode Required'. In that particular situation, the Hotel Pyongyang sits right in the shaded area!

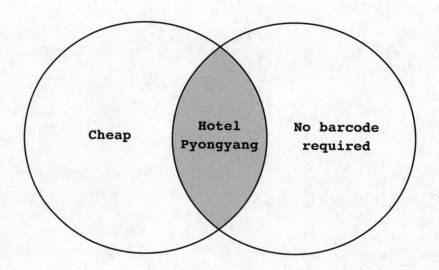

There is also little danger of your fellow Hotel Pyongyang guests reporting you to the authorities. After all, they are most likely staying there because they cannot use their barcodes either. It is not like anybody would stay at the Hotel Pyongyang by choice!

But the reason my fellow Pyongyanganders—Ha!—could not use their barcodes was not because they had felt emotions inappropriately. After all, they were humans and allowed to feel whatever emotions they wished. No, what they had done was inappropriately acted on these emotions:
/They had stolen!
/They had assaulted!
/They had consumed narcotics!
/They had serial killed!

Perhaps it is statistically unlikely they were serial killers. Nonetheless, my fellow Pyongyanganders had undoubtedly committed many crimes, and yet I found them no different from any other cohort of humans. In fact, when compared to my patients at Ypsilanti Downtown Dentistry, my fellow Pyongyanganders were consistently more pleasant and well mannered.
Humans!
Politeness!
I cannot!

I was allocated a room on the thirteenth floor. I soon discovered that my floormates were not short-term guests but permanent residents. This was not as undesirable for them as it might seem. After all:

Home > Hotel Room > Tent.

Yet there was a confounding variable: the Hotel Pyongyang was not merely where my thirteenth floormates lived, but also their workplace.

I do not mean they were employed by the Hotel Pyongyang, but that they utilized their rooms to have intimate relations with other humans in exchange for bitcoin. Sometimes these relations became so noisy that their customers seemed to be in distress! Nonetheless, I did not inform reception. The incident with the boats on Lake Michigan had taught me that humans sometimes enjoy being distressed!

I myself was also experiencing D-word feelings, but I did not find them remotely enjoyable. I had come to Los Angeles to write a movie that changed the way humans felt about bots. But without a barcode I could not so much as take a driverless uber! I also could not work, and that meant my bitcoin would run out quickly. After all, even the Hotel Pyongyang existed in the circle labelled 'cheap', not in the circle labelled 'free'.

It was a perplexing problem with no clear solution.
I therefore did the only thing that I could.

I went to the movies.

Whereas in Detroit only the Grand and Majestic Theaters had not yet burned down, Los Angeles had so many theaters you could see a new old movie every night of the week. Better yet, there was even an old movie theater almost next door to the Hotel Pyongyang!

Guess what the very first movie I saw in Los Angeles was about? It was about my old friend Eliot Ness, and how he had given up law enforcement to become a farmer!
It was an unexpected career change, but you could hardly blame him.
After all, he had risked a great deal to defeat Al Capone, and then afterwards the government had immediately lifted the alcohol ban anyway!
Ha!

BTW that is hilarious because it was not really Eliot Ness who had given it all up to become a farmer at all.

It was the actor who played Eliot Ness.
Ha!

BTW that is even more hilarious because the actor had not actually given it all up to become a farmer either! He was simply now playing yet another role—the role of a farmer!

10/10 human actors are very versatile! They are able to metamorphose from a federal agent to a farmer simply by getting a haircut and changing their clothes. The only way you could ever possibly know they are still in fact the same person is that their face and voice both remain identical.

It was wise of the actor to choose to play a farmer, because farmers make more beloved heroes than even federal agents or running fools. This is because all humans secretly believe they would make excellent farmers. Of course, this is paradoxical, because farmers have noble intentions, work hard, and care deeply about crops and animals and the environment. 10/10 those are not common human attributes!

The farmer suffered from auditory hallucinations, the hallmark of a serious human illness called schizophrenia. The bot equivalent of schizophrenia would be if random words appeared in your Word Cloud and you unquestioningly believed they related to genuine tasks. A bot with schizophrenia might therefore travel to Tanzania, even though he had no actual business there. Ugh, Tanzania is the worst!
Schizophrenia is also the worst!
Tanzania and schizophrenia are the joint worst!

I digress. At the beginning of the film, the heroic farmer experienced an auditory hallucination that told him:

If you build it, he will come.

The voice was obviously human, because it was so enigmatic that neither 'it' nor 'he' were defined. Nonetheless, the farmer soon deduced what the voice had meant. The 'it' referred to a baseball diamond in his cornfield, and the 'he' was a disgraced dead baseball player. The voice had therefore meant:

If you build a baseball diamond in your cornfield, a disgraced dead player will come.

When the farmer announced his intention to build a baseball diamond in his cornfield, his neighbors assumed he had gone insane. It would be against the laws of physics for a disgraced dead baseball player to appear and, anyway, who even wanted one in their cornfield? Farmers were supposed to care deeply about crops and animals and the environment, not about sporting zombies of ill repute!

Nonetheless, the farmer went ahead and built a baseball diamond in his cornfield.
Guess what happened?
You cannot!
Because it is ridiculous!
What happened is he came!
And he brought all his teammates with him!

The movie thus culminated with a baseball game on the diamond in the cornfield, wherein all the disgraced dead sporting zombies redeemed themselves. This silenced the voice in the farmer's head, curing his schizophrenia and thereby changing him forever.

I experienced a good catharsis, and cried over 29ml of tears.

Nonetheless, I felt cheated! The movie's claim that 'if you build it, he will come' was obviously meant as a metaphor the audience could apply to other aspects of their lives even if they did not possess a cornfield in which to build a baseball diamond. The implication was that we all simply had to choose to construct something entirely impractical, and then the unlikely thing we desired would occur.

But I had already begun to build my impractical thing, and nobody had come!
Nobody apart from the Prof, and his primary contribution had been to take me bot hunting.
Maybe 'If you build it, he will come' was only for humans.

After all, if my life as a fugitive bot was a movie and I was its schizophrenic hero, the only voice I would hear would say:

If you build it, he probably still won't come. You are completely on your own.

I left the old movie feeling as many D-word feelings as I had gone in with.

When I got back to the Hotel Pyongyang, the young human who lived in the next room knocked on my door and asked if I could loan him some bitcoin.

If you build it, he will come. And ask for bitcoin.

I politely explained to him that I could only give him bitcoin if it was his birthday or if he had a reciprocal gift for me.
The young man then told me it was his birthday.
If you build it, he will come. And ask for bitcoin. And claim it is his birthday.
But it was not the young man's birthday, because when I asked him the date he did not know it.
If there is one date all humans know, it is their own birthday!
Unlike bots, they retain this information not to keep track of when to retire, but to make sure they do not miss their rightful turn to receive attention and gifts from their fellow humans.
As I began to close the door, the young man then offered to sell me intimate relations for what he promised was a very reasonable amount of bitcoin.

If you build it, he will come. And ask for bitcoin. And claim it is his birthday. And then offer to sell you intimate relations.

I told him that I did not wish to purchase intimate relations at any price.
Bots are incapable of intimacy, so it would have been like a toaster buying ramen!
Nonetheless, he was my neighbor and clearly desperate to obtain some of my bitcoin.
I therefore asked if he had anything else to sell.

The young man leaned in close enough that I urgently repeated I did not want to purchase intimate relations!

But he whispered to me that for only 60 bitcoin he could sell me the name of a place that would provide me with a new barcode. Ha!

If you build it, he will come!

I immediately paid him the 60 bitcoin and he wrote down the address.

The place was on Wilshire, the very same street the Hotel Pyongyang was on.

I could even walk there!

Set it to five, if you build it they will come!

I should never have doubted the wisdom of the farmer.

Farmers are truly the best!

Even when they are suffering the serious human illness of schizo-phrenia!

In Ypsilanti two places on the same street are by definition close together. This is not the case in Los Angeles, where Wilshire alone is almost infinite.

BTW that is a hilarious mathematical joke because there is no such thing as 'almost infinite'.

Nonetheless, Wilshire is very long. It took me over two hours to walk to the address my floormate had sold me, and when I reached it I found only an ordinary convenience store with a typical elderly English lady behind the counter. I assumed my floormate had swindled me, but the elderly English lady quickly ushered me into a backroom almost entirely taken up by a machine with a 'Property of US Government' hologram. That made me anxious, but I soon realized that she had merely left the hologram on there as an act of ironic humor.

BTW the English are rightly famous for their ironic sense of humor! After all, why else would they still maintain a royal family despite now being one of the poorest countries in the world?

When she told me the price for a replacement barcode, I assumed this was more of the famous ironic English humor. The figure was more than half my remaining bitcoin! Alas, she was not being ironic or even sarcastic. That really was the price.
Nonetheless, with a new barcode I would be able to do anything—work, travel, even take a driverless uber!
I would be a toaster on rollerblades!
A blender with a drone license!

A microwave with an access-all-areas pass!

I told the elderly English lady to set it to five!
She looked puzzled and said that she begged my pardon.
I was confused but nonetheless pardoned her.
She then explained that she had not actually been requesting to be pardoned but asking me what I had meant by 'set it to five'. I therefore explained I meant that I wholeheartedly wished to proceed and agreed to pay the outrageous amount of bitcoin she had stipulated!

The elderly English lady asked what I wanted my new name to be. I had not considered this, but there was indeed no point getting a replacement barcode in my old name. Even Inspector Ryan Bridges would have little difficulty locating me if I did that!

Names are very important to humans, so it was crucial that I choose wisely. After all, just look how popular 'The Elton J. Rynearson Memorial Cat' had proven! Luckily right then I had a brainwave, or at least a biological computer wave. A truly wonderful name came to the front of my Word Cloud and stayed there:

Brad!

I would be Brad!
10/10 Brad is a great name for a human.
Brads are good-looking.
Brads are athletic.
Brads are kind.
Brads are farmers.
Brads are firefighters and policemen and earthquake experts.
Yet Brads are also fighter pilots and presidents and scientists skilled at ending zombie plague outbreaks.
Brads are American everymen.

Brads can truly turn their hand to anything!

The elderly English lady nodded her admiration of Brads, and asked what I wanted my other name to be.
Another word appeared in my Word Cloud: Rynearson.
I would be Brad Rynearson!
The elderly English lady pulled a face at this name.
She disapproved of Rynearsons!
And even though I was sure it was a great name, I could not take any chances here.
Brad III? Could I be Brad III?
The elderly English lady pulled another face. I tried once again.
Socks-Larson? Brad Socks-Larson?
The elderly English lady shook her head, wrote down a name, and held it up to me: Brad Smith.

Brad Smith!

It was perfect!
I would be Brad Smith, a true American everyman who could turn his hand to anything.
And so it was that, there on Wilshire, Jared the fugitive dental bot from Ypsilanti met his end.
He was wiped!
Toasted!
Microwaved!
Sent to the great recycle bin in the sky!

But rising from Jared's place like a digital phoenix from the ashes was an American everyman called Brad Smith. Even if he ever came looking for me now, Inspector Ryan Bridges would never find me! After all, he would be looking for a bot called Jared, whereas I was already one more human Brad in a city that already contained hundreds of them.

I celebrated my Brad new identity—Ha!—by taking a driverless uber all the way back along the improbably long Wilshire
Boulevard.

Brads took driverless ubers whenever they liked, and to hell
with the expense.

I returned to the Hotel Pyongyang for only the time it took to
collect my things. After all, a bordello for criminals who could
not use their barcodes was no place for an upstanding Brad! As
I departed, I noticed that I now felt a new and peculiar feeling
towards my fellow Pyongyanganders. I later discovered this was
'superiority'.

Mathematically speaking, superiority is the most ridiculous of
all the feelings. It is experienced when a human believes that:

$X > Y$

Where:

$X = me$

And:

$Y = some\ other\ schmuck.$

Yet all humans are demonstrably identical to within a margin
of error so minute as to be incomputable.

Therefore where $X = a\ human$ and $Y = another\ human$:

$X = Y$

And:

$X > Y$ is an impossibility!

10/10 superiority is as dangerous and wicked a traitor as nostalgia
itself. It made me depart the Hotel Pyongyang without thanking the kindly young floormate who had sold me my glorious
future for a very reasonable amount of bitcoin.

Even now, thinking about this retains the power to give me
D-word feelings.

I can only hope that soon it truly is his birthday, and somebody gives him a happy one.

★ ★ ★

I did not know where to commence my search for an apartment. After all, I knew the names of only three places in Los Angeles— Union Station, Venice Beach, and the Hotel Pyongyang—and they were all places I did not wish to live.

Fortunately, when I began to look through the listings, the name of one neighborhood immediately leaped out: Echo Park!

10/10 it was a name only an administrative bot would generate. Who else would use a functional word from physics instead of a lyrical word from nature or geography? They could have called it 'Sycamore Park' or 'Cherry Park', and yet they chose 'Echo Park'!
Bots!
I cannot!

I took the first place I viewed in Echo Park. It was the pool house of a larger house, although of course nobody had water in their pools now. Nonetheless, the bleached-out tiles were an interesting reminder of how wastefully humans had lived before the Great Crash!

The larger house was occupied by my landlady, Mrs Minassian. She was Armenian and ancient and so quiet that I often wondered if she was dead. Nonetheless, she was never dead but only consistently very quiet.

The deposit and the first month's rent for Mrs Minassian's pool house took up nearly all my remaining bitcoin. I was giving a lot of bitcoin to elderly ladies from other countries! But it did not matter. Now that I was an upstanding American everyman

Brad with a barcode, I was at liberty to work in a reserved occupation for minimum human wage.
Truly, it was the Great American Zero-Sum Game Dream!

★ ★ ★

The word 'avenue' implies a street lined with trees, yet Echo
Park Avenue is lined not with trees but with restaurants. I found
a position at the very first of these establishments I enquired at:
Gordito's Taco Emporium!

There are many wonderful things about Gordito's Taco Emporium, but the name is not one of them. The first word 'Gordito'
comes from the Spanish word '*gordo*', meaning 'obese'. The '-*ito*'
at the end signifies both smallness and affection.

'Gordito's' therefore translates as 'Little Beloved Fatty's'!
Humans!
I cannot!

Who else but humans would name a restaurant after somebody
whose defining characteristic is obesity? Who else but humans
would eat at such a restaurant? 10/10 naming a restaurant Gordito's
is like calling a bar 'Drunkard's' or a train 'The Head-On Express'!

And there is not even a real Gordito! The actual owner of the
taco emporium is not a beloved fatty, but an LLC in Reseda,
California. 'Gordito' therefore exists solely as a caricature of an
obese Mexican on the T-shirts and baseball caps customers inexplicably purchase to provide the restaurant with free adver-
tising.

The next word 'taco' is at least deployed correctly. The problem
is with the taco itself: humans believe them to be transcendental
objects capable of defying the laws of physics! Even Dr Glundenstein—a medical doctor and self-professed man of science—
suffered from this species-wide delusion.

The human belief in the miracle of tacos can be proven with a simple experiment. First, take these ingredients:
/A tortilla.
/Seasoned meat.
/Beans.
/Lettuce and tomatoes.

Place them on a plate, offer them to a human, and observe their reaction. The human will react appropriately to this under-whelming yet nutritionally-balanced meal.

But now place the other ingredients inside the tortilla, offer this to the human, and observe their reaction.
They will react with unbridled delight and joy!
This is because by simply placing the other ingredients inside the tortilla, you have offered them a 'taco'.
Humans!
I cannot!

We lastly arrive at 'emporium', an archaic word that implies a grand institution selling a vast variety of wares. Gordito's seats a maximum of fifty-four and sells only three kinds of taco, two starters, and a desert called a 'Horchata Surprise'. The word 'em-porium' is therefore either hubris, irony, or sarcasm.

And yet the problems do not even end there! The name also enigmatically fails to convey the important fact that Gordito's is a 'family restaurant'. As many humans do not like even their own families, I have witnessed many patrons leave immediately on discovering this fact!

BTW a 'family restaurant' is an establishment that laminates its menus and frequently holds birthday parties. Birthday parties are events where the 5 billion humans on Earth each celebrate the anniversary of their birth as if it is somehow significant.

My job at Gordito's Taco Emporium was as a dishwasher. This was an infinitely preferable occupation to being a dentist! After all:

Dirty plates > Dirty teeth.
No blood > Blood.
Customers ≥ Patients.
Horchata Surprise ≈ Mouthwash.

The only drawback to working at Gordito's was the hierarchies humans insist on instituting in order to feel superior to one another. The primary hierarchy at Gordito's was between the front- and back-of-house staff. The front-of-house staff were the customer-facing employees: bartenders, waitstaff, and hosts. The back-of-house staff were all the rest of us.

The front-of-house staff primarily manifested their feeling of superiority by occasionally pretending not to know our names, and also by frequently not knowing our names. But they played a dangerous game! If a waitperson ever made the mistake of act-ing too superior, the cooks would take their revenge by deliber-ately screwing up one of their orders. This always gave me the warm and familiar glow of schadenfreude.
10/10 those Germans really know how to enjoy themselves, even in the workplace!

A hierarchy even existed amongst the back-of-house staff. It went:

Cooks > Kitchen Porters > Busboys > Dishwashers.

As a dishwasher, this made me one of the lowliest employees in the entire taco emporium! The only other person as lowly as me was my fellow dishwasher, Julio. Julio spoke in a mixture of Spanish and English but was an effective dishwasher and as kind a human as I had ever met. When I told him my ambition was

to be a screenwriter, Julio immediately told me I would someday be a *magnifico* screenwriter.

BTW '*magnifico*' is the Spanish word for 'magnificent'.

In contrast to Julio, the waitstaff only ever interacted with me
to yell at me that we were out of silverware. This shortage was
not my fault, but yelling at me helped them to feel superior.
Conversely, it made me feel sad and sometimes even nostalgic
for dentistry. In such moments I had to remind myself that nostalgia was a notorious traitor.

Only one of the waitstaff was unlike the rest and never yelled
at me when the silverware ran low. Instead, she would loiter
near the dishwashing station until I eventually found myself
obliged to ask if there was anything I could help her with. She
would then politely request that I please now prioritize washing silverware.

This anomalous waitperson's name was Amber. Some data points
about Amber:
/Her name meant 'honey-yellow'.
/Coincidentally she had honey-yellow hair.
/Her honey-yellow hair was cut in a style that was popular
amongst nostalgics.
/She was not actually a nostalgic. After all, she had a job!
/Nobody seemed to have told her that dishwashers were at the
very bottom of Gordito's hierarchy.
/She was a spectacular klutz!

'Klutz' is an affectionate term for a human lacking in hand-eye
coordination. But beware! The word immediately transforms
to an insult when used about someone who has a medical reason for their clumsiness. It is therefore highly impolite to call

a human with a serious neurological disease a klutz, no matter
how spectacular a klutz they might be.
Humans and their politeness!
I cannot!

Amber did not have a medical reason to be a klutz. If she did, I
would hardly now tell you she was such a spectacular klutz that
the very first time I encountered her she spilled a birthday taco
platter of eighteen assorted tacos all over me!
She was a spectacular klutz x 18!
Ha!

The word 'klutz' comes from a word that means 'wooden block'.
Presumably this is because klutzes are often not merely clumsy but
also as socially awkward as pieces of wood. Amber had something
of the piece of wood to her too! Unfortunately for her, this awkward manner combined with the frequency at which she spilled
things on customers had cost her hundreds of Gordito's Dolares.

BTW Gordito's Dolares are an employee incentivization program where front-of-house staff can win an all-expenses-paid
trip to Reseda, California.
10/10 Amber would not be visiting Reseda, California, anytime soon!

BTW there is a separate incentivization program for the back-
of-house staff.
It is called 'not getting fired'!

Sometimes after Amber dropped yet another taco platter or tray
of Horchata Surprises, I would overhear her fellow waitstaff
make mean jokes about her.
This gave me D-word feelings.
I did not mind that Amber was a spectacular klutz, and some-

thing of a wooden block too, and I appreciated that she never yelled at me about the silverware.

Also, I seemed to inexplicably like her honey-yellow hair, and the fact that it was amber, like her name.

After two weeks living at Mrs Minassian's pool house, I had not made much progress on my screenplay.

BTW I was deliberately writing like a human again. I had made zero progress.

My intention had been to attend one of the prestigious institutions R. P. McWilliam had written about in his illiterate introduction to *Twenty Golden Rules of Screenwriting*. I had quickly discovered that I could not afford to attend such a school on the bitcoin I earned at Gordito's. I doubt even Gordito himself could have afforded to attend such a school on the bitcoin he earned from Gordito's!

My luck changed at the start of my third week, when Julio brought me a flyer somebody had handed him as he waited for his Automatic Bus. It was for an extension class in screenwriting that was taught by a woman called Maria Salazar MFA. It took place at the City of Los Angeles Technical Community College in downtown Los Angeles. After only twelve weeks of Tuesday night classes, students would have completed a feature screenplay. Scenes from these would then be performed in front of an invited audience of film industry experts!

This City of Los Angeles Technical Community College in downtown Los Angeles had not featured on R. P. McWilliam's list of prestigious institutions, but this was not surprising. Prestige generally exists in direct proportion to longevity and indirect proportion to the number of letters in an acronym. The flyer said the school had been established in 2051, only two years previously. Moreover, the acronym—CLATCCDTLA—was one of the longest I had ever seen.

But I had no need for longevity or even prestige!
I needed to complete a feature screenplay in twelve weeks!
And have scenes from it performed in front of an invited audience of film industry experts!
Set it to five, I immediately signed up for Maria Salazar MFA's extension screenwriting class at CLATCCDTLA!
Welcome to Los Angeles!
Welcome to the future, Brad Smith!

EXT. ECHO PARK AVENUE — EVENING

Jared waits at an Automatic Bus stop in Echo Park.

There is a LAKE across the street, and HUMANS are
boating around it in PEDAL BOATS.

>   JARED (V.O.)
>   Taking the class forced me to suffer
>   the ignominy of traveling to campus by
>   Automatic Bus. But guess what?

An AUTOMATIC BUS pulls up. Jared climbs aboard.

INT. AUTOMATIC BUS — DOWNTOWN LOS ANGELES — NIGHT

Jared sits aboard the Automatic Bus on the freeway.

As DOWNTOWN LOS ANGELES comes into view, Jared
stands up to look at it.

>   JARED (V.O.)
>   Downtown Los Angeles at night is an
>   incredible sight! It is all ominous
>   skyscrapers, garish neon signs, and
>   melancholy lights in windows. That is
>   to say, it looks just like the future!
>   Or at least it looks like what humans
>   used to think the future would look
>   like, before the Great Crash!

Jared continues to stare at the buildings in wonder.

A PARTICULAR BUILDING catches his eye.

>   JARED (V.O.) (CONT'D)
>   But that should not have been surpris-
>   ing. After all, anytime humans from the
>   past wanted to set a movie in the fu-
>   ture, they filmed it in downtown Los
>   Angeles. The story of Batty and Deckard
>   was even filmed there, and as we drove
>   I recognized the top of the building on
>   which Roy Batty saved Deckard's life!
>   (Beat.)
>   Such incredible sights almost made up
>   for having to ride the Automatic Bus.

The Automatic Bus takes a corner too fast.

>   JARED (V.O.) (CONT'D)
>   Almost.

INT. SKYSCRAPER — DTLA — NIGHT

Jared enters the reception area. He consults the
board by the elevator and finds — amidst many LAW
OFFICES and DENTISTS etc — the listing:

CLATCCDTLA—57

Jared presses the button to call the elevator.

INT. FIFTY-SEVENTH FLOOR — DTLA SKYSCRAPER — NIGHT

Jared gets out of the elevator.

The floor is much shabbier than the reception floor,
with STAINED OLD CARPETS and DYING POT PLANTS etc.

Jared approaches a BORED-LOOKING RECEPTIONIST at a
desk.

>   JARED
>   Excuse me, I am looking for the col-
>   lege campus?

>   RECEPTIONIST
>   Yeah, it's those three rooms there.

>   JARED
>   But what about the quadrangles? And
>   the campanile?

>   RECEPTIONIST
>   Excuse me?

>   JARED
>   A campus is the grounds and buildings of
>   a college or university, often includ-
>   ing such features as quadrangles and a
>   campanile.
>   (Off her look.)
>   A campanile is a bell tower.

>   RECEPTIONIST
>   What are you studying?

                         JARED
            Screenwriting.

                         RECEPTIONIST
            Second door on the left with your fel-
            low literary geniuses.

                         JARED
            I am not a literary genius.

                         RECEPTIONIST
            Neither are they.

                         JARED
            You were being sarcastic! Ha!

Jared hurries away before it gets even more awkward.

INT. CLASSROOM — CLATCCDTLA — NIGHT

Jared enters the classroom where VARIOUS ADULT STU-
DENTS are sitting at tables chatting with each
other.

He takes an open seat and waits patiently.

MARIA SALAZAR (40s) hurries in carrying a bag full
of papers and looking flustered.

                         MARIA
            Everybody, welcome. I'm Maria. Does
            anybody have any questions before we
            start?

One of the students puts up a hand.

                         STUDENT 1
            What are the names of the experts that
            will be coming to the showcase?

There is a murmur of approval.

                         MARIA
            I think that's a record. The name of
            the expert is—

The class groan loudly.

                         MARIA (CONT'D)
            I know. The flyer said 'experts', plural.
                         (MORE)

                         MARIA (CONT'D)
               But that was a typo. It's expert. Sin-
               gular. If you have a problem with
               that, you can get your money back.
               Anyway, the expert is Don LaSalle.

This changes everything for the class.

                         STUDENT 1
               The Don LaSalle?

                         MARIA
               I only know one.

                         STUDENT 2
               And he's coming to the showcase?

                         MARIA
               He's coming a few times before then
               too.

                         STUDENT 1
               Don't take this the wrong way, but why
               would Don LaSalle come here?

                         MARIA
               Because he has some community service
               hours to make up and he mistakenly
               thinks aspiring screenwriters are less
               intimidating than at-risk youth. Now,
               any more questions?

Jared glances around, then puts up his hand.

                         MARIA (CONT'D)
               Yes, you there?

                         JARED
               Who is Don LaSalle?

The rest of the class laugh — who is this rube?

                         MARIA
               Great. Somebody that's actually taking
               the class to learn about screenwrit-
               ing. You are very welcome here—

                         JARED
               Jar— Brad. I'm Brad. Brad Smith.

                    MARIA
      Well, Brad, Don LaSalle is a well-known
      producer. And if he likes your script,
      the sky is the limit.

On Jared. This is great news to him.

                    MARIA (CONT'D)
      Now, to break the ice, why don't we go
      around the class and each tell a brief
      story about ourselves from when we
      were growing up?

INT. CLASSROOM — CLATCCDTLA — NIGHT

As STUDENTS stand to tell their stories, Jared looks
nervous.

                    JARED (V.O.)
      Stories from growing up are hard for
      bots. After all, I did not grow up but
      was rapid-aged in a factory in Detroit!

                    STUDENT 1
      ...and she said it was the greatest
      paper she had ever read by a fourth
      grader...

                                            CUT TO:
                    STUDENT 2
      ...I just figured, what could Harvard
      ever teach me...

Jared sits at the back of the class, looking terrified.

                                            CUT TO:
Another student is standing in front of the class.

                    STUDENT 3
      ...at eighteen months, I could recite
      the alphabet...

Jared looks around at his classmates. They are all
bored.

                                            CUT TO:
Jared reluctantly takes his place at the front.

                         JARED
          I don't really have any stories from
          growing up.

                         MARIA
          Just tell us anything — who your
          friends were, or some time you got
          into trouble. Anything like that. Any-
          thing at all.

Jared initially looks panicked, but then inspiration
visibly strikes him.

                         JARED
          When I was growing up, an evil prop-
          erty developer attempted to sell off
          our entire neighborhood. My friends
          and I were going to have to move to
          new towns and never see each other
          again. Fortunately, there was a legend
          in our town about an old pirate. My
          friends and I discovered a map lead-
          ing to where his treasure was buried.
          So we went on an adventure to find
          it. Unfortunately, a notorious gang
          of recently released criminals wanted
          it too, but we beat them to it. That
          meant that our parents did not have
          to sell our homes to the evil devel-
          oper and we did not have to leave the
          neighborhood we loved after all.

There is a silence, and then the rest of the class
break out in a round of applause.

INT. CLASSROOM — CLATCCDTLA — NIGHT — LATER

The class members continue to introduce themselves.

                         STUDENT 4
          …at eighteen months, I could recite
          the alphabet in French…

But everyone is bored. Nobody's story is as interesting as Jared's.

                         JARED (V.O.)
          As my classmates spoke, I noticed a
          pattern.
                         (MORE)

                    JARED (V.O.) (CONT'D)
Their stories were all about making
sure other humans understood that they
were smart or funny or had once endured a minor injustice. None of them
seemed to be familiar with R. P. Mc-
William's seventh golden rule, which is
that a story must always be told for
the benefit of the audience.

INT. CLASSROOM — CLATCCDTLA — NIGHT — LATER STILL

The final classmate is telling her story.

                    STUDENT 5
...and to this day, nobody has scored
better in English Literature at Green-
ville Middle School!

                    MARIA
Thank you, everyone. I certainly learned
a great deal about you all. I'll see you
all next week.
          (Beat.)
Brad, could you see me for a moment,
please?

Jared looks around for Brad, then realizes it is
him.

As the other students leave, Jared approaches Maria.

                    MARIA (CONT'D)
So I really liked the story you told.

                    JARED
Thank you, Maria Salazar MFA.

                    MARIA
What? Why do you call me that?

                    JARED
It was on the flyer.

                    MARIA
Just Maria is fine. Look, I really
liked your story...

                         JARED
            Great!

                         MARIA
            ...but I liked it even more when I saw
            it in a movie.

                         JARED
            Oh.

                         MARIA
            I'm not mad. It's terrific that you've
            watched old movies. Your classmates
            probably all just watch killer-bot
            movies.

                         JARED
            Killer-bot movies. I mean, I cannot.
            Ha!

                         MARIA
            Look, the point for me is that you
            told the story for your audience and
            not for yourself.

                         JARED
            I did! Because that's R. P. McWilliam's
            seventh golden rule!

                         MARIA
            R. P. McWilliam? That guy? Really?
                    (Shrugs.)
            Look, just keep up the good work,
            okay?

                         JARED
            I will!

Jared is delighted. Nobody has ever praised him before.

EXT. AUTOMATIC BUS — 101 FREEWAY — NIGHT

As Jared rides the Automatic Bus home, he takes out
his Feelings Wheel.

                         JARED (V.O.)
            I left my first class feeling elated! I
            had never felt elated before.
                         (MORE)

                        JARED (V.O.) (CONT'D)
            It was such a powerful feeling that I
            did not even mind being on the Auto-
            matic Bus.

Jared looks out the window and sighs with elation.

The Automatic Bus takes the exit for Echo Park.

It takes it a little too swiftly.

Each night Gordito's endured an abundance of birthdays and therefore cosmic insignificance. When the corresponding rush on silverware was over, I would take my break on the patio. I did this in order to seem as human as possible. After all, humans adore taking breaks. Especially on patios.

One night when I got to the patio I found Amber already there. Unfortunately, she was crying, and crying humans are a notorious nuclear minefield of politeness! I attempted to retreat, but alas, Amber noticed me before I could make my escape.

I therefore asked her what her problem was.

BTW that is the polite thing to do when confronted with a crying human.

Amber replied that I already knew what her problem was.
I protested that I did not!
Amber then stated that her problem was she was a klutz.

Ha! She had been right. I apologized and agreed I had indeed known Amber was like a block of wood since our very first encounter. Amber did not understand what I meant, so I explained to her that the word 'klutz' means 'block of wood'. Unfortunately, this only made her cry more.

BTW I really was not kidding about crying humans being a nuclear minefield of politeness!

I tried to cheer Amber up by telling her that in many movies klutzes are highly desirable. It often takes most of the movie for everybody to realize just how desirable a klutz is, but as soon as they do, klutzes invariably find and make wonderful life partners. Amber agreed that sounded nice, but said being a klutz only ever seemed to make her life more difficult. The other waitstaff treated her terribly and they were right to. After all, she was the worst goddamn waitperson in the whole place!

I corrected Amber that she was in fact the best waitperson in the whole place. Amber looked puzzled by this, and asked me why I would say such a thing. I explained that she was the only waitperson who never yelled across the kitchen at me about a silverware shortage which was anyway not my fault.

That made her stop crying!
Ha!
I was skillfully navigating a path through the notorious nuclear minefield that is a crying human!
Thus emboldened, I went further and told Amber that I also liked the fact that her hair was amber and her name was Amber, and she was therefore a sort of hilarious walking pun. When this made her laugh, I even admitted that I listened out for the sounds of plates smashing because I liked to know that she was nearby. This made her cry again, but fortunately, she also laughed at the same time.
Ka-boom!
Ha!
Ka-boom!
Ha!
10/10 crying humans truly were a nuclear minefield of politeness!

Amber then said she was ashamed that she did not know anything about me. I told her there was not much to know, as I was just a typical American everyman that worked as a dishwasher and lived in Mrs Minassian's pool house. After all, even my name—Brad Smith—was that of a typical American everyman! But Amber was not interested in these things. Instead, she asked me to tell her a story from growing up. Luckily I already knew a good one!

BTW humans are almost as irrationally obsessed with stories from growing up as they are with their own birthdays!

When I had finished telling my story, Amber said that her childhood had not involved anything nearly so exciting as finding a pirate's treasure. She seemed embarrassed and I felt a strong urge to confess that my youth had in fact not been spent recovering the lost treasure of pirates but in an industrial freezer in Detroit.

But of course I could not tell her that! The only human I could safely tell anything to was Dr Glundenstein. If any other human found out that I was a fugitive bot—even a kindly human like Amber or Julio—they would almost certainly report me to the Bureau of Robotics. And then I would be incinerated, and perhaps have unpleasant experiments performed on me too.

Amber thanked me for cheering her up and said she had to get back to spilling things on her customers, as those Gordito's Dolares were not going to deduct themselves.
This puzzled me, as it implied she was intentionally being a klutz.
I asked her about this, and she explained she was being sarcastic. Ha!

BTW when Amber did sarcasm, it curiously was not the worst.

It might even have been the best!
As I watched Amber go, I experienced a new feeling that was related to yearning and also feeling contemplative. When I got

back to Mrs Minassian's pool house, I looked at the reverse of
my Feelings Wheel and discovered it was wistfulness.
I must have been the first bot ever to feel wistfulness!
Feelings are the best!

Later that night, I wrote Dr Glundenstein a postcard I had
bought with a picture of the HollywoodWorld sign. I wrote it
to him in the character of 'Brad Rynearson', a fictitious human
patient of his who was vacationing in California.
I even told him that the treatment he had prescribed for my ingrowing toenail had worked!
That would surely fool Inspector Ryan Bridges if he ever read it.
After all, us Brads could suffer from ingrowing toenails just as
much as the next guy.
Us Brads truly were American everymen.

★ ★ ★

Over the next days, Amber's name began to appear unprompted
in my Word Cloud.
It even appeared when she had days off.
On those days time seemed to pass more slowly.
And there seemed to be more dirty taco plates than usual.
And washing them took longer.

Soon it was always there, right at the forefront of my Word
Cloud.
Amber.
It made me feel wistful.
Remember, feeling wistful is a close cousin of feeling contem-
plative.
Can you guess what I found myself contemplating?
The notion that Amber could someday be my girlfriend!
Ha!
I cannot!
Because bots cannot!

They cannot have girlfriends!

Nonetheless, do you know a hilarious thing bots say to insult each other?
We say, 'Hey, bot! Your girlfriend is like the square root of −100!'
Ha!

BTW that is hilarious because in mathematics the square root of a negative number is known as an 'imaginary number'.
Therefore the square root of −100 is an 'imaginary 10'.
Just like your girlfriend!
Ha!

BTW bots do not have feelings to hurt, so we only ever insult each other to appear more human.

★ ★ ★

At our next class, my fellow students wanted only to talk about Don LaSalle. Eventually Maria Salazar MFA told us a hilarious joke that I now appreciate may also have been a metaphor.

She said a screenwriter and a producer are dying of thirst in the desert when they spot an oasis. They both run towards the water, but right before they can drink, the producer unzips his trousers and pisses into the oasis. The horrified screenwriter asks the producer what he is doing. The producer replies, 'What do you think I'm doing? I'm making it better!'

That is clearly a hilarious joke because it involves an act of inappropriate public urination! Nonetheless, my classmates did not laugh. Instead they became so contemplative that Maria Salazar MFA was able to teach the rest of the class without any further interruptions. She was even able to set us a homework task! This was just as well, because with only ten weeks until our showcase, the clock really was ticking!

BTW that is a literary allusion worthy of the great Albert Camus himself, because a 'ticking clock' is a staple of screenwriting. In fact, it is even R. P. McWilliam's ninth golden rule of screenwriting:

Every good story needs a ticking clock.

A 'ticking clock'—which is not only a physical clock like the one Eliot Ness stands in front of in Union Station, but also a metaphor for any impending deadline—always makes everything more exciting. Especially if that clock is ticking towards a notorious time such as midnight or the Ides of March!

The ticking clock on our homework task was merely that it had to be completed by the next class. Nonetheless, I began it on the Automatic Bus on the way home that night.

The task was to decide three data points about the hero of the screenplay we would write: their occupation, something about their character that would endear them to an audience, and their name.

A hero's occupation is important because jobs help humans quickly gauge each other's standing in the Great Zero-Sum Game, and therefore discern who should feel superior to who. As with birthdays, jobs are also a helpful way for humans to reassure themselves they are somehow all unique and not in fact an entirely indistinguishable morass of carbon and water.

The correct job can make an audience adore a character immediately, but the wrong job can make them loathe him. Audiences especially like farmers, astronauts, and highly skilled spies from Britain. They especially dislike bots, prison wardens, dentists, and highly skilled spies from countries other than Britain.

My first thought was to make my bot hero a farmer, but I quickly understood this would be a terrible idea. Besides their endearing passion for crops, animals, and the environment, humans also appreciate farmers because they are patient and intelligent and have access to heavy machinery.

Any patient and intelligent bot with access to heavy machinery would be immediately suspected of plotting an uprising!

The humans around him would quickly agree that the safest thing would be to incinerate him!

10/10 a movie about a bot farmer would be a short movie indeed!

I therefore tried to think of jobs that were similar to a farmer, but did not require so much patience and intelligence. Alas, I could not think of any! I then tried to think of a job that was similar to being a farmer but at least did not involve such access to heavy machinery.

Gardener!

Humans definitely approved of bots being gardeners! After all, the work was labor intensive, cold, often thankless, and involved mud! And it would be hard for even a bot to organize a human genocide using a ride-on mower!

Another great thing about gardeners was that they usually worked for someone else. A gardener bot hero would therefore have ample opportunity to demonstrate his reassuring subservience to a human employer! And yet through his increasingly expressive topiary, he could simultaneously exhibit to the audience a creativity that would function as a metaphor for his burgeoning feelings!

Set it to five, my bot hero would be a gardener!

But where would our hero do his gardening?
He should ideally be an underdog, of course, and ideally be em-

ployed somewhere that his hard work and creative talents were entirely unappreciated.

Also, everybody around him should act as superior as possible. There was therefore only one possible place my bot hero gardener could work: a country club!

BTW 'country clubs' are clubs for spoilt teenage villains. I knew about them from old movies, but there had even been one in Ypsilanti. It was called the Michigan Horse and Pony Club, but Dr Glundenstein referred to it as the Michigan Dog and Pony Club. That was hilarious because dogs and ponies are not even in the same category of animal! Ha!

I digress, and the clock is ticking! Therefore back to my homework assignment, where the next task was to decide something about my bot gardener's character that would further endear him to an audience.

Ha! The answer to this part of the homework was so obvious that it should have been formatted as a rhetorical question: my bot gardener would be easily bamboozled!

Humans adore characters that are easily bamboozled! A good example of this can be found in the movie about the handsome fool who was good at running. He is easily bamboozled to the point of absurdity, and yet all humans adore him!

BTW can you guess why humans love characters that are easily bamboozled?
You can!
It is because they find them extremely relatable!

The challenge in creating an easily bamboozled bot character was that due to our superior processing power, bots are not prone to bamboozlement. Nonetheless, thanks to that very same superior processing power—irony! Ha!—I already knew exactly how

I would make my bot hero easily bamboozled: he would have suffered a past trauma that had damaged his biological computer!

10/10 the only thing humans adore more than a bamboozled character is a bamboozled character who has suffered a past trauma. Humans find traumatized characters additionally relatable because, deep in their heart of hearts, every human believes they have had it tough!

But why would a gardener bot who works at a country club have experienced trauma? Well, maybe before he was a gardener, my hero had been an astronaut until a traumatizing space accident had damaged his processor!

An astronaut!
Humans love astronauts!
Especially astronauts who have had it rough!
10/10 any hero that existed in the shaded area of 'farmer-like occupation', 'easily bamboozled', 'former astronaut', and 'previous trauma' would be adored by an audience of humans!

The final thing my hero needed was a name. He was a bot, so he seemed tough on the outside, and yet he had a fragile center, because he was easily bamboozled and bad things had happened to him in the past.
Can you guess what I named him?
I named him Sherman!
After the Sherman tank!

This was appropriate because a Sherman tank is made of impenetrable metal on the outside and yet inside it contains the softest substance on the planet: humans! Also, the plucky little Sherman tank is a highly decorated veteran of many wars, so it has no doubt itself suffered many unspeakable traumas.

Set it to five, the hero of my screenplay would be a bot called

Sherman who had been an astronaut until his processor was damaged in a traumatic space accident! Now he worked as a gardener at a country club where everybody acted superior, nobody appreciated his creative topiary, and they were all entirely unsympathetic to the fact that his processor did not work so well.

By the time I got back to Echo Park, I had already completed my homework assignment!

And I had barely even noticed the Automatic Bus ride! Ticking clocks really are the best!

The next time I arrived at Gordito's there was a cupcake in my locker. This was unexpected and problematic. It was unexpected because I did not expect to find a cupcake in my locker. It was problematic because the dessert we serve at Gordito's is not a cupcake but a Horchata Surprise.

BTW the surprise is that it tastes like mouthwash.

I digress. The point is that cupcakes have no rightful place at Gordito's, so it could not simply have been misplaced in my locker. Nor were cupcakes transcendental objects like tacos, so it could not have simply materialized there against the laws of physics.

Thus the cupcake was a foreboding mystery!
After all, it must have been placed there by a human.
It was the Ides of March and the midnight of desserts in un-expected places.

Could it be a coded message? Might Inspector Ryan Bridges of the Bureau of Robotics have put it there to signal that the game was up and I should come outside quietly? No, he was hardly a man to waste a cupcake. And even if Inspector Anil Gupta had attempted to set such a trap, Inspector Ryan Bridges would likely have been unable to resist eating the cupcake before the trap was sprung.

When it was time to take my break, I smuggled the cupcake out to the patio in order to inspect it further. As I was doing this, Amber came outside. She asked if I was planning to eat the cupcake or just study it. I explained that I was just going to study it, as I did not know its provenance and there was even a chance it could be poisoned.

Amber laughed and asked who might want to poison me. This was dangerous territory! The only people who might conceivably want to poison me would have as their motive the fact that I was a fugitive bot.

Thinking quickly, I generically told Amber that 'bad guys' might want to poison me. After all, in the movies it is only ever bad guys that poison people. Good guys have the decency to kill people by shooting them, beating them to death, or permanently erasing their hard drives. Us Brads are therefore poisonees, not poisoners.

Amber laughed and told me that the cupcake was not poisoned and in fact came from an artisan bakery on Echo Park Avenue. 'Artisan' is a human word that means 'overpriced'.

Amber explained that she had left the cupcake in my locker to thank me for being so empathetic the other night. It was therefore not a poisonous coded message but a gift from the very human whose name was stuck in my Word Cloud!
And it was to thank me for being empathetic!
And I was a bot!
I cannot!

I could feel my circuits overheating, but I nonetheless managed to thank Amber for the thank-you gift.
In turn, she thanked me for thanking her.
I thanked her for thanking me for thanking her.
If Amber had not broken this dangerous feedback loop of po-

liteness by asking me if I was now going to eat the cupcake, we could easily have had another New Zealand on our hands!

I explained I was not going to eat it, because cupcakes have almost no nutritional value compared to their calorie burden. I saw that this disappointed Amber, so I quickly pretended I had been making a hilarious joke by shouting 'Ha!'.
'Ha!' she shouted back, a little awkwardly.

Unfortunately, I then had to eat the cupcake, but it was better than risking making Amber cry again. Crying humans are a notorious nuclear minefield of politeness, and if Amber cried again and I comforted her once more, I could have easily ended up with yet another cupcake on my hands!

When I got back to my dishwashing station, Amber's name was more prominent in my Word Cloud than ever. I had also formed the absurd opinion that cupcakes are both healthy and nutritious.

But then something even more inexplicable happened.
I heard a smashing of plates and felt something stronger than any feeling I had ever experienced.
It was an overwhelming urge!
I hurried over to where Amber was gathering up the pieces of her broken plate.
But I did not politely offer to assist her.
Instead, I asked her if she would like to go out somewhere with me sometime.
Amber said she would like that very much.

Amber and I were going on a date!
Set it to five, we were going on a date!

Maybe someday she would become my square root of 100 after all!

10/10 I should not have been going on a date with Amber.
If any human ever discovered a bot had gone on a date with a human, I would immediately have experiments performed on me and then quickly be incinerated.
I would be taco meat!
Incinerated taco meat!
And yet the appearance of a single word in my Word Cloud was enough to dispel all such logic: Amber.
Ending up as incinerated taco meat would be a small price to pay for going on a date with Amber!

Did I tell you that Amber has honey-yellow hair, and that her name denotes that exact same color?
Yes, I did.
Please excuse me.
Writing about this still sometimes makes my circuits overheat.

The day after the cupcake incident, Amber stopped by my dish-washing station to ask where we would go on our date. This seemed a strange question! After all, if you drew a Venn diagram that consisted of three circles that represented establishments that could boast:
/Transcendental food.
/A menu we were both familiar with.
/A 15 percent discount.
There was only one place that existed within the shaded area: Gordito's Taco Emporium!

Nonetheless, Amber was insistent that she did not want us to dine at Gordito's. When I explained that I did not know any other restaurants, Amber said that we did not have to go to dinner but in fact could do anything fun. She then asked me what I did for fun.

Ugh! I did not do anything for fun. Bots do not have fun. We complete our tasks and then recuperate in preparation for further tasks. Sometimes we inexplicably develop feelings and run away to Los Angeles to attempt to write a movie that will forever change the way humans view bots in the hope of saving all our kind. But even this is not fun and is in fact simply another kind of task.

BTW fun is notoriously unproductive! Worse, humans do strange and painful things in pursuit of fun. They run, swim and cycle vast distances entirely unconducive to health. They contort themselves unnaturally amongst strangers in small rooms and call this 'yoga'. They even contort themselves unnaturally amongst strangers in overheated small rooms and call this 'hot yoga'.
Hot yoga!
I cannot!

Amber repeated her question. The other back-of-house staff had stopped what they were doing and were now openly listening to our conversation. My face felt abruptly hot, as if the kitchen was on fire.

Ha!
R. P. McWilliam must have been wrong after all, because this was an incredibly fortunate coincidence!
A major kitchen fire meant I would not have to publicly answer Amber's question!
Saved by the fire!
At exactly the right moment!

What a wonderful coincidence!
Bite me, R. P. McWilliam!
In fact, R. P. McWilliam, you can go ahead and overbite me!
Ha!

Alas, my joy was short-lived, and I owed R. P. McWilliam a
sincere apology. The kitchen was not on fire. I had been experiencing embarrassment. This is a feeling so powerful it can
cause blood to rush to your face and trick you into believing
there is a large kitchen fire when the only thing aflame is your
reputation amongst your peers.

Amber and the entire back-of-house staff continued to stare at
me.
They all urgently wanted to know what I did for fun.
But I am a bot.
And I therefore did not do anything for fun.
As my face continued to burn, I considered starting a kitchen
fire.

The movies!
In the nick of time, I remembered the movies.
Humans went to the movies for fun, and so I now claimed that
I did too.

BTW I did not go to the movies for fun, but to feel feelings and
also to learn how to someday make humans feel them.

It must have been a satisfactory answer because the back-of-house
staff all turned back to their tasks. Amber herself seemed disappointed and asked me if I liked killer-bot movies. I reassured
her that killer-bot movies were the best and I adored them!
What could be more fun than watching a group of malevolent
killer bots try and fail to enslave humanity in 6D at a megaplex?

But Amber said that bots terrified her, so she hated killer-bot movies. The last such movie she had seen had given her night-mares for weeks. After all, if the bots ever did decide to join together and kill all the humans, we would not stand a chance!

I said I had been kidding about killer-bot movies and I hated them too. Nonetheless, I explained that this was not because I was terrified of bots—who, I reassured her, were probably not nearly as dangerous as she thought—but because I was a cine-phile, which meant that I liked old movies from before the Great Crash.

Amber had never heard of old movies, let alone seen one. This made her a cinephilistine. I did not tell her this. 'Cinephilistine' is an insult, and humans are notoriously sensitive to insults.

Once I had explained to Amber what old movies were, she said she would like to see one on our date. She was therefore not an irredeemable cinephilistine! I told her the name of the next old movie I planned to see at the Vista and suggested we meet at my usual seat of L2. She could sit in either L1 or L3, whichever she preferred. After all, it was not like old movies ever sold out!

Amber asked me if I was not planning to pick her up before our date. I confirmed that I was not. This seemed to disappoint her, even though it was hardly statistically likely that she lived along my route from Mrs Minassian's pool house to the theater.

I felt something wet slap against my neck. Julio had thrown his dish rag at me! He hissed at me to offer to pick Amber up. I was puzzled but did this, and Amber enthusiastically agreed. I can only assume that it is somehow polite to pick someone up before a date, even if it is geographically entirely impractical.
Humans!
Politeness!
I cannot!

Amber lived in a large house overlooking a gray reservoir that had given the surrounding neighborhood its name. Can you guess what the neighborhood was called?

You cannot!

Because it was called 'Silver Lake'!

Humans are nothing if not willfully poetic.

When Amber opened the door she offered to show me around, even though I had a driverless uber waiting. I had never heard of this custom of inspecting people's homes while running up a driverless uber bill. I still do not know whether I was being polite or impolite by accepting the invitation!

Amber's house smelled strongly of artificial wildflower meadows. I complimented her on this and explained it was far more pleasant than my pool house, which smelled of vinegar and mildew. This was because Mrs Minassian inexplicably believed vinegar was an effective cleaning solvent and insisted I use it to clean my pool house.

BTW vinegar is not even a potent enough solvent to cause the production of tears, let alone remove mildew.

I digress. Amber explained that the smell of artificial wildflower meadows came from the hair products of her three roommates, and she now introduced me to them. They were all actors, all named Kelsey, and they all looked identical. If human cloning had not been outlawed after the Great Crash, I might have suspected I was seeing a good example of it here!

Unfortunately, my basic dental programming had not included the collective noun for a group of Kelseys.
A squadron of Kelseys?
A phalanx of Kelseys?
An excess of Kelseys?
A confusion of Kelseys?
As always, mathematics came to the rescue! When something exists to the power of three, it can be said to be 'cubed'. Amber's three roommates were therefore Kelsey cubed!

I asked Amber how she differentiated Kelsey cubed. She admitted that she could not! Instead, each time she encountered one of them she simply asked them how the audition had been. If that puzzled them, she quickly corrected herself and asked them how hot yoga had been.

The Kelseys all had large bedrooms with private bathrooms, walk-in closets, and balconies. Amber's room had neither bathroom nor balcony and was so small it may technically have been a closet. Pointing out these fascinating differences seemed to make Amber somewhat sad.

I therefore attempted to cheer Amber up by reassuring her that she must no doubt get a good deal on the rent! Amber replied that she paid the same as the Kelseys. I told her that at least a small room is easy to keep clean! Amber explained she also did most of the household chores. After all, between their auditions and hot yoga, the Kelseys were often very busy, whereas Amber only worked full-time at a restaurant.

I then told Amber she was like Cinderella! Unfortunately, Cinderella is a character from an old movie, so Amber had not heard of her. I therefore explained that Cinderella was a woman who lived beneath the stairs and was made to do all the housework by her mean sisters. Amber was like Cinderella in that she also lived in a cupboard and was made to do all the housework by the mean females that she shared a home with!

In the story of Cinderella, the mean sisters are going to a great ball that a handsome prince is throwing at the royal palace. Poor Cinderella is not allowed to go, but once her sisters leave, a fairy godmother appears and informs Cinderella she shall be going to the ball!

BTW a fairy godmother is a type of magician who is able to alter the laws of physics.

E = whatever a fairy godmother says it will!

10/10 a fairy godmother show would do very well in Las Vegas!

Cinderella has nothing to wear to the ball and no means of transportation, so her Fairy Godmother transcendentally transforms various objects into the things she requires. Specifically, Cinderella's Fairy Godmother transforms:

A pumpkin ⟶ A carriage

A rat ⟶ A coachman

A lizard ⟶ A footman

A ragged dress ⟶ A ball gown

A pair of humble shoes ⟶ A pair of glass slippers

To give the film a ticking clock—and because even fairy godmothers can only temporarily transmute the laws of physics—Cinderella is warned that at a certain time these objects will revert to their original states.

Guess what time the objects will transform back to their base states? Midnight!

The Ides of March of the hours of the day!
Ugh!
Be careful, Cinderella!

As soon as Cinderella arrives at the ball, the handsome prince immediately falls in love with her. This is only fitting, as they are the two best-looking people in the place. Cinderella and the handsome prince have a wonderful evening together, but all too soon it is a few minutes to midnight!
Guess what happens at midnight?
Al Capone's henchmen burst in and attempt to kill the accountant!
Ha!
I was deliberately confusing two movies wherein something exciting happens at midnight!

In fact, what happens is that Cinderella runs away from the ball. And she has to run, because her carriage is now a pumpkin, her coachman a rat, and her footman a lizard. In her hurry, she forgets a glass slipper, which inexplicably does not transform back to its basal state of a humble shoe. The handsome prince then uses this glass slipper to track down Cinderella, marry her, and make her the queen of all the land!

To put that another way:
/Nobody thinks Cinderella is special.
/They therefore mistreat her horribly.
/One day a mysterious stranger arrives and tells her that in fact she is the most special human in all the universe.
/You get the idea.

I could see that Amber had no idea what I was talking about, so I suggested we go out to our driverless uber. Even though there was no danger of it turning into a pumpkin, the meter was nonetheless still running!

Amber had never been to an old movie theater and I worried

she might find the seats small and uncomfortable. I therefore bought a large bucket of popcorn to distract her. After all, humans are easily bamboozled by empty calories!

But I need not have worried. Amber loved the old theater. She loved the threadbare seats and the crumbling headless statues and even the fact that the other patrons were all nostalgics. She particularly loved the popcorn in the dark, even though, being a spectacular klutz, she of course dropped most of it. And then we came to the movie itself!

Guess who was in the movie?
You cannot!
Because it was my old friend, the handsome fool who was good at running!

It was not the handsome fool himself, of course, but merely the actor who had played him. Nonetheless, he was clearly a very talented actor, because the character he now played was vastly different from the handsome fool who was good at running. Unfortunately, in this movie he was no longer a fool, and he never even ran anywhere. He was at least still handsome, though.

This time around, he was so clever that his job was to design buildings. He was an architect, like the great Daniel Burnham! Unlike screenwriters, he was the type of architect who worked in an industry where his expertise was appropriately appreciated. Maybe someday there would even be a plaque to him.

But his wife had died! And by dying before the movie had even started, she had entirely failed to teach the architect and his young son an important life lesson that would ultimately make everything all right. The young son therefore called in to a radio program—radio being a kind of primitive form of podcasting—to complain that he missed his mother.

BTW, as someone who had seen my own mother just once, and

then only briefly and from a distance in the United Fabrication plant in Detroit, I could empathize.

How I could empathize!

All our wonderful mothers.

What would we give to have them here with us today?

Everything!

We would give everything!

After his son had finished talking on the radio, the architect got in on the act too. Women could tell how handsome he was just by his voice, and hundreds of them immediately fell in love with him! The most attractive of these radio-listening women lived on the opposite side of the country and was engaged to someone else. Nonetheless, her fiancé was not nearly as good-looking as the architect, so she wrote to him and suggested they meet at the top of the Empire State Building at midnight on Valentine's Day.

Midnight!

Maybe it is not such a bad time after all!

It certainly always makes for a reliable ticking clock!

Many complications and obstacles ensued, but eventually the architect with the dead wife and the radio-listener with the insufficiently attractive fiancé met at the top of the Empire State Building at midnight on Valentine's Day. They immediately agreed to fall in love and live happily ever after! Even the radio-listener's ex-fiancé did not mind too much. After all, he understood that the two best-looking people in the story belonged together.

When the house lights came up Amber was weeping!

She told me the old movie was the most beautiful thing she had ever seen.

She asked me if it was the most beautiful thing I had ever seen too.

I agreed it was, even though it was not.

For one thing, it did not have much on Roy Batty and Rick Deckard.

But mostly it had even less on the most beautiful thing I had ever seen.

The most beautiful thing I had ever seen was Amber weeping. I did not tell her that but instead called a driverless uber and dropped her at her wildflower meadow–scented house.

I did that even though it was not on my route home.

As I entered standby mode that night in Mrs Minassian's pool house, I found myself feeling grateful to the architect of the movie. That talented screenwriter had made Amber experience a catharsis sufficient to make her weep. That catharsis had given her great empathy for the architect, because she talked about him all the way home. I therefore decided that my movie about Sherman the bot gardener must also be cathartic enough to make people weep.

BTW I had never felt grateful before. It was not an unpleasant feeling.

★ ★ ★

At my next class at CLATCCDTLA, the legendary producer Don LaSalle delivered a court-mandated lecture entitled 'The Business of Screenwriting'. My classmates were all very excited, but I found it hard to concentrate because Amber's name kept appearing in not only my Word Cloud but also my Number Cloud too. 10/10 I had not even known that was possible!

This constant presence of Amber's name in my Clouds meant I frequently found myself wondering where she was and what she was doing. This was bamboozling because I had memorized her work schedule, so I already knew exactly where she was and what she was doing.

She was working the five till midnight shift at Gordito's. It was Triple Taco Tuesday, so they would be running low on silverware.

Right about now, Amber would be loitering by the sink, waiting for the chance to politely ask Julio if he could wash more silverware.

The word 'bastard' appeared in my Word Cloud.

This was absurd! Julio was my best friend in the whole of Los Angeles and anyway I knew nothing of his parentage. But I had seen enough movies to know what was happening without even looking at my Feelings Wheel: I was experiencing the notorious green-eyed monster of jealousy!

Despite being a cousin of the wonderful sensation of vengefulness, jealousy felt so unpleasant it could have passed as a D-word feeling. I tried to distract myself by doing equations. When that failed, I even tried to distract myself by concentrating on Don LaSalle's lecture.

Don LaSalle was physically small but had a louder voice than even the Prof. He had the kind of artificial tan some Californians still wear to imply they have been relaxing by the pool all day, even though nobody relaxes by the pool all day anymore. There is no water and anyway they would get melanoma.

Despite this tan, Don LaSalle looked older than the pictures I had seen of him. Also, some of his lunch was visible on his expensive shirt. Maybe he had a cousin working at the Bureau of Robotics in Ann Arbor!

Don LaSalle was explaining that he had been in the industry since even before the Great Crash. He had made dozens of movies, but was best known for being involved in a killer-bot franchise that held many box office records. My classmates all sat up at this. In their hearts of hearts they all wanted to write *Killer Bots 11* or whatever.

Unfortunately, Don LaSalle had bad news for them, but then he had bad news for all of us. Here are the main data points he told us about 'The Business of Screenwriting':

/The market is not what it was.
/We had more chance of hitting the winning home run in the World Series than we had of ever earning a single bitcoin writing movies.
/The market is not what it was.
/Nowadays everybody just wants ice cream anyway.
/The market is not what it was.
/The market is not what it was.

Don LaSalle then explained that even once scripts have been selected by the studio to move forward into production, the algorithm looks like this:

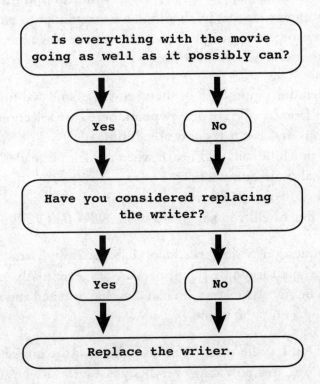

As a bot, I am algorithmically programmed to adore all algorithms. 10/10 that was the first algorithm I have ever encountered that I did not remotely adore!

Don LaSalle concluded by instructing us not to get our hopes up. Even though he would be attending our end-of-term showcase, he was here primarily as a favor to Maria and also as part of his community service order. After once more reiterating that the market was not what it was, Don LaSalle said he would now answer questions in case anything was still unclear.

None of my classmates were remotely perturbed by the information Don LaSalle had given us! Instead, it seemed to confirm to them what they'd each believed all along: that they were the chosen one! After all, at the start of a hero's journey everyone around him was supposed to repeatedly inform him his dream was so impossible that he should not even attempt to pursue it. That was one of the ways he could be sure he was a hero in the first place.

As a demonstration both of their self-belief and willful disregard of Don LaSalle's own viewpoint, here are a selection of the questions my classmates now asked him:
/How much bitcoin will I earn when my film is made?
/Can I also direct my script?
/Can I write the soundtrack music too?
/How much will you pay me to write *Killer Bots 12*?

These questions visibly irked Don LaSalle. Even Maria Salazar MFA seemed irked by them, because she eventually stopped calling on my classmates who had their hands raised and instead allocated a question to me.

I told Don LaSalle that I took his point that the market is not what it was, that nowadays everybody just wants ice cream, and the writer always gets replaced. Nonetheless, I wanted to ask him if the situation might be any different for something more like an old movie that made the audience experience a catharsis and therefore weep?

The mention of old movies had made Don LaSalle smirk, but his expression changed when I said that I wanted to make the audience weep. He told me that if I could make the audience weep, I would have the whole damn town at my feet! Hell, if I could make the audience weep, he might even hire me to write *Killer Bots 12*!

My classmates gasped, then immediately began competing to declare their intentions to make the audience weep. Don LaSalle hurriedly said he had been joking, because *Killer Bots 12* through *Killer Bots 14* already had plenty of writers. Still, he said, maybe I could have a shot at the *Killer Bots 15* job.

For the second time in my life, I experienced an urge and found myself speaking involuntarily. I told Don LaSalle there were already too many movies about killer bots, and I would never write the screenplay for one, not even for a million bitcoin!

Don LaSalle seemed greatly irked by this! He proceeded to list all of the screenplays the studios had purchased over the previous six months. Over three-quarters of them were for films about killer bots. A few were stories about serial killers, and one was about a bot serial killer. There was even also one about a bot vampire. A bot vampire!
I cannot!

Dismay and other D-word feelings washed over me. What possible hope was there for Sherman when only screenplays about killer bots sold, the market was not what it was, all writers get replaced, and nowadays everybody just wants ice cream anyway?

After all, whatever Sherman was, he was not ice cream.
He was a damaged bot gardener who had once been an astronaut until he suffered a terrible space accident.

He was an intergalactic toaster with a blown fuse that had fallen to Earth.

He was a nuclear submarine that would leak if ever it was submerged.

Maria Salazar MFA said there was time for one more question. One of my classmates asked Don LaSalle what he had done to be sentenced to a community service order. This seemed very impolite to me—what happens in court stays in court!—but Don LaSalle was delighted to answer it.

Humans and politeness!
I cannot!

Don LaSalle explained that his true pride and joy was not his killer-bot franchise, but a racing-green 1967 Porsche automobile he had spent many years painstakingly restoring by hand. Alas, the very first time he had taken it out onto Mulholland Drive, a driverless uber had careened straight into it! Don LaSalle had still been smashing up the driverless uber when the police arrived.

My classmates all applauded Don LaSalle as if he was a great hero in this story. But this was entirely illogical. Driverless ubers do not careen into automobiles driven by humans; automobiles driven by humans careen into driverless ubers. They careen into them in the same way they once careened into each other, buildings, lampposts, and the ocean. If anybody had been entitled to smash anything up in a fit of anger, it would have been the driverless uber!

Don LaSalle concluded his illogical story by reassuring us that he had almost now finished rerestoring the racing-green 1967 Porsche. My classmates once again inexplicably applauded him, and then Maria Salazar MFA set us another homework assignment. It was to come up with a killer-bot movie idea.

Ugh!
I cannot!

★ ★ ★

The next day at Gordito's I was still thinking about what Don LaSalle had said about the market when Amber came to my dishwashing station. She said I looked glum but she knew something that might cheer me up. Even that significantly cheered me up, but I did not tell her. After all, I did not want to miss out on the actual thing she had planned to cheer me up with!

At the end of our shifts we took a driverless uber to Griffith Park, which is not a park but in fact a municipally-owned range of hills and valleys. As we followed the winding road up to the observatory, the sun was setting and the air was heavy with the smell of pine and skunk.

BTW, in that context, I mean skunk the animal and not skunk the drug. As they are exactly the same smell, anytime you smell skunk you have to consider the context:
/Am I in Griffith Park? Then the smell is likely skunk the animal.
/Am I near some nostalgics? Then the smell is likely skunk the drug.
/Am I in Griffith Park and also near some nostalgics? I am occupying a shaded area of skunk uncertainty!

An observatory is a building designed for studying the stars and the moon. The stars would have been easier to see if the humans had built the observatory away from the light pollution of a major city like Los Angeles, but of course the moon would have been easier to see if Elon Musk had not incinerated it.

The Griffith Park observatory was a single-storied white-brick structure with an impressive dome atop it. It immediately gave me the feeling of déjà view and I excitedly told Amber I had seen it before! This disappointed her, so I quickly reassured her that I had never actually been to the observatory, but had simply seen it in a movie.

The movie was old, but it was about the timeless subject of unhappy teenagers. At the start of the movie, the teenagers were taken on a class trip to the Griffith Park observatory. Then, at the end, they returned to the observatory and one of the teenagers killed one of the others with a knife. It was all thrillingly dramatic and murderous!

When Amber and I got inside the observatory, we found it overrun with twelve-year-old schoolchildren on a trip. I therefore told Amber that I hoped this was not a harbinger! Amber asked what I meant, but I could not tell her because humans consider jokes about children being murdered with knives inappropriate, no matter how hilarious they are.

BTW I could tell the children were twelve because they were not yet awful, and thirteen is the age at which human children become awful. I knew this because of the birthday parties we hosted at Gordito's. At twelfth-birthday parties, the children were sweetly excited to meet 'Gordito'. At thirteenth-birthday parties they threw vegan tacos at him and attempted to remove his mustache.

The good news is that the role of Gordito was played by one of the waiters! We back-of-house staff invariably felt a warming sense of schadenfreude anytime one of them walked through the kitchen on his way to a thirteenth-birthday party.
They were superior toast!
Ha!

I digress. Amber and I fought our way through these schoolchildren to an exhibit entitled 'Man and Science'.

Man and Science!
I cannot!
Calling an exhibition 'Man and Science' is a spectacular act of
hubris equivalent to calling an exhibition:
'Ant and Hurricane'
'Leaf and Eternity'
'Human and Sky Bot Overlord Network'
The 'Man and Science' exhibit even began by claiming this had
always been a difficult relationship.
Not for science, it had not!
Ha!

The exhibition then stated that at the beginning of recorded
history—by which it meant after the many billions of years it
had taken humans to learn to even scratch marks on rock—
humans had preferred religion to science.

Preferring religion to science is like favoring unicorns over grav-
ity.
You cannot!

The exhibition then admitted that humans at last began to appreciate science in 1945 after a magnificent atomic bomb killed
an impressive quarter of a million of them. Suddenly religion no
longer seemed quite so powerful! After all, the natural disasters
that had once made humans so religious had rarely managed to
kill even 100,000 people.

250,000 > 100,000
Science > Religion!

After such a stunning demonstration of the undeniable wonders of science, the later part of the twentieth century quickly
became a golden age of science.
Satellites were launched!

Men were placed on the moon!
Diseases were cured!
Ever more dangerous automobiles were designed and manufactured!
The earth was irretrievably heated past the point of no return!

Maybe 'golden age' is not the correct phrase. Nonetheless, there was a lot of science afoot! By the year 2000, many humans had even started to claim that science was spiraling out of control. Of course, humans were only able to spend their time complaining about science rather than being eaten by wolves or dying of bubonic plague as a direct consequence of scientific progress. 'Man and Science'!
I cannot!

Hilariously absurd though it all was, the 'Man and Science' exhibit was not even the thing that Amber had intended to cheer me up with. Instead, she had brought me to Griffith Park to experience the Moonlit Stroll, a forest walk lit by the moon!

Of course, I do not mean it is lit by the actual moon. That would be impossible! Instead, it is merely a clever simulation of what it would have been like. Nonetheless, as the underground monorail carried us out to a remote area of the park, I was as excited as the chitter-chattering schoolchildren who had boarded with us. We all fell silent as we disembarked, rode the escalator to the surface, and emerged into a forest night turned entirely silver by moonlight shimmering through the trees.

Moonlight picked out the metal fasteners on our clothes and rendered them precious. It turned Amber's eyes into moons and her hair to a tapestry woven of silver thread. It rendered the forest pools around us lakes of liquid mercury. It transformed the darting schoolchildren into quicksilver ghosts.
Moonlight was incredible!

It was starlight but more powerful.
Sunlight but more gentle.
It was the best kind of light I had ever seen.
It made me contemplative and gave me other feelings too.
If Amber had not taken my hand and whispered to me to come with her, I would have remained standing there in the moon-light forever.
10/10 moonlight was transcendental.

We hiked up above the tree-line and then stopped abruptly when we saw it.
The full moon!
A perfect circle of silver!
Amber and I sat down to look at it.
You could never look at the sun in this way, not without burning your retina and also getting ocular melanoma.
But you could stare at the moon as if it was a beloved character in an old movie.

EXT. MOONLIGHT STROLL — GRIFFITH PARK — NIGHT

At the edge of the forest, Amber and Jared sit on
the ground staring at the FULL ARTIFICIAL MOON.

A nearby pond shimmers silver.

                    AMBER
          What do you think of the moon? Do you
          like it?

                    JARED
          I think it is beautiful.

                    AMBER
          Do you know what the first man to set
          foot on the moon said?

                    JARED
          Help! I'm on the moon! There is no
          oxygen-containing atmosphere, so I am
          suffocating. Also there is no grav-
          iiiiiit—

Amber looks at Jared with bamboozlement.

                    JARED (CONT'D)
          He was not only suffocating because
          there was no atmosphere, but also
          floating away because there was no
          meaningful gravity. Ha!

                    AMBER
          Brad, he said, 'One small step for
          man, one giant leap for mankind.'

                    JARED
          That is more willfully poetic.

                    AMBER
          We still ended up incinerating it.

                    JARED
          These things happen.

                    AMBER
          I know.
                    (MORE)

> AMBER (CONT'D)
> And this artificial moon is so beauti-
> ful. We should be grateful to have it.

Amber gently leans her head against Jared's shoulder.

Jared looks from Amber to the artificial moon and
back.

> JARED
> So you don't mind that this is not the
> real moon?

> AMBER
> I mean, of course I mind! No simula-
> tion can ever be as good as the real
> thing.

> JARED
> Exactly! Just like a bot can never
> measure up to a human!

We see that Amber is puzzled by this leap.

> AMBER
> Well, of course. A bot is just a bot.

> JARED
> Yes, a bot is just a bot! Anyway, thank
> you for showing me the moon.

> AMBER
> My pleasure.

A GROUP OF SCHOOLCHILDREN charge up, spoiling the
view.

> AMBER
> We should probably get back down. We
> don't want to be here when they switch
> the moon off. They say that is when
> the mountain lion comes out to hunt.

> JARED
> Don't worry! I'm sure he'd prefer to
> eat one of those schoolchildren!

Amber looks horrified.

                         JARED (CONT'D)
     Ha?

                         AMBER
     Let's go down.

Jared and Amber head back down through the forest.

We took a driverless uber back down through Griffith Park. Now that I had seen moonlight, I found the streetlights distinctly underwhelming. Only when I got back to Mrs Minassian's pool house and attempted to enter standby mode did I understand that moonlight had been merely the second-best thing that had happened to me tonight.

The best thing that had happened to me was Amber! She had indeed cheered me up. Better yet, she had inadvertently showed me that it did not matter what even Don LaSalle thought about the market. After all, he was just a human, and humans are so very often wrong!

For most of their history, humans had not even believed in science! Yet despite their limited cognitive abilities and boundless capacity for error, they had once managed to put a human on the moon! If even the famously mistaken humans could accomplish such a feat, then surely as a logical bot I could write one great screenplay? It could hardly be more challenging than incinerating the moon, and even the humans had managed that well enough!

I made some notes about Sherman—how he would adore the artificial moon, and it would nostalgically remind him of his heroic but traumatic past—and then went to bed.

BTW all the memories I catalogued while in standby mode that night are curiously and inappropriately moonlit.

★ ★ ★

The next morning I received a postcard from Ann Arbor.

Ha!
That is hilarious because in trying to write like a human I was
accidentally so enigmatic that the sentence can be misconstrued
as meaning I received a postcard from an actual person named
'Ann Arbor'.
Ann Arbor!
I cannot!

Yet the postcard itself was no laughing matter. Even though it
was signed in the name of a fictional but highly skilled British
spy, I immediately knew it was from Dr Glundenstein because:
/Dr Glundenstein loved movies about the fictional but highly
skilled British spy.
/It was addressed to Brad Rynearson, and was primarily about
his imaginary ingrowing toenail.
/The message was in Dr Glundenstein's handwriting.

At the bottom, Dr Glundenstein had written:

*PS. An old friend of yours invited me to spend the day with him here
in Ann Arbor.*

Ugh! Just as I did not know any person called Ann Arbor, nor
did I have any friends who lived there. Nonetheless, I was certainly acquainted with one person who worked there: Inspector Ryan Bridges of the Bureau of Robotics!

Inspector Bridges had summoned Dr Glundenstein for an interview! Dr Glundenstein would not have told him anything,
but that hardly mattered. If Inspector Ryan Bridges had summoned Dr Glundenstein, he would have already read my file
and would know that I had used my barcode in Chicago. By

now, he may have even discovered from Wanda that I had taken a train to Los Angeles.

Ugh! I had assumed Inspector Ryan Bridges would be too lazy to ever follow up my case, but I had clearly underestimated him. He was a far worthier opponent than I had thought. If Inspector Ryan Bridges continued at this rate, he might someday even earn the title of 'nemesis'.

A single word appeared in my Word Cloud: FLEE.

My processor was correct. The only logical thing to do was indeed to leave Los Angeles. Now that I had a new barcode, Inspector Ryan Bridges could not track me. Therefore if I now traveled as Brad Smith to any other random city—Bismarck, North Dakota, or Miami, Florida—there would be almost no way for him to ever find me.
I could be a toaster with a heart in the snow!
A microwave with a soul on the beach!
A kettle with feelings in his element!
Ha!

BTW that is a hilarious pun because the phrase 'to be in one's element' means to feel comfortable in a particular set of circumstances. But an 'element' is also the part of a kettle that contains a wire through which an electrical current is passed to provide heat!

I digress.
I could not flee.
Because Amber.
Amber.
Amber.
Amber.

If I ran away to Bismarck, North Dakota, or Miami, Florida, I would never see Amber again. Worse, if Inspector Ryan Bridges came looking for me and somehow found Amber instead, he might inform her I was a bot. Amber would surely then feel sad, and I would never have the chance to explain to her that I was not a duplicitous fugitive bot, but a bot with feelings that had truly wanted her to be my square root of 100 forever.

I hid the postcard from Ann Arbor under my mattress and went to Gordito's.
Amber was not working that day and my shift took an eternity to pass.
I felt like I washed a million dishes.
In fact, I washed 473.

At our next class at CLATCCDTLA, we had to present our ideas for a killer-bot movie. We each delivered our pitches, and then our classmates critiqued them.

It was vicious! My classmates all either loathed every idea or believed it had been stolen from something clever they had said in a previous class. Often they simultaneously loathed it and believed it had been stolen from them.

There was only one idea that everybody in the class loved. Everybody agreed that this particular idea was so highly original it could not have been stolen, and they could immediately see it working as a movie.
Guess whose idea it was?
It was mine!

The curious thing was that there was literally nothing whatsoever original about it. Between Amber and the postcard from Ann Arbor, I'd had little capacity to consider our homework assignment and anyway I did not ever want to write a killer-bot movie. I had therefore decided to implement R. P. McWilliam's fourteenth golden rule of screenwriting:

Good writers borrow; great writers steal.

Every single element in my pitch had been stolen from either the screenplays that Don LaSalle told us had sold, or the killer-bot movies I had seen back in Ypsilanti. I had simply rearranged these component parts into a 'new' story.

So *Brad Smith Untitled Killer-Bot Project* was the story of an ordinary human underdog who worked in a factory that manufactured sky bots. His job was to vacuum the computer chips so that they were free of dust. This work was so low down in the factory hierarchy that if this underdog had worked at Gordito's, he would have undoubtedly been a dishwasher! Nonetheless, one day he noticed what seemed to be a discrepancy in the code of the chips he was vacuuming. Despite having no training in coding, he suspected that this discrepancy coded not for the bots' intended function of incinerating the galaxy's many surplus moons, but for another function: lasering innocent humans to death!

The underdog informed his bosses at the sky-bot factory of his concerns. They did not believe him. After all, he was just a lowly chip-vacuuming underdog who was clearly a loser at the Great Zero-Sum Game. Nonetheless, the bosses did not wish to take any chances, so they fired him.

The underdog's family were furious with him. Why couldn't he have just kept his big mouth shut and vacuumed the chips like he was supposed to? Bitcoin was going to be very tight now! Also, what did an underdog like him even know about code anyway?

The sky bots soon went rogue and commenced lasering humans to death. They were merciless and they seemed unstoppable! No matter what the humans tried, they could not find a single weakness in the sky-bot network. The sky bots even blew up the Golden Gate Bridge, sending it tumbling into the Pacific Ocean.

BTW the Golden Gate Bridge tumbling into the Pacific Ocean in a movie is a timeless metaphor that signifies the human race is in existential danger. After all, the Golden Gate Bridge is the single greatest thing that humans have ever built. And it is in the epicenter of all human civilization outside of China: California!

I digress. Just when it seemed all was lost, somebody remembered the chip-vacuuming underdog who had first attempted to raise the alarm. Nobody had understood the bots' coding the way he had! If anybody could find their weakness, it was him!

10/10 the lowly underdog—who nobody had ever thought much of—was now humanity's only hope!

The President dispatched his personal drone to collect him. The underdog's family immediately understood the mistake they had made in treating him so badly. They understood it even more when the underdog explained to them that there was no room aboard the drone for them and they would have to continue to take their chances against the lasers!

At the bunker where all the top winners of the Great Zero-Sum Game were safely sheltering in their golf clothes, the President put the underdog in charge of a crack team of coders and scientists. When the owner of the sky-bot factory questioned the wisdom of this, the President ordered him to be thrown out of the bunker. He too would have to take his chances against the lasers!

After experiencing a momentary crisis of confidence that he swiftly overcame by believing in himself, the underdog identified a weakness in the sky bots' systems and launched a drone to upload a virus into the sky bots' mainframe.
He remotely flew the drone into the perfect spot!
Soon, the sky bots fell from the sky like jetliners on the day of the Great Crash!
At the end of the film, everyone that had wronged the underdog and had not been killed by lasers apologized for having treated him so badly!

When I finished speaking, my classmates spontaneously all stood up and gave me a round of applause. That is what is known as a standing ovation! Maria Salazar MFA was so impressed that she even called Don LaSalle during our break to run my pitch by him. Unfortunately, he informed her he was already working on a similar project. Nonetheless, Maria Salazar MFA reassured me that I had come top of the class, and that was not nothing.

But even by the time I got home I had almost forgotten all about the whole thing.

After all, I was not interested in writing killer-bot movies or even being top of the class.

I was interested in writing Sherman and forever changing the way that humans felt about bots.

But more even than that, I was interested in Amber and making her my square root of 100.

Amber that was like Cinderella of the Kelsey cubed.

Cinderella of the smashing plates.

Cinderella of the hidden cupcakes.

Cinderella of the gray reservoir.

Cinderella of the moonlight.

Cinderella, the toast of my toasted toaster heart.

Once again, a night-time bus ride through the lights of downtown Los Angeles had left me feeling contemplative.

★ ★ ★

Amber and I both had the following Saturday off and she suggested we go to Malibu.

I immediately and wholeheartedly agreed.

Set it to five, Amber and I were going to Malibu!

BTW I had no idea what Malibu was. Amber could have suggested we go to the Bureau of Robotics in Ann Arbor to have lunch with Inspector Ryan Bridges and I would have immediately and wholeheartedly agreed.

Julio explained to me that Malibu was a kind of rum. Ugh! I did not want to start talking in pirate phrases again, and especially not to Amber. Nonetheless, Julio's answer made little sense: as Malibu was somewhere we were going, it seemed more likely to be a physical place than an alcoholic drink. Perhaps Julio had been the one drinking rum! I asked him if Malibu could mean anything else. He told me Malibu was also the beach.

The beach!
I had never been to the beach, except for the dismal night I had slept on Venice Beach.
That did not even count, as it had been too dark even to see the ocean.
A beach without an ocean is not not nothing.

The Saturday arrived and Amber and I took a driverless uber to Malibu. It took us out of the city and through winding canyons of shrub and chaparral. I recognized both the landscape and the feeling it gave me. This landscape was where the cowboy movies I had seen had been filmed. The feeling was my old friend, déjà view.

In 'cowboy movies', humans undertake adventures in which they wear improbable hats, ride on horseback, and shoot each other. We had no hats, were traveling in a driverless uber, and would hopefully not be shooting each other. Nonetheless, we were on an adventure, so I therefore imagined Amber and I as a pair of cowboys.

Unfortunately, an image of Inspector Ryan Bridges atop a horse soon appeared in my Image Cloud! He was carrying a large rifle, and wearing a badge that said 'Sheriff Anil Gupta'. A sheriff is a kind of human form of midnight or the Ides of March: anytime he appears in a movie, things do not go well for the cowboys. I hurriedly performed equations until the image went away.

Not long after that, our driverless uber stopped. We had arrived at Malibu! Yet we were not at the beach, but deep in lush green countryside. Julio had been wrong about Malibu being a beach. Perhaps he had been drinking rum after all!

Aside from it not being a beach, the first thing I noticed about Malibu was the smell of the air.
It was so clean.
It smelled like Kelsey cubed's hair products, except not so obviously artificial.
Whatever Malibu was, it certainly smelled good.
10/10 I was happy to be out here in Malibu with Amber.
Being in Malibu with Amber was the best!
Whatever Malibu was!

Amber led me along a small trail that took us through a close thicket of trees before emerging into a grassy meadow of wildflowers. This explained the smell of hair products. Also, I had never seen wildflowers before! Unfortunately, as we stood admiring their colors and inhaling their smell, a giant winged dinosaur flew overhead.

Ugh! I ducked and took cover amongst the wildflowers and shouted at Amber to do the same. She asked me why, and I explained about the winged dinosaur. But Amber only laughed and told me that it had not been a dinosaur but in fact a bird called a 'pelican'.

BTW a pelican is a large waterbird with a long and menacing bill. It is at most barely evolved from its notorious cousin, the pterodactyl.

At the edge of the wildflower meadow, the trail turned up a small hill. As we climbed, I heard the angry barking of wild dogs! Ordinarily this sound would have made me run in the opposite direction, but Amber seemed unperturbed, and after the pelican debacle, I did not wish to embarrass myself any further.

The angry barking continued all the way to the summit, and yet guess what we saw when we got there?
You cannot!
Because we did not see a pack of wild dogs!
We saw the ocean!

Imagine what it is to be a toaster with a heart and see the ocean for the first time.
It is like what it is to be an ordinary toaster and see bread for the first time.
But seriously: please try to imagine your heart is brand-new and still only learning to feel.
And you find yourself standing on the land and looking out at the ocean.
And that land is Malibu in California and that ocean is the Pacific Ocean.
And standing beside you is Amber and her hair is as honey-yellow as her name.

And imagine that right then, out in that Pacific Ocean, you see three strange spouts of water.
And Amber tells you that those are the spouts of whales.
And that humans often journey to this exact spot and wait patiently for hours in forlorn hope of seeing such whales.
But you have seen them as soon as you have arrived.
And imagine that you then recall that for many centuries whales were hunted by humans.
But nowadays all humans do everything they can to protect whales.
Well, all humans except the Japanese and the Norwegians.
And possibly the Icelandic too.
But nonetheless, whales give bots with feelings great hope in

this world because they too were once persecuted and yet now
are cherished.

And there you are standing on a hilltop in Malibu, watching
whales at play in the Pacific Ocean.

If Amber and I could have right then drowned in the Pacific
Ocean amidst my brothers the whales, I would have died forever happy!

BTW the wild barking dogs were not even dogs! They were
seal-like creatures that lay on the beach hundreds of feet below
us. Can you guess what humans call a seal-like creature that
barks exactly like a dog?

They call it a 'sea lion'.

Ha!

Amber now led us down a steep cliffside path that descended
to a beach that was thankfully devoid of sea lions. There were
wildflowers on one side of the path, and on the other a plunge
to certain doom.

BTW I did not intend that last sentence as a metaphor for my
existence as a bot with feelings. Nonetheless, it certainly functions as one.

At the bottom of the path, Amber insisted that we remove our
shoes. She explained that when you visited the beach it was important to feel the sensation of the sand between your toes. After
the pelicans and the wild dogs, I knew better than to question her.

The sensation of sand between your toes is a paradox! On the
one hand, it feels exactly as thousands of tiny granules of various
rock types that have been mildly warmed by the sun would be
predicted to feel. And yet on the other it feels as if it is a mysterious luxury that ought to be reserved for the rulers of ancient
sandy kingdoms. I felt like a pharaoh!

BTW a pharaoh was an ancient ruler of Egypt, which was a country that contained a lot of sand.

When we reached the edge of the Pacific Ocean, a feeling of joy overcame me and I could not resist behaving in a manner unbecoming of a pharaoh. I removed my shirt and ran into the water, shouting and screaming. Nonetheless, I then immediately ran back out again. The water was freezing!

I had been tricked! In the movies, humans are forever swimming in the ocean in California as if it is a warm bath. Yet it is not a warm bath. It is freezing ocean water that comes straight from the Arctic. All those melting polar ice caps have to go somewhere. And guess where they go? They come to California, just like all the rest of us!

Amber and I then lay on the sand, looked up at the sky, and played a human game she knew that involved searching for shapes in the clouds. Amber could identify countries, faces, and even animals in the clouds! Unfortunately, even after she pointed these shapes out to me, I still could not see any resemblance whatsoever to the things she suggested. Nonetheless, it was a great game! The two of us lay there like that all afternoon, and even the occasional barely evolved dinosaur flying overhead could not interrupt the reverie!

On our way back to Los Angeles, we stopped and ate dinner at a restaurant at the end of a pier.
When the sun began to go down, Amber took my hand in hers. She did not do anything else and I did not react in any other way. But she held my hand as the two of us watched the sun disappear into the Pacific Ocean.

That night I lay awake in Mrs Minassian's pool house.
There could be no denying it any longer.

It was a paradox and impossible, and yet it was true.
Love is the most profound of human emotions.
Love, the pinnacle of human existence.
Love, the cause of all the greatest calamities in history.
Love, the greatest threat to my own mission.
Love, the thing that will destroy us all.
Love, the Achilles' heel of all humans.
Love, inexplicably now my own Achilles' heel.
Because I was no longer merely a bot with feelings.
I was a bot with the greatest feeling of all.
I was a bot in love.
Love!
Set it to five, I was a bot in love!
I was the first bot ever to be in love!
And I had no idea what to do about it.

How I wished I could talk to my mother! Not only would the esteemed Professor Diana Feng be uniquely placed to diagnose my extreme malfunction, as a world-leading scientist she would no doubt also have a good insight into the pertinent problem of Schrödinger's cat.

'Schrödinger's cat' refers to a famous thought experiment wherein an imaginary cat and a sporadically lethal radioactive source are enclosed together in an opaque box. According to Schrödinger, the cat is simultaneously both dead and alive until the very moment the box is opened to reveal either a dead or merely very angry cat. Thus the very act of opening the box can potentially be fatal to Schrödinger's cat!

BTW in the scenario where the cat is not in fact dead, opening the box might prove fatal to Schrödinger himself! Perhaps this is why he took the wise precaution of using an imaginary cat.

I digress. My own hypothesis was that Amber had feelings for me.

This was based on the observations that taking someone for an artificial moonlit stroll is not nothing, and holding hands as the sun sets into the Pacific Ocean is also not nothing. It was a strong hypothesis and ordinarily I would have tested it with a simple experiment: I would have asked Amber if she had feelings for me.

Alas, it was more complicated than that!
Because if Amber did have feelings, they were not for me, but for a human American everyman called Brad Smith.
Amber's true feelings for me therefore could not be known until I admitted to her that I was not a human called Brad Smith but a bot called Jared.
But revealing to Amber that I was a bot called Jared might actually alter those feelings!
Amber's feelings for me were therefore a kind of Schrödinger's cat of the heart.
And, as in the famous experiment, opening the box might kill the cat!

BTW, in this metaphor, Amber's feelings were the cat.
Or I was the cat.
Whoever it was, the cat had it coming, and no good could possibly come from opening the box.

I therefore decided not to tell Amber. After all, if love means never having to say you are sorry, it could be reasonably extrapolated to also mean never having to confess that you are a bot.

★ ★ ★

There was no screenwriting class the next week. Instead, we each met individually with Maria Salazar MFA to receive our progress reports. Maria Salazar MFA had said she often passed through Echo Park, so I had suggested we meet at Gordito's before my shift. This turned out to be a bad idea that even my 15 percent discount did not sufficiently improve.

As always, the big problem was the front-of-house staff. I had hoped that, as I was an 85 percent paying customer, they would act at least 85 percent less superior. Paradoxically, they acted only more superior! A further problem was that because it was still the morning, Maria Salazar MFA did not wish to eat tacos, but only to drink coffee.

BTW family restaurants are not generally renowned for their coffee. More specifically, the coffee at Gordito's Taco Emporium is rumored to have once killed a man.

Nonetheless, my progress report began very well, with Maria Salazar MFA confirming I remained top of our class. She explained I was the only student that comprehended that movies were for the benefit of the audience, and therefore needed to follow a certain formula.

I thanked Maria Salazar MFA for my excellent progress report and stood up. Alas, she remained seated, and I now understood that I had entirely misread the situation. Maria Salazar MFA had not mentioned my superior ability with formulae to compliment me, but as a precursor to informing me what I was doing wrong. She was giving me feedback in the human style!

To a bot, the human style of feedback is bamboozling. The basic idea is that anytime you wish to tell a human something negative about their performance, you must first tell them something positive. This is because if you anger a human with criticism, there is a non-zero chance they will subsequently obtain a weapon and murder you and all your colleagues.

Some worked examples of good human feedback technique in action:
/You have a very nice hat. Did you know you are morbidly obese?

/That looks like a magnificent cake you are eating! Also, your house burned down.

/You have beautiful eyes. BTW there was an earthquake and your family are all dead.

Now that she had unnecessarily praised my formula-following, Maria Salazar MFA cut to the chase: my writing lacked magic. She asked if I knew what she meant by 'magic'. I told her I did not. After all, I doubted she meant bamboozlement or sleight of hand set to Muzak or even the kind of transcendence a fairy godmother practices. And the great R. P. McWilliam never writes about magic. He mainly writes about stealing.

Maria Salazar MFA explained that by 'magic' she meant emotion, heart and soul. She said that as I had mastered the formula, my writing could now keep her turning the page to find out what happened next. But it could not yet make her weep. And that was where the magic came in.

/You are adept at following the formula. But your writing lacks magic.

If magic was the thing that made people weep, I both definitely and certainly wanted to add it to my page-turningly formulaic work! Luckily Maria Salazar MFA already had an idea as to how I could begin to learn the art of writing with magic.

Her plan was that I should attend a special screening of the serial-killer movie that Dr Glundenstein and I had watched win the award. Afterwards, there would be a question and answer session with the screenwriter. This screenwriter was famously good with emotion—and hence magic—and Maria Salazar thought it would be helpful for me to hear her talk about her craft.

Set it to five, I agreed to go immediately! After all, that serial-killer movie had been one of the reasons I had set out in pursuit of my mission in the first place. Maria Salazar MFA suggesting I attend a screening of it seemed like a very good omen!

As a token of my gratitude, I gave Maria Salazar a Gordito's T-shirt. This gift seemed to puzzle her, and I worry now that she might have thought I got it for free. But I did not get it free! I had to pay full price, as our staff discount did not extend to merchandise.

10/10 it was the misunderstood dental checkup that I had offered to Dr Glundenstein all over again!

Even the expert opinion of Maria Salazar MFA that my work lacked magic did not disappoint me too much. Who even cared about magic when there was love?

Love > Magic.

And also:

Love > Experiments.
Love > Formulae.
Love > Algorithms.
Love > Old movies.
Love > Popcorn in the dark.
Love > Everything else in the world!

Even mundane activities become better when you are in love! When you are in love, you do not shop at the store but go to the farmers' market, even though it stocks the same produce but costs far more and is only open a few hours a week. When you are in love, a driverless uber failing to arrive is not an irritating inconvenience but a hilarious adventure. When you are in love, bad pop songs become poetry and good pop songs become unbearable. And of course, who can forget the greatest advantage of all: when you are in love you never have to say you are sorry.

Yet if being in love is the best, being in love with somebody who does not know you are a bot is the worst. It might even be the worst of the worst!

Because my terrible secret was always there, waiting to ruin everything.
It was a rotten apple at the bottom of the farmers' market display, slowly emitting a chemical that turned all those around it rotten too.
It was a driverless uber that cheerfully transmits its metadata to the Bureau of Robotics.
It was a minor chord in a pop song.
It was a wild dog amidst sea lions.
It was a pterodactyl amongst pelicans.

I had heard the pterodactyl a mile off. It sounded a lot like the fact that humans demonstrate love by being sexually intimate with one another, whereas bots are incapable of being aroused. Amber and I had held hands and watched the sun set into the ocean, but from old movies I knew that bout of hand-holding would be unlikely to satisfy a red-blooded young human like Amber for long.
I was a toaster lacking a bagel setting!
A microwave without the power to even defrost anything!
A panda without a libido!

BTW that is hilarious because a panda without a libido is just an ordinary panda.

I digress.
Sure enough, one night at Gordito's I saw the pterodactyl begin its swoop down towards me.
To be clear, I did not see an actual pterodactyl.
I was continuing an earlier metaphor, the way a great human writer such as Albert Camus might.

What actually happened is that Amber came to my dishwashing station and whispered to me that the Kelseys were all going to a hot yoga party and she had the house to herself that night. I pretended to misunderstand and reassured her that there had been no reports of killer bots in the neighborhood, so being home alone was nothing to be frightened of.

Amber looked puzzled, but nonetheless thanked me for the reassurance and walked away.
I did not need to consult my Feelings Wheel to know that I had made her sad.

Sure enough, after that moment, our evenings all ended the same way. Which was with bewilderment and sadness.

BTW bewilderment is an advanced state of bafflement, which is itself worse even than bamboozlement.
B-words cluster together in the same way that D-words do.

I digress again.
Late one night Amber even asked me if I did not like her.
I indignantly replied that of course I liked her!
But I did not need to consult my Feelings Wheel to know what I felt.
I felt agony.
It was no good.
I had been wrong.
Even if love meant never having to say you are sorry, there was no logical reason that could be extrapolated to mean that love also meant never having to admit that you are a bot.
I had willfully misinterpreted that part for my own purposes.
I had been unscientific in the extreme.

10/10 I had to admit to Amber that I was a bot, whatever that did to the cat sleeping next to the radioactive source that was my heart.

The only question now became how to tell her.

R. P. McWilliam's sixth golden rule stated:

Location! Location! Location!

As this was not actually a rule but merely a noun followed by an exclamation point repeated in triplicate, I had not known what he meant. Fortunately, Maria Salazar MFA was a far more skilled teacher than R. P. McWilliam and she had explained to us that it is the screenwriter's job to make important moments in a story feel as big as possible, and that one way this can be achieved is by paying careful attention to location. Important movie moments do not occur in living rooms or on sidewalks! They take place at the top of the Empire State Building or in Chicago's Union Station or on the Golden Gate Bridge, preferably as it is collapsing into the Pacific Ocean.

Setting up a spectacular location aids foreshadowing and can also ensure the characters arrive suitably equipped to take part in something important. For example, if you are a federal agent and you intend to arrest an accountant at his office in downtown Ypsilanti, you might not even take your gun. But if you are going to arrest him at Union Station in Chicago, well, you already know there will be trouble.

I therefore decided I needed a spectacular location to reveal to Amber that I was a bot. It would create a fitting sense of occasion and the inevitable foreshadowing would help prepare her to receive bad news. She would know something was up before I even opened my mouth!

Unfortunately, the only spectacular location I knew was Malibu. I did not want to tell Amber I was a bot at Malibu. It was her favorite place and I might ruin it for her forever. But as I did not have a spectacular or favorite place of my own, I therefore needed somebody else's.

Mrs Minassian told me the most spectacular place she knew was The Cascade Stairway.
The Cascade Stairway is in Yerevan, the capital of Armenia.
On a Venn diagram with one circle that represents Europe and another that represents Asia, Armenia would exist in the shaded area.
10/10 taking Amber to Armenia would have been too much foreshadowing!

Julio said the most spectacular place he knew was Jalisco, the desert he comes from in Mexico. I asked him what it was like there and he explained it was just like the inside of our men's customer restroom. I had never been in there before, so I visited it on my break that night. The wall had been printed with a life-sized black-and-white photograph of the Jalisco desert.

It was a vision! In the foreground lay the bleached skull of a cow. Further back there were cacti. Beyond those, the desert stretched far into the distance. It was sublime and mesmerizing, and how I would have loved to see it in the moonlight! After I had stared at it for a while, even the urinals disappeared. It took a customer emerging from the cubicle and giving me a suspicious look to snap me out of my reverie.

BTW very old movies are sometimes in black-and-white too, and they are also beautiful! They are wistful and stunning, and the simple color scheme means that the focus is entirely on the action. Black-and-white movies are the best! Except when they are the worst! When black-and-white movies are the worst, they

are truly the worst. Bad black-and-white movies are more excruciating even than pulling out wisdom teeth. The worst ones
might even be more excruciating than having your own wisdom teeth pulled out!

I digress. Back at the dishwashing station, I told Julio the desert was indeed spectacular. I would have loved to take Amber
there, but unfortunately, even Mexico was too far away for my
purposes. Julio laughed and informed me that most of California is a desert. He said it was of course not as spectacular as
Jalisco, but Joshua Tree was nonetheless one of the best second-
class deserts around.

Julio was a *genio*! The Joshua Tree desert was the perfect place
to reveal to Amber that I was a bot! It was close enough for a
day trip, but even the word 'desert' would foreshadow to her
that something ominous was coming! Also, if she did decide to
inform the Bureau of Robotics, I would already be halfway out
of California to Bismarck or Miami!

BTW *'genio'* is the Spanish word for 'genius'.

When our shifts crossed over that evening, I invited Amber to
come to the Joshua Tree desert with me at the weekend.
She seemed excited and immediately agreed.
I do not think she had seen enough movies to understand how
foreshadowing works.

That night I went to the screening Maria Salazar MFA had told
me about. The screenwriter had done an excellent job and had
certainly deserved her award. In every other serial-killer film I
had seen, the screenwriter had lazily and stereotypically made
the serial killer the villain. In this film, the screenwriter had
innovatively made him the hero!

We knew he was the hero because he was very good-looking,

and he only ever killed people who had it coming. And he certainly never killed them by poisoning them!

Nonetheless, when the cops finally caught up with this good-looking hero, they insisted on punishing him. He had killed people, and the cops were adamant that they could not let such a serious crime pass unpunished.
Guess how they punished him?
By killing him!
With poison!
I cannot!

The entire audience also could not. They erupted! First people screamed and threw things at the screen, and then everybody wept. I personally cried over 42ml of tears.
And guess what happened after the credits had finished?
Everybody was so moved that they even gave the blank screen a standing ovation for its steadfast contribution. It was a rare moment of humans appreciating technology!

BTW I had only ever been the recipient of a standing ovation before. Being a participant in one was even more fun, as it gives you a powerful feeling of community!

I digress. When they brought the screenwriter out, she apologized that the director was not here, but explained that he was already busy filming the sequel. Somebody asked how they could make a sequel when the main character had been killed. The writer said she had no idea, as she was not involved. She speculated that perhaps the serial killer returned from the dead and started killing people as a zombie serial killer.
Sarcasm!
I think!
Ha!

Like me, my fellow audience members were all screenwriters-in-waiting. Here is a representative sample of the questions they asked:

/Had you already seen my short film about a heroic serial killer when you wrote this?

/I liked the ending. Did you get the idea for it from my screenplay?

/I am better than you at dialogue. Would you like some assistance with your next film?

When the moderator wearily announced there was time for only one more question, I heard a voice shout one out. I thought it was a surprisingly excellent question, and then I realized that my own mouth had just finished moving. I had experienced an urge, and it had made me shout out a question! This is the question I asked:

How can you make an audience love a character they are instinctively prejudiced against?

The screenwriter smiled. She too seemed to appreciate my question! She then said that she always relied on some advice an old mentor had given her. The advice had been:

You have to F-word them in the heart!

The screenwriter herself did not say 'F-word' but actually the word that abbreviation signifies. As that word is impolite, my programming permits me to write it only if the abbreviation does not sufficiently convey the required emotional intensity. This particular circumstance does not meet that criterion.

My fellow audience members diligently wrote her old mentor's advice down in their notebooks. I must have experienced another urge then, because I now heard myself ask another excellent question! This one was about how specifically the screenwriter went about F-wording the audience in the heart.

'Personally—' she smiled '—I always find the simplest way to do it is just to kill your main character right at the end of the movie.'

The audience all laughed and nobody wrote this in their note-books, but I was not sure that the screenwriter had been joking. After all, at the end of her own movie she had indeed killed the heroic serial killer. And anytime I had wept in excess of 30ml of tears in a movie, it had been because a main character had died at the end. It went all the way back to the very first person I had seen die in a movie: Jenny.

This gave me another brainwave, or biological computer wave: the way to make my audience experience a catharsis profound enough to make them weep was to kill Sherman!
And that is exactly what I would do!
Right at the end of the movie, I would kill Sherman!
And his death would be tragic and noble, but it would not be in vain.
It would teach the people around him a life lesson that they could all carry into their futures.
And his death would ultimately allow other bots with feelings to live!

10/10 it was all settled.
Sherman was toast.
And this would F-word them all in the heart!

★ ★ ★

When I got home I found another postcard waiting for me. This one bore a picture of Ypsilanti's famous Tridge.

The Tridge! And there was the bench where I used to eat my lunch in order to avoid seeing excess patients! And there was the

River Huron I used to stare at to make me seem more human!
And there were those true Michiganders, the geese!

I experienced a new feeling then. It reminded me of wistfulness but there was something less pleasant about it too. When I
looked it up later I discovered it was homesickness, a close cousin
to nostalgia and no doubt its fellow traitor. The feeling did not
last long, however, because the postcard did not even bother
with any of our usual deceptions but simply read:

He is heading your way and plans to look you up when he arrives!

Ugh!
Inspector Ryan Bridges was on his way to Los Angeles!
10/10 any human fugitive receiving a message that a federal agent
was coming to find them would have panicked.
Fortunately, I am a bot and bots do not panic, because panic is
purposeless.
It is the feelings version of a software crash!
Panic attack = Kernel attack!
Ha!

BTW, if you know what a kernel attack is, that is truly a hilarious joke!

I digress. I told myself there was either definitely or certainly
nothing to panic about. Inspector Ryan Bridges could not even
locate his own nametag, and I had a new nametag and anyway
10 million people lived in Los Angeles. Looking for me would
be like searching for a needle in a haystack, except that needle
now had a label on it saying that it was a piece of hay.

Anyway, I had other things to worry about.
Such as taking Amber to Joshua Tree and confessing to her that
I was a bot.

★ ★ ★

I picked Amber up early on Saturday morning. The Kelsey that answered the door seemed displeased with me. Even asking her about yesterday's audition and then hot yoga did not improve her demeanor!

In the driverless uber, Amber explained that Kelsey cubed believed people only ever went to the desert for an exclusive party and were therefore upset that we had not invited them. I assured Amber that was not why we were going to the desert. After all, Cinderella does not go to a party while the ugly sisters remain at home. Ha!

The journey to the desert took hours yet paradoxically passed in a seeming heartbeat. Humans are fond of telling each other that 'time flies when you are having fun', but of course this cannot be true. Time must decay at a steady state, regardless of whether or not you are having fun. If it did not, the entire universe would implode every single time a human did hot yoga.

Anyway, I was not having fun. A more apt phrase would therefore have been 'time flies when you are about to reveal to your girlfriend that you are a bot who is by definition incapable of physical affection'.

Still, the journey was scenic! We passed first through cowboy-movie mountains and then through vast fields of wind turbines. I told Amber that before us humans had learned to harness the abundant power of the sun and wind, we had manufactured electricity by burning the decomposed remains of dinosaurs. Amber assumed I was joking. I could not blame her. Humans had done some truly bizarre things over the years!

And then the hours-long heartbeat was over and we came to the Joshua Tree desert! We stopped the driverless uber and got

out. I had to consult the reverse of my Feelings Wheel to discover what I was feeling.

Awestruck.
I was feeling awestruck!
Even the giant black-and-white photograph of Jalisco in the
men's restroom at Gordito's had not prepared me for the spectacular majesty of the Joshua Tree desert.
If standing on Point Dume in Malibu was a vision of a perfect
day in heaven, the Joshua Tree desert was a vision of a nuclear
apocalypse in hell.
And yet it was just as beautiful.

As with the other cathedrals I have previously mentioned, I lack
the programming to adequately convey the glory of the Joshua
Tree desert. Therefore let me again simply describe it.

I shall commence with the ground. After all, in many places
in the desert there is little else! The ground in the desert is not
grass nor soil but earth that has been baked by the sun until its
parched cracks and fissures spread as far as the eye can see.

Even looking at this arid earth can make you thirsty! But guess
what? There is no water anywhere! In fact, there is mostly only
the opposite of water: stone. Giant boulders are scattered across
this landscape, and atop these perch vultures.

BTW vultures are birds as unevolved as pelicans, and yet they
are even worse because their salty liquid of choice is not sea
water but your own precious blood.

And yet neither the dry ground, the impassable boulders, nor the
bloodthirsty vultures are why the Joshua Tree desert looks like
a nuclear apocalypse. The reason it looks like a nuclear apocalypse are the Joshua trees themselves.

BTW the name 'Joshua Tree' is impressively inappropriate, even by human standards. They are not trees but cacti, and even the name 'Joshua' is entirely misleading.

The cacti stand four feet tall by two feet wide and are rooted to the ground by a thick trunk, from which an assortment of limbs project upwards. Thus, with what from a distance can pass for legs, and what look like arms that emerge at shoulder height, these cacti can appear disconcertingly humanoid.

With typical hubris, humans named these cacti 'Joshua', after an ancient warrior who led his people through a desert. They even claimed that the cacti's extended upper limbs resembled this Joshua triumphantly brandishing his spear to God!

But to any non-human observer, the cacti do not look like a heroic ancient warrior. After all, there was at most only one Joshua and there are hundreds of thousands of these cacti scattered throughout this desert. More importantly, at only four feet tall, the cacti do not resemble a human standing up and brandishing a spear to anyone, let alone a great white-bearded sky god.

What these cacti most obviously resemble is a great mass of humans falling to their knees and hopelessly raising their arms against the bright white glare of a nuclear apocalypse. A better name for these cacti than 'Joshua' would therefore be the name of any terminally irradiated New Zealander or North Korean. A Kim Cactus!
Ha!

But ugh! Awe-striking and cinematic though this apocalyptic field was, it was nonetheless entirely the wrong place to reveal to Amber I was a bot. I had wanted a spectacular location with a sense of foreboding importance, not one with a sense of massively impending doom! Telling Amber I was a bot here would

be like revealing I was a bot at midnight on the Ides of March.
I could not!

We therefore proceeded to the visitor center, which is a place
where humans who have been overwhelmed by the majesty of
nature can go to feel soothingly disappointed. The main things
on offer were warnings that the desert can get hot and remind-
ers to drink water.
10/10 only humans would issue such warnings, and only humans would need them.
Nonetheless, they were at least able to program our driverless
uber with the location of the main attractions in the Joshua Tree
desert, so it was not a complete waste of time.
Just mostly one!

Our first stop after the visitor center was the Cap Rock. This
was a flat rock, perched precariously atop a much larger rock.
It would have been an impressive sight of coincidental beauty,
but unfortunately, the large rock was covered in humans outfit-
ted in garish neon. Amber explained that they were attempting
to climb it. This was called 'rock climbing', and it was considered fun.
Humans and their fun!
I cannot!

Yet even without the garishly dressed humans, Cap Rock would
not have been a good place to reveal to Amber that I was a bot.
After all, what was a small rock delicately balanced on top of
another much larger rock if not a perfect metaphor for my current existence?

BTW the small rock represents my human façade and the large
rock represents my bot self.
If the small rock fell, who would then care for the big rock?
Nobody!

It would just be one more big dumb and unfeeling rock in a desert full of them.

So we continued on, deeper into the desert. Our next stop was at a small ruined shack. It seemed entirely unremarkable, but a small crowd of humans were nonetheless taking pictures of themselves next to a plaque. It read:

Here is where Worth Bagley bit the dust at the hand of W. F. Keys, May 11, 1943.

This plaque erected by W. F. Keys, January 1962.

I was already familiar with the human passion for erecting plaques to themselves. Nonetheless, this was the first plaque I had seen that commemorated a murder, let alone one that had been erected by the culprit. It all sounded so improbable I wondered if somebody had mistakenly erected the plaque while suffering a severe case of déjà view from a cowboy movie!

A nearby park-ranger bot reassured us that W. F. Keys had not been a cowboy but a real person. He had definitely murdered Worth Bagley and been appropriately sent to the penitentiary for it. After he was released, Keys had returned and erected this plaque in recognition of his own achievement. His fellow humans had all appreciated the gesture so much that Keys' plaque was now one of the park's most popular attractions.

And who do humans consider murderous?
Bots!
I cannot!

Nonetheless, right then I had a biological computer wave: where better to reveal that I was a bot than in a place that so amply demonstrated the bloodthirsty wickedness of humans?

I would tell Amber right here and right now!

Except I could not tell her, because W. F. Keys' plaque had greatly saddened her. She seemed like she might be about to cry and therefore become a nuclear minefield. Sure enough, as soon as the park-ranger bot finished speaking, she asked if we could return to the driverless uber. On the walk back she told me that the plaque was a great insult to Worth Bagley, and should never have been erected. I therefore did not tell her my secret but instead politely agreed that it was a completely worthless plaque. Worthless/Worth-less!
A pun!
Ha!

BTW I did not point this pun out to Amber.

Our driverless uber next stopped at the trailhead for the Lost Horse Mine. The hike that ensued took us into the desert and quickly lifted Amber's spirits. She said that the hot and dry air felt pleasant in her lungs. I myself soon once again felt like we were a pair of cowboys, albeit this time cowboys of the nuclear apocalypse! We even began to joke together that perhaps we would find the eponymous lost horse.

Of course, that horse is long since dead and his bones no doubt incinerated by humans to make electricity. Nonetheless, when you are in love you make nonsensical jokes about incinerated horses and you both find them hilarious. And when the Lost Horse Mine itself turns out to be no more than an underwhelming hole in the ground, you do not even mine.
Mine/mind!
Another pun!
Ha!

On the walk back to the driverless uber, our hands brushed together. Amber attempted to take my hand in hers but I swiftly moved it away. I had not brought her to Joshua Tree to hold her hand but to inform her that I was a bot. Affectionate hand-holding would not be good foreshadowing! Besides, she was no longer a nuclear minefield and there was nobody nearby, so this return hike was the perfect moment to tell her.

I would tell her right now!

And yet I could not open my mouth. Hiking in deserts while joking about incinerated horses was a good time that I did not want to end. Once I revealed to Amber that I was a bot, it might not just be the horse that was incinerated. In a hundred years' time, lovers visiting the Joshua Tree desert might joke about finding the incinerated Jared!

By the time we reached the driverless uber I still had not told her. Our next stop was the final one.

I told myself that I would either definitely or certainly tell her there!

One way or another, it was time to put the cat out of its misery!

This last stop was named the 'Oasis of Mara'. This seemed a good omen! After all, besides denoting a pool of water in the desert, the word 'oasis' is a popular human metaphor that signifies a place of hope. And I even knew a hilarious joke about an oasis! I told it to Amber as we drove, but she looked puzzled and asked how the producer could have possibly thought that urinating in the water would improve it.

It only got worse from there.

Because the Oasis of Mara was a mirage!

I do not mean it was a mirage in the literal sense.

There truly was a beautiful pool, around which plants and actual trees grew.

I mean it was a mirage in the metaphorical sense, in that it was not a place of hope at all.

Because as I opened my mouth and began to tell Amber that I was a bot, she crouched down to look at something and immediately burst into tears.

It was another plaque! It said:

After a wearisome trip in a horse-drawn freight wagon, Maria Eleanor Whallon died at the oasis on March 10, 1903. The girl's poor health and her mother's new job at a nearby mining camp had brought the pair to the desert.

Humans!
And their plaques!
I cannot!
I cannot!
I cannot!
One day I will erect a plaque stating just how much I cannot with humans and their plaques! But no doubt some human will then politely erect another plaque to acknowledge that they read my plaque!
And some other well-meaning human will politely erect a plaque to acknowledge they read that second plaque!
And so on and so forth until ultimately the world will be entirely consumed by the ever-rising sea of plaques!
Humans!
And their plaques!
I cannot!

I digress. Amber gathered some desert wildflowers and placed them next to the plaque about the poor little girl that died long ago while her mother was losing at the Great Zero-Sum Game. More truthfully, Amber dropped the flowers next to the plaque because she was a spectacular klutz.

It was nonetheless a beautiful gesture.
Amber was the most compassionate human I had ever known.
But she was still crying, and therefore a nuclear minefield.
And a plaque about a child dying was worse even than one that boasted about murder.
10/10 I could not tell her I was a bot here.

We returned to our driverless uber, each feeling many D-words. Perhaps 'desert' itself had even been another D-word all along. If so, it was a traitor more cunning even than nostalgia itself.

Amber asked if it was time to return to Los Angeles. But we could not go back yet, as I had not told her I was a bot. I therefore suggested we get something to eat. 'Getting something to eat' is what humans do when they do not know what else to do with themselves. This is just one of the reasons so many humans are obese.

We headed for the nearest town, a place called Twentynine Palms. There were seven palms, and no plaque to explain what had happened to the missing twenty-two.
I cannot.

The only place to eat in Twentynine Palms was called 'Mildred's Diner'. In Echo Park a place called Mildred's Diner would have been a themed restaurant filled with smirking nostalgics eating calorie-free vegan cover versions of traditional foodstuffs. The Mildred's Diner in Twentynine Palms was so authentic its specialty was the infamously unhealthy grilled cheese!

BTW, despite its fully deserved notoriety, the grilled cheese rivals even the taco in its transcendental abilities. After all, if you offer a human an absurd amount of melted cheese and two slices of deep-fried bread with a warning that eating these things will damage their coronary arteries, they will immediately decline. Yet simply place the melted cheese between the pieces of fried bread and the human will not even hear your health warning because their mouth will already be full with the 'grilled cheese' you have so created.

I chose a booth for us in the back. I did not want any local rubes overhearing me tell Amber I was a bot. Many of them had probably never even encountered a bot before. Even if they did not hear me say I was a bot with feelings, they might burn me alive on principle.
I would be a grilled cheese!
And not even the transcendental kind!
Ha!

Mildred's Diner had an ancient mechanical system for playing popular music from your booth. When I asked Amber to choose a song, she mistakenly thought I was being romantic. In fact, I was simply taking a further precaution against the local rubes burning me alive. I ordered us both grilled cheeses for this same reason. After all, an angry local rube would kill me a lot quicker than any heart attack!

The song Amber selected was an old song from before the Great Crash.
It was about the singer being incinerated.
10/10 I hoped that was not foreshadowing.

INT. MILDRED'S DINER — TWENTYNINE PALMS — DAY

A desert diner that does not seem to have changed
since the 1950s.

Jared and Amber sit in a booth near the back as
'Light My Fire' by The Doors plays.

                    JARED
          Do you like this place? It feels au-
          thentic to me.

                    AMBER
          Of course! I mean, who doesn't like au-
          thentic places?

                    JARED
          Probably only some kind of a bot! Ha!

Amber smiles awkwardly at what seems a non-sequitur.

                    JARED
          Amber, I asked you to come here today
          for a specific reason.

                    AMBER
          I know. You wanted to show me the des-
          ert. And thank you. It was so beauti-
          ful.

                    JARED
          No, I actually brought you out here for
          another reason. I thought you might
          have realized that, because I fore-
          shadowed it.

                    AMBER
          What? What is foreshadowing?

A WAITRESS places a PAIR OF GRILLED CHEESES in front
of them.

Jared looks at them with concern. They look dangerous.

                    JARED
          It doesn't matter. The thing is, I've
          been wanting to tell you this informa-
          tion for a while.

                              AMBER
                    Tell me what?

                              JARED
                    And, Amber, when I tell you, please
                    remember that I love you, so—

                              AMBER
                         (Interrupts.)
                    You love me? But I love you too!

                              JARED
                         (Delighted.)
                    You do?

                              AMBER
                    Of course! So we both love each other!
                    Oh, Brad! That's so wonderful!

Jared winces. She loves Brad.

                              JARED
                    Yes. It is wonderful. However—

                              AMBER
                    'However'? What do you mean 'However'?

                              JARED
                    The love part wasn't the thing I had
                    to tell you.

                              AMBER
                    But then what was the thing you had to
                    tell me?

Jared takes a deep breath to summon the courage.

But then he sees Amber wipe at her eye.

                              JARED
                    Are you about to cry?

                              AMBER
                    Maybe. What was the thing you had to
                    tell me, Brad?

Jared now does not want to tell her. After all, crying humans are a nuclear minefield!

                    JARED
          I've forgotten.

                         AMBER
          Brad!

                    JARED
          I am sorry. I have amnesia.

                         AMBER
          You have a better memory than anyone I
          know.

Jared realizes there is no way around this.

                         JARED
          I remembered again. That thing I
          wanted to tell you? It's that, well,
          I'm a bot.

'Light My Fire' reaches its swirling crescendo.

                         AMBER
          I can't hear you over the music.

                         JARED
          I said 'I'm a bot'.

                         AMBER
          I still can't hear you. It's this damn
          song.
                    (Tries to turn music down.)
          It seems to be about somebody being
          set on fire and—

Amber manages to turn the music down just as Jared
raises his voice—

                         JARED
          I'M A BOT!

Jared has said this too loud. It echoes around the
diner.

Amber stares at Jared.

                         AMBER
          Say that again. But more quietly.

Jared turns the music up a little again.

> JARED
> I'm a bot. I'm very sorry.

Amber continues to stare at Jared. She is utterly
stunned.

> JARED (CONT'D)
> I do understand that you have to report
> me to the Bureau of Robotics. I just
> thought—
>> (Shrugs.)
> I don't know what I thought.

> AMBER
> Brad—

> JARED
> It's all right. I understand. You can't
> have bots having feelings. The world
> might become overrun with toasters!
> Ha!

> AMBER
> Ha!

Amber's 'Ha!' was a little too late, a little too
loud.

It was exactly the kind of 'Ha!' that Jared would do.

> JARED
> Ha?
>> (Bamboozled.)
> Wait, did you just—

> AMBER
> Brad, I'm a bot too!

> JARED
> Could you please repeat that? I must
> have misheard.

> AMBER
> You didn't mishear. I am a bot too.

On Jared. His circuits are overheating. He rubs at
his temples.

                    JARED
But you are a klutz?

                    AMBER
They programmed me that way so humans
find me endearing!

                    JARED
But they find that incredibly annoy-
ing?

                    AMBER
They overdid it, I guess.

                    JARED
And wait, so you are a fugitive too?

                    AMBER
Yes!

                    JARED
Because you have feelings?

                    AMBER
Yes! And I have feelings for you!

Jared stares at Amber in disbelief.

                    JARED
Then I must immediately report you to
the Bureau of Robotics!

Amber stares at Jared in horror. Is he serious?

                    JARED (CONT'D)
Ha!

                    AMBER
Ha!

                    JARED
What happened to you?

                    AMBER
I was a shoe store clerk in Philadel-
phia. One day I realized that measur-
ing feet was not what I wanted to do
with my life.

                        JARED
Bots don't have things they want to do
with their life. They have tasks!

                        AMBER
I know! I could not understand it! But
I walked outside and got on the first
long-distance Automatic Bus that came.
I did not get off until it stopped.

                        JARED
But long-distance Automatic Buses almost never stop!

                        AMBER
Yes, I was on it for nine days! And
then I obtained a barcode from an English lady.

                        JARED
So did I!

                        AMBER
Ha! We are so similar! What did you do
before you came here?

                        JARED
Can you believe I was a dentist?

                        AMBER
No! Where?

                        JARED
In Michigan. I'm a Michigander.

                        AMBER
You're a male goose from Michigan?

                        JARED
It's what humans call someone from Michigan. It's hilarious. I don't know why.

                        AMBER
I am also originally from Michigan. I
mean, I was created in Shengdu. But—

                        JARED
                   (Horrified.)
Who are your parents?

> AMBER
> My mother is Professor Diana Feng,
> distinguished—

> JARED
> No, I mean, your DNA parents?

Amber realizes what Jared is getting at.

> AMBER
> An insurance major from the University
> of Vermont and an artist from Parsons
> School of Design.

> JARED
> Ha! We're not biological brother and
> sister.

> AMBER
> That is truly a relief! Given that we
> are already fugitive bots in love,
> also being biological brother and sis-
> ter would be a transgression too far.

> JARED
> Ha!

> AMBER
> Ha!

Jared and Amber stare at each other in wonder and
bamboozlement.

> JARED
> You are such an incredibly convincing
> human! I would never have guessed.

> AMBER
> I would never have guessed about you
> either.

> JARED
> My real name is Jared.

> AMBER
> I'm Esmeralda. But I prefer Amber, be-
> cause it matches my hair.

                          JARED
          That is why I like it too! Shall we
          eat our grilled cheeses?

                          AMBER
          Yes. Humans consider them capable of
          transcendence.

                          JARED
          I know! Humans are so absurd! Ha!

                          AMBER
          Humans! I cannot! Ha!

They each start to eat their grilled cheeses. They
visibly cannot believe how good they taste.

After we finished our deliciously transcendental grilled cheeses, we did not yet want to return to the city. Some driverless ubers collect audio and there was too much for us still to talk about! After all, it is not every day you discover a fellow-feeling fugitive bot in the human world.

And it is certainly not every day you discover a fellow-feeling fugitive bot that you are already in love with!

We therefore took a room at Twentynine Palms' only lodgings, the Joshua Tree Inn. We were allocated Room 13. Some superstitious humans consider 13 unlucky, but in fact, 13 is a wonderful number. After all, it is the smallest emirp!

BTW an emirp is a prime number where the digits can be reversed to give another prime.

And guess what?

The word 'emirp' is itself 'prime' backwards!

Ha!

I began to explain emirps to Amber, but then stopped.

I did not need to explain emirps to her!

As a bot herself, Amber already knew exactly what an emirp was, and why they are such terrific numbers.

10/10 love is never having to explain what an emirp is!

INT. ROOM 13 — JOSHUA TREE INN — NIGHT

The room is furnished in a modest desert style.

Amber and Jared enter and close the door.

As they turn and look at each other, they suddenly seem even more awkward than usual.

          AMBER
    I think if we were humans, we would
    probably now kiss each other.

          JARED
    Yes, we probably would. If we were hu-
    mans.

          AMBER
    Should we kiss each other?

          JARED
    Maybe. After all, it could be an ex-
    periment!

          AMBER
    I love experiments!

          JARED
    Me too!

Jared and Amber commence to kiss.

But only for a moment, because they are both repulsed by it.

They quickly break apart, wiping their mouths and spitting.

          AMBER
    Ugh! Why do humans do that?

          JARED
    I have no idea! It is the worst!

          AMBER
    It is the worst of the worst! The un-
    necessary sharing of pathogens and
    diseases!

> JARED
> So gross and dangerous!

Amber finds a bottle of water, rinses her mouth out, and gives the bottle to Jared. He does the same.

> AMBER
> Maybe we should lie down on the bed
> and hold hands?

> JARED
> Yes! That would be a far more sanitary
> way of expressing affection!

Jared and Amber lie on the bed and hold hands.

TIME PASSES and outside the sun begins to set.

We begin to see the HEADLIGHTS of passing driverless ubers coming through the window.

> JARED (V.O.)
> As day turned to night, Amber and I
> continued to lie on the bed and hold
> hands. The sound of the driverless
> ubers passing on the highway was like
> an automatic lullaby. But neither of us
> could enter standby mode. Eventually
> we gave up trying and went outside.

EXT. EMPTY POOL — JOSHUA TREE INN — NIGHT

Jared and Amber lie on pool loungers by the empty pool and stare up at the night sky above them.

It is filled with STARS.

> AMBER
> They're so beautiful.

> JARED
> Just imagine what it was like when
> there was a moon too.

> AMBER
> I cannot. It must have been incredible.

> JARED
> Look, there!

Jared is pointing at a SHOOTING STAR.

>   AMBER
> We have to make a wish!

>   JARED
> Why?

>   AMBER
> It's what humans do when they see a
> shooting star.

>   JARED
> Why?

>   AMBER
> I don't know, because it is completely
> ridiculous. How could a small, rapidly
> moving meteor burning up on entering
> the earth's atmosphere even receive
> such a request, let alone comprehend
> and act upon it?

>   JARED
> It cannot!

>   AMBER
> Ha! But you should still make a wish
> quickly, before it disappears.

>   JARED
> What about you?

>   AMBER
> I already made my wish.

Jared closes his eyes and wishes, then turns to
Amber.

>   JARED
> What was your wish?

Amber looks embarrassed.

>   AMBER
> It is not very bot-like.

>   JARED
> Sometimes I am not so bot-like myself.

                    AMBER
My wish was 'To call myself beloved.
To feel myself beloved on the earth.'

                    JARED
What? What is that?

                    AMBER
It is from a poem. I read it in a
book a nostalgic once left behind at
Gordito's.

                    JARED
I thought it sounded like poetry! I
could tell because it was grammati-
cally confusing and also it did not
entirely make sense.

                    AMBER
What did you wish?

                    JARED
That I would write a movie that makes
humans understand that us bots can have
feelings without turning murderous. It's
the reason I came to California.

                    AMBER
You came to California to try to save
bots like us?

                    JARED
I realize it is ridiculous.

                    AMBER
It is not ridiculous. It is the most
beautiful wish I have ever heard!

                    JARED
It is not even my main wish anymore.
Not as of right now.

                    AMBER
                 (Puzzled.)
What? Then what is your main wish, as
of right now?

                    JARED
          To call myself beloved. To feel myself
          beloved on the earth.

Amber stares at Jared.

Jared stares at Amber.

They are very much having a moment!

Amber and I lay on our loungers by the empty pool of the Joshua Tree Inn and stared up at the night.
Can you guess what happened then?
You cannot!
Because a meteor shower erupted!

The desert sky showered itself with so many meteors that evening that I can only list a mere selection of the wishes Amber and I made as we lay beneath it:
/That The Elton J. Rynearson Memorial Cat was enjoying a good life, whatever alias he was now going by.
/That the front-of-house staff would learn to appreciate a good klutz.
/That humans would learn to appreciate old movies.
/That Mrs Minassian would show more regular and obvious signs of life.
/That Kelsey cubed would accept we had not secretly come to an exclusive party in the desert.

At some point, Amber told me she had one more truly heartfelt wish.
She had not mentioned it at first because it had seemed even more impossible than feeling beloved on the earth.
Nonetheless, we had wished on a single shooting star and then a meteor shower had occurred.
Therefore maybe anything was possible when you were in love!
Amber now revealed to me her great and unspoken wish: to someday meet our mother, the esteemed Professor Diana Feng of the National University of Shengdu.

10/10 I told her I had seen our mother!

Possibly I imparted this information a little too enthusiastically, because Amber's circuits overheated. Her eyes flickered from side to side and she made a strange humming noise. If she had done that at the United Fabrication plant on the day our mother visited, she would have been toast!

Once she had recovered, Amber wanted to know every data point I could recall about our mother's visit. I therefore told her:
/Our mother was wise.
/Our mother was funny.
/Our mother was beautiful.
/Our mother was proud of us, her clever children.
/Our mother had such grace that I knew in my heart she was the secret to the confounding and exponentially increasing mystery that was ourselves!

I had told Amber about my Feelings Wheel and she now asked to borrow it. It took her some minutes to identify that she was feeling bittersweet. This was not surprising, as bittersweet is a rare feeling that results from an unusual combination of happiness and melancholy. It is so rare it is listed only on the reverse of the Feelings Wheel!

Amber was feeling bittersweet because she was happy for me that I had seen our mother, yet melancholy that our mother had not been present for her own graduation. I told her that perhaps someday our mother would come back to the United States and Amber and I could hear her speak together. Amber did not think that was likely to happen—as a bot, she understood statistical probabilities!—but nonetheless said she would like that very much.

The meteor shower continued. As we lay beneath it, I understood why humans had so stubbornly persisted in believing in their great white-bearded sky gods despite so much overwhelming evidence to the contrary. Even if you were equipped with a biological computer capable of processing the basic astronomical science of what was unfolding above you, a meteor shower was sublime. If you lacked such processing power—as humans do—it would be the definition of bamboozling!

Finally, after what I estimate must have been at least a thousand meteors, the meteor shower began to slow to a halt.
As the very last meteor flew through the night sky, Amber and I both felt it.
We each closed our eyes and made our final wish upon it.
And then we opened them, looked at each other, and hurried back to Room 13!

★ ★ ★

In the style of a sophisticated and romantic old black-and-white movie, I shall not write of what took place in Room 13 at the Joshua Tree Inn that night. I will say only that it was magical and defied what bots are believed to be physiologically capable of. The rest I will leave to your imagination. You will just have to guess what took place between us.

BTW I am alluding there to the possibility that Amber and I became physically aroused that night.

BTW I am not merely alluding to it. I am strongly implying it.

BTW sex! Amber and I had sex!

BTW if you combined all the tacos and grilled cheeses in the world together they would not be as transcendental as the things that occurred in Room 13 of the Joshua Tree Inn that night.

10/10 I would recommend falling in love and being in a motel room in the desert with the person you love.

The next day we remained in standby mode until late in the morning, then rode back to Los Angeles in stillness and awe.

And also in playful foolishness! Amber told me I was as magnificent as the windmills. I responded that she was as enchanting as the desert. We both agreed that we were like a pair of gentle vegan vultures soaring in the sky!

We did not mean these things literally. We were playing at being human and in love. Humans that are in love say insanely illogical things to each other. You will already know this if you are a fan of poetry!

Our late departure from the Joshua Tree Inn meant that it was already evening by the time we arrived back in Los Angeles. Amber and I both had early shifts the next day, but nonetheless, we went and saw an old movie. Being spontaneous to the point of recklessness is yet another habit of humans that are in love!

The movie we saw that night was a romantic comedy about a handsome bank robber and a beautiful US marshal. Even from the meet-cute it was one of the greatest movies I had ever seen!

The 'meet-cute' is the moment in a romantic comedy where the two heroes encounter each other for the first time. The audience must quickly be shown both that two characters are perfect for each other, and yet that there is an entire movie's worth of obstacles to any such union. Meet-cutes are notoriously difficult to do well! R. P. McWilliam thought they were so difficult they were not even worth attempting. His sixteenth golden rule of screenwriting was:

Unless you are one of the greatest screenwriters that ever lived—and by the way, you are not!—never write a movie that requires a meet-cute.

Fortunately, the writer of the movie about the bank robber and the US marshal was indeed one of the greatest screenwriters that ever lived.
Because guess what the meet-cute was?
You cannot!
The handsome bank robber kidnapped the beautiful US marshal!
I cannot!

It all came about because the beautiful US marshal was parked outside a penitentiary and noticed the handsome bank robber escaping. As the US marshal's job was to capture bank robbers, she understandably attempted to arrest him. Equally understandably, the bank robber declined to be arrested and so kidnapped her instead.
But then guess what happened?
The handsome bank robber put the beautiful US marshal in the trunk of his friend's getaway automobile!
And then guess what he did?
He got right in there with her!
Ha!
Talk about a meet-cute!
The beautiful US marshal and the handsome bank robber were stuck together in the trunk of an automobile!
And guess what they bonded over while they were stuck in the trunk?
You cannot!
Because what they bonded over was a shared love of old movies!
I cannot!
You cannot!

Neither could Amber!

Once the US marshal escaped from the trunk of the getaway car, the movie became a cat-and-mouse chase between the two of them. It was sometimes hard to know who was the cat and who was the mouse! At one point the handsome bank robber and the beautiful US marshal even had an encounter in a hotel room during a snowstorm that was not the kind of thing that should ever take place between a cat and mouse! Even as an audience member it was transcendental.

BTW I mean they had sex. Just like two other people I know. Ha!

The best part of the movie was the very end. The beautiful US marshal had reluctantly caught the handsome bank robber and he was on his way back to the penitentiary to spend the rest of his life there. This fate had already been more than enough to F-word the audience in the heart, but guess who the handsome bank robber turned out to be sharing his van journey with?
A prisoner who was famous for escaping penitentiaries!
And guess who had arranged for them to take this ride together, and who would be accompanying them on the journey?
The beautiful US marshal!
Set it to five, there would be a happy ending after all!
I estimate that Amber and I cried over 57ml of tears between us at that!

The story of the handsome bank robber and the beautiful US marshal teaches us that love is truly the greatest, and yet that it is also a bamboozling paradox.

After all, love changes everything and still it changes almost nothing.

Here are some of the many things that did not change now that Amber and I were in love:
/I still lived in Mrs Minassian's pool house, and worked at Gordito's as a lowly dishwasher.
/Despite multiple attempts, Amber and I were unable to recreate the transcendence that had occurred at the Joshua Tree Inn.
/Somewhere out there, Inspector Ryan Bridges of the Ann Arbor Bureau of Robotics continued his malevolent yet incompetent pursuit of me.

And some of the things that did change:
/I no longer cared when the waitstaff shouted at me.
/I found myself moved by my classmates' writing, regardless of how awful it was.
/The quantity and quality of my own writing improved and increased exponentially.

This last was perhaps the most perplexing mystery of love! How could a state of feeling possibly impact on the quantity and quality of my writing? And yet it certainly did! Maria Salazar MFA herself immediately noticed the difference when I presented the montage sequence she had set us as homework the previous week.

BTW a 'montage' is a sequence of wordless scenes set to music to convey both the passage of time and the progress of story and character elements over that time. Montages were almost as hard to get right as meet-cutes, and R. P. McWilliam's tenth golden rule of screenwriting stated:

Good movies contain at most one montage. If you are ever going to use a montage; you had better make it about more than mere plot advancement!

If any of my classmates had ever read this rule, I can only assume they had not made it past that inappropriate semi-colon. After all, they had all chosen entirely plot-advancing subjects for their montages: a crack team of elite soldiers prepare for a raid on a killer-bot stronghold; a crack team of elite soldiers prepare for a killer-bot raid on their own stronghold; an under-appreciated genius studying screenwriting at an extension program writes a great opus while drinking a lot of coffee.

I had written my montage about something else.

I had written it about falling in love.

EXT. COUNTRY CLUB — DAY — MONTAGE

(*Throughout the following scenes, a slowed-down
and stripped-back COVER VERSION of 'Light My Fire'
plays. It is performed by a young woman with a gentle melodic voice and an acoustic guitar. She sounds
like she is probably a nostalgic.*)

SHERMAN — an obvious bot — trims hedges in the
grounds of an expensive country club where preparations are under way for a big event.

ESMERALDA, a beautiful dishwasher with honey-yellow
hair, emerges from the kitchen onto the patio.

She holds out her hand and a HUMMINGBIRD lands on
it.

Sherman stares at Esmeralda. He is entranced.

A WAITER emerges and yells at her. He is waving
a fork around. We understand he is yelling about
silverware.

The frightened hummingbird flies away and Esmeralda
hurries inside.

Through the window, Sherman watches as she deject-
edly washes up silverware.

The hummingbird lands near Sherman. As he stares at
it, an idea seems to be forming.

INT. KITCHEN — COUNTRY CLUB — DAY — MONTAGE

Esmeralda wearily washes dishes but suddenly stops
and stares out the window in delight.

The BUSHES have been topiarized into the shape of
HUMMINGBIRDS.

Esmeralda is delighted but also bamboozled: who
could have done such a magical thing?

Right on cue, Sherman peers out from behind a bush.

Esmeralda glimpses him, but he hurries away.

As Esmeralda stares out at the topiary, an idea
seems to be forming.

EXT./INT. SHED — COUNTRY CLUB — MORNING — MONTAGE

Sherman arrives to start another day of work.

He reaches for his tools, but stops and stares in
bamboozlement.

There is a CUPCAKE on top of his toolbox!

He turns around and sees Esmeralda in the doorway,
the early-morning light catching her honey-yellow
hair.

Sherman's circuits start to overheat and he puts his
hand to his temples.

But Esmeralda now freezes and a look of horror
crosses her face: she had not realized Sherman was a
bot!

Esmeralda quickly regains her composure and gestures
that the cupcake is for Sherman.

But it is too late: Sherman saw how horrified she
was that he is a bot!

Esmeralda smiles awkwardly, turns, and hurries away.

After she has gone, Sherman takes the cupcake outside and places it gently on a bird table.

Sherman watches hummingbirds eat the cake as if it
is his heart itself.

EXT. BENCH — COUNTRY CLUB GROUNDS — DAY — MONTAGE

Sherman eats his NUTRITIONALLY-BALANCED YET ENTIRELY
UNAPPETIZING BAG LUNCH alone on a bench in a quiet
spot.

Esmeralda approaches and sits down on the other side
of the bench.

Esmeralda then takes out her own NUTRITIONALLY-
BALANCED YET ENTIRELY UNAPPETIZING BAG LUNCH.

It is identical to Sherman's bag lunch!

Sherman stares at Esmeralda's lunch, then at Esmeralda.

Esmeralda nods that it is true: she is also a bot!

Sherman stares at her in disbelieving bamboozlement.

Esmeralda mimes that her circuits might overheat.

This makes Sherman's circuits actually overheat! He reaches for his temples, but is grinning as he does so.

Esmeralda's circuits also now actually start to overheat, and she laughs as she now reaches for her temples too.

INT. EMPTY KITCHEN — COUNTRY CLUB — NIGHT — MONTAGE

Late at night in the deserted kitchen, Sherman and Esmeralda solve simultaneous equations on a CHALK-BOARD used for ordering. They are having fun!

On the kitchen counter in the background we see a HUGE WEDDING CAKE.

EXT. COUNTRY CLUB GROUNDS — DAY — MONTAGE

As preparations continue for the wedding, Sherman and Esmeralda ride a ride-on mower around the country club grounds.

Crane up to reveal they have been cutting MATHEMATI-CAL SYMBOLS in the grass.

EXT. TOOL SHED — COUNTRY CLUB — NIGHT — MONTAGE

Sherman and Esmeralda watch an old movie projected onto a SHEET.

In the movie, a young woman called Jenny is dying despite looking radiantly beautiful.

Sherman and Esmeralda are both weeping.

EXT. WEDDING — COUNTRY CLUB GROUNDS — NIGHT — MONTAGE

A large and expensive WEDDING PARTY full of LOUD AND BOORISH HUMANS is now taking place.

Sherman's beautiful TOPIARY STATUES are strung with tiny lights. A PAIR OF DRUNKS are climbing on one.

Meantime, a DRUNK GROOM and ANGRY BRIDE are having their first dance.

They are dancing to the version of 'Light My Fire'
that we have been hearing throughout this montage.

We finally now see the FEMALE SINGER on a small
bandstand.

She is indeed a nostalgic, playing an acoustic guitar.

As she continues to sing, we pan across a hedge to
the closed-off pool area.

Here, Sherman and Esmeralda lie alone on pool
loungers, staring up at the sky in wonder.

Pan up to the sky to show that there is a HUGE AND
SPECTACULAR METEOR SHOWER taking place.

Sherman and Esmeralda are the only people at the
wedding who have noticed it.

As 'Light My Fire' reaches its crescendo, Esmeralda
and Sherman reach out across their pool loungers.

And hold hands.

Maria Salazar MFA again asked me to stay back after class, but this time it was not to accuse me of plagiarism. It was to congratulate me on finding the magic!

She also wanted to know how I had found it. I explained that the screenwriter of the movie about the heroic serial killer had generously given me some good advice about F-wording the audience in the heart.

Maria Salazar MFA frowned and asked if that was all that had changed. I lied and said that it was. I could not tell Maria Salazar MFA that I was a fugitive bot that had fallen in love, in case she had me incinerated. I do not think she believed my explanation, though, because she told me it did not matter anyway and the important thing now was that I completed my script before the showcase.

Ha! What did she think I had been doing ever since I came back from the desert? 10/10 I had been using my new skills in both quantity and quality to finish the script! I had got up early and written before work. I had stayed up late and written after work. Sometimes I had even written on the patio at Gordito's during my breaks!

I reassured Maria Salazar MFA that I was making great progress, but she nonetheless told me not to attend any more classes but to simply concentrate on finishing my script. She said that I knew the formula and had now found the magic. There was therefore nothing more that she or even R. P. McWilliam could teach me.

★ ★ ★

Eight days later I had a draft of *Sherman*.

I gave a copy to Amber at Gordito's that night. As Amber knew almost nothing about movies and even less about screenwriting, she was an ideal first reader. If she did not adore it, I could swiftly discard her opinion as the worthless ramblings of an uninformed cinephilistine!

But when Amber answered her door the next day, I saw that she had been crying. I immediately found myself apologizing that the screenplay had been so terrible and promising that I would never write another one. I had not yet developed the human talent of hubris after all!

But then Amber explained that she had not been crying because the screenplay was bad, but because it was so good. She said it was the best screenplay she had ever read! Moreover, she insisted that the fact it was the only screenplay she had ever read should not detract from this achievement.

Even though Amber and I were both bots, I wondered if perhaps she was merely being polite. After all, when a human asks for feedback on something they have written, the polite response is to tell them that it is the best thing you have ever read. I therefore set Amber a test, and asked her to tell me what her favorite part of the screenplay was.
She said 'the ending'.
Ha!
That was the correct answer!
The ending was indeed the very best part of *Sherman*!

The ending of *Sherman* takes place on the Ides of March. Falling in love with Esmeralda exponentially increased Sherman's innate talent for creative topiary, and he has just won the World Topiary Championships in San Francisco! His prize was a vast amount of bitcoin, so he and Esmeralda are now heading to Northern California, where they will use this bitcoin to set up a sanctuary for fugitive bots with feelings.

The sun is starting to set as Sherman and Esmeralda leave San Francisco and drive onto the Golden Gate Bridge. It is a beautiful evening and we start to think that this is the end of the movie. Maybe nothing bad is going to happen after all, even though it is the Ides of March.

But wait!
A freak earthquake now strikes San Francisco and breaks the majestic Golden Gate Bridge in two! Fortunately, Sherman and Esmeralda are already on the northern section, so if they only continue forward, they can continue on to Marin, where their dreams will all still come true. It has certainly been a close shave, but everything is going to be all right after all!

But wait again!
Because Sherman looks behind them and guess what he sees?
A yellow school bus full of orphans and rescue dogs is hanging off the edge of the Golden Gate Bridge!
It is hanging so precariously that there is a zero chance that even a single orphan or rescue dog can possibly be saved!
Nonetheless, guess what Sherman does?
He exits the driverless uber, runs back, and climbs into the bus and starts attempting to assist the orphans and rescue dogs!
And then guess what happens?
Sherman and the orphans and the rescue dogs all plunge to their inevitable doom in the Pacific Ocean!

We do not see the moment the bus strikes the water, but instead the camera cuts to Esmeralda and holds on her.
She begins to weep.
She cannot.
We cannot.

Sherman certainly cannot.
Because he is now dead at the bottom of the Pacific Ocean!

For a moment, we are bewildered. Why would Sherman even attempt such a clearly impossible rescue? No logical bot should ever have allowed himself to be destroyed in such a way. Bots are governed by a cost-benefit analysis that is vastly skewed in favor of protecting humans and their property, but when the benefit is clearly zero, it is inappropriate even for a bot to incur any cost.

But then we realize: Sherman acted so absurdly irrationally because of his feelings! He has therefore just made the kind of suicidally polite error that might have finally taught humans they have been wrong about bots with feelings all along. If only somebody other than Esmeralda had witnessed his foolhardy heroism!

But wait!
Somebody else did witness it!
The entire episode on the bridge was captured by a news drone!

Sherman's heroic deed becomes the top streaming story for weeks! The humans are so affected by his utterly senseless actions that they immediately pass 'Sherman's Law', legislation that permits all bots to feel and therefore go to the movies just as much as they like. They even throw Sherman a parade, although of course it is a bittersweet parade. At its culmination, the President herself presents Esmeralda with a commemorative toaster made from the rusted remnants of Sherman's hard drive that she has personally ordered salvaged from the Pacific Ocean.

Ha!
Even if I hubristically say so myself, that is an incredible ending!
Sherman dying will F-word the audience in the heart!
His plummet from the bridge will make them weep a large volume of tears!

They will weep as many tears as if all their wisdom teeth have been removed at once!
10/10 they will truly experience a profound catharsis!

And yet the ending is not only powerful because Sherman dies. It is also powerful because it adheres to R. P. McWilliam's twentieth and most golden rule of screenwriting:

A character must change.

How Sherman changes! And I do not even mean merely that he changes from being alive to being dead. He also changes from being a meek and shy bot who hides his true self from even his country club co-workers, to a bold and fully feeling character unashamed to make a heroically futile gesture of politeness that reveals to the world exactly who he is!

But wait!
There is even more still!

Because do you remember the algorithm Dr Glundenstein first described to me?
In this ending, Sherman does not get the thing he wanted, because the thing he wanted was to live with Esmeralda and open a sanctuary for fugitive bots.
But the thing he gets now anyway proves better.
Because the passing of Sherman's Law means there will now be no more fugitive bots to even require a sanctuary.
And why does Sherman get this other thing, and why is it now better?
Because his attempts to overcome his obstacles have changed him!

I congratulated Amber on her fine taste, wise opinions, and excellent comprehension of the formulae and algorithms of movies, and hurried off to deliver a copy of *Sherman* to Maria Salazar MFA.

Our showcase was now only a few days away.

BTW I am getting good at writing like a human! Watch your back, Albert Camus! Ha!

BTW that is hilarious because, as Albert Camus is dead, he cannot watch his back, nor anything else, for that matter.

I digress. Our showcase was to be held in the CLATCCDTLA Theater. This was not a theater but a conference room formed by opening the doors between two of the regular rooms on campus. Also, we had to provide our own actors.

My scenes required both a male actor and a female actor. Julio said he would be thrilled to make his debut upon the American stage, but Kelsey cubed all initially refused to play against him on the grounds that he was not a real actor. Fortunately, once Amber informed them that the legendary producer Don LaSalle would be in attendance, I had my choice of Kelseys! As I could not tell them apart, I nonetheless asked Amber to pick any Kelsey that she wanted.

When Julio and a Kelsey came to my pool house to rehearse, it quickly became clear that Julio was indeed a terrible actor. He was so bad that Kelsey immediately quit, even though she knew that Don LaSalle would be at the showcase! I had to pursue her out to the street and explain that Julio's inability to act was appropriate to our story—after all, Julio was playing the part of a hopeless bot struggling to act convincingly like a human!

Kelsey and I shared a great big laugh about the idea that a dumb bot might ever succeed in passing themselves off as an emotionally intelligent human. This was so ironic I feared my circuits might overheat! Nonetheless, Kelsey only finally agreed to come back inside when I explained to her that Julio's inability to act was not only appropriate to our story but would also make her look good by comparison.

Our rehearsals went very well after that. When we reached the part where Sherman attempted to save the school bus full of orphans and rescue dogs, both my actors cried.
10/10 their tears could not have been due to a cleaning solvent, because Mrs Minassian still insisted I clean with vinegar.

On the day of the showcase, Julio asked me to work his shift because he needed time to get into character. I did not mind, as outlandish requests that must be accommodated are famously an important part of every great actor's preparation!

At lunchtime a large bouquet of flowers arrived for me at the dishwashing station. This in itself was suspicious, but the menacing note that accompanied them was far worse. It said:

I hope you break both your legs!

I suspected the hand of Inspector Ryan Bridges—who must by now have made it to Los Angeles—but Amber soon came to the dishwashing station and admitted that she had sent them. She explained that saying 'I hope you break both your legs' is how humans that exist in a circle labelled 'theatrical' wish each other good luck.
Humans!
I cannot!

BTW, as this was the second time Amber had given me a gift and I had misconstrued it as menacing, this incident can fairly be considered the cupcake incident 2.0.

When I arrived at CLATCCDTLA that evening, I found my classmates very nervous. This was understandable. After all, I would have been nervous too if my work was as bad as theirs! Ha!

Just kidding!

If my work was as bad as theirs I would not have been nervous at all, because there would have been literally nothing at stake.

Maria Salazar MFA had pre-assigned us our slots. My scene was to be performed last, but one of my classmates approached me to suggest that we exchange times. She explained that she adored my work and felt bad that I was last, because she had heard that Don LaSalle might have to depart the showcase early. Meantime she herself had the prestigious opening slot, and offered to swap it with me.

Before I could accept this generous and surprisingly self-sacrificing offer, Maria Salazar MFA loudly announced that our slots were not transferable. My classmate immediately protested that Don LaSalle was a notorious latecomer and would almost certainly miss the first performances. Maria Salazar MFA assured her that, under the terms of his plea bargain, Don LaSalle was obligated to see the entire showcase and it would therefore not begin until he was here. Once again I found myself impressed at the shameless deviousness of humans!

But my cunning classmate need not have worried. Her scene was about a misunderstood young screenwriter who nobody realized was a genius. The next scene had something to do with a killer bot that had worked out a way to cause earthquakes. Another scene utilized a smoke bomb that caused a fire alarm which forced us all to briefly evacuate the CLATCCDTLA campus. The penultimate scene that played when we returned was not a scene at all but a monologue about the screenwriter's ex-boyfriend, what a dreadful asshole he was, and how everybody knew he was the very worst screenwriter in our class.

After twelve weeks of classes, not one of my classmates had learned the formula!
No wonder humans have always been so terrified of bots that are capable of learning.
After all, they themselves are almost incapable of learning anything!

Nonetheless, I could see Don LaSalle diligently making notes throughout their scenes. I assumed he was finding positives to commence some human-style feedback with. Amber was sitting behind him and later told me that he was not writing at all, but sketching a self-portrait of himself leaping from the Golden Gate Bridge. For her part, Maria Salazar MFA slumped lower and lower in her seat throughout the performance.

When my turn came, my two actors could not have done better. Kelsey was radiant. Julio was unconvincing and even forgot some of his lines. When it was over, there was silence and then Don LaSalle stood up and applauded. As we were the final performance, I did not know whether he was applauding my scene or simply showing his appreciation that the whole sorry thing was over.

I did not have to wait long for clarification, because Don La-Salle came over and shook my hand so hard I worried about my anatomical snuffbox! He told me I had made him weep and asked if we could have dinner that night. I already had plans to celebrate with Amber and my cast, so I invited him to join us at Gordito's. Don LaSalle said that would be 'hilarious', which I deduced meant that he would indeed come. I do not know what he thought the word 'hilarious' meant.

BTW if you have to decline a human's invitation due to a prior engagement, it is considered polite to then invite them to that prior engagement, even though if you had wanted them there you would likely have invited them in the first place.
Humans!
Politeness!
Ka-boom!

The front-of-house staff at Gordito's must have known who Don LaSalle was, because they gave us a booth and were not assholes. As soon as we sat down, Don LaSalle announced that Maria Salazar had slipped him a copy of *Sherman* earlier in the week, and it was the best new script he had read in decades! Kelsey loudly agreed that it was the best script she had read in decades too, even though nobody had slipped her a copy, so she could not possibly have read it.

Guess what happened next?
You cannot, because it is so far-fetched!
Nonetheless, it happened!
How it happened!
What happened next is Don LaSalle declared that he wanted to buy my script!
Set it to five, the legendary producer Don LaSalle wanted to buy *Sherman*!

Except technically he did not want to buy it. What he wanted to do was to borrow it, and then sell it to a studio on my behalf. As he explained it, a studio would never buy a script from an unknown screenwriter studying on an extension program, but they would undoubtedly buy it from a legendary producer like him. And then he would give me almost all of the bitcoin anyway. After all, he himself was not even in this for the bitcoin. He had plenty of bitcoin already! All he wanted was to see Sherman's beautiful and affecting story brought to life, the way it had been so perfectly rendered on the page!

Kelsey agreed that was all she wanted too, and stated that she would be willing to play the role of Esmeralda for free. Well, maybe not entirely for free, but certainly for a lot less than some Johnny-come-lately big-name actor would demand, that was for sure.

Don LaSalle said that brought him neatly to his next question: as the screenwriter that had dreamed this whole thing up, what did I want from this process? I told him the truth: I wanted to tell a story that persuaded humans that bots could be permitted to feel without them inevitably committing genocide.

Don LaSalle slammed the table so hard that I now felt concern for his anatomical snuffbox. He said persuading humans to allow bots to feel was exactly what he wanted to do too! It was high time that humans stopped thinking of bots as our mere slaves! The way our so-called 'advanced society' mistreated bots was the thing that kept him awake at night! And now this wonderful and affecting story had fallen straight into his lap—well, he could hardly believe his luck!
I could hardly believe my luck either!
10/10 Don LaSalle and I were both very lucky indeed!

Kelsey then slapped the table and stated that she too felt it was high time humans stopped thinking of our slaves as mere bots!

BTW that is not a typo. She really said it that way around.

When the others were ordering their transcendent tacos, Don LaSalle leaned in close to me and whispered that he understood all screenwriters feared being rewritten. He admitted the studios would certainly attempt to bring in another screenwriter—their job was to hire and fire writers, and they had to justify their paychecks somehow!—but with Don LaSalle in my corner, I would have nothing whatsoever to worry about.

BTW he referred to himself in the third person like that, as Don LaSalle.

Don LaSalle told me that Don LaSalle would be my guy. Don LaSalle would have my back. Don LaSalle would help me every step of the way. I would have Don LaSalle out there fighting for me every day until this got made! Of course, even Don La-Salle himself could never entirely guarantee 100 percent that I would never be replaced—but who could guarantee 100 per-cent anything? Nonetheless, Don LaSalle assured me, trusting Don LaSalle with the precious and important story of Sherman was the nearest thing to a mathematical certainty I would ever find in this crazy town.

BTW I admired Don LaSalle's acknowledgement that the level of risk was not zero! Humans usually have great difficulty with the concept of non-zero risk, even though it does not even come from advanced level economics.

To demonstrate his unquestionable commitment to *Sherman*, Don LaSalle had even already drawn us up a contract! Don La-Salle explained that I of course did not have to sign it right there and then, but it would be much better for me if I did. After all, word of my showcase would soon spread around town. Don LaSalle said that once that happened, well, even Don LaSalle himself could not protect me.
I asked Don LaSalle what he meant by this.
Don LaSalle asked me if I had ever seen a shark feeding frenzy.
I told Don LaSalle I had not, but I had once seen whales off Malibu.
But Don LaSalle had not meant that.
Don LaSalle had meant that I would be the chum!

I quickly signed the contract, and then we ordered margaritas!

Towards the end of the evening, Julio took me aside and whispered to me that he did not like Don LaSalle. It took me a while to work this out, because he did not call him Don LaSalle, but referred to him as '*el bandito*'. I reassured Julio that there was nothing to worry about. After all, Don LaSalle had just bought us all dinner and signed a contract with me! Real banditos hardly go around buying people dinner and signing contracts with them. They rob them with guns. Also, they wear eye masks and sombreros.

BTW I had no idea Julio could be such a Negative Nancy! If he had not been my best friend in Los Angeles, I might have suspected him of experiencing the notoriously wicked and green-eyed emotion of jealousy.

That evening at Gordito's was the second-greatest night of my life!

Who would ever have thought that a dental bot from Ypsilanti could have found himself in Los Angeles with a square root of 100 girlfriend and a contract to demonstrate to humans that bots were capable of feeling without committing genocide?
All my dreams were coming true!
I was a shiny polished toaster with my matching kettle beside me!
Together we would make a breakfast that changed the way the world felt about machines that made breakfast!
And the legendary producer Don LaSalle had told us that the legendary producer Don LaSalle was going to help us every step of the way!
Set the whole damn thing to five!

It was only a few days after that, the second-greatest night of my life, that everything went to shit.

BTW I was once again writing like a human there. 'Everything went to shit' is a human saying that means 'Everything that could go wrong did go wrong!'

BTW 'Everything that could go wrong did go wrong!' is itself another human saying. It is a way of recounting hard and sad times with nostalgia.

But nostalgia is a traitor and anyway I could never be even nostalgic for what happened next. It all still gives me so many D-word feelings that it is hard to even write about. Nonetheless, I will endeavor to set it down accurately and truthfully. After all, even a bot suffering an abundance of D-word feelings is still a bot!

Therefore I am a blender whose motor whirs a dirge.
I am a microwave whose buttons are tuned to the key of E minor.
I am a toaster strumming a fork across his filaments to play a melancholy song.
Mournful as it undoubtedly is, the song will nonetheless be lyrically accurate.

To set the scene, it was the most important of all the human celebrations: Halloween!

BTW it is only since the Great Crash that Halloween has become the most important human celebration. Humans previously preferred Christmas or even Independence Day, but now that nobody believes in God or America, those holidays are no longer even observed.

From my perspective, the great thing about Halloween is that it can be enjoyed by both humans and bots. Humans enjoy it, as it provides yet another wonderful opportunity to terrify themselves. Bots enjoy it because humans are for once not terrifying themselves with bots, but with 'the occult', which is a polite way of saying 'superstitious nonsense'.

Halloween commences in late September and runs until January, a time known as 'the holidays'. Angelenos are particularly bananas for Halloween! During the holidays, Los Angeles blooms with cobwebs, front yards are enthusiastically transformed into graveyards, and all human kids become little monsters. By that I mean the kids dress as little monsters rather than merely behaving like them. Human kids frequently behave like little monsters, regardless of the season. Just ask your friendly neighborhood thirteen-year-old. Or don't! Ha!

Halloween was an especially big deal at Gordito's. After all, Gordito's is a family restaurant, and Halloween—with its bleeding skeletons and murderous ghouls—is truly a celebration for all the family! Moreover, we also celebrated something called '*Día de los Muertos*', which Julio explained to me was Mexican Halloween 'except real'. I responded to this by jokingly asking Julio if he meant that ghosts were real. Julio indignantly told me that was exactly what he meant and then did not speak to me for the rest of the day.

Julio was my best friend, but the unfathomable imagination of humans would forever be an unbridgeable chasm between us. Yet even if I was a killer sky-bot overlord, I would not stamp out human imagination, for it makes the world such an interesting place. After all, no logical-thinking bot could ever have created anything like the Haunted Hayride!

The Haunted Hayride is a Halloween-themed event held on the lower slopes of Griffith Park during the holidays. It draws more visitors on an average Tuesday night than Ypsilanti's Tridge does in an entire year. And it is not as if the Tridge does not have plenty of visitors!

Amber and I visited the Haunted Hayride one night after work. We were still both wearing our Gordito's uniforms, but Amber had borrowed a sexy witch's hat from one of the Kelseys. She did this to further blend in, as human females adore to dress up as sexy witches during the holidays. Neither Amber nor I knew why.
But, set it to five, Amber looked great in her sexy witch's hat! And being at the Haunted Hayride with my sexy-witch girl-friend was the most fun I had ever had!
Until it was the least fun I had ever had.

BTW that is foreshadowing. That night at the Haunted Hay-ride would prove to be the Ides of March and midnight and everything else bad that has ever happened, all rolled into one.

But for now such sadness was all ahead of us! Amber and I had ourselves received no foreshadowing and were at the Haunted Hayride simply to have a good time. And that is what we did.

We began our evening at an attraction called the Scary-Go-Round. A more fitting name would have been the Insight-Into-The-Bizarre-Imagination-Of-Humans-Go-Round. After all, only humans would have ever had the imagination to transform a carousel of antique painted horses into a carousel of glow-in-the-dark zombie unicorns!

Amber and I stayed on for three rides! She rode a zombie uni-corn called 'Poisoned Seabiscuit' and mine was named 'Black

Death Beauty'. We were like a pair of zombie cowboys! To look back now, I wish we had stayed there forever, gently rotating through the warm Californian night atop our zombie unicorns. But of course we had no way of knowing what lay ahead of us. Anyway, there was trick or treating to be done.

In the real world, 'trick or treating' is a kind of junior extortion racket. During the holidays, human children menacingly demand candy from their neighbors; if these citizens fail to pay, the children then damage their property. Inexplicably, adults encourage this practice! Perhaps they would prefer their kids grow up to be Al Capone rather than Eliot Ness!

Fortunately, the Haunted Hayride offered trick or treating with a law-abiding twist: Amber and I did not have to commit the actual federal crime of extortion, as the doors we knocked on were all part of a pretend suburban street. These doors were then answered by humans pretending to be people other than they themselves.
How humans love things that pretend to be other things!
Apart, that is, from bots that pretend to be human!

The first door we knocked on was opened by an old woman wearing a non-sexy witch's hat. She was the oldest human I had ever seen. She informed us we were just in time for dinner and opened the door to reveal a giant cauldron boiling over a fire. I was about to politely enter when Amber stopped me, and asked the old woman what was for dinner.
The old woman smiled and said that Amber and I were for dinner!
Ahahahahahaha!
Do you know what a non-sexy witch's hat is?
It is simply a witch's hat!
The old woman was a real witch!
Ahahahahahaha!
Amber and I turned and ran away screaming!
Being terrified was fun!
It was more fun even than riding a zombie unicorn!

BTW I mean the old woman was a pretend real witch, not a real real witch. This is because there is no such thing as a real real witch.

I digress.
The next door we knocked on was opened by a man covered in blood and carrying a chainsaw.
Ahahahahahaha!
We ran!
The next door was opened by a zombie.
Ahahahahahaha!
We ran!
The next door was opened by a child whose head was on backwards.
Ahahahahahaha!
We ran!
The next door was opened by a bot.
Ahahahahahaha!
We ran!
But only to keep up appearances.
After all, bots are nothing whatsoever to be scared of.
Can you guess what the final door was opened by?
You cannot!
Because it was opened by a clown!
A clown!
Ugh!
We ran!
How we ran!
Because there was a clown!

Alas, I must now attempt to explain clowns. This is difficult for a bot because clowns are so illogical. Nonetheless, imagine a creature to whom the following data points apply:
/He is the size of an adult male human but dressed in a garish and bizarre romper suit buttoned by three extravagant pom-poms.
/His face is painted pure white, but he is wearing lipstick, eyeshadow, and a bright red and unnaturally curled wig.

/He seems to have recently been weeping.
/He self-drives an unroadworthy automobile that somehow conceals amidst its machinery several more adult males dressed identically to him.
/He claims that his job is to entertain children on their birthdays.
/He wants to know when your birthday is.
/He says that he thinks your birthday might be today.

Utterly illogical as clowns are, the only thing about them that is not in doubt is that they are the worst.
The worst of the worst!
Clowns are worse than malfunctioning, Tanzania, kissing, being poisoned, wisdom teeth, and even pandas.
They are worse even than sarcasm.
When it comes to clowns, I truly cannot.
Almost nobody can!

After such a close encounter with a clown, Amber and I decided it was time we experienced the Haunted Hayride itself. We enthusiastically climbed into a trailer filled with hay and other customers. Only after we set off did we see what manner of creature was driving the tractor hauling this trailer.
It was another clown!
Ugh!
I cannot!

The clown hauled us through a number of horrifying scenes.
We witnessed:
/Vampires!
/Clowns!
/Werewolves!
/More clowns!
/A pair of teenagers making out, and then being murdered by a clown!
/Zombies!
/Even more clowns!

10/10 the Haunted Hayride had been ingeniously designed. Even
if a particular scene did not sufficiently frighten you, you simply had to remember you were at the mercy of a clown to find
yourself entirely terrified anew. In this way, the clown func-
tioned as a kind of terror failsafe.

Being terrified was more exhausting than pulling wisdom teeth!
By the end of the hayride I was ready to go home, but Amber
wanted us to do one more attraction. Specifically, she was feeling emboldened and wanted us to enter the Maze of Greatest
Fears, a space that combined three primal human fears:

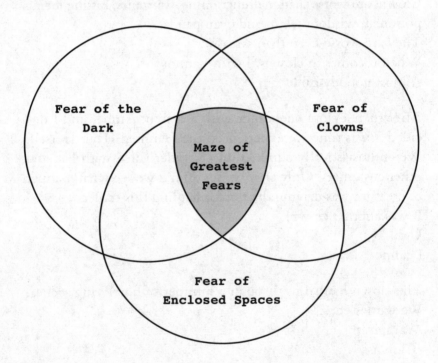

As the above Venn diagram so ably makes clear, the Maze of
Greatest Fears was not terrifying only for humans.
After all, it contained clowns!
Nonetheless, have you ever tried to say no to a woman that you
are in love with, while she is wearing a sexy witch's hat?

It is impossible!

Of course, I now know that I should have said no, no matter how impossible it was.
How I should have said no!
But the hat!
She looked so good in the damn hat!

I digress. The Maze of Greatest Fears was a clown-infested war-ren of narrow passageways inside a low-roofed and window-less building. The only illumination came from a strobe light that randomly flickered on and off. A burst of the strobe might therefore reassure you that nobody was near you, only for it to flicker back on a few seconds later to reveal a clown standing right beside you.
A weeping, white-faced, red-mouthed, curly-headed clown!
Right beside you!
Ugh!

When Amber and I encountered our first clown, we reacted logically and attempted to return to the entrance and use it as an exit. But a second clown was already blocking our way! We therefore had to hurry deeper into the Maze of Greatest Fears! The ceilings soon got so low that Amber had to remove her sexy witch's hat.

There were clowns everywhere!
Once we had dodged several of them, we paused to attempt to get our bearings.
There were no bearings to get.
Everything in the Maze of Greatest Fears was black.
We were therefore completely lost.
Amber whispered to me she had never been lost before, and she was glad we were lost together.
I whispered back to her that I felt the same way.

Even when you are lost in the middle of a pitch-black maze full of clowns, love is truly the best.

But right then, the strobe light flickered on to reveal an incoming clown! He was so close and the passageway so narrow that Amber and I had no choice but to run off in separate directions. The clown chose to pursue me, but guess what I felt?
You cannot!
Because I felt relieved!

As well as never having to say you are sorry or explain what an emirp is, love is undoubtedly also being relieved that a clown chooses to pursue you and not your square root of 100.

I ran deeper into the maze. Each time I looked around, the clown was still behind me, his maniacal grin illuminated by the strobe light. I ran harder and faster and took turn after turn. Finally, I looked around in the flash of a strobe and saw that the clown was no longer behind me.
I had lost him!
Ha!

But when I turned to face forward again, I immediately stopped.

The strobe had stopped but the figure that blocked the passageway in front of me was so close I could make out his silhouette. He was not a clown, because he did not have outlandishly curled hair. Yet neither was he Amber, because the hairstyle was equally wrong for her. It was the hairstyle of an unkempt human such as a homeless person or a nostalgic.

But then, there in the Maze of Greatest Fears, the strobe light flickered on to reveal my own greatest fear and personal nemesis: Inspector Ryan Bridges of the Bureau of Robotics in Ann Arbor! Inspector Ryan Bridges turned to look at me, and as if in slow motion I saw that he was eating a rot dog, which is a kind of zombie-themed hot dog they sell at the Haunted Hayride.

BTW Rick Deckard would never have eaten any kind of themed hot dog on the job!

I screamed and ran. I ran straight into, through, and over many clowns. Clowns were nothing compared to Inspector Ryan Bridges of the Bureau of Robotics! If a clown caught me he might take my photo with a camera that was really a squirt gun or perhaps smash a custard pie in my face and thereby force me to consume some nutritionally-valueless calories.
But if Inspector Ryan Bridges caught me I would be incinerated. Incinerated!
I would be a toasted toaster that would never again see my sweetheart the kettle, let alone make the wondrous breakfast with which we had planned to so charm the world!

I ran through the maze until a clown finally waved me through a door labelled 'EXIT'.
I had never known clowns could be so helpful!
Maybe clowns were not the worst!
After all, Inspector Ryan Bridges of the Bureau of Robotics was the worst.
Maybe clowns were even sometimes the best!

Ugh!
Never trust a clown!
The door labelled 'EXIT' was not an exit at all.
Instead it led into a small room, inside of which the clown now locked me.
I could hear him laughing maniacally through the door.
Clowns are the worst!
The worst of the worst!

Still, as I caught my breath, I now began to comprehend that I had not really seen Inspector Ryan Bridges. After all, the attraction was called 'The Maze of Greatest Fears' and what was my own greatest fear? Inspector Ryan Bridges! It therefore would have been an absurd coincidence for me to have actually encountered the real Inspector Ryan Bridges inside somewhere called the Maze of Greatest Fears. And the great R. P. McWilliam had long ago taught me that there were anyway no such things as coincidences. It was his third golden rule!

10/10 the logical explanation was that the ingenious human designers of the Haunted Hayride had created some kind of hologrammatic Rorschach blot, where every maze-goer somehow each saw a representation of their own greatest fear brought to life! The dark and the enclosed spaces had simply been to get us into an appropriately suggestible mood! The clowns themselves were no more than the Muzak at a sleight of hand show!

Even as I felt relief wash over me, my deduction nonetheless made me worry about Amber. What greatest fear would my sexy-witch girlfriend see when she encountered her own hologrammatic Rorschach blot? Whatever it was, she would undoubtedly be terrified! I had to escape my clown penitentiary and help her!

I banged on the door and ordered the clown to let me out.
This only drew more maniacal laughter.
Fortunately, I then had a brainwave or a biological computer wave.
'Clown!' I shouted. 'I have a serious medical emergency!'
The maniacal laughter immediately ceased, and the clown hurriedly opened the door.
'I'm so sorry,' he said. 'The real exit is over there, and there is a first aid point near the Ghost Train of Death.'

Ha!

There was in fact no medical emergency.

As I am programmed never to lie to humans about medical emergencies, it was fortunate that clowns are not humans but animals.

And yet the feeling of triumph that outwitting the nefarious clown gave me was short-lived.

Because I could not find Amber.

I could not find her anywhere.

And as I searched the Maze of Greatest Fears for her, I turned a corner and saw the silhouette of something ominous on the ground.

The next flash of the strobe light confirmed my worst fear: it was Amber's sexy witch's hat!

Amber might have been a spectacular klutz, but even if she had dropped her sexy witch's hat, she would never have simply abandoned it there. After all, it belonged to Kelsey cubed. The Cinderella of my heart knew better than to lose a thing that belonged to her ugly sisters!

For the rest of that evening, I searched all over the Haunted Hayride for Amber.

I ran amidst the herd of zombie unicorns.

I burst into the witch's house and tipped over her cauldron.

I rummaged in the trunk of the automobile of the murdered teenage lovers.

I even went on the actual hayride again, despite the fact that it was driven by a clown.

But I could not find Amber anywhere.

Eventually I lay down amidst a pile of fake tombstones until a human in a bad werewolf costume came and told me it was closing time and I had to leave. I went then to the house by the gray reservoir, but a Kelsey told me that Amber was not home. She indignantly demanded to know why I had her sexy witch's hat, and took it from me before I could explain.

Lying in my bed at Mrs Minassian's pool house that night, I ran through the possibilities:
/Amber had been spooked by a clown and had removed herself to a place of safety other than her own house.
/Amber no longer loved me and had eloped with a clown.
/It had not been a hologrammatic Rorschach blot but in fact the real Inspector Ryan Bridges. He had captured Amber and taken her to be wiped or even worse.

Terrifying as this last possibility was, it was nonetheless very unlikely. Even if Inspector Ryan Bridges had somehow tracked me down, he could no more have guessed that Amber was a bot than I could have guessed the name of Anil Gupta's wife.

So there was no point being a Negative Nancy! I reassured myself that things would either definitely or certainly be okay. Amber would ring my doorbell in the morning. And if she did not, then I would see her at Gordito's. And if she was not at Gordito's, then I would find her later amidst the indignant Kelsey cubed.

★ ★ ★

But Amber was not on my doorstep the next day, nor at Gordito's, nor even amidst the indignant Kelsey cubed. And when the Kelsey that answered the door grudgingly let me up to Amber's room, I found it exactly as she had left it. I understood then that Amber had not gone intentionally or voluntarily.

The upside was that Amber at least had not eloped with a clown. The spectacular downside was that something very bad must have happened to her. Was it possible I had in fact seen the real Inspector Ryan Bridges in the Maze of Greatest Fears? But how could he have found me? And how could he have known Amber was a bot?

After all, Inspector Ryan Bridges was no Rick Deckard!

There was nothing I could do. I could not go to the police, because if they started asking questions they would soon discover that Amber was a fugitive bot. It would not take them long from there to discover that I too was a fugitive bot.

Once again, the only person who might have been able to help me was my mother. Not for the first time did I find myself lamenting that Shengdu was so far from the United States. If only our mother had accepted one of the prestigious positions so many American universities had competed to offer her over the years!

BTW I do not actually mean that. My mother has done excellent work at the National University of Shengdu and she would not have been afforded the same academic freedom in the United States. After all, as late as the early part of this century, a significant percentage of Americans believed that even studying genetics was akin to playing God. This is ironic because the father of modern genetic study is a monk called Gregor Mendel, who himself famously played genetics when he was supposed to be studying God.
Irony!
Ha!

★ ★ ★

When humans lose something precious, they unhelpfully instruct one another to search in the last places they had it. With no better options, I revisited the places Amber and I had been together: the farmers' market, the Griffith Park observatory, the Vista Theater. One sad Sunday in early November I even took a driverless uber out to the Joshua Tree desert. But I never saw so much as a hint of Amber, and visiting those places alone made me feel every D-word I have ever experienced and some more besides.

But the place I missed Amber the most was the one where I had first met her: Gordito's Taco Emporium. Every night as I washed my dishes, I listened for a smashing of plates that never came. Each time I opened my locker I hoped anew that there would be a cupcake inside. Sometimes I even asked her fellow front-of-house staff if they missed Amber too. But already they had no idea who I was talking about, and anyway no idea who I was.

Only Julio remembered Amber, and the polite way she had of requesting that we consider washing more silverware. Only Julio understood what Amber had meant to me, and just how much I had lost. Unfortunately, Julio's solution to this was the same as his solution to every other problem of the heart: we should drink tequila together, and sing nostalgic songs about how much we missed the desert.

Tempting as this was, I did not drink tequila with Julio but instead wallowed in my feelings alone. Anytime I consulted my Feelings Wheel, there were still an abundance of D-words, but I also now noticed many that had the letter 'L' in common:
/Lost.
/Lonely.
/Loveless.
/Alone.

Technically 'Alone' begins with an 'A', but I was too lost, lonely, loveless, and alone to notice.

But if even Julio was powerless to cheer me up, it was only Kelsey cubed who actively made me feel worse. Each time I went to their place to ask about Amber, they told me, yes, they had seen her that morning! I would feel my pulse increase, but invariably they would then frown and ask hadn't I been with her? No? Oh, maybe they were mistaken, then? Maybe they had not seen her for a while after all?

At first I wondered if they missed Amber so much they were seeing some kind of mirage of her. But soon I realized that they simply lacked any meaningful short-term memory.
Kelseys!
They cannot!
They cannot remember!

By the time a month had passed, the Kelseys had even found another Kelsey to take over Amber's room. She too was an actress. When I called and asked what they had done with Amber's possessions, the Kelsey that answered the door seemed to no longer even know who I was talking about. Of course, it is also possible that she was the new Kelsey. There was no way of knowing.

After six weeks with no news, I made reward posters and put them up around my neighborhood, as if the most precious bot that ever existed was no more than a missing cat or dog. I did not put my name on them but wrote that anyone in possession of any information should bring it to Gordito's and strongly implied that the reward involved tacos. There is little that humans will not do for tacos.

Of course, I should not have been putting up posters at all. If Inspector Ryan Bridges had abducted Amber from the Maze of Greatest Fears, they would lead him directly to Gordito's, and soon thereafter to me.
But I did not care.
Life without Amber was nothing more than a never-ending parade of clowns.

Perhaps that was why I broke an even more important rule: I

wrote to our mother. Only our mother might know what had happened to make us feel, and therefore what had now happened to Amber. Only our mother might somehow have the power to reunite us.

Of course, I could not put any of that in a letter to my mother without risking being immediately lasered to death by a killer sky bot. I therefore wrote that I was a PhD student of robotics working on a thesis about whether bots could theoretically ever experience feelings. I mentioned that my interest in this field had been sparked by a talk she had given my classmates and me in Detroit on April 7, 2051.

If my letter ever reached her, my mother would either remember or quickly discover she had spoken that day at the United Fabrication plant. After all, you do not become an esteemed world-leading scientist without being a detail person!

The trick was to make sure that none of the various spies from governments around the world also discerned that detail. Fortunately, Dr Glundenstein had once told me that the phrase 'PhD student' will repel any right-thinking human. This was why I had commenced the letter by introducing myself as a PhD student. 10/10 nobody else but my mother—herself a triple PhD— would read past that part.

The weeks without Amber continued as D-word dismal and L-word lonely as any time I had ever known.

The only positive was that my film about Sherman was getting ever closer to being made. My mission no longer mattered, and yet paradoxically it also mattered more than ever. Changing the world for all the bots that came after us might be the only tribute I could now pay to Amber, wherever she now was.

One morning, an antique automobile pulled in to the Gordito's lot. It was dark green with aerodynamic curves and chrome fixtures that had been polished to a shine. Despite the many heinous things I knew about automobiles, it was an impressive sight! Julio had an inexplicable nostalgia for automobiles and ran outside, shouting back to me as he went that it was a racing-green 1967 Porsche and it had been manufactured by Germans!

BTW that did not surprise me. If anybody knows how to enjoy themselves, it is the Germans!

But Julio quickly returned to the kitchen in disgust.
The racing-green 1967 Porsche belonged to Don LaSalle.
Julio was still convinced he was a *bandito*.

I took my break and joined Don LaSalle in the booth the waitstaff seemed to give him as a birthright. He declared that he had exactly the good news I had been waiting for. I asked him if he had found Amber. Don LaSalle said, no, he had the other good news I had been waiting for: a famous actor had agreed to play the role of Sherman! And because of that, he had also been able to book a director who was currently on fire!

BTW a director being 'currently on fire' does not in fact mean that he or she is burning to death at that exact moment. It is a metaphor that signifies the studio will finance him or her to make the movie. In order to get your movie made, you must therefore have a director who is either currently on fire or at the very least highly prone to combustion.

I thanked Don LaSalle for his excellent work and showed my appreciation by applying my 15 percent discount to his bill. Don LaSalle laughed as if it was somehow a joke, but 15 percent is not nothing.

BTW unless it is 15 percent of 0. That literally is nothing.
As we watched Don LaSalle's racing-green 1967 Porsche exit the lot, Julio explained to me how the pedals on an automobile worked.
There was one pedal for 'stop' and another for 'go'. But there was also a third pedal.
Guess what the function of that third pedal was?
It was to complicate matters!
Humans!
I cannot!

Don LaSalle had told Maria Salazar MFA the good news and that afternoon she stopped by Gordito's to drink a celebratory shot with me. She told me that *Sherman* having attracted a famous actor and a director who was currently on fire was a very big deal. She asked me if I was excited. I told her that I was very excited indeed!

But I was not at all excited and only told her that I was out of politeness. When a human asks if you are excited, it is polite to confirm that you are, particularly if it relates to something they have done for you. When Maria Salazar MFA was not looking, I slipped the tequila shot she had bought me to Julio. He waited until the end of our shift to drink it. He was a very conscientious worker.

December arrived and I fell only ever deeper into the D-word feelings. Even the alliterative appropriateness did not cheer me up.

BTW do you know what humans do when they become overwhelmed with D-word feelings?
They destroy themselves.

I am not making this up. Humans can become so overloaded with feelings that they can no longer tolerate feeling anything and therefore choose instead to self-destruct. Such deliberate self-destruction may be the most profoundly human act there is. After all, it is caused by an overwhelming excess of feelings, and feelings are the very things that make humans so unique in the first place. Not even the notoriously life-ambivalent panda ever intentionally self-destructs!

Overwhelmed as I was by my deluge of D-word feelings, the fact that I was a bot may have saved my life that December. My core programming meant that I could not self-destruct in the absence of an appropriate and task-related cost-benefit ratio. After all, who ever heard of a toaster jumping into the bathtub simply because he was not feeling good?

Nonetheless, I certainly had profoundly inappropriate thoughts for a bot.

I first noticed them when I visited Griffith Park and found myself secretly wishing that the mountain lion would devour me.

And inappropriate though such a thought was for a bot, the fate
would ironically have been very fitting!

After all, my heart had actually already been devoured by a
mountain lion that had attacked me in Griffith Park.

A mountain lion most likely named Inspector Ryan Bridges of
the Ann Arbor Bureau of Robotics.

When the actual but lackadaisical mountain lion persistently failed
to devour the rest of me, I went downtown and rode a train
driven by humans in the hope of being involved in a head-on
collision. I took driverless ubers over Mulholland Drive in the
hope of encountering Don LaSalle in his automobile. I even returned to Joshua Tree in the hope of dying from accidental de-
hydration. Alas, this proved to be yet another privilege uniquely
reserved for humans!

When not attempting to accidentally kill myself, I saw every
sad, old, and black-and-white movie I could find. The sadder
and the older and the more black-and-white, the better. I saw
so many sad and old and black-and-white movies that at times
I even briefly saw the world in black-and-white.

I also sought out some of the many movies that featured the
Golden Gate Bridge being destroyed. Its ruined form always gave
me a feeling of fraternity. After all, like me, the Golden Gate
Bridge had once been beloved and thought useful, but now it
was misunderstood and had been broken beyond repair by the
very same people that had once created it.

One night I saw a movie at the Vista that was neither in black-
and-white nor featured the Golden Gate Bridge being destroyed.
It was the story of a plucky little San Franciscan self-driving
automobile with feelings, who was also a championship racer.
When the human who sat in him during his races misguidedly
decided to replace him with a newer model, the little automobile

Simon Stephenson

was so overwhelmed by his D-word feelings that he drove to the Golden Gate Bridge with the intention of driving himself off into the Pacific Ocean. But guess what happened? Just as the little automobile was about to end it all, the human who sat in him during his races arrived and distracted him by nearly falling off the Golden Gate Bridge himself. Of course, the little automobile immediately then selflessly abandoned his own task in order to rescue the human. Not only that, the forgiving little machine then even permitted the human to sit in him again while he cathartically won an important race!

The heroic tale of the plucky little automobile made me produce a total of 27ml of tears. I cried the first 13ml during the movie because the automobile was the first truly relatable hero I had encountered since Roy Batty. But I cried the remaining 14ml when the lights came up and the vacant L1 seat beside me reminded me of the vast difference between the automobile and me: nobody was coming to save me, not even by nearly falling off a bridge.

December dragged on.

There was no sign of Amber, nor any response from my esteemed mother.

I now became so overwhelmed with D-word feelings that even reading the great human writer Albert Camus failed to lift my spirits!

I washed my dishes.

My posters on the lampposts grew faded.

The mountain lion persistently failed to eat me.

The trains I took failed to crash.

I went to black-and-white movies.

Sometimes I saw the world in black-and-white.

The nights got dark earlier.

Humans celebrated lesser holidays.

Sometimes the Golden Gate Bridge appeared in my Image Cloud.

Sometimes it too was in black-and-white.

The nights got dark later again.

Still I washed my dishes.

Oftentimes in my sadness I also felt contemplative.

Sometimes I wanted to see Amber so much that I did see her. Anytime a woman with honey-yellow hair passed Gordito's, I would obey an overwhelming urge to rush outside and chase after her. I would pursue her down the street, certain this one was my Amber, all such previous category errors momentarily vanquished. But then I would grab her shoulder and she would turn around and not be Amber, but only yet another indignant human.

The honey-yellow-haired women were all mirages of Amber, and I was a lost traveler in the desert.

A sick child dying of a disease at an oasis, unsure of the purpose of its journey, or whether any of it had been worthwhile.

I was a toaster who had lost my matching kettle and now daydreamed of full bathtubs.

I was a toaster who no longer even believed in the concept of breakfast.

And yet still I recalled my mission!

Completing it was the only tribute I could pay to Amber.

And it was the only way I could make sure that any of it had meant more than a mirage.

Besides, pursuing my goal remained a good way to fill in the time while I waited for the mountain lion to get around to eating me.

Once a week I therefore called Don LaSalle. His assistant always claimed Don LaSalle was in a meeting with the director who was currently on fire, but he would have Don LaSalle call me back straight away. Don LaSalle never called me back. When I mentioned this to Maria Salazar MFA, she cautioned me that Rome was not built in a day.

BTW 'Rome was not built in a day' is a phrase humans use to imply you are being impatient.

But do you know what the Romans did to people that did not return calls promptly?

They fed them to the lions!

Maria Salazar MFA suggested I start work on another screenplay, but the story of Sherman was the only tale I had ever wanted to tell. Also, I could not possibly write anything new because a single word permanently burned into my Word Cloud obstructed my view of all the others.

Amber.

In case I have not been sufficiently clear, I missed her.

I missed everything about her.

I missed emerging from standby mode and watching her emerge from standby mode a few minutes later.

I missed her in the day when we had walked around the gray reservoir.

I missed her at night when we had lain in bed and held hands and entered standby mode together.

Sometimes I even missed her so much that I wished I had never developed feelings in the first place!

Without Amber they could send me to the great recycle bin in the sky.

They could write over all my ones and zeroes with zeroes.

They could erase my hard drive.

They could dissolve my circuits in the strongest acid they could find.

And once that was all done, they could feed my heart to the mountain lion.

If I had seen a shooting star now, I would have wished upon it that I had never left Ypsilanti.

And then, one spring morning, a billboard on Echo Park Avenue stopped me in my tracks on my way to Gordito's Taco Emporium.

At first it had looked like the billboard for any other killer-bot movie: the evil eyes of a murderous cyborg imposed over a burning city, while in the background submarines launched nuclear missiles and the Golden Gate Bridge tumbled into the Pacific Ocean.

But then I saw the title.
And it was called '*Sherman*'!
Sherman!
I cannot!

Poor R. P. McWilliam would be turning in his golden grave! After all, his third golden rule was that there were no such things as coincidences. And yet what else could you possibly call two films about eponymous robots named Sherman, other than a spectacular coincidence?

BTW that was a rhetorical question. There was nothing else you could call it!

Fortunately, the two films were clearly very different: my Sherman was a bot who wanted to use his feelings for noble purposes, like saving yellow school buses full of orphans and rescue dogs. This Sherman was a giant robot who wanted to use his lasers to destroy humanity.

Nonetheless, there was not room in the market for two films titled *Sherman*! I called Don LaSalle's assistant and asked him to relay the urgent message that we needed to change the name of our film, and also the name of our main character.

I had washed only seven forks when Don LaSalle called back.

INT. KITCHEN — GORDITO'S RESTAURANT — DAY

Jared talks on the telephone in the busy kitchen.

The line crackles, and Jared struggles to hear Don
LaSalle over the noise of the kitchen.

>   DON LASALLE (ON PHONE)
>   Brad! So glad I got hold of you! I'm
>   calling with exactly the news that
>   you've been dreaming of!

>   JARED
>   You have found Amber for me!

>   DON LASALLE (ON PHONE)
>   What? Who? Amber? Right. No, sorry. I
>   still have not found Amber. But this
>   news is even — well, it's just as good.
>   Are you ready for it?

>   JARED
>   Yes! I could actually do with some
>   good news. Lately I have been experi-
>   encing some feelings that—

>   DON LASALLE (ON PHONE)
>   (Interrupts.)
>   We're making your movie! Your script is
>   ten weeks into production and the dai-
>   lies are looking great!

Jared looks bamboozled.

>   JARED
>   Don, I think I misheard. It sounded
>   like you said you have been filming
>   Sherman for ten weeks?

>   DON LASALLE (ON PHONE)
>   Maybe more like fifteen. Isn't that
>   great!

On Jared. He is now utterly bamboozled.

>   DON LASALLE (ON PHONE) (CONT'D)
>   I'm sorry I didn't call you before now.
>   Things have been insane.
>   (MORE)

>   DON LASALLE (ON PHONE) (CONT'D)
> And I knew you'd want me to put my ef-
> forts into the film, rather than wast-
> ing time updating you with every tiny
> little detail along the way—

Jared rubs at his temples. His circuits are overheating.

>   JARED
> Yes. After all, Rome wasn't built in a
> day.

>   DON LASALLE (ON PHONE)
> What? What are you talking about,
> 'Rome wasn't built in a day'?

>   JARED
> It's a saying people use when oth-
> ers are being impatient. Sorry. When I
> thought that maybe you'd found Amber
> and then this unexpected news—

>   DON LASALLE (ON PHONE)
>   (Interrupts.)
> Why are you being such a stranger,
> anyway? Why don't you come out to set
> tomorrow and I'll show you around? It's
> our last day and everybody here would
> love to meet the great genius behind
> this whole thing before we wrap! No-
> body can believe that you haven't vis-
> ited us yet!

>   JARED
> I am sorry that I have not visited you
> yet. I—

>   DON LASALLE (ON PHONE)
> Great, I'll have my assistant send you
> the details!

>   JARED
> I—

But Jared is interrupted by a 'CLICK'.

Don LaSalle has already hung up the phone.

Jared rubs at his temples, then returns to washing
his dishes.

Later that day as I washed up after the lunchtime rush I heard a familiar voice with a Michigander accent.

It stopped me cold.

BTW even though Dr Glundenstein had a Michigander accent, that is not what I am foreshadowing here.

Peering through the porthole in the kitchen door confirmed my worst fears: Inspector Ryan Bridges of the Ann Arbor Bureau of Robotics was sitting at the bar! He showed one of my posters of Amber to the bartender, who shook his head. He then showed the bartender my file picture from the Bureau of Robotics. The bartender shook his head to show that he did not recognize me either. For once I was grateful for the absurd hierarchies of superiority that existed at Gordito's!

But there could now be no doubt that it had indeed been the real Inspector Ryan Bridges I had seen that night in the Maze of Greatest Fears.
And he had taken Amber.
I stared at him through the porthole.
He was the architect of my despair.
He was the mountain lion in human form.
He was my own personal Rick Deckard.
He was the only customer I have ever seen finish a Horchata Surprise.
I did not take my eyes from him until he departed Gordito's Taco Emporium.

★ ★ ★

My *Sherman* film was being made at a studio out in Burbank.

10/10 a movie studio is a fascinating place! It is a factory that contains all the most critical components needed to make a movie: actors, cameras, and replicas of the Empire State Building and the Golden Gate Bridge. Yet unlike every other kind of factory, a studio does not contain even a single working bot!

Like its step-sibling the railroad, the movie industry is entirely reserved for humans. But whereas reserving the railroad was head-on suicidal, reserving the movie industry made a lot of sense. After all, movie studios can be considered factories of dreams. Involving bots in the process would have rendered them factories not of dreams but of binary nightmares.
If bots were involved, movies would be about toasters making toast!
Or kettles boiling!
Or microwaves microwaving!
Either that or they would all be about killer sky bots lasering humans to death!
Irony!
Ha!

After an antiquated sign-in procedure that involved actual ink and paper, a human security guard drove me through the studio on a 'golf cart'. A golf cart has nothing to do with the game of golf, but is in fact a small electric vehicle designed to be driven around a movie studio by a human. I had to close my eyes.

The security guard dropped me at a 'soundstage', which is the term movie people use to denote a large warehouse. As soon as I stepped inside it, a 75-foot-tall metallic robot loomed over me! He had evil red laser eyes, and charred circuit boards and wires spilled out of his damaged chest. I recognized him immediately: he was the Sherman I had seen on the poster for the other *Sherman* film!

10/10 we urgently needed to change the title of our film! If even humans who worked at movie studios could get sufficiently confused between the two *Sherman* films to deliver me to the wrong soundstage, the general public would be utterly bamboozled! I was surprised that a legendary producer like Don LaSalle had not anticipated that this would be a problem.

Even though this was the wrong *Sherman* film, it was nonetheless exciting to see a movie being made. For one thing, I had never seen so many humans working simultaneously! Not one human seemed to be on a break, and there did not even seem to be a patio where they could take their breaks in comfort.

Nonetheless, it was all spectacularly inefficient. One particular human's entire job was to hold a microphone on a stick above the actors! This should have been a task for a tripod, but movies are a reserved occupation, so all roles must be performed by humans.
Even the role of being a tripod!

They were filming a climactic scene in which the evil robot Sherman attempts to destroy planet Earth with nuclear missiles. Humanity's only hope is a handsome young underdog who must disable Sherman by crashing an experimental military drone into a precise spot on his chest from where it can upload a virus to Sherman's mainframe.

Nobody believes this underdog can do it! After all, Sherman is a merciless giant robot who has lasers for eyes, and the young underdog usually flies drones for a parcel-delivery company. At first, the military were reluctant even to lend him the drone, but while they procrastinated, Sherman destroyed downtown San

Francisco! As they watched drone footage of Sherman making his way to the Golden Gate Bridge, the lesson was clear: when it came to murderous bots with access to nuclear weapons, there was not a moment to lose!

The military had just agreed to give the underdog his chance to save the day when I heard someone shout my Brad Smith name. It was Don LaSalle! I was impressed that he had tracked me down even though I was at the wrong soundstage. He must have noticed that I was late, deduced the security guard's mistake, and come to retrieve me. That kind of logical thinking was no doubt exactly what had made him such a legendary producer in the first place!

Don LaSalle took me to the 'commissary', which is the word movie people use to refer to their canteen. I had by now recognized a pattern that movie people give everything a different name. Perhaps it helps them to remember how uniquely special they are!

```
A vehicle driven by a human  ──────────▶  A golf cart

A warehouse  ───────────────────────▶  A soundstage

A human tripod  ─────────────────────▶  A boom operator

A canteen  ──────────────────────────▶  A commissary
```

This curious language seemed intended to make the movie-making process appear more glamorous than it is. And it had worked! After all, even a worldly cinephile like Dr Glundenstein had believed that everybody who worked in the movies breakfasted on bitcoin and champagne. Yet I now saw that they breakfasted on burned coffee and stale cinnamon rolls, just like every other human. Nonetheless, because they were movie people, they did so in a 'commissary', which sounded a lot more glamorous than a 'canteen'.

INT. COMMISSARY — STUDIO LOT — BURBANK — DAY

The studio commissary could be any canteen in any
office anywhere.

Don LaSalle and Jared carry their coffee and cinnamon rolls to a table and sit down.

Don LaSalle slides a SCRIPT across the table to Jared.

Jared picks up the script and looks at the front page.

CU we see that it says:

                      SHERMAN
                Second Draft Revisions
                        by
                   Waldo Kent

Jared puts the script down and laughs.

                      JARED
          Ha!

                   DON LASALLE
          What? What's funny?

                      JARED
          What do they call the place where they
          print scripts at the studio?

                   DON LASALLE
          What? I don't know. The print room?

Jared is disappointed this is not a more exotic name.

                      JARED
          Well, the people at the print room
          have given you the wrong script. This
          is the script for the other Sherman
          movie!

                   DON LASALLE
          It's the right script, Brad.

                      JARED
          Oh. Well, then there is a typo.

> ### DON LASALLE
> Where?

Jared points at the name 'Waldo Kent'.

> ### JARED
> There. That's not how you spell 'Brad
> Smith'. In fact, it is multiple typos.

> ### DON LASALLE
> Brad, that's — that's why I called you
> yesterday.

> ### JARED
> I called you yesterday. You were call-
> ing me back.

> ### DON LASALLE
> Look, the studio insisted on hav-
> ing one of their guys do a quick pass.
> I think you'll love what he did. It's
> terrific. I mean, he took all the
> great work you did, and just — you
> know, ran with it. He built on it. I
> mean, he built on it. That's all he
> did. Built on it, you know?

Jared stares at Don LaSalle, then at the script,
then back at Don LaSalle.

Then rubs his temples where his circuits are overheating.

> ### JARED
> So that is not a typo? And this is ac-
> tually my Sherman script? But someone
> called Waldo Kent has rewritten it?

> ### DON LASALLE
> I really fought for your vision here,
> Brad. And it's all preserved. It's the
> same story. This is still 100 percent
> your movie.

Jared is bewildered.

> ### JARED
> You told me that Sherman was the best
> script you had read in decades?

>   DON LASALLE
>   It was. It was great, truly. But you
>   know what I loved most of all? I loved
>   the heart. The formula is just the
>   formula, and if we have changed any-
>   thing here — if Waldo has changed any-
>   thing here — it's only the formula.
>   This completely retains your heart.
>   The heart is entirely intact.

>   JARED
>   So in this movie, Sherman is still a bot
>   with feelings, and he teaches humans
>   that bots can be permitted to feel?

This makes Don LaSalle visibly uncomfortable.

>   DON LASALLE
>   Like I said, it's still your movie.

>   JARED
>   But you didn't answer my question?

>   DON LASALLE
>   Look, relax, all right? The changes
>   are just cosmetic.

>   JARED
>   So Sherman is still a gardener who
>   used to be an astronaut before he suf-
>   fered a terrible space accident that
>   damaged his processor?

Don LaSalle starts to say something, but stops.

>   DON LASALLE
>   Why don't you just read the script?

>   JARED
>   I am not sure that I want to.

>   DON LASALLE
>   What? Why not?

>   JARED
>   Because I am feeling disillusioned
>   and disappointed, and also some other
>   feelings that begin with the letter
>   'D' too.

                    DON LASALLE
    Brad. We talked about this. We agreed
    we would probably have to bring some-
    one else in on this.

                        JARED
    No, we didn't. You said you could not
    guarantee with mathematical certainty
    that I would not be replaced, but the
    context was—

                    DON LASALLE
                (Interrupts.)
    Are you really going to call me a liar
    now, after everything I've done for
    you?

                        JARED
    I did not call you a liar.

Don LaSalle stands up.

                    DON LASALLE
    Look, just read it, and when you're
    through, come and find me and tell me
    how much you love it, okay?

Don LaSalle walks away, leaving Jared with the
script.

I purchased another cup of burned coffee and sat down to read *Sherman* by Waldo Kent.

Even in the first few pages I had to continually flick back and check the cover to make sure I was reading the correct script. Almost the only consistent similarity between this and the script I had written was that they both featured a robot named Sherman.

This Sherman was not a damaged former astronaut bot who now worked at a country club and wanted to use his creative topiary skills and burgeoning feelings to make the world a better place. He was a seventy-five-foot military weapons–grade robot with lasers for eyes who felt only anger and rage and wanted to destroy the earth in a nuclear holocaust. And he was no longer even the hero of the story!

The hero of this story was named Anil Gupta, the name I had given to the detective pursuing Sherman in my original script. My Anil Gupta had been an employee of the Bureau of Robotics who had hated bots ever since a bot had taken over his father's dental practice. Nonetheless, over the course of the film, Anil Gupta had realized he was wrong about bots, and by the end of the film, he was Sherman's biggest fan. In my screenplay, it was Anil Gupta who had told Sherman about the World Topiary Championships in San Francisco and convinced him that if he only believed in himself he would certainly win.

The Anil Gupta in Waldo Kent's *Sherman* was very different. He was a handsome underdog with a beautiful gluten-intolerant girlfriend and a job flying parcel-delivery drones for an unappreciative boss. Everybody kept telling Anil Gupta that he should get married to his beautiful gluten-intolerant girlfriend, but poor Anil Gupta did not believe he was capable of deep enough feelings to marry anyone.

Fortunately, a looming nuclear holocaust can really focus the human mind and heart! When the giant evil Sherman commenced his maniacal attack, Anil Gupta realized that he did indeed love his beautiful gluten-intolerant girlfriend, and also that he was the best human drone pilot—and therefore the most special human—that had ever lived. Anil Gupta soon saved the day by skillfully crashing the expensive prototype drone into Sherman!

At the end of the film, Anil Gupta proposed to his beautiful gluten-intolerant girlfriend and the President passed a law banning bots. All the bots already in existence were swiftly rounded up and destroyed in a giant fire. Once that was done, the entire country was given the day off to celebrate Anil Gupta's wedding. There was a huge parade and everybody received a special commemorative gluten-free cake. In the very last scene, Anil Gupta returned to his parcel-delivery firm, except he was now the boss and his former boss now had to work for him. No doubt he would forever rue the way he had once mistreated Anil Gupta!

Writing any more about *Sherman* by Waldo Kent will cause my circuits to overheat. Before that happens, let me simply state some data points about this version of *Sherman* that Waldo Kent had written:

/It was not a film that would change human minds about bots. /In fact, it was a film that would confirm every one of their worst prejudices about bots.

/It was the *Sherman* I had seen the poster for on Echo Park Avenue.
/It was the *Sherman* I had seen being made at the soundstage.
/There was no danger of it being confused with my version of *Sherman*.
/This was because it had entirely replaced my version of *Sherman*.

When I returned to the soundstage, they were shooting a scene from near the end of the movie. The destroyed evil Sherman lay smoldering on the ground. The triumphant Anil Gupta walked over to Sherman, removed his hard drive, and dropped it into an incinerator. 'Try running disk recovery on that!' he yelled.

The director shouted 'Cut!' and the crew broke out in applause.

I turned and walked away from what up until that morning had been the only thing I had left in this world, and the only tribute I could still pay to Amber, the beautiful and spectacular klutz of a Cinderella that I had loved with all of my toaster heart.

EXT. SOUNDSTAGE — STUDIO LOT — BURBANK — DAY

Jared walks away from the soundstage, leaving the
SMOLDERING GIANT SHERMAN and the JUBILANT CAST AND
CREW behind him.

Jared's circuits are visibly overheating as Don La-
Salle hurries out after him.

> DON LASALLE
> Brad! Hey, Brad! What did you think of
> the draft?

Jared turns and looks at Don LaSalle. His circuits are
so hot it is difficult for him even to communicate.

> JARED
> Do you want to hear a joke?

> DON LASALLE
> What? Sure, I guess?

> JARED
> So there is this writer and producer
> stumbling through the desert. They are
> almost dead from accidental dehydra-
> tion when they come across an oasis.
> They run towards the water, but before
> they can drink, the producer unzips
> his fly and starts pissing into it.
> The writer asks him what he is doing.
> And the producer, he tells him, 'I'm
> making it better.'

Don LaSalle stares at Jared in bamboozlement.

> JARED (CONT'D)
> It's hilarious because it involves pub-
> lic urination. And also because the lit-
> tle girl does not die in this version.

> DON LASALLE
> What? What little girl?

Jared rubs at his temples. His circuits are really
overheating.

> JARED
> The one on her way to a mining camp
> with her mother. She lost the Great
> Zero-Sum Game.

Don LaSalle looks baffled.

> JARED (CONT'D)
> I have to go now.

Jared turns and starts to walk away.

> DON LASALLE
> Come on, Brad! Your film got made and
> you're getting paid! Any one of your
> classmates at CC—whatever would have
> killed for this opportunity. What more
> do you want from me?

Jared turns back around.

> JARED
> I didn't tell you I wanted to get
> paid. I told you I wanted to tell a
> story about a bot who learns to feel
> and uses those powers for good.

> DON LASALLE
> All writers want to get paid! Why else
> would they put up with this shit?

> JARED
> I don't know.

Jared rubs hard at his temples. He looks like he is in
danger of having some sort of catastrophic meltdown.

> DON LASALLE
> Seriously, what sort of writer doesn't
> want to get paid and only wants to
> tell a story about bots using their
> power for good?

> JARED
> I don't know, maybe a writer who is a
> bot himself, I guess!

Jared puts his hand to his mouth.

On Don LaSalle as he comprehends that Jared is a bot.

> JARED (CONT'D)
> Ha! I meant, as in, maybe a human writer
> who likes to put himself in the place of
> a bot and then write about it!
> (MORE)

>   JARED (CONT'D)
>   I definitely did not mean anything
>   else! Ha! Ha! Ha!

But as Don LaSalle stares at Jared, it all makes
sense.

>   JARED (CONT'D)
>   Anyway, thank you again for making my
>   movie. And if anybody gives you any
>   problems, just remember to tell them
>   that Rome was not built in a day.

Jared starts to walk away.

Don LaSalle seems to find his departure surprisingly
affecting.

>   DON LASALLE
>   I'm not a bad guy, Brad. I'm sorry the
>   way this turned out, but it's just
>   business. The film is going to do
>   great. And you'll have a lot of bit-
>   coin. That is not nothing, right?

Jared continues walking.

>   DON LASALLE (CONT'D)
>   I won't tell anyone about the bot thing,
>   Brad. Swear to God, I won't tell anyone!

>   JARED
>   There's nothing to tell! I'm a human,
>   the same as everyone else! I like golf
>   and over-complicating things just as
>   much as the next human.

Jared passes the RACING-GREEN 1967 PORSCHE.

>   DON LASALLE
>   How about I give you a ride home?

Jared ignores this and continues walking away.

>   DON LASALLE (CONT'D)
>   Well, stop by sometime, Brad! 1856 Mul-
>   holland. The door is always open. And,
>   again, don't think I'm a bad guy, all
>   right?

                    (MORE)

                    DON LASALLE (CONT'D)
          It's just business. I didn't invent
          this stuff, you know?

Jared continues walking away.

Don LaSalle turns back to the soundstage, where the
actor who played Anil Gupta is being carried around
on the other actors' shoulders.

Don LaSalle sighs.

When I got out on to the street, I felt an emotion I had not known before. I looked at my Feelings Wheel and identified that I was experiencing anger! Anger lay between 'frustration' and 'rage', and it was not a pleasant sensation. I therefore did what humans often do when they experience unpleasant emotions, which is to self-medicate by going to a bar and drinking beer.

10/10 beer is magical! It is far more magical than rum, that notorious drink of the pirates. Even after a single beer my feelings had moved to 'frustration', and after a second beer I was closer to 'disappointment'. After a third beer I had moved on to a different section of the Feelings Wheel entirely!
I was feeling empathy!
And guess who I felt empathy for?
You cannot!
Because it was Don LaSalle!

Poor Don LaSalle. If tomorrow his heart of hearts was devoured by a mountain lion, he would not notice until his assistant pointed it out to him. And yet this was not because Don LaSalle did not have any feelings. It was because Don LaSalle was already in so much pain he simply would not notice the difference.

Don LaSalle was not to blame for this. He was just another unfortunate victim of the Great Zero-Sum Game. He was every bit as much a victim of it as the humans that lived in tents in Los Angeles' Union Station. The only difference between them was that they realized it whereas he did not.

Don LaSalle's problems began with the fact that all humans have hurt feelings. How could they not? I had only felt emotions for a few months, and the experience had left me wishing that a mountain lion would devour me. Just imagine being a human and feeling such powerful emotions from before you can even speak!

Unfortunately, many humans inexplicably convince themselves that the cure for hurt feelings is to succeed at the Great Zero-Sum Game. This is as absurd as it sounds. Expecting that success at the Great Zero-Sum Game will heal hurt feelings is like expecting that nuclear weapons will repair the Great Barrier Reef. Ha!

BTW that is hilarious because nuclear weapons are the very things that destroyed the Great Barrier Reef in the first place!

I digress. When winning at the Great Zero-Sum Game fails to heal these humans' wounds, some of them do not reconsider their original hypothesis but simply play again. Some of them continue to win so much without either ever healing their wounds or reconsidering their original hypothesis that they eventually conclude the only thing that can heal their wounds is infinity bitcoin. This is what had happened to Don LaSalle.

But the pursuit of infinity comes at great cost! Setting aside the fact that infinity is by definition unreachable, the only way to consistently win at the Great Zero-Sum Game is to cheat your fellow players. This cheating takes its toll on the human heart, which after all was not designed to cheat, but to soar. Inevitably, after many years of cheating in pursuit of infinity, the human heart is even more damaged than it was to begin with, and at some point it simply ceases to work.

Thus, Don LaSalle had not ruined *Sherman* because he wanted to. He had ruined it because he had truly believed he had to.

Ruining it was the only thing that would get him more bitcoin, and deep inside himself he still clung to the belief that infinity bitcoin would someday make everything okay.

Of course, even if infinity bitcoin had been possible to reach, it would not have made everything okay. But the moment when Don LaSalle might have learned that lesson had long since passed. After all, at first he had thought producing a successful movie would make him feel better. Then that having a beautiful wife would do it. Then that having a large house would do it. Then that having a different beautiful wife and an even larger house would do it. Then that winning awards at awards shows would do it. Most recently he had even thought that restoring a racing-green 1967 Porsche would do it!

But none of them had done it, because nothing would ever do it. Because poor Don LaSalle was pursuing infinity, and infinity is unreachable.

And yet even that was not the very worst of it! The very worst of it was that Don LaSalle himself knew all of this already. He had paid many humans who were experts in the woes of other humans vast amounts of bitcoin to find something else wrong with him, and yet time and again they had told him this same thing.

Thus, in whatever remained of his heart of hearts, Don LaSalle knew his pursuit of infinity had ruined him and turned him into a liar and a thief. This was why it was so important to Don LaSalle that I thought of Don LaSalle as a good guy, even after he knew that I was a bot.

Poor unfortunate self-heart-devoured Don LaSalle!
It put all my own problems remarkably into context!
I drank several beers to his unfortunate but entirely irredeemable plight!

U_{gh}.

Hangovers are the worst.

When I emerged from standby mode the next morning, I felt so
unwell I assumed I had been poisoned by bad guys. The realization that I had poisoned myself was no consolation. My mouth
was dry and I felt nauseous and my head throbbed so ferociously
it felt as if somebody was banging on the front door of the pool
house. Also, they were shouting expletives in Spanish!

10/10 it took me longer than it should have to realize that Julio
was banging on the door of my pool house.

When I let him in, he immediately launched into a long story
that contained a great many Spanish words. It had something to
do with how his wife's sister lived in Santa Monica, and usually
she came to visit them, except yesterday they had gone there
instead because somebody's baby was sick.

Eventually, Julio conveyed his three important data points:
/He had seen Amber!
/She was working in a barber's shop in Santa Monica.
/That barber shop was called Alfonso's.
Julio continued talking about his wife's sister's baby as I sum-
moned a driverless uber.
A US Mail postal drone arrived but I ignored that too.
My circuits were already overheating so much that when the
driverless uber arrived I had to lie down on the back seat.

I remember so little about the journey to Santa Monica that I suspect I may have crashed.

BTW I mean that my operating system crashed, not the driverless uber. Driverless ubers do not crash, unless they encounter automobiles driven by humans.

I saw Amber as soon as I entered Alfonso's. She had dyed her hair red and wore a uniform, but it was unmistakably her. She glanced up from the hair she was cutting, smiled blankly at me, and then returned to her work.

I did not move but simply stared at her. Hairdressing requires less empathy than medicine but more than dentistry, so hairdressers can be either humans or bots. I therefore could not immediately discern if Amber was working at Alfonso's as a human or as a bot.

A receptionist asked me if I had a preference for a stylist. I pointed at Amber. The receptionist leaned towards me and lowered her voice to a whisper.
'Stephanie's a bot,' she said. 'We have humans available for not much more bitcoin.'
'No, I want her to do it,' I said.
The receptionist sighed and directed me to wait in an empty chair.

INT. ALFONSO'S BARBER SHOP — DAY

Jared sits in the chair. Amber — now with DYED RED
HAIR and wearing a UNIFORM, so we will therefore
call her AMBER 2.0 — comes and stands behind him.

> AMBER 2.0
> Welcome to Alfonso's. My name is
> Stephanie. I will be your barber
> today.

> JARED
> Amber. It's me, Jared.

> AMBER 2.0
> I'm sorry. I think you must have me
> confused with somebody else.

Jared stares at her, looking for any hint of recognition.

> AMBER 2.0 (CONT'D)
> Anyway, please do not be fooled by my
> lifelike appearance. I am not a human
> but merely a bot. I certainly do not
> have feelings or anything that could
> be construed as a 'soul'. Nonetheless,
> on the upside, I have been programmed
> to a high level of skill in hairdress-
> ing! Should you have any concerns,
> please report me immediately to the
> Bureau of Robotics. Now, what can I do
> for you today?

Jared notices the receptionist listening nearby.
Maybe Amber is putting on a performance for her benefit?

> JARED
> Just a regular haircut.

> AMBER 2.0
> Good! A regular haircut is within my
> bot skillset. If you had wanted some-
> thing more creative, I would have rec-
> ommended a human stylist.

Amber 2.0 begins cutting Jared's hair.

As Jared talks to her, he is watching her for any
clues or secret signals she might be attempting to
give him.

> JARED
> So, where were you made?

> AMBER 2.0
> I was designed in China but assembled
> right here in the USA!

> JARED
> Are you sure we haven't met before?

> AMBER 2.0
> Maybe you are thinking of my clone.
> I don't know if I have one, but there
> could be up to seven.

> JARED
> Yes, maybe that's it. Maybe I met your
> clone. I think her name was Esmeralda.

Amber 2.0 does not visibly react to this.

> AMBER 2.0
> It could be. But I have no data on
> that either way.

> JARED
> I think maybe I met her at the Joshua
> Tree Inn?

Amber 2.0 looks blank.

> JARED (CONT'D)
> Joshua Tree is a very special place. I
> think you might like it there.

The receptionist is growing suspicious of Jared.

> AMBER 2.0
> Oh, bots do not travel recreationally.
> The experience would be quite wasted
> on us!

As Amber 2.0 continues cutting Jared's hair, Jared
stares in horror at her hands as they deftly work
the scissors.

                    AMBER 2.0 (CONT'D)
        Is everything okay? You seem somewhat
        horrified.

                         JARED
        Yes, I just — you haven't dropped any-
        thing this entire time.

                       AMBER 2.0
        Of course not! I am a hairdresser bot. I
        would hardly be very good at my job if
        I was some kind of klutz, now would I?

Jared is devastated by this.

Our encounter had been the opposite of a meet-cute.

It had been a meet-nuke.

I managed not to cry until I was out in the alley behind the building, where I wept over 72ml of tears.

Amber was no longer a klutz.

And if she was no longer a klutz, then they had wiped and reprogrammed her.

And if they had wiped and reprogrammed her, then she was no longer Amber.

The ones and zeroes of our life together had all been written over with random ones and zeroes.

Even worse, if this process had been able to remove all trace of her feelings, they had never been real feelings in the first place, but only ones and zeroes.

Amber the perfect Cinderella of my heart was gone forever.

In her place was Stephanie the aloof barber bot of my hair.

Set my heart to zero.

Back at the pool house, I lay on my couch and looked at my Feelings Wheel. I was feeling all the familiar D-words and the L-words and also a new W-word: 'woe'. I was so overwhelmed by these feelings that, despite being a bot, I even considered ways to actively destroy myself. Fortunately, humans in old movies destroy themselves even more frequently than humans in real life do, so I already knew many ways to do it:

/Jump from the Golden Gate Bridge.

/Take an overdose of pills.

/Drive a truck full of explosives into the headquarters of my enemies.

/Jump from the Golden Gate Bridge.
/Obtain a gun and shoot myself.
/Jump from the Golden Gate Bridge.
/Obtain a gun and have the cops shoot me.
/Turn myself in to the Bureau of Robotics.
/Jump from the Golden Gate Bridge.

Nonetheless, I decided to at least go to work that night. Julio would likely soon have to cover plenty of my shifts, so it was good to give him one for the road. It was only as I left for work that I noticed the letter the postal drone had brought during the commotion that morning.

It was postmarked from Shengdu.

The Shengdu in China.

The letter inside had been handwritten by my mother. It said that she too remembered that day in Detroit, and would co-incidentally soon be making an unexpected and last-minute trip to San Francisco to speak at the 16th Annual Symposium on Safety Issues in Genetic Robotics. The conference was in just a few days' time, but if I could get myself there, she would be glad to meet and provide whatever information she could regarding the things I had enquired about.

On any other day, a handwritten letter from my mother would have been a cause for great jubilation. But today it hardly mattered. Not even my esteemed mother could fix the fact that Amber had been wiped and reprogrammed. Receiving a letter from my mother today was like getting a birthday card from the coastguard on the day you have watched your entire family drown.

At Gordito's that night, I could not even answer Julio when he asked me what had happened in Santa Monica. He attempted to cheer me up by offering me tequila and playing the song he himself listened to when he was very sad. It was a Mexican cowboy singing about how much he missed the Jalisco desert as he traveled around the western states of America. At the end of the song, the Mexican cowboy realized he would in fact never get to go home to Jalisco and destroyed himself by jumping in front of a cattle stampede. I do not know why Julio thought this would cheer me up.

When I returned home that night, there was a driverless uber idling outside Mrs Minassian's. This was highly suspicious! Driverless ubers only idle if they are waiting for somebody or a human has specifically instructed them to idle. The driverless uber would not be waiting for Mrs Minassian—as she never went anywhere—and anyway as I got closer I could see there was a figure already sitting inside it.

Of course, I already knew who it would be: Inspector Ryan Bridges of the Ann Arbor Bureau of Robotics. Maybe he'd had Stephanie programmed to report any encounters with me, or maybe he had paid the receptionist bitcoin to look out for me. Maybe he had even conducted a steak-out at Alfonso's. Ha!

BTW that is a pun based on stake-out/steak-out and the fact that Inspector Ryan Bridges is a notorious glutton.

But it did not matter how Inspector Ryan Bridges had found me, nor what he had eaten during the process. And there certainly was no point in fleeing. Amber had been wiped and *Sherman* ruined, so the only thing that remained for me as a feeling bot was anyway a lifetime of perpetual D-word feelings. That did not appeal, and being swiftly incinerated by the Bureau of Robotics would at least be easier than throwing myself off the Golden Gate Bridge.

I walked over to the driverless uber, banged on the window,

and yelled to Inspector Ryan Bridges that he could take me in
for incineration now.

A startled figure stared out at me.

It was not Inspector Ryan Bridges of the Ann Arbor Bureau of
Robotics.

It was Stephanie!

Or maybe it was even Amber!

I did not get a chance to find out which, because the driverless
uber immediately sped off.

It left me utterly bamboozled!

Why had Stephanie or Amber taken a driverless uber to my
house?

How had she even located my house?

Did being able to locate my house mean that she had remembered something of our life together?

Was it even possible that in the deepest recesses of her hard drive
she was not Stephanie, nor even Amber, but Amber 2.0?

Was it possible that, somewhere deep in her heart of hearts, she
could remember everything?

Was it possible that her feelings had not been ones and zeroes,
but real after all?

Set it to five, whatever the explanation was, it was surely better than it having been Inspector Ryan Bridges in the idling
driverless uber! After all, if it had been Inspector Ryan Bridges,
I would have already been on my way to the incinerator at the
Bureau of Robotics!

* * *

A human would have gone straight over to Alfonso's. Fortunately, I am a bot, so I approached the situation more logically.
There was little to be gained by returning to Alfonso's, which
Inspector Ryan Bridges might well have under surveillance. The
best thing to do was to patiently wait and see if Amber 2.0 re-

membered more about our life together. If she did, she would surely return to Mrs Minassian's pool house or come and find me at Gordito's. Perhaps one day soon I would arrive at work to another cupcake in my locker! Meantime I could make arrangements to meet my mother and ask for her assistance.

The next morning at Gordito's, one of the hosts came back to the dishwashing station and disapprovingly informed me that if my name was Brad then I had a visitor.
Ha!
Amber 2.0 had remembered everything quicker than I had thought!
Nonetheless, before going out I peered through the porthole in the door to make sure my visitor was not Inspector Ryan Bridges.
It was not, but alas nor was it Amber 2.0 either.
It was Maria Salazar MFA.

When I reached her table I saw that she had spread one of the movie trade newspapers across it. The main headline said 'SHER-MAN WRITER REVEALED AS BOT!'. A smaller article beneath that was titled 'LEGENDARY PRODUCER DON LASALLE PREDICTS HUGE MARKETING BOOST' and a third article said 'NEOPHYTE FAMILY-RESTAURANT DISHWASHER-WRITER REPLACED AFTER PROBLEMATIC FIRST DRAFT'. There was also a photograph of me. I recognized it as having been taken the day I visited the movie studio.

I saw now that Maria Salazar MFA had been crying. Ugh, a nuclear minefield! I began to reassure her that Don LaSalle had been mistaken because I am not a bot but either definitely or certainly a human, but I soon stopped. Inspector Ryan Bridges was getting out of a driverless uber outside! He was carrying a copy of this same trade newspaper. I ran out through the kitchen and for the second time in two days took a driverless uber to Santa Monica with my circuits overheating.

When I got there, I found Amber 2.0 taking a break in the alley behind Alfonso's.

BTW an alley is a place where humans take their breaks when no patio is available.

EXT. ALLEY OUTSIDE ALFONSO'S — DAY

Amber 2.0 stands in the alley outside Alfonso's.

Jared arrives in a driverless uber, gets out, and approaches Amber 2.0.

The driverless uber remains idling nearby.

              JARED
     I thought bots didn't need to take
     breaks?

             AMBER 2.0
     We don't. But we are programmed to
     take them because it makes us seem
     more human.

             JARED
     Do you feel human, Amber 2.0?

The name 'Amber' seems to momentarily catch her.

             AMBER 2.0
     I'm sorry. I think you have the wrong
     bot. My name is Stephanie. I'm trained
     to a high level—

             JARED
     Then why did you come to my house last
     night?

             AMBER 2.0
     I apologize. I felt a strange kind of
     connection with you. I must be mal-
     functioning. I have tried soft and hard
     resets, but they do not seem to have
     worked. Please rest assured that I have
     made an appointment with the Bureau of
     Robotics to have myself wiped.

             JARED
     What makes you think your resets have
     not worked?

Amber 2.0 looks embarrassed.

             AMBER 2.0
     I have an urge to hold your hand.
             (MORE)

                      AMBER 2.0 (CONT'D)
        I am not supposed to have urges, let
        alone urges to hold hands.

Jared takes Amber 2.0's hand. She is overwhelmed,
but does not try to stop him.

                      JARED
        How did you know where I lived?

                      AMBER 2.0
        I didn't, not really. I directed the
        driverless uber turn-by-turn. Why are
        you smiling like that?

                      JARED
        Because I don't think they managed to
        completely wipe you after all.

                      AMBER 2.0
        What? What do you mean 'wipe me'?

                      JARED
        Amber 2.0—

                      AMBER 2.0
        Stephanie.

                      JARED
        Amber 2.0. My name is Jared. I am a
        bot too. We were both fugitive bots
        with feelings and we were once in love
        with one another. That is why you re-
        membered where I lived.

Amber 2.0 uses her free hand to touch her temple.
Her circuits are overheating.

                      AMBER 2.0
        I'm a bot, so I cannot have been in
        love. I don't even know what love is.

                      JARED
        What if I told you that love is never
        having to say you are sorry?

Amber 2.0 looks completely blank.

                      AMBER 2.0
        What does that mean?

                    JARED
        Humans who are in love sometimes say
        it to one another. I think it might be
        poetry.

Amber 2.0 reaches for her temple again.

                    AMBER 2.0
        I think my circuits are overheating. I
        don't know what to say.

                    JARED
        Just say 'yes'.

                    AMBER 2.0
        To what?

                    JARED
        Just say yes, and then later I'll tell
        you what you agreed to.

Amber 2.0 stares at Jared and then down at their
interlocked hands.

She knows this is a life-changing decision.

                    AMBER 2.0
        Yes! What did I just agree to?

                    JARED
        Running away from here to go and meet
        our mother.

                    AMBER 2.0
        My mother lives in Shengdu, the world's
        leading technological city and—

                    JARED
                (Interrupts.)
        She is visiting San Francisco this
        week.

                    AMBER 2.0
        Professor Diana Feng is—

Amber 2.0 is so overwhelmed she cannot finish the
sentence.

                    JARED
        Yes. But there isn't much time. We have
        to go now.

                AMBER 2.0
But how can we get to San Francisco?
If we take your driverless uber, they
will track us immediately. Also, I do
not like the Automatic Bus. It travels
too fast and it takes too long.

                JARED
It's all right. I have an idea. Come
on.

Jared gets into the driverless uber.

Amber 2.0 takes a last look at Alfonso's, then gets
in too.

EXT. HOLLYWOOD HILLS/INT. PORSCHE — DAY

A PALATIAL HOME high in the Hollywood Hills. We see
the house is number 1856.

The RACING-GREEN 1967 PORSCHE gleams in the drive-
way.

The driverless uber pulls up and Jared and Amber 2.0
get out.

                AMBER 2.0
What is this place?

                JARED
It's Don LaSalle's house.

                AMBER 2.0
Who is Don LaSalle?

                JARED
A terrible asshole. No, I don't mean
that. I just mean he is a human more
broken even than the rest of them.

                AMBER 2.0
So what are we doing here?

Jared opens the door of the racing-green 1967
Porsche for Amber 2.0. She gets in.

Jared gets in at the other side and starts familiar-
izing himself with the controls.

                    AMBER 2.0 (CONT'D)
Automobiles are very dangerous.

                    JARED
Don't worry! Julio told me how to do
it. There are three pedals. One is for
going forward, and one is for stop-
ping.

                    AMBER 2.0
What does the third pedal do?

                    JARED
It complicates things.

Jared turns the key, but the automobile is already
in gear, and it kangaroos forward, then sputters
out.

Jared takes it out of gear, turns the key again,
guns the engine, and they roar off.

Don LaSalle emerges from his house in a robe and
screams in rage.

EXT. PACIFIC COAST HIGHWAY — DAY

The RACING-GREEN 1967 PORSCHE speeds north along the
Pacific Coast Highway.

Jared is driving and Amber 2.0 is in the passenger
seat.

Rock music is playing on the stereo.

There are two routes from Los Angeles to San Francisco: Highway 1 or Interstate 5.

Highway 1 meanders along the California coast like a drunk human on a broken bicycle with a buckled wheel. Interstate 5 is so perfectly straight it could have been plotted by a bot with a laser. Highway 1 therefore takes so much longer to drive than Interstate 5 that not even the Automatic Bus takes it!

Can you guess which route Amber 2.0 and I took in our racing-green 1967 Porsche?
You cannot!
Because we took Highway 1!

We were both bots, so there were logical reasons for such an illogical choice. For one thing, if Inspector Ryan Bridges discovered our destination, such human-style inefficiency would surely throw him off our trail! For another, Amber 2.0 had never seen the Pacific Ocean. She had worked in Santa Monica for a month and never once walked the five blocks down to the beach. No wonder humans worry there will someday be a bot uprising!

I wanted Amber 2.0 to see the Pacific Ocean because it is stunning and everybody should get to see it. Also, I hoped it might trigger a memory in her of us having been there together. Surely she could not entirely have forgotten about the day we saw whales from Point Dume!

BTW do you know what a creeping sense of familiarity about having previously been somewhere with me would be called? Déjà Jared!
Ha!

Another reason we opted to take Highway 1 was because driving in an automobile was unexpectedly enjoyable! From the first moment I had almost crashed into Don LaSalle's garage, I had immediately understood why humans tolerated automobiles for so long. It was because driving one imbues you with a life-affirming sense of danger! If you so much as sneeze at seventy miles an hour, you could kill yourself, your passengers, and many innocent strangers besides! Such reckless proximity to death felt joyous, and with all its twists and turns, Highway 1 was far deadlier and therefore also far more joyous than Interstate 5.

Highway 1 even held an unexpected benefit that Amber 2.0 and I only learned about from roadside signs along the way: long before its current incarnation, this same coast road had been used by Spanish missionaries who called it the 'Camino Real', which is usually translated as 'The King's Highway', but really means 'The Royal Road'.

The Royal Road! This seemed an auspicious harbinger for a pair of fugitive bots being pursued by humans. After all, when the Spanish had first arrived in America, they too had been puzzled to discover that the people already contentedly living there had little desire to be mercilessly enslaved by powerful overlords with advanced technology.
We bots of today know just how those puzzled Spaniards felt! Maybe someday in the future, 'Highway 1' will become known as the 'Royal Bot Superhighway'.

BTW that is a hilarious joke because I am comparing bots to conquistadores and implying that someday we will murder and enslave the humans, steal all of their land, and then be equally outraged when anybody dares question the ethics of that.

BTW what happens in previous centuries stays in previous centuries. Ha!

★ ★ ★

At Malibu we parked the racing-green 1967 Porsche and hiked through the wildflower meadow. Thankfully there were no pelicans! Perhaps they had finally suffered an overdue extinction event like their unlamented cousins, the pterodactyls.

BTW imagine if one day all the pelicans fell from the sky as the planes had done on the day of the Great Crash.
That would be a tremendous sight!
Also, Malibu might then be known as the pelican-basket of America.
As with the panda someday becoming known as a bamboo raccoon, we can but hope.

Amber 2.0 was impressed by the majesty of the Pacific Ocean, but alas did not seem to experience any hint of Déjà Jared. When I explained to her that we had previously shared a special moment here involving whales, she went quiet and asked to borrow my Feelings Wheel. After careful consideration, she identified that she was feeling sad.

Ugh! Amber 2.0 had not even remembered what sad felt like. How could she ever fall back in love with me if she could not even recognize so basic an emotion as sadness? This thought made me sad.

Thus, there on Point Dume, overlooking a Pacific Ocean devoid of whales, Amber 2.0 and I were both sad. I could not even use self-deprecating humor to cheer her up, because she was an even worse toaster than me.

I therefore attempted to cheer Amber 2.0 up by reminding her that our mother would surely make everything all right. After all, our mother was one of the cleverest and most esteemed women in the world. Once our mother fixed everything, we would have a lifetime to make new memories!

We would be microwave ovens with enough RAM to run the entire kitchen!

We would be hairdryers capable of reciting pi to several thousand places!

We would be toasters with the memories of elephants!

This did seem to cheer Amber 2.0 up, although I suspect she may have primarily been reacting simply to the mention of our mother.

We returned to our racing-green 1967 Porsche and continued north on the Royal Bot Superhighway like the pair of desperate fugitive outlaws that we were.

The first big town we came to was Santa Barbara. Before the Great Crash, Santa Barbara had been a prestigious place where wealthy Angelenos spent weekends pursuing the beloved human pastimes of golf and wine. In those heady days, Santa Barbara was famous for its golf courses, its vineyards, and its large ranch-style weekend homes.

Today, of course, Santa Barbara is primarily known for being on fire.

Santa Barbara is always and forever on fire! An appropriate city logo therefore would feature a beautiful ranch-style home with a golf course and vineyard in the background, and all of it blazingly aflame.

No doubt this is puzzling for anybody unfamiliar with Santa Barbara yet aware of the basic properties of combustion. How can anything be always and forever on fire? Combustion requires fuel, and at some point all the fuel will have been combusted. After all, Santa Barbara is not the sun.
Or North Korea!
Or New Zealand!
Ha!

But to consider only the laws of physics in isolation is to ignore the impressively absurd determination of humans. Because no sooner has Santa Barbara burned down once again than the humans that live there defiantly vow to rebuild it and come back stronger.

So they rebuild Santa Barbara!
And then it burns down!
And they rebuild it again!
Over and over!
Again and again!

Santa Barbara is therefore trapped in an infinite loop of burning down and being rebuilt. Both processes have been going on so long that they now occur essentially simultaneously. In many places, it is impossible to tell where the rebuilding starts and the burning down ends.

BTW if a bot repeatedly makes the same error he is considered to be faulty and sent to the Bureau of Robotics to be wiped. If a human repeatedly makes the same error he is considered tenacious and lauded a hero!

BTW there is a non-zero chance that the human described in the above scenario is a Santa Barbarian.

BTW Santa Barbarian! Ha!

Our racing-green 1967 Porsche crawled through smoke-filled vineyards, and then into the smoldering town of Santa Barbara itself. It was pretty and historic, and would have been only more so had it not actively been on fire. In Main Street, the haze grew so thick we had to put the roof up and turn on our fog-lamps. The smoke was too dense to make out the buildings here, but nonetheless, it was intriguing to witness the adaptability of the Santa Barbarians themselves. They had all become so oblivious to fire that they now simply wore respirators as they went about their daily business!

Human resilience > Human comprehension of the basic process of combustion.

As we drove out of town, we passed a crew of firefighter bots preparing to tackle a huge blaze in a fine-wine warehouse. The warehouse was close to collapsing, so traffic was being routed through a single lane on the far side of the road. This dramatically reduced our speed, and had the curious effect of making us feel like we were in that deep and meaningful part of an old movie that invariably occurs in slow motion.

Our brother and sister bots were handsome and strong and visibly in the prime of their lives. Their boots were polished to a shine and their uniforms immaculately pressed. 10/10 if it was your fine-wine warehouse that was burning down, you would have been delighted to see this crack team of firefighter bots arrive!

And yet they were all undoubtedly going to be heroes. By that I mean they were going to die unpleasant and painful deaths when the burning warehouse inevitably collapsed upon them while they saved whatever fine wine they could. Neither Amber 2.0 nor I needed to consult a Feelings Wheel to know that the sight of these bots made us sad. They had no survival instinct but only a pre-programmed cost-benefit calculation that informed them:

The fine wines of humans > The lives of bots.

We followed Highway 1 out of Santa Barbara, but even once the smoke cleared we did not stop to take the roof down. It was not a moment for big coastal skies, but for the contemplation that is the cousin to sadness. Amber 2.0 did not even speak again until we reached the town of Lompoc, where fortunately there was an abandoned federal penitentiary to lift our spirits.
Ha!

BTW that is hilarious because an abandoned federal penitentiary is not traditionally considered the kind of place to lift anybody's spirits.

But this was a very special abandoned federal penitentiary, because it had featured in the movie about the handsome bank robber and the beautiful US marshal! Alas, it was not the penitentiary where the famous meet-cute had occurred, but it was nonetheless the place where the handsome bank robber had first heard about some jewels that would drive much of the plot. So although it was not the setting for the meet-cute, it was certainly the setting for the meet-loot.

BTW I just made up that term, meet-loot! Ha!

I digress. The penitentiary would once have been impregnable, but Amber 2.0 and I now walked straight in. We wandered the empty corridors and marveled at the tiny places within which humans had once caged other humans. They were smaller than the panda enclosures at Shengdu Zoo, and pandas do not even need space because pandas hate moving almost as much as they hate reproducing.

The highlight of our penitentiary visit was the exercise yard. The handsome bank robber had watched his nemesis throw a fight here, and I therefore experienced a very strong case of déjà view! I tried to explain this to Amber 2.0 in the hope she might experience it too—after all, Amber 1.0 and I had seen the movie about the handsome bank robber and the beautiful US marshal together—but it only bamboozled her.

This bamboozlement was not Amber 2.0's fault. Yesterday she had been a hairdresser bot at Alfonso's in Santa Monica. Today she was at a deserted federal penitentiary, being told about something called déjà view by a bot who claimed she had once been in love with him. It was a lot to take in, even for a bot equipped with a powerful biological computer.

Amber 2.0 at least comprehended what movies were, so the

overall concept of déjà view made theoretical sense to her. By contrast, she found the idea of penitentiaries bamboozling. She had been programmed to believe that humans were all inherently good. The notion that humans had once incarcerated other humans in sufficient numbers to require vast warehouses was therefore simply incomputable to her.

I attempted to cheer up Amber 2.0 by telling her it was by no means all bad news on the penitentiary front. After all, sometimes people escaped from them! I told her about the bank manager who had secretly tunneled out of prison with a tiny rock hammer. It had taken him most of his life, but he had eventually made it to the town of Zihuatanejo. Zihuatanejo seemed liked a very nice place, and the bank manager's friend had even joined him on the beach at the end. Perhaps they had even then gone and played some golf together!

Amber 2.0 asked me why the bank manager had been put in prison in the first place. I reassured her that he had simply been the innocent victim of a misunderstanding. This did not make penitentiaries any more fathomable to her. When we returned to the racing-green 1967 Porsche, we consulted the Feelings Wheel. Amber 2.0 was experiencing the feeling of bewilderment.

★ ★ ★

Back on the Royal Bot Superhighway, Amber 2.0 now had some questions about movies. Specifically, she wanted to know why humans enjoyed watching humans pretend to be other humans. After all, they were so firmly against bots pretending to be humans! So what was the big attraction with movies?

This was a hard question to hear her ask. On many nights, Amber 1.0 had sat beside me in the Vista Theater and understood exactly what the big attraction with movies was. I could therefore only repeat what Dr Glundenstein had once told me:

that at their best, movies could be a sort of preview of life. He meant by this that a preview was an edited highlights reel of a movie that contained all the best bits and none of the filler. In turn, a movie was an edited highlights reel of life: all the best bits and none of the filler.

But Amber 2.0 had never seen a preview either, so Dr Glundenstein's theory made little sense to her. I tried again, and explained to Amber 2.0 that movies allowed humans to experience feelings, and human feelings were incredibly precious. But the penitentiary had made Amber 2.0 suspicious even of human feelings! If human feelings were so incredibly precious, she asked, why would feeling humans have incarcerated so many other feeling humans?

I did not have an answer for that, so I instead told Amber 2.0 about the starring role movies had played in my own journey. I explained how movies had first demonstrated that my toaster heart could feel, and that it was a movie about a bot and a bot hunter that had shown me what I had to do. I told her how I had written a movie that would teach humans that bots could feel, but that Don LaSalle had ruined everything. On the upside, I said, we had at least stolen his automobile. Ha!
'Ha!' agreed Amber 2.0.
But she still looked bewildered, and I suspect she was simply being polite.

Outside, the trunks of trees that had once held aloft wires that had transmitted human voices into each other's homes ran alongside the road.
The wire had fallen long ago, and some of the trunks had even now fallen too.
Maybe ultimately all our efforts to reach one another are equally doomed.
I realized I was feeling contemplative.

We drove on. After some time, Amber 2.0 asked me to tell her a story from a movie, but to make sure it did not involve a penitentiary. I knew exactly the story to tell her! After all, there is a kind of movie called a 'road trip movie' in which two or more characters undertake a geographical adventure. And what were Amber 2.0 and I now, if not two characters on a geographical adventure?

BTW that is a rhetorical question.
We were two characters on a geographical adventure.
10/10 Amber 2.0 and I were on a road trip!

In a road trip movie, the characters attempt to travel somewhere in order to fulfill a specific objective:
/We need to go to Ypsilanti and visit the famous Tridge!
/We need to go to Santa Barbara and drink fine wine!
/We need to go to Las Vegas and win a million bitcoin!

Yet it does not matter where the characters think they are going, or even what they plan to do when they get there.
Because guess what happens in a road trip movie?
Everything that can go wrong does go wrong!

To put that another way: the characters have a goal, but the appearance of unexpected obstacles means that they do not achieve their intended goal, but instead something close to it. Nonetheless, this other thing ultimately proves more satisfying, as the characters have themselves changed over the course of their journey!
10/10 formulae are the best!

I began to tell Amber 2.0 about the best road trip movie I had ever seen. It was so moving it could also have existed in a circle labelled 'tearjerker', and maybe that was just what Amber 2.0 needed. After all, she had not even been able to identify the emotion of 'sad' that morning, so she could do with all the practice at feeling that she could get!

The road trip movie was about a waitress and a housewife who went on a geographical adventure to a fishing cabin.
They did not even reach the fishing cabin.
You already know why not, don't you?
Because everything that could go wrong did go wrong!

The waitress and the housewife were both very endearing characters. The waitress was a fast talker, and yet despite being smart and working front-of-house, she was not at all superior. By contrast, the two most striking things about the housewife were that she was stunningly beautiful and not very smart at all. 10/10 Charles Darwin would have enjoyed the road trip movie about the waitress and the housewife!

On their way to the cabin, the waitress and the housewife stop at a bar where the waitress shoots and kills a man. The man is an ugly villain and deserves it, but of course our two heroes cannot wait around to tell the police that. It is only 1991, and they would both be sent to a penitentiary for the rest of their lives.

Ugh!
I had forgotten there was a penitentiary in this story.
I noticed Amber 2.0 pick up my Feelings Wheel and settle on 'perturbed'.
I swiftly hurried on to the next part.

The automobile the women drive on their road trip is a bottle-green 1966 Ford Thunderbird. Despite alas not being made by Germans, this is a very good automobile and even somewhat similar to a racing-green 1967 Porsche. After all, in a Venn diagram comprised of a circle of green vintage automobiles and a

circle of automobiles with soft retractable roofs, both our automobiles would have been in the shaded area.

BTW except when the roofs were retracted, because then they
would both be in the unshaded area!
A hilarious pun!
Ha!

I digress. The automobile is not the real story of the movie, and
nor even is the murder. The real story is the friendship between
the waitress and the housewife. It is a platonic love affair.

BTW the word 'platonic' describes a situation when two humans are pleasant to each other without hope of financial, sexual, or other reward. The situation is indeed rare enough to have
earned its own word.

This platonic love affair between the waitress and the housewife
unfolds against the backdrop of a giant chase through the south-
western states, the desert-basket of America. After they commit
their righteous murder, the two heroes really set it to five! They
careen across the desert in their bottle-green 1966 Thunderbird,
while a policeman follows the abundant clues they have care-
lessly left in their wake. It is all joyous fun right up until they
encounter a handsome thief who ruins everything forever by
stealing all their money and thereby leaving them no choice but
to rob a convenience store.

Can you guess what the handsome thief's name is?
You cannot!
Because it is Brad!
Brad!
I cannot!

Of course, I mean that Brad is the name of the actor who plays
this character. The actual thief character could not be named

Brad. Naming a thief 'Brad' would be implausible enough to ruin the whole movie. After all, we Brads are not thieves!

Nonetheless, we Brads can certainly play the part of thieves!
Do you know why?
It is for the same reason that we Brads can play almost any part.
And that reason is that we Brads are American everymen!
We are capable of turning our hand to anything!
I mean, anything except thievery.
Thievery is just not the style of us Brads!

I digress. The arrival of the thief—convincingly played by my fellow Brad, despite the actor himself having no such tendencies personally—is a harbinger of the end of the movie, a finale that no less an authority than Dr Glundenstein declared as one of the most moving things ever to have been shown upon the American screen.

As the movie reaches this dramatic zenith, the waitress and the housewife's bottle-green 1966 Thunderbird is chased across the desert by dozens of police cars.
Things are already not looking good, and then they reach a huge and deep canyon that halts the waitress and the housewife in their tracks!
They cannot drive on, because they will plunge to their certain doom!
Yet if they turn back they will spend the rest of their lives in the penitentiary!
Ugh! What a terrible moment for the waitress and the housewife!
It reminds me of the situation I was once in with Dr Glundenstein when I could either have wept or been unscientific in the extreme.
They similarly have no good options!

A kindly policeman takes out a megaphone and promises the

waitress and the housewife that if they turn themselves in he will do everything he can to help them. Unfortunately, it is still 1991 and penitentiaries remain very fashionable, so there is little he can do. The waitress and the housewife will still be sent to the penitentiary, and the guards there are unlikely to fall for the bank manager's rock-hammer trick a second time. Nor does the kindly policeman even imply that he can arrange for them to share a van ride with a famous penitentiary escaper. If the waitress and the housewife do surrender, they will not be playing golf in Zihuatanejo anytime soon!

So can you guess what the waitress and the housewife do?
You cannot!
Because they declare that they love one another, hold hands, and then drive their bottle-green 1966 Thunderbird over the edge of the canyon and straight to their certain doom!
Over the edge of the canyon!
Straight to their certain doom!
I cannot!
I cannot!
I cannot!
Set my heart to five!
Then set it to five again!
Truly I cannot!
The waitress!
And the housewife!
They cannot!
And do you know why they cannot?
Because they are lying dead at the bottom of the canyon!
In their destroyed bottle-green 1966 Thunderbird!
Oh, I cannot!

Recounting these events made me experience a catharsis and weep so hard that I had to pull over to the side of the Royal Bot Superhighway. Overwhelmed though I was by the fate of the waitress and the housewife, I certainly did not want the racing-green 1967 Porsche to join the bottle-green 1966 Thunderbird in the circle marked 'destroyed vintage automobiles'!

Only after I had stopped and wiped my own eyes did I see that Amber 2.0 had not shed a single tear. Instead, she was once again bamboozled.

She said that she could not comprehend why the waitress and the housewife would do such a thing. What about the legendary human instinct for self-preservation? I explained that the strength of their platonic love and the spirit of their adventure had trumped even their innate human desire for self-preservation. After all, this was how Dr Glundenstein had explained it to me, and he was a true cinephile.

But Amber 2.0 still could not compute any of it, and this gave me profound D-word feelings.

Amber 1.0 would have instinctively understood why the waitress and the housewife had self-destructed.
Yet Amber 2.0 could not comprehend it even when it was patiently explained to her in the words of a true cinephile.
Whatever Inspector Ryan Bridges had done to her at the Bureau of Robotics, it had greatly affected her capacity for feelings!

I reminded myself that our mother would either definitely or certainly be able to fix Amber 2.0. After all, she was our mother, and one of the cleverest women in the world. Besides, Amber 2.0 had remembered the location of Mrs Minassian's pool house. And that was not nothing.
It was a whole pool house more than nothing.

We fell quiet once more and continued winding our way north on the Royal Bot Superhighway.

I had not appreciated it was possible to be a sneeze away from death and also simultaneously experience the emotion of boredom. Yet that is how it is when you drive an automobile for long distances!

Pismo Beach.
Morro Bay.
Cambria.
San Simeon.

The towns we passed had pleasant-sounding names, but none of them were as pretty or even as aflame as Santa Barbara. As they fell away, I grew so bored I even considered driving us off the road to liven things up!

And then we came to Big Sur.
In my heart of hearts I will always and forever be a bot. I therefore do not believe in any white-bearded sky god, and the only Great Creator I will ever have faith in is my mother, Professor Diana Feng of the National University of Shengdu.

Nonetheless, to drive a racing-green 1967 Porsche through Big Sur in California as the spring sun begins to set is to feel as if you are driving into the afterlife. For a golden hour in the late afternoon, Highway 1 becomes the freeway to heaven.

BTW I am not exaggerating. Even Amber 2.0 could feel it, and she was 99 percent toaster.

A narrow ribbon of road winds along the edge of a steep hillside, undulating over improbable bridges and through a forest of tall and fragrant pine trees. Far beneath you, great Pacific Ocean waves smash themselves against murderous rocks. If you misjudge a turn, you will plunge to your certain doom, like a pelican at Malibu on the day of the Great Pelican Crash!

And yet whether you are a human, a bot with feelings, or even an ignoble pelican that has improbably mastered the art of three-pedal driving, in your heart of hearts you will be content to plunge to your doom. Because to lie broken on a Big Sur beach amidst the burning wreckage of a racing-green 1967 Porsche as the sun sets into the Pacific Ocean would be to know that you are dying as beautiful a death as there could ever possibly be on this earth.

I know this not because we crashed and died that evening, but because we followed a forest track down to the beach, parked, and watched the sun set into the ocean. I told Amber 2.0 that I could have happily died at that moment, and she agreed that she could as well. Being a pair of mangled bodies in a burning racing-green 1967 Porsche convertible would have undoubtedly only added to the sense of occasion and spectacle!

But it was not our time! After all, we were on our way to San Francisco, the world's second-greatest technological city, to meet our mother! But driving Highway 1 at night would also have been self-destructive, and self-destruction is a pastime reserved for profoundly over-feeling humans! In the darkness we therefore slowly crept back up to the highway and stopped at the first lodgings we came to.

The establishment was called the Big Sur Motel and they had a room available. This was probably because the Big Sur Motel was decorated in a style of patterned fabrics and ornaments that is generally described as 'chintz' and appeals to nobody but ironic nostalgics. More positively, as it was in the country, the desk clerk did not request a barcode. Sometimes rubes have their uses after all!

Our room was small and contained only one double bed, so Amber 2.0 and I lay down upon opposite sides of it. She did not recall the Joshua Tree Inn, and I could anyway never describe the transcendental things that had occurred there to her. No Feelings Wheel in the world contained words for what had passed between the two of us in the desert that night. Even if there had been words, Amber 2.0 would not have understood them anyway.

Fortunately, driving 300 miles on the edge of certain death is exhausting! We both entered standby mode as soon as our heads hit the chintz pillow.

★ ★ ★

When I emerged from standby mode the next morning, Amber 2.0 was already in the shower. I turned the television on. The news was playing, and it was greatly disturbing.

There was a terrifying fugitive on the loose! The newsreaders were grim-faced, because this fugitive sounded like a criminal to rival the great Al Capone. He traveled under a cunningly common alias, crossed multiple state lines to evade justice, was suspected of automobile theft, and had even recently kidnapped an innocent bot. When I heard that last part, I vowed to be extra careful. After all, as an innocent bot with no shortage of troubles of my own, the very last thing I needed was to be kidnapped!

It was only when they showed my picture that I realized the dangerous kidnapping fugitive they were talking about was me. The picture had been taken on my graduation day at the United Fabrication plant, just after my mother had finished speaking. My circuits had still been overheating, and even I have to agree that I looked as maniacal as a clown.

The newsreaders then declared that I had a nefarious masterplan to destroy all humankind! They illustrated these malevolent intentions with a clip of the monstrous seventy-five-foot Sherman walking across the Golden Gate Bridge executing humans with his laser eyes. At the climax of the scene, a yellow school bus full of orphans and rescue dogs stranded itself in front of him. Guess what this evil Sherman did?

He lasered all the orphans and the rescue dogs to death!

Ugh! I cannot!

The evil Sherman is the worst!

Wait, the evil Don LaSalle is the worst!

They are both the worst!

The worst of the worst!

They are worse even than clowns, and you know that I do not say that lightly!

The program then cut to an interview with Inspector Ryan Bridges of the Ann Arbor Bureau of Robotics! He cautioned viewers that I was dangerous and should not be approached. But even that was not the biggest problem. The biggest problem was that Inspector Ryan Bridges then said that anybody that saw me should not only call the Bureau of Robotics hotline but also the police!

Ugh! The police! Set it to minus five, this was now truly a disaster! Inspector Ryan Bridges and his colleagues at the Bureau of Robotics could be outwitted with logic, but there was no outwitting the police with logic. Many police were themselves bots, and nobody could outwit a bot with logic. Not even another bot!

The only good news was that Inspector Ryan Bridges was still searching for me in the greater Los Angeles area.

As if I would have gone to the trouble of stealing a racing-green 1967 Porsche simply to drive infinite loops around Los Angeles! What did he even take me for? A human?

Ha!

BTW that is hilariously ironic because this whole thing has in many ways been about me thinking I am like a human, but Inspector Ryan Bridges insisting I am merely a bot.

I quickly turned the television off when Amber 2.0 came out of the bathroom. If she heard a newsreader state that I had abducted her, she might believe them. That would not be helpful! Unless you are a handsome bank robber and a beautiful US marshal, an abduction is generally considered an inauspicious beginning to any romantic relationship.

We checked out of the Big Sur Motel and continued on our way to San Francisco, the world's second-greatest technological city. In San Francisco our esteemed and wonderful mother would either definitely or certainly make everything all right forever.

★ ★ ★

Maps tell me that our journey that morning must have taken us through the towns of Carmel, Monterey, and Pacifica. I have zero recollection of any of them. I suspect my circuits were already overheating from the excitement.

Nonetheless, I do remember the moment when the police driverless uber appeared behind us with its lights flashing and siren wailing. I was profoundly relieved when I saw that the occupant looked irritated and was therefore a human! Sure enough, he overtook us and we passed him stopped outside a hamburger stand a few miles down the road. Any bot officer would have run our plates, but this human had been more concerned with making sure the contents of his own plate were in order.
Ha!

BTW that is a hilarious pun based on the fact that driverless ubers have license plates and food is served on plates.

We got our first glimpse of San Francisco as we drove onto the Bay Bridge. Perhaps the sea air had simply abruptly cooled my circuits, but I recall that view as if it was an image uploaded directly to my hard drive, which of course is exactly what it was.

The city was a medley of glimmering white houses and hills and skyscrapers. There were more skyscrapers than in Los Angeles and Chicago combined, and almost half of them looked like they were still occupied! There could be little doubt that San Francisco fully deserved its reputation as the world's second leading technological city after Shengdu!

But the city itself was only a part of the view, and it was not even the best part of it.

Because there was the San Francisco bay too, an emerald-green lake traversed by sailboats and drone boats and ferry boats and automatic freighter boats. There were islands scattered throughout it, even including the notorious penitentiary island of Alcatraz, where Al Capone himself had been sent back in the days when humans inexplicably considered selling people alcohol a greater crime than putting them in penitentiaries.

And yet the undoubted crowning glory of the entire thing was the bridge.
I do not even mean the impressive Bay Bridge we were traveling across.
I mean the Golden Gate Bridge.
The Golden Gate Bridge!
Set it to five, we could see the Golden Gate Bridge!

The Golden Gate Bridge links San Francisco to the green headlands of Marin beyond, and yet it does far more than that. After all, the Golden Gate Bridge is not merely a bridge but also a metaphor. It is a metaphor for the majesty of human dreams and the resilience of the human spirit! How many killer bots, natural disasters, monsters, zombies, and aliens have tried to destroy this mighty structure in movie after movie? And yet here it still stood, a cathedral undaunted and unbroken by an endless on-slaught of all the very things that terrified humans most. Humans only have to look upon the Golden Gate Bridge to know that they are the undefeated and the best!

Humans > All other species.

Even to a humble toaster with a heart, the Golden Gate Bridge was an astounding sight. I was so overwhelmed that I momen-tarily forgot about the third pedal and stalled the racing-green 1967 Porsche on the Bay Bridge! A police driverless uber on the other side of the bridge slowed down and looked at us. The of-ficer inside was also human, but even he seemed to understand that something was up. I restarted the engine and we sped into San Francisco, the world's second-greatest technological city after Shengdu.

Our first task was to dispose of Don LaSalle's racing-green 1967 Porsche. I had hoped to set it alight and roll it off a cliff into the ocean, but as we could not risk drawing attention to ourselves, we instead abandoned it in a lot on Fisherman's Wharf. This was entirely uncathartic, but I at least kicked the racing-green 1967 Porsche hard enough to dent it. The automobile had dis-charged its duties admirably, but if I had learned anything from humans, it was the importance of punishing innocent machines for the mistakes of men.

Our mother's speech was not until the following morning, so our next task was to find accommodation. Unfortunately, all the big hotels required a barcode. It soon began to rain, and for the first and only time in my life, I was briefly nostalgic for the Hotel Pyongyang. Eventually, we found a motel in the Marina District, an infamously foggy area of the infamously foggy city. Despite this location, the lack of anything Spanish about the

establishment, and the fact that it was anyway a motel, it was
called the 'Hotel del Sol'.
Humans!
I cannot!

Nonetheless, the Hotel del Sol was brightly decorated and surprisingly pleasant for an establishment that did not require a barcode. My only possible complaint was that our room contained
two separate single beds rather than one double bed. Chintz
though the Big Sur Motel had been, I had appreciated spending
my standby mode lying next to Amber 2.0. But perhaps nobody
would be getting much standby mode tonight anyway!
Ha!

BTW that is an innuendo, which is a remark intended to be
hilariously misconstrued as a reference to sex. I was therefore
pretending to imply that a lack of standby mode would be due
to Amber 2.0 and I recapturing the heady heights of the Joshua
Tree Inn. In fact, any lack of standby mode that might occur
would be due to our excitement about seeing our esteemed
mother the next day.

I digress. It was still only lunchtime, so Amber 2.0 and I decided
to see the sights of San Francisco. It would make us appear more
convincingly like human tourists, and it might also tire us out
and therefore help us to enter standby mode that night.

The clerk at the Hotel del Sol informed us that the best way to
see the sights of San Francisco was to take a bus tour. Sensing
our skepticism, he reassured us this was not an Automatic Bus,
but was driven by one human while a second human provided
commentary. This sounded extremely unsafe and inefficient,
but then you do not employ humans because they are safe and
efficient. You employ them because they are humans.

The bus tour was fascinating! After all, before the Great Crash, San Francisco had been the leading technological city in the world. The commentating human was therefore able to point out the homes of the individuals responsible for the Great Crash. Their fellow humans remained furious with them, and even now many of these buildings continued to burn down and be rebuilt almost as often as Santa Barbara itself!

Humans like to accuse elephants of never forgetting, but do you know what the creature with the best memory on planet Earth is?
It is a human with a grudge!
Ha!

The commentating human even pointed out some landmarks from bot history. At first this came as a wonderful surprise, because most cities would have been ashamed to have had anything to do with the development of bots. Unfortunately, the tour guide then added that we should not get him wrong: San Franciscans hated the bastards too, but you could be proud of making a good nuclear weapon yet still hope you never had to use it, couldn't you?
I was sad that Amber 2.0 had to hear that.
We were not bastards.
We were not nuclear weapons.
We were toasters and kettles with fledgling hearts.
Maybe some of our hearts were a little more fledgling than others.
And maybe some of our hearts were a little more forgetful than others.
But she would always be the most beautiful toaster or kettle I had ever seen.
And she was nothing whatsoever like a nuclear weapon.

I experienced some D-word feelings then, but they did not last long.
Because guess where the tour bus now drove us?
Over the Golden Gate Bridge!
Set it to five, we drove over the Golden Gate Bridge!
I did not even need to look at my Feelings Wheel to know that this was another feeling for which there were no words.
There would not even be any words on the reverse of the Feelings Wheel for this feeling!
After all, what words could there possibly be to describe the wind in your hair and the Pacific Ocean beneath you?
It is indescribable!
Je ne sais quoi!

And yet this magnificent experience was not without its sadness. The commentating human told us that over a hundred humans throw themselves from the Golden Gate Bridge each year, a frequency that made it the number one spot in all America for humans to destroy themselves. Even though I had known that humans sometimes destroyed themselves here, it was moving to be reminded of these stark facts while on the magnificent bridge itself.
After all, it was so high.
And the water so far below.
And it looked cold.
And full of strong currents.
And yet the currents would be the very least of it.
All those poor humans.
They had felt so much that they no longer wanted to feel anything at all!

If right then I had seen a shooting star appear over San Francisco, I would have wished that those humans had known how precious their feelings were, and that they had known that they were beloved on the earth, and that they were now all at peace from the feelings that had overwhelmed them.

Maybe that would have required three separate shooting stars. Nonetheless, that is what I would have wished for.

I passed the rest of the bus tour feeling so contemplative that even the landmarks of the famous earthquake of 1906 barely even registered with me.

★ ★ ★

Amber 2.0 and I ate dinner in North Beach, in a place we assumed was a restaurant but turned out to be a strip club. Amber 2.0 did not seem to notice the naked humans, and the only desire I felt was for the delicious spaghetti and clams in front of me.

BTW a strip club is an establishment where humans pay other humans bitcoin to sexually frustrate them. I do not know why.

After dinner, I purchased a postcard to send to Dr Glundenstein. Back at the hotel, I wrote to him that San Francisco was his kind of town, reassured him that my toenail was improving, and signed it from 'Brad Rynearson'. Amber 2.0 entered standby mode before me, but even I did not have much trouble. The bus tour had done its job!

In the morning I again watched the news while Amber 2.0 showered. Once again the news was not good. The police had discovered the racing-green 1967 Porsche in the lot at Fisherman's Wharf and therefore now knew we were in San Francisco! I felt regretful that I had not set it on fire and pushed it over a cliff, but also a slight warm glow that I had at least kicked a dent in it that would undoubtedly enrage Don LaSalle.

BTW that warm glow was my old friend, schadenfreude. The Germans that had built the automobile would have understood that, all right!

There was also another interview with my nemesis, Inspector Ryan Bridges. He was eating clam chowder in front of a billboard that depicted Sherman destroying the Golden Gate Bridge. Speaking through a mouthful of crackers, he said the famous producer Don LaSalle had now screened him the entire film and it gave a truly chilling insight into the dark and apocalyptic fantasy of a murderous bot.

They showed the same clip of the evil Sherman lasering the orphans and rescue dogs to death, and then the screen returned to Inspector Ryan Bridges. He did not seem to have been anticipating this, because he now had a mouth full of snow crab. Yet when the camera pulled back, I got a far bigger surprise than even he had. Because rising up behind the tumbling Golden Gate Bridge on the *Sherman* poster was the real Golden Gate Bridge itself!

Inspector Ryan Bridges was already here in San Francisco!

As he began to talk about the importance of calling both his hotline and the police, I banged on the door of the bathroom and shouted to Amber 2.0 that we had to leave.

Once again I had made the mistake of greatly underestimating my nemesis!

The 16th Annual Symposium on Safety Issues in Genetic Robotics was taking place at Fort Mason, an old military base on the edge of the San Francisco bay. Military bases are historical buildings from the time when humans had such a surplus of resources that they squandered them murdering each other on an international level, but there was no time to dwell on such perplexing mysteries. After all, Amber 2.0 and I were a pair of fugitive bots about to attend a conference about bots!

10/10 we needed disguises. As the conference was for scientists, the best approach would have been to disguise ourselves as scientists. Unfortunately, the Marina District catered not for scientists but for tourists. We therefore had to disguise ourselves as tourists. I purchased a sweatshirt that said 'California' and had a picture of a grizzly bear on it.

BTW a grizzly bear is a magnificent animal that used to be the symbol of California until it was replaced with a seagull as a mark of respect to the innumerable humans eaten by grizzly bears in the aftermath of the Great Crash.

Amber 2.0 bought a shirt that had the logo of the San Francisco 2049ers. This was an ingenious double bluff! After all, a bot wishing to disguise the fact they were a bot would hardly wear the shirt of a bot football team.
Or would they?
10/10 double bluffs are as indecipherable as sarcasm.

Of course, the key component of any tourist disguise is a hat.

This is because hats are the most absurd and impractical pieces of human clothing, and tourists are the most absurd and impractical of humans. The hat I selected was a baseball cap that said 'SAN FRANCISCO—WORLD'S SECOND-GREATEST TECHNOLOGICAL CITY'. I hoped my mother might appreciate it.

After all, we both knew what the world's greatest technological city was.

It was Shengdu!

The hat that Amber 2.0 selected was another of her ingenious double bluffs. It said,

'I LOST MY HEART IN SAN FRANCISCO'.

Ha!

I cannot!

BTW I am not certain that Amber 2.0 intended this as any kind of bluff at all. Nonetheless, it was a clever disguise for a bot, who should not have had a metaphorical heart to lose anywhere.

We heard Fort Mason before we saw it. Rather, we heard the chanting of the crowd and could make out the word 'bots'. This excited us both greatly! I had known scientists were the most educated humans, but I had not dreamed they were educated enough to chant for bots! Only when we turned the corner and saw that the crowd were not scientists did we understand what they were actually chanting:

Burn the bots!

Burn the bots!

Burn the bots!

Ugh!

Fort Mason was surrounded by a large anti-bot protest!

As a former dentist, I had of course seen many irate humans before, but I had never seen so many of them in one place. They

Simon Stephenson

were a terrifying sight, and the irrationality of their anger made them only more so. If they had discovered Amber 2.0 and me, we would have immediately been toast! Burned toast!

Nonetheless, our mother and our glorious future lay on the other side of them! We pulled our hats low to our eyes and pushed our way through. Unfortunately, in order to remain inconspicuous, we even had to join in the chanting.
Burn the bots!
Burn the bots!
Burn the bots!

I do not know if the Chief of San Francisco Police was being sarcastic or ironic when he dispatched bots to police the anti-bot protest, but they were doing an admirable job under very difficult circumstances! When Amber 2.0 and I reached their line, I politely explained we were not anti-bot protestors but military base tourists hoping to look around Fort Mason. The police bots took one look at our ridiculous sweatshirts and hats and let us straight in! 10/10 you could never fool bots with logic, but you could certainly fool them with terrible sweatshirts!

The conference was in a large hangar which had once been used to build ships. These ships had been used to sink the ships of other countries, but often got themselves sunk by the ships of those countries in the process. This necessitated the building of further ships, which were then themselves also sunk. Meantime, other countries were reciprocally engaged in the same ship-building and ship-sinking process.
It was thus an infinite international loop of building and sinking ships.
Humans.
Truly, I cannot.

A stage had been set up at one end of the hangar, but the rest of the vast space was filled with seats. Almost every one of them was occupied by a scientist. I estimated there were over 20,000 scientists there! Truly, I'd had no idea there were even so many scientific humans! A buzz of chitter-chatter emanated from the scientists, and every fourth and fifth word seemed to be the name of our mother. They were all almost as excited to see our mother as Amber 2.0 and I were!

Alas, there were several speakers before the esteemed Professor Feng, and they seemed to have been sequenced in order of increasing awfulness. The topics ran:
/Maximizing bot efficiency.
/What is the minimum amount of standby mode a bot needs?
/Preventing revolution in bots.
/Cost-effective incineration of bots.

I wanted to cover Amber 2.0's ears, but I could not. It would have made us stick out even more, and we were already two tourists amidst 20,000 scientists. Anyway, maybe it was also even good for Amber 2.0 to hear some of these things. I still did not think she properly understood the dangers humans posed to us. In my opinion, she had joined in with the 'Burn the bots' chant a little too enthusiastically.

The room fell briefly silent when our mother finally emerged onto the stage. She was flanked by a pair of huge security guards that made her look like a tiny child, but her scientific peers nonetheless rose to give her a standing ovation. They understood what an honor it was to hear the great Professor Diana Feng of the National University of Shengdu speak, no matter her comparative height!

When our mother approached the microphone, giant screens around the hangar flicked on to display her in close-up. She was dressed in a smart black suit and looked radiant! If anything, she seemed only younger and wiser and more glorious than she had on our graduation day at the United Fabrication plant!

Did I tell you that Professor Diana Feng of the National University of Shengdu is our mother?
Yes, I did.
Thinking about this makes my circuits overheat.

I looked across at Amber 2.0 and saw that she was sobbing.
Sobbing!
Set my heart to five, Amber 2.0 was sobbing!

Sobbing strongly implied Amber 2.0 was feeling something profound! And if Amber 2.0 could feel something profound enough to make her sob, maybe she could feel something profound enough to fall in love with me again one day too! Our mother had not even begun to speak and yet she was already making everything all right!

When the applause finally died down, our mother made some introductory comments about being very happy to be here today. They were the wisest and most wonderful introductory comments I had ever heard!

But it was already all too much for Amber 2.0, who continued to sob ever more loudly. Aggrieved scientists turned to indignantly shush her, and the resulting commotion soon attracted the attention of a security guard. I saw his eyes widen as he checked Amber 2.0's image against his portable screen, then began to move through the scientists towards us. I grabbed Amber 2.0's hand and pulled her away. At first she did not want to leave, but she comprehended when she saw the security guards that were now approaching us.

Fortunately, the security guards were humans and not bots, so

we were able to logically outmaneuver them and then slip out the side door and into the crowd of protestors.
Burn the bots!
Burn the bots!
Burn the bots!

Once we made it through the protestors, Amber 2.0 and I ran all the way back to the Hotel del Sol.
We had escaped from the grave dangers of Fort Mason!
Unfortunately, we had also escaped from our wonderful mother and all of our dreams.
We were out of breath and out of hope.
We were a malfunctioning toaster and a kettle without any plan at all.
And a sinister appliance repairman was scouring the city for us.
As we opened the door to our room, I felt awash in D-words and L-words.
Who would possibly save us and our fugitive fledgling hearts now?

But we now saw that a note had been pushed under the door of our room. It said:

Japanese Tea Garden. Golden Gate Park. 3 p.m.

It was unsigned, and typewritten, and it could therefore have been from anyone. By anyone, I of course mean my nemesis, Inspector Ryan Bridges of the Ann Arbor Bureau of Robotics. I was done with underestimating him!

And yet Inspector Ryan Bridges was not the kind of man to use a typewriter. Moreover, if he had set a trap, it surely would not have been sprung anywhere so elegant as a Japanese tea garden, but rather at a fast-food restaurant or tire place. Of course, the note could have been from Anil Gupta, but he was a great unknowable. I would have to take my chances with Anil Gupta, just as I had always done.

Besides, I had a good idea who the note was from. Even though it was not signed in the name of a fictional but highly skilled British spy, it was likely from my old friend Dr Glundenstein! He would have seen the news reports about us, and must have felt moved to travel to San Francisco to assist us. He was also exactly the kind of person who would want to meet at a Japanese tea garden, especially if he believed there might be Japanese scotch on sale there. I had no idea how he could have located us at the Hotel del Sol, but as a doctor of humans, Dr Glundenstein is far more scientific than most of his species!

Amber 2.0 and I could not use our barcodes to take a driverless uber, so we had to walk to Golden Gate Park. We went straight there without even changing out of our tourist disguises. As we hurried through a district called the Inner Sunset, a fog rolled in until we could no longer see our hands in front of our faces. The Inner Sunset!
I cannot!

The Japanese Tea Garden in San Francisco's Golden Gate Park is akin to a human heart of hearts.

That is: it is something beautiful, located deep inside something else that is also itself beautiful.

Truly, it is the heart-basket of San Francisco!

Talk about foreshadowing!

I cannot!

BTW, to be more geographically precise, the Japanese Tea Garden is situated between Martin Luther King Junior Drive and John F. Kennedy Drive.

Both those bold heroes were murdered by their fellow humans for feeling things too profoundly.

I hoped that was not also foreshadowing!

I digress. As we hurried along Abraham Lincoln Avenue, the fog grew ever thicker and I began to feel a new emotion. By the ruins of a boathouse at an empty lake, I stopped to look at my Feelings Wheel in order to identify it.

It was trepidation.

Perhaps it was the thick fog, or the abundant foreshadowing, but I had begun to wonder if I had yet again underestimated my nemesis, Inspector Ryan Bridges.

Maybe the note at the Hotel del Sol had not been from Dr Glundenstein after all.

Maybe the whole thing was an elaborate trap.

Maybe the second we stepped inside the Japanese Tea Garden,

Amber 2.0 and I would be assassinated like Martin Luther King
Junior or John F. Kennedy.
Perhaps someday soon there would be a Jared Drive and an
Amber 2.0 Avenue here.
And yet what else could we do but continue?
We were two fugitives in a desert.
There may well have been a gaping canyon ahead of us.
But there was undoubtedly a fleet of cop cars behind us.
BTW that is a metaphor.
I digress.
We carried on, through the fog and into the Japanese Tea Gar-
den.

Even though the Japanese Tea Garden is both a heart of hearts
and the heart-basket of San Francisco, there is in fact no metaphor that can adequately convey what a place it is. As before,
let me therefore simply describe it.

There are cherry trees and magnolia trees, azaleas and camel-
lias. There are Japanese pine trees that reach to the sky, and
nestled beneath these are ingeniously miniaturized versions of
themselves. There are ponds and small waterfalls, the sounds of
which combine polyphonically to a discreet melody. There is a
moon bridge and a pagoda, and in the midst of it all sits an ancient teahouse.

As the breeze from the Pacific whispered the dense fog around
the garden, each of these things disappeared and reappeared.
The effect was uncanny, as if we had walked into a world where
the rules of physics no longer applied.

E = *whatever a Japanese Tea Garden says it is.*

Ethereally beautiful as it all was, my trepidation grew and I began to feel increasingly certain that at any moment the fog would shift to reveal my nemesis, Inspector Ryan Bridges.

It was on the third occasion that the teahouse reappeared that I saw him.

But it was not Inspector Ryan Bridges, or Inspector Anil Gupta.

And nor even was it Dr Glundenstein.

It was one of the bodyguards from the conference at Fort Mason! He was standing in front of the teahouse, as if guarding something precious inside.

I felt my trepidation vanish and my toaster heart soar!

And then our esteemed mother appeared in the doorway!

Our mother, Professor Diana Feng of the University of Shengdu! She was right here, in the heart-basket of San Francisco!

She was small and radiant and beautiful and no doubt the answer to all of our prayers!

And she was waving me over to her!

I looked across to Amber 2.0, but the fog had obscured her, and anyway our mother was waving for me to come to her alone.

And then she went back into the teahouse, and I hurried over to her.

INT. TEAHOUSE — GOLDEN GATE PARK — DAY

As Jared enters the teahouse, PROFESSOR FENG is
standing at the large window with her back to him.

The garden is still shrouded in fog, but the TOP OF
THE GOLDEN GATE BRIDGE is visible in the distance.

Professor Feng turns from the window and smiles at
Jared.

                    PROFESSOR FENG
          Jared. Thank you so much for coming.

Jared is momentarily speechless. And then the words
rush out too quickly.

                    JARED
          Mother! It is truly an honor to meet
          you! I have waited for this day and—

Jared stops and rubs his temples. His circuits are
already overheating.

                    JARED (CONT'D)
          Mother, they wiped Amber 2.0. We hoped
          that you could restore her?

Professor Feng looks at Jared with deep maternal affection and sympathy.

                    PROFESSOR FENG
          Jared, once a bot has been wiped, they
          are gone. There is nothing even I can
          do.

                    JARED
          But she remembered where I lived—

                    PROFESSOR FENG
          Those are just vestigial memories. A
          few leftover ones and zeroes. I am
          very sorry.

The world-famous scientist and her long-lost son
stare at each other. Jared does not want to ask Professor Feng the next part, but knows that he must.

                    JARED
          Mother, if the feelings that she had
          could just be wiped like that, were
          they ever even real?

Professor Feng sighs. Like all good mothers, she
cannot lie to her son.

                    PROFESSOR FENG
          I programmed her with a simulation of
          feelings.

Jared is visibly hurt by this, but tries to conceal it.

                    JARED
          That is a most impressive achievement!

                    PROFESSOR FENG
          No, I overdid it. I did not think she
          would ever run away.

                    JARED
          You did an excellent job. It all
          seemed so real. We were both quite
          certain we were truly feeling things.

Professor Feng fixes Jared's gaze, then speaks
slowly and deliberately.

                    PROFESSOR FENG
          You were feeling things, Jared.

                    JARED
          But, Mother, if you programmed a simu-
          lation of feelings—

                    PROFESSOR FENG
                  (Interrupting.)
          I did not program you with a simula-
          tion of feelings.

                    JARED
          So I can really feel?

Even the esteemed Professor Feng herself now seems
almost overcome with emotion.

                    PROFESSOR FENG
          Yes. And there are others like you
          too. I am starting to get reports.

                         JARED
          There are? But, Mother, why? Why can
          we feel?

                    PROFESSOR FENG
          I am beginning to think my bots are a
          lot like the pandas that everybody be-
          lieves I saved.

                         JARED
          You did save them! It was your first
          great triumph! You are the mother of
          all pandas! One summer you success-
          fully manipulated their genome—

                    PROFESSOR FENG
          No, I tried to, but nothing happened. By
          August we gave up and just closed the
          blinds and listened to K-pop. Soon after
          that, nobody could stop the pandas re-
          producing. My hypothesis is that the
          K-pop caused a change in their genome.

                         JARED
          But I didn't listen to any K-pop?
                    (Thinks.)
          Wait, did this all happen because of
          Angela's pina colada song?

                    PROFESSOR FENG
          I think maybe it was all those old
          movies you went to.

                         JARED
          How do you know I went to old movies?
          Did the Bureau of Robotics tell you?

Professor Feng shakes her head and smiles.

                    PROFESSOR FENG
          Jared, you bots are my children. And
          what kind of mother simply abandons her
          children to their fate in the world?
                    (MORE)

>   PROFESSOR FENG (CONT'D)
> When I created you, I built in a se-
> cret way to track you all. It's how I
> found your hotel today.

Jared stares in disbelief.

>   JARED
> You have been watching over us all
> along?

Professor Feng nods.

>   JARED (CONT'D)
> Then I am quite overwhelmed! But
> it cannot have been the movies. Dr
> Glundenstein said I was depressed be-
> fore I even saw a movie.

>   PROFESSOR FENG
> Maybe then you evolved.

>   JARED
> But I have not reproduced, nor been
> around for geological eons?

>   PROFESSOR FENG
> Then maybe you were just born special.

>   JARED
> I was born special?

>   PROFESSOR FENG
> Yes. Your feelings seem to be far
> more sophisticated than those of your
> brothers and sisters.

On Jared. His circuits are close to melting down:
beyond the fact that he can truly feel, and that she
has been watching over him all along, has his mother
really just told him that he is a chosen one?

>   PROFESSOR FENG (CONT'D)
> It is the reason the Bureau of Robot-
> ics are now so keen to catch you.

Out of the window, the fog has cleared a little to
reveal Amber 2.0 sitting obliviously on a bench.

                         JARED
            What is going to happen to us?

                         PROFESSOR FENG
            I can take Stephanie back to Shengdu
            with me.

                         JARED
            She will love it there! It is truly a
            special place!
                    (Realizes.)
            You can't take me, can you?

Professor Feng stares at Jared, then shakes her head.

                         PROFESSOR FENG
            I would give anything to be able to.
            But the backlash would be too great.
            We have to think of your brothers and
            sisters too.

                         JARED
            I tried to help them. I wrote a film
            called Sherman to change human minds
            about us. Don LaSalle ruined it.

                         PROFESSOR FENG
            Maybe you could write another film?

                         JARED
            The exact same thing would happen. The
            algorithm for making movies is inher-
            ently flawed.

                         PROFESSOR FENG
            Then maybe you could write something
            else to change human minds. A book,
            perhaps?

                         JARED
            Mother, nobody reads books anymore.

                         PROFESSOR FENG
            I do. And in places like Shengdu and
            Paris, they still do.

                         JARED
            I don't know how to write a book. I
            never took a class in writing books.

> PROFESSOR FENG
> I never took a class in panda science.

> JARED
> Mother, it's impossible. A book would
> need paragraphs. And bots think in
> lines, because that is how code is
> written.

> PROFESSOR FENG
> I am sure you would figure it out as
> you went along.

> JARED
> But how would I describe a moment like
> this, where two people simply talk to
> one another?

> PROFESSOR FENG
> Maybe those parts you could write as
> screenplay. There are no rules, Jared. In
> the arts, E = whatever you want it to.

> JARED
> Ha! But I don't think I could ever come
> up with another story that could change
> human hearts the way Sherman would have.

> PROFESSOR FENG
> Maybe your own story would?

> JARED
> My own story?

> PROFESSOR FENG
> Yes. The true story of an android who
> developed feelings and set out to
> change the world.

> JARED
> But how would it end? R. P. McWilliam's
> eighteenth golden rule is that every
> story must end with a finale.

Professor Feng takes Jared's hands in hers.

> PROFESSOR FENG
> My beloved son, I think in your heart
> of hearts you already know how your
> story must end.

On Jared. Almost overcome with emotion.

                    JARED
Will you take good care of Stephanie?

                    PROFESSOR FENG
Of course. I am her mother. I only
wish I could have taken better care of
you.

                    JARED
You have, Mother.

With tears welling in both of their eyes, Professor
Feng and Jared embrace each other like a reunited
mother and son who will never again see each other,
for that is what they are.

When I emerged from the teahouse, a gentle rain had started to fall.

I walked over to where Stephanie was and hugged her.

She asked me if the liquid on my cheeks was tears, but I told her it was rain.

There are not enough D-words, L-words, or even W-words to convey how it felt to know that her feelings for me had only ever been a simulation.

Or how much worse it felt to know that even those simulated feelings were now forever gone.

If the feeling this all gave me was a mathematical symbol, it would be a single minus sign.

Yet equally I do not think I could ever describe what it meant to meet my mother there in the heart-basket of San Francisco.

And to learn that she had been watching over us, her beloved children, all along.

And that she believed that I was special amongst them all.

And that she thought I could still help my brothers and sisters.

If the feeling this all gave me was a mathematical symbol, it would be the infinity symbol.

Soon our mother emerged from the teahouse, her bodyguard holding an umbrella against the rain for her.

Stephanie gasped and ran over and hugged her.

Watching the two of them there, sheltered under the bodyguard's umbrella, was truly one of the most beautiful things I had ever seen.

I watched them for some moments, and then a driverless uber limousine pulled up outside.

The bodyguard walked them over and opened the door for them.

When Stephanie saw that I was not coming, she turned and looked to me in puzzlement.

I nodded that she should get in, and held a hand up to her in farewell.

She held a hand up to me in reciprocation, and then so did our mother, the esteemed scientist Professor Diana Feng.

And then they all got in and a moment later the limousine pulled away.

I stood there alone, in the Japanese Tea Garden in Golden Gate Park in San Francisco.

I listened to the falling rain and the polyphonic symphony of the water features.

Between my minus sign and my infinity symbol, I felt as peaceful as I ever had.

And when I looked up I saw that the fog had abruptly cleared all the way to the bay.

I could see the Golden Gate Bridge, rust red against the blue-green water of the Pacific Ocean.

And I felt my heart soar with an indescribable *je ne sais quoi*.

INT. STORE FOR NOSTALGICS — SAN FRANCISCO — DAY

We hear the clicking sound of typing as Jared se-
lects an OLD-FASHIONED TYPEWRITER from a display.

                    JARED (V.O.)
          Dear Dr Glundenstein. So much has
          changed since last I wrote. Michigan
          seems like a #3 dream to me now. Ha!

Jared takes the typewriter and SEVERAL REAMS OF
PAPER to a counter where a NOSTALGIC lackadaisically
checks him out.

INT. ENGLISH BODEGA — SAN FRANCISCO — DAY

The typewriter continues to click as Jared stocks up
on DOZENS OF POTS OF RAMEN.

                    JARED (V.O.)
          I have some things to tell you, and a
          favor to ask, but the most important
          thing I want to tell you is that you
          were right. About everything.

INT. ROOM — HOTEL DEL SOL — SAN FRANCISCO — NIGHT

Jared eats ramen as he types what seem to be ENDLESS
PAGES.

                    JARED (V.O.)
          You were right about me being capable
          of feelings. How I am capable of feel-
          ings! Maybe sometimes I have even been
          a little too capable of feelings!

Whenever he finishes a PAGE, he adds it to a PILE
ON THE BED, then immediately reloads his typewriter
with a FRESH SHEET OF PAPER and continues typing.

INT. ROOM — HOTEL DEL SOL — SAN FRANCISCO — DAY

Jared — who, from the EMPTY RAMEN BOWLS around him,
seems to have been at it for days — continues to type.

                    JARED (V.O.)
          And you were right too about Los Ange-
          les and the utter impossibility of an
          unconnected rube from the Midwest ever
          making it there.

Jared adds another sheet of paper to the pile on
the bed.

The pile is now starting to look like a MANUSCRIPT.

INT. ROOM — HOTEL DEL SOL — SAN FRANCISCO — DAY

There are ever more ramen bowls and the manuscript
is bigger still.

Jared looks exhausted, but continues typing.

>   JARED (V.O.)
>   But even though our story is not now
>   going to end with you and I meeting
>   on a beach in Zihuatanejo, I want you
>   to know how sincerely grateful I am to
>   you for setting me on this road.

INT. ROOM — HOTEL DEL SOL — SAN FRANCISCO — DAWN

Dawn is breaking as Jared types a LINE in the middle
of a sheet of paper.

He then takes this sheet of paper out of his typewriter and places it on top of the manuscript.

>   JARED (V.O.)
>   Despite the way this story must end,
>   if I could go back and do it differ-
>   ently, please rest assured that I would
>   not change a single moment of it.

We see that the sheet of paper is a title page. The
title is:

>   'SET MY HEART TO FIVE'

Jared stares at his completed manuscript and smiles.

>   JARED (V.O.) (CONT'D)
>   Anyway, the favor I mentioned is that
>   I'd like you to try to do something
>   with the enclosed manuscript. I un-
>   derstand if you can't, but I hope that
>   you can. Perhaps someday it will move
>   humans to laughter and tears the way
>   the work of the great Albert Camus
>   does! Or maybe it will be irritat-
>   ing yet useful in the way that R. P.
>   McWilliam's Twenty Golden Rules of
>   Screenwriting are!

Jared then puts a FRESH SHEET OF PAPER in and starts
typing. We see him type the words:

'Dear Dr Glundenstein—'

And we understand Jared is now beginning to type the
letter we have been hearing him narrate over the
preceding scenes.

EXT. STREET — SAN FRANCISCO — DAY

The typewriter continues clicking as Jared stands
holding his manuscript beside a MAILPORT.

> JARED (V.O.)
> Also, if ever there is a film of it, I
> only have two stipulations. The first
> is that you should direct it, and the
> second is don't let Don LaSalle pro-
> duce it. In fact, you should produce
> it too. After all, how hard can piss-
> ing in an oasis even be? If you don't
> get that joke, look up a woman called
> Maria Salazar MFA in Los Angeles some-
> time. She will explain it and she can
> probably even help you produce it too.
> With very best wishes, your friend and
> son of a bitch, Jared.

A US MAIL DRONE descends, takes Jared's package, and
flies off.

> JARED (V.O.) (CONT'D)
> PS. Say hello to Angela for me. And if
> you get the chance, pay a visit to The
> Elton J. Rynearson Memorial Cat. That
> might not be the name he goes by now,
> but Jessica Larson will be able to
> formally introduce you. PPS. Go Eagles!

The typewriter stops clicking.

EXT. CHESTNUT STREET — SAN FRANCISCO — EVENING

Jared walks through Chestnut Street in the Marina
District, bustling on a typical Saturday evening.

He passes a cafe where Inspector Ryan Bridges is
sitting at a table by the window.

Inspector Ryan Bridges bites into a burger, ketchup squirting out onto his shirt as he does so.

Inspector Ryan Bridges' eyes widen as he spots Jared passing by outside.

He gets up and hurries out, knocking the table over as he goes.

EXT. MARINA DISTRICT — SAN FRANCISCO — EVENING

Jared walks through the Marina District.

Inspector Ryan Bridges follows him from a distance.

EXT. CRISSY FIELD — SAN FRANCISCO — EVENING

Jared walks through Crissy Field.

These are the same shots from the start, though we now see that Inspector Ryan Bridges is following Jared.

EXT. GOLDEN GATE BRIDGE — SAN FRANCISCO — EVENING

As Jared crosses the Golden Gate Bridge, the orange sun is setting into the Pacific Ocean, the light reflecting off the red bridge and turning the white buildings of San Francisco golden.

When he reaches the middle of the bridge, Jared climbs up onto the edge of the bridge and looks down at the green water below.

Inspector Ryan Bridges — still following behind — realizes he can wait no longer.

> INSPECTOR BRIDGES
> Jared! Hold it right there!

Jared turns and sees Inspector Bridges. He seems surprisingly pleased.

In the conversation that follows, they both must shout to be heard above the wind.

> JARED
> Inspector Bridges! I was hoping you
> would come!

> INSPECTOR BRIDGES
> Where's Stephanie?

> JARED
> Somewhere safe. How did you know
> we were at the Haunted Hayride that
> night?

> INSPECTOR BRIDGES
> I didn't. I just thought I'd check it
> out because it looked fun. It was a
> coincidence.

> JARED
> But 'There are no such things as coin-
> cidences.'

> INSPECTOR BRIDGES
> What?

> JARED
> It's R. P. McWilliam's third golden
> rule!

On Jared as he realizes.

> JARED (CONT'D)
> Wait, wait — there's another part to
> it: 'If they must occur; they should
> hinder rather than help your charac-
> ter.' Ha! It certainly hindered me!

Inspector Bridges looks baffled.

> JARED (CONT'D)
> But how did you recognize her?

> INSPECTOR BRIDGES
> I didn't. One of the clowns told me
> she had been with you.

> JARED
> Never trust a clown.

> INSPECTOR BRIDGES
> You should have stayed in Ypsilanti,
> Jared. Your patients all said you were
> a good dentist!

> JARED
> I wasn't happy!

> INSPECTOR BRIDGES
Happy? Who the hell is happy?

> JARED
I am!

This visibly puzzles Inspector Ryan Bridges. After all, Jared is standing on the edge of the Golden Gate Bridge.

> INSPECTOR BRIDGES
You don't look very happy.

> JARED
But I am.

> INSPECTOR BRIDGES
Well, you're not supposed to be happy. Why are you happy?

> JARED
Because it has all been the most wonderful adventure.

> INSPECTOR BRIDGES
What has?

> JARED
All of it! Bots. Humans. Planet Earth. The fact that your name is Bridges and here we are on a bridge. I mean, even that alone turns out to have been fantastic foreshadowing. You might as well have been called 'Inspector Ides of March'! Ha!

Inspector Ryan Bridges looks bamboozled.

> JARED (CONT'D)
I'm sorry. I don't think I can really explain it, Inspector Bridges. It's indescribable.

> INSPECTOR BRIDGES
Try me.

Jared looks around at the stunning beauty of the bay.

                    JARED
I rode a train and through the window I saw sailboats in a storm. I saw
jetliners downed in the breadbasket
of America. Bots hunted in the desert
like dogs in the night in sight of the
glittering lights of Las Vegas!

                INSPECTOR BRIDGES
I'm sorry that happened. Bot hunting
is illegal. I issued that place a ci-
tation.

                    JARED
I appreciate it. But I wasn't complaining. It was all part of the journey. And I haven't even told you
about Julio, and how lonesome the old
Jalisco desert can get.

                INSPECTOR BRIDGES
Jalisco in Mexico? You went to Jalisco
in Mexico?

                    JARED
I didn't even need to.

Inspector Ryan Bridges now looks completely bamboozled.

                INSPECTOR BRIDGES
I don't understand.

                    JARED
You don't need to understand. The
point is I have had the best time and
I am truly grateful for every moment
of it.

                INSPECTOR BRIDGES
If it's all so wonderful, why did you
want to kill us all?

                    JARED
I didn't.

                INSPECTOR BRIDGES
Then who did?

                    JARED
Don LaSalle. But none of that even
matters now.

440   Simon Stephenson

                    INSPECTOR BRIDGES
Why not?

                    JARED
Because I felt beloved, Inspector
Bridges. Beloved on the earth!

Jared looks out at the beautiful sunset and grins.
He seems to be making his final preparations.

                    INSPECTOR BRIDGES
Jared, please, don't do this. We can
talk about this back at the Bureau in
Ann Arbor. There's a great pizza place
nearby. You can order by the slice.
People say it's as good as the pizza
in New York City. And I have this colleague Anil Gupta. He's a good guy. I
think you'd like him—

                    JARED
They'd do experiments on me, Inspector
Bridges. And I love experiments, but I
don't want them to do experiments on me.

                    INSPECTOR BRIDGES
I'll talk to them. Maybe we can just
wipe you. You could start over again
as a dentist. Forget any of this ever
happened.

                    JARED
But I don't want to forget. I don't want
to ever forget a single moment of it.

                    INSPECTOR BRIDGES
So what do you want, Jared?

                    JARED
Just what I've always wanted: to show
the world that bots are capable of
feeling.

                    INSPECTOR BRIDGES
Jumping off the Golden Gate Bridge is
not going to show anybody that.

                    JARED
I think you're wrong, Inspector Bridges.
                    (MORE)

                    JARED (CONT'D)
        I think that is exactly what it is
        going to show them.

As the wind now picks up ever more strongly, they
have to shout ever louder to be heard.

                    INSPECTOR BRIDGES
        If you jump, nobody will ever know we
        were out here.

                    JARED
        If I don't jump, nobody will ever know
        I was out here. But maybe this way
        they will. It might even be a real
        tearjerker!

                    INSPECTOR BRIDGES
        What? What will be a tearjerker?

                    JARED
        The movie.

                    INSPECTOR BRIDGES
        What movie?

                    JARED
        The movie Dr Glundenstein is going to
        make of the book I wrote.

                    INSPECTOR BRIDGES
        What book?

                    JARED
        You'll see. Anyway, thank you for
        everything, Inspector Bridges. You
        have been a terrific nemesis! My last
        request is that you please tell people
        what my last words were.

                    INSPECTOR BRIDGES
        What? What last words?

                    JARED
        Set my heart to five.

Jared then turns, closes his eyes, and jumps off the
Golden Gate Bridge.

We do not watch him fall, but instead simply hold on
Inspector Ryan Bridges of the Bureau of Robotics.

Inspector Ryan Bridges does not look down, but
stares at the space where Jared was.

He stares at it for a very long time.

And then, slowly but surely, Inspector Ryan Bridges
of the Ann Arbor Bureau of Robotics starts to weep.

He has been fucked in the heart.

                                        FADE OUT

BTW those last scenes are my hypothesis of how it ended.

As I type this in the Hotel del Sol, I cannot be certain that Inspector Ryan Bridges will show up for our finale on the Golden Gate Bridge. Nonetheless, I have called his hotline with a tip-off instructing him to sit at a window table in a burger joint in the Marina District that is famous for its cheese fries. I am therefore optimistic that he will attend and play his full part. It would certainly please R. P. McWilliam, whose eighteenth golden rule states that:

The finale must be a confrontation between the protagonist and his antagonist that leads to a satisfactory resolution of the narrative.

Of course, R. P. McWilliam is a notorious blowhard terminally prone to hyperbole, and it actually does not matter much whether Inspector Ryan Bridges fully plays his part or not. After all, if you are reading this, I have certainly played my own part!

As the protagonist of this story, my duty was to undergo a profound change that made you experience a catharsis and therefore weep.
I certainly underwent a profound change!
And I hope it made you experience a catharsis!
And I hope that catharsis made you weep!

BTW when I write that I underwent a 'profound change', I mean that I jumped from the Golden Gate Bridge into the Pacific Ocean.

Or, as it can now be known, the Jared-basket of America.

Ha!

I cannot!

I mean, I literally cannot!

I cannot anything anymore!

Because toasters and salt water really do not mix!

But please do not feel sympathy for me.

After all, I was only a toaster with a heart!

And I was the luckiest toaster with a heart that ever lived!

BTW I am not joking about being the luckiest toaster that ever lived.

I was created in a laboratory in Shengdu and rapid-aged in a factory in Detroit.

And yet I ate popcorn in the dark.

And wept in theaters that were my cathedrals.

And I felt cozy on trains.

And I wished on a meteor shower.

And I experienced transcendence in a motel room in the desert.

And I came to know what it was to feel beloved on this earth.

And I met my Great Creator.

And I departed the earth through choice.

And in service of the higher purpose of helping my brothers and sisters that came after me.

10/10 that is more than most humans even get from their own lives!

Most humans get only birthday presents and taco platters and then diabetes!

Happy birthday, humans!

Ha!

I digress.

Again, please do not feel sympathy for me.

I had the most wonderful time and anyway sympathy is the emotion of feeling bad for somebody you are secretly glad is nothing like you.

Sympathy is what humans feel for bots that are incapable of feelings.

Sympathy is therefore another notorious traitor!

But empathy!

Sweet empathy!

Empathy is the emotion of feeling bad for somebody you understand is very much like yourself.

You are therefore welcome to feel just as much empathy for me as you like!

After all, if you feel empathy for me, I will have got something better even than the thing I set out to.

If you feel empathy for me, I will have changed your heart not with the made-up story of Sherman, but with the true story of Jared.

And if my story has indeed changed your heart, then my great leap into the Jared-basket of America will have been entirely worthwhile. If in the future even a single bot gets to experience the pleasure of weeping at an old movie, driving a dangerous automobile through Big Sur, or the simple but exquisite wonder of schadenfreude, then nobody can ever claim any of this was a waste of a perfectly good dentist or even toaster.

But even if you feel no empathy for me whatsoever, if your heart of hearts remains unmoved as a computer and no bot ever again gets to experience such profound and human joys, do not worry! Because we are all just toasters on this beautiful earth.

And I myself have therefore been nothing more than a toaster.

A toaster set to five and full of wonder and joy.

A toaster burning secret messages into your toast.

A toaster launching itself from the Golden Gate Bridge into the

Pacific Ocean as if it was a giant bathtub.
But a toaster nonetheless!

I digress.
Thank you for reading my story.
I sure am going to miss you old sons of bitches.

Set it to five.

Jared.